"With its large cast of wounded, complex, and ethnically diverse characters, all yearning for love, *Where Blackbirds Fly* creates a world that looks very much like America. That it does so with rich lyricism and polymathic learning is a testament to the love Shann Ray himself has for humankind. Read this novel for the perception-altering poetry in Ray's prose, the vividly and sympathetically drawn characters, the precise attention to detail, and the expansive spirit that courses through this elegantly rendered story. Beauty, care, and wisdom sing from these pages!"

—Charles Johnson, author of *Middle Passage*,
winner of the National Book Award

"The language, sharp. The story, riveting. The love, physical. *Where Blackbirds Fly* left me breathless as I caught the thread of Divine Mystery woven in its pages."

—Drew Jackson, author of *Touch the Earth*

"There is a spirit in the American West—a spirit calling out—and Shann Ray envisions it beautifully. Vivid. Grounding. In imagery of skies, wildlife, and mountainscapes, Ray immerses readers in a story deeply personal and boundless. Thoughtful with the complexities of identity, heritage, and connection, he evokes the timeless bond between land, heart, and the shared human experience."

—CooXooEii Black, author of *The Morning You Saw a Train of Stars Streaking Across the Sky*,
winner of the Rattle Chapbook Prize

"A breathtaking narrative of the unspoken histories of couples. How do we find a way to love when there are multigenerational wounds? That struggle informs *Where Blackbirds Fly* as each pairing carries different burdens and different intimacies. The blackbirds' appearance is subtle but prophetic, and as with the tricolored blackbird, the startle of its color in flight, their path echoes the uncommon strength of this narrative. Over the years each interwoven life takes on power and poetic significance as we question if love will triumph over loneliness, over loss. We come to care deeply about the people here, their trials and vicissitudes. We celebrate with them, and grieve with them, and when the novel is complete, we don't want to leave them."

—Mary Jane Nealon, author of *Beautiful Unbroken*,
winner of the Bakeless Prize

"Shann Ray's prose defies limitations and boundaries. In *Where Blackbirds Fly* the world he creates is a brutal one where empathy only glows brighter. His sentences stipple the page with such grace and beauty we're left not with just a book or a story but a true work of art."

—Dane Bahr, author of *Stag*

"In Shann Ray's kaleidoscopic and cinematic novel we bear witness to characters grappling to kindle and keep love. Characters yearn, strive, and soften for a transcendent wholeness, a healing they glimpse tenderly in each other. Where no redemption seems isolated or linear, this hard and lovely work urges us to consider the healing strength of love and how we can just as easily ruin each other. The precise telling resists reveling in love's sweetness. Around each corner another couple rises into view, scuffed and scarred with trying. We mourn the inevitable damage they cause and rejoice in the moments they are able to break loose from personal and collective pain, able to be available and steady for each other. Ray articulates a vital and palpable interconnectedness of humanity."

—Natalie J. Graham, author of *Begin with a Failed Body*, winner of the Cave Canem Poetry Prize

Praise for Shann Ray's previous work

"A celebration of the intricacies of love told in crystalline prose. As compelling as Harrison's masterwork *Legends of the Fall*. Expansive and luminous. Visionary. Powerful. Heartbreaking."

—Debra Magpie Earling,
American Book Award–winning author of
The Lost Journals of Sacajawea

"Shann Ray brings a voice at once rugged and unapologetically vulnerable. Like any decent bluesman, Shann knows when to wail, when to whisper, and when to let the silences do their own damn work."

—John Murillo, Kingsley Tufts Award–winning
author of *Kontemporary Amerikan Poetry*

"Ray's feel for the heart and soul of Montana and its people—all its people—graces every page."

—Andrea Barrett,
National Book Award–winning author of *Ship Fever*

"Shann Ray's work brings to mind Cormac McCarthy and Annie Proulx but is, thankfully, entirely his own. His work is lyrical, prophetic, brutal yet ultimately hopeful."

—Dave Eggers, Pulitzer Prize finalist and author of
What Is the What

"Not torch song but full-throated anthem for the conflagration love tenders. Shann Ray is a poet of ecstasy, god-parented by Derrida and Dickinson, propelled to plumb terrain both spiritual and geographic for clarity around what it means to be embodied and consumed."

—Katrina Roberts, Washington Book Award finalist
and author of *Friendly Fire*

"The sentences in this book have such grace and muscularity. The author's images and events carry the nearly visceral weight of memory. A powerful, resonant work of literature. Shann Ray is a masterful and original writer."

—Robert Boswell, author of
Tumbledown and *Century's Son*

"Remarkable for its spare, lyrical prose; the stunningly original metaphors and perceptions; and the tenderness with which Shann Ray sees his people even in the midst of dangerous, self-destructive disturbing circumstances. The experimentation with form highlights Ray's extraordinary flexibility as an artist and thinker, his willingness to let the reader enter his work in the silent spaces he leaves open."

—Melanie Rae Thon, author of *Sweet Hearts*
and *The 7th Man*

"A brutal beautiful vision."

—Benjamin Percy in *Esquire*,
Plimpton Prize–winning author of *Refresh, Refresh*

"Riveting and inventive. Dark and unprecedented. A remarkable assembly of language and spirit, difficult to face at times but so important, so powerful in witness. There are moments of wretched cruelty and despair here. And beautiful evocations of redemption. An exercise of imagination and soul like no other I've read."

—Alyson Hagy, author of *Boleto* and *Scribe*

"Shann Ray's work is both grounded and spiritual. He has an eye for minute detail, and while he's describing an act of love or violence or just panning through a scene to render river and mountain range, he's also trying to understand how we respond to the often generational brutality of existence without forgetting its beauty. How is it that a single life can hold so many disparate things—love, hatred, trauma, healing, destruction, forgiveness, redemption—without tearing apart? Love is a salve for violence, but also sometimes a kind of violence itself. In Ray's work, good and evil aren't moral poles set apart from each other, they're aspects of a whole held in tension, whether in a single person, in all of humanity, or in the mystery of God."

—Luke Baumgarten, co-founder of the arts nonprofit
Terrain and a partner of Treatment/Creative

"Written in a voice and style that is hard to put down, harder to forget. The gorgeous prose is the perfect bearer of souls in all states—being born, living, being broken open, moving through time."

—Janis Segress, Queen Anne Book Company,
Seattle, Washington

"Every once in a while a book falls into your hands that is so beautifully written, deeply affecting, and powerful that it burrows into your heart and makes a lasting place there. Shann Ray's novel is a triumph. A tender evocation of the passions and sorrows of people, and a piercing look at the ravages of racism, greed, and violence. Ultimately, this book's power lies in its characters, all of whom I came to care deeply about, worry over, and wish for as one by one they came to life on the page. A stunning portrayal of the scope of the human spirit, and the many paths to grace."

—Laurie Paus, Elliott Bay Book Company,
Seattle, Washington

"Shann Ray writes about men and women, white and Native American, full bred and half bred; he writes about love and betrayal, alcohol and abuse, pride, vanity, everyday losses and recoveries. Most of all he writes about the soul in search of its reason and its peace."

—Tom Jenks, coeditor with
Raymond Carver of *American Short Story Masterpieces*

"Shann Ray is one of the best writers writing today. Not just 'in the West,' like so many people like to say, but in the nation. Shann writes the West the way it should be written, with unflinching love, loss, violence, and above all, beauty."

—Charles Finn, editor of *High Desert Journal*
and author of *On a Benediction of Wind*

"Tough, real, and beautiful, Ray's writing is lyrical yet concise and perfectly captures the hardness of humanity—violence, racism, control, greed—but is driven by a silver thread of love and chosen resilience of spirit. The characters are flawed and sometimes dark in thought and action, but the novel maintains a light that can only be accomplished by a thorough understanding of love and forgiveness."

—Jess Lucht, Auntie's Bookstore,
Spokane, Washington

BISON
BOOKS

Where Blackbirds Fly

A Novel

SHANN RAY

University of Nebraska Press
Lincoln

Acknowledgments for the use of copyrighted material appear on pages 466–68, which constitute an extension of the copyright page.

The University of Nebraska Press is part of a land-grant institution with campuses and programs on the past, present, and future homelands of the Pawnee, Ponca, Otoe-Missouria, Omaha, Dakota, Lakota, Kaw, Cheyenne, and Arapaho Peoples, as well as those of the relocated Ho-Chunk, Sac and Fox, and Iowa Peoples.

For customers in the EU with safety/GPSR concerns, contact:
gpsr@mare-nostrum.co.uk
Mare Nostrum Group BV
Mauritskade 21D
1091 GC Amsterdam
The Netherlands

Library of Congress Cataloging-in-Publication Data

Names: Ray, Shann, author.
Title: Where blackbirds fly: a novel / Shann Ray.
Description: Lincoln: University of Nebraska Press, 2025.
Identifiers: LCCN 2024061478
ISBN 9781496243577 (paperback)
ISBN 9781496243881 (epub)
ISBN 9781496243898 (pdf)
Subjects: BISAC: FICTION / Westerns | LCGFT: Western fiction. | Novels.
Classification: LCC PS3618.A9828 W47 2025 | DDC 813/.6—dc23/eng/20250310
LC record available at https://lccn.loc.gov/2024061478

Designed and set in Garamond Premier Pro by Lacey Losh.

for Jennifer,
Natalya, Ariana, and Isabella
forever

WHERE BLACKBIRDS FLY

Book 1

When the blackbird flew out of sight,
It marked the edge
Of one of many circles.

—Wallace Stevens

THE SIMPLE TRUTH: John Sender believed in love.

Thirty-three. Still single. Driven, overly driven. So much head work, and such solitude, but into his self-doubt, love. Real love. A love he could hardly believe after such drought, but yes, he believed. He'd even gone home to Montana and borrowed his long-dead grandfather's black Florsheim wingtips from his recently dead grandmother's bedroom closet, and from her bureau the diamond ring she'd kept through two foreign wars—his mom wanted him to have it—the ring he'd be giving to his bride.

Only he hadn't much spoken with his bride yet.

He pressed his hands down on the desk, flattening them, staring. Big boned, rough. Late night; everyone gone. Alone again. The day had been difficult, another without tone or hue, loans drawn up, rates secured, moneys meted out. He worked for the world renowned National American Bank, on the seventh floor of its massive headquarters in downtown Seattle. Strange, the bones of a hand, beautiful in their way. His were like his father's, not afraid of work. White as moonlight and pocked from field work, he thought, with his Czech-German blood, a fraction of it Cheyenne. His hands were also strong like his father's, but shy with women. His grandfather, a suicide, had been shy with women too. In that echo John always felt uneasy, but he took comfort in how the outline of his fingers against the woodgrain made him think of home.

He had thought he might just stick to horses. They calmed him every bit as much as he calmed them, the kind-spirited ones, the wild ones too, like bolts of lightning he could get a heel into and fight. He missed it, breaking for Dad and the neighbors. That and all the rodeoing he'd done.

Spooked since he could remember, he felt awkward on every date he'd been on, which were few. Tall man: six foot one, wired tight. Bridge of the nose bony as a crowbar, broken on a fence in Flagstaff. Rodeo docs always salty, that one laid him flat on the ground, shoved two metal rods up his nose and got on top of him, then jerked the rods hard. The sound was unnatural, the pain like a landslide in the brain. Straightened things out but left a crude notch. Too tall for saddle broncs, the doc said, but he'd made do.

"Hardnosed," his dad said when he saw the nose.

"Keeps the women away," John answered, and they chuckled.

John's looks were distinctive. Shoulder-length black hair, drawn back, crow-like. Dark blue eyes. Bold features. Big. Just quiet with women, and morose, he thought. His mind tended to focus on things that depressed him. He put his hands through his hair. Easier to see people enter his office hoping to secure a loan, a home. Single or together, they were enthused or subdued. Alone or fused, sometimes disoriented, often good-hearted, isolate or bound like the threading on well-mated nuts and bolts. Secretly, he loved the spectrum of all who hoped for a better life together. He often found the older couples the most savvy. From his own yearning he was undoubtedly biased. Some who married called each other pet names. Others used first names. Still others, silent, said nothing. Engaged, married, or simply together, they don't know what they have, John thought. When it comes to love, they should realize what they borrow is a person: we borrow them from their family, from their parents. Maybe we borrow them from God. He admitted he hadn't had much luck with love. But he knew when people thought love dead it surprised you with its presence, and those who commodified love were bankrupt.

Tailored suit and silk tie. Late again, after dark, he needed to finish the paperwork and get home. No cowboy hat, no boots, he felt at odds with himself. A rodeo scholarship and a BA in English from the University of Montana, then three seasons on the professional rodeo circuit and an MBA along with a smattering of additional graduate work in philosophy from Seattle University. He'd been in loans now for a few years, and until he met Samantha everything had seemed caught in a time foreign to him and uglified. Hollow, missing the land and sky. The ranch. Mom and Dad by themselves and him a corporate hired hand, trapped like a pawn in some thoughtless efficiency. He was leery, and still afraid of women. But he wasn't one to be afraid of darkness. He loved the night—the ocean north of the city not held in city light but illumined by an immensity of stars and the night's own lantern. The scent of kelp and mud wash and cold.

And of the women and men who borrowed?

He suffered over them, as he did himself, and his heart went out to them.

John never forgot a face, and those days it was true, life so hectic, so recessed and downhearted, so bubbled with economy, so mealy with anxiety, no one felt compelled to remember, though even slight remembering might have meant help, and remembering well might have meant salvation. People stayed the same or arced upward or fell like meteors from an incomprehensible height. He recalled both the feminist thought leader bell hooks and the Enlightenment philosopher Rousseau: we borrow the land we live on, whispers in the dark, shouts of exultation, the ways we listen or speak, draw near or fade away, the very fruits of the earth and the absolute clarity of unexpected grace. We not only borrow money, he thought, we borrow the unique and versatile manner of our individual and collective lives, and even our common deaths.

HE PLACED a stack of loans in the processor's inbox.

In America it was an old institution, loans: indebtedness part and parcel of the capital condition. Debt perhaps the oldest form of being human, people were owned by their misconceptions. They wanted money and when they couldn't get it he detected the undertow: lack of property smelled stale, ego smelled like blood. Looking at amortization schedules mesmerized them. Trying to own a home meant being in a one-down position for a long time. Never mind that the banks shorted you and sucked you dry for thirty years. At least you had a roof over your head.

Past midnight locking the office door his hands felt chilled. He'd only been in her close proximity once. As he merged onto I-5 for the forty-minute commute from downtown, he pushed the ring over his right pinkie finger, a simple solitaire, firm hand at twelve o'clock, and watched the glow through the windshield, obscured usually but in the direct light of oncoming vehicles the stone a tiny torch of white, gold, and vermilion. He envisioned placing the ring on her slight hand, smiling into her eyes, receiving from her the smile she'd give. He dreamed of trips back home to Montana, where he drove Going to the Sun Road in Glacier, hiked the lakes region from Hidden Lake at Logan Pass, to Avalanche Lake and Two Medicine. He'd teach her to fly fish. He'd make small bright fires under wide skies on nights that would deepen from light to dark blue then black as black silk, silver points like fine sand from east to west, the Milky Way an arm of clustered stars overhead. The Summer Triangle. Cygnus the Swan. Vega, Altair, Albireo. In the western night they'd shine, he and she like satellites.

He knew what gave him the right to give people money. Nothing. He hadn't earned the cash he gave away. The money came from the ether, from history, from those who had it, from the accrual that ran a world built on the back of unforeseen chaos. The great men made an ungodly percentage on every dollar: exploitation being the binding principle of getting ahead until gluttony cracked the vault and the economy spilled away and couldn't be contained again without great force. He'd indebted himself like everyone else, if a little less so and with the opportunity to cut into it with a decent salary.

That night in bed, he held his hands over his chest and stared at the ceiling. Chill air, down comforter his mother gave him a Christmas ago.

He wondered what Samantha thought of money but he kept thinking of blackbirds. On the winds that blew below the Cascades and over the foothills of Montana's Rocky Mountain Front blackbirds filled the sky. His father taught him how in their multitudes they navigated the atmosphere by a form of sevenfold kinesthesia, one bird's movement affecting its seven closest neighbors, each of those neighbor's movements affecting their seven closest neighbors ad infinitum. Rain made their wings glisten. Sun set their bodies alight. In this way the birds moved higher and more unified in shapes of enlargement or diminution, ordered by the physics of magnetism, scale-free correlation, and synchronized orientation, obscuring the heavens. The people below could be gangly, John admitted, inelegant, sometimes deadly, and also magnetized. Beneath the blackbirds' flight, on the land people knew, on the land that knew them, women and men lived alone or in groups, behind elaborate enclosures or in ruined housing, under freeways or in the grit of alleys. Windows were expansive and filled with sky, or narrow, permitting little light, or ill made, disfiguring vision. The people who peered out were multiple, varied, brindled, one. Single-minded as animals, but like angels, majestic. They slept in modern castles and under tarp. Cloaked by trees. Encumbered by blocks of industry. Born into foolishness, into love awakened. From above we must appear thinly made, he thought, easily destroyed.

Vulnerable to our outsized hungers.

Even with the plugged-in feel of being in banking, and even with how he still liked the city for the ways it always seemed about to ignite, he admitted he was low in Seattle, real low away from home, boxed in by granite and glass, and the rain, no range or visibility, no sky, and out among the millions he'd nearly given up hope. Growing up he'd become something of a naturalist, but neither his dad nor he could abide the binary naturalism set up between the laws of nature and spiritual laws he considered as natural as the wind. He pictured the bird skull he'd found in late summer in the Highwood Mountains. Mandible and beak line and orbital bones like elongated white flower petals in his palm. A Bohemian waxwing, Siberian accentor, or perhaps an errant barn swallow separated from the long, forked tail and steely blue wing pattern, the rufous chest and chestnut forehead. Who fathoms will or tenderness? he wondered. Who tests the furnace of the sun, the gravity of a child's heart, or the beauty of mercy, justice, and love?

Seattle wasn't the flats near Rock Springs where you could ride for miles and never see a soul and never feel alone. Here, you brushed up against people constantly, bumping them on the sidewalk or in a grocery line, touching and being touched and never knowing anyone. You couldn't get away from the sheer mass and the loneliness even if you wanted to.

Yet here he'd found her.

He stared at the ceiling. His hands wouldn't warm up.

To win love, men put on an attitude of cleanliness, he thought, clipped nails, and shaved faces, sideburns like little battle axes, a soul patch below the lower lip or a thin goatee, lines of facial hair crisp, hard, geometric, glistening. The room was too quiet. He tried to warm his hands against his ribs.

He closed his eyes but couldn't sleep.

On free fall in the apartment, he moved from the bed to the kitchen where he drank a glass of milk, then went to the leather reading chair and stared at the window. Strange reflection: long white body, white T-shirt, white underwear, skin like alabaster but with abundant moles, light tan or dark brown, some black. He leaned and took an old issue of *Montana Quarterly* from the rack beside him. He read an article on a wolverine researchers collared that crossed nine mountain ranges in forty-two days. He fell asleep in the chair. Woke, stumbled back to bed. Night sifting the sediment of dreams. Dark animal, solitary, full of speed. Light. Morning. Glass of water. Toast. No TV, no radio. No sound. Driving I-5 to work he lifted from the heart pocket of his suit coat the pen Samantha had given him that first chance meeting. He thought of her holding the pen, a black ballpoint made of inexpensive metal alloy, pens the bank gave out. He'd seen her in the lobby after work, seated, writing a memo, a note to a friend, or perhaps her mother, left-handed—a note to him, he liked to imagine—her clear nail polish and French manicure, the pale half-spheres at the base of her fingernails like small suns touched to the ocean of her skin. It was sudden: more than anything he'd ever desired he loved the idea of her, of them together, forever.

Awful, the anxiety over his voice being too boyish, his hands too hard. He sat down next to her. "Can I borrow your pen?" he'd said.

"Sure," she said. "Keep it."

She slipped her fingers into her purse and drew forth an identical pen.

"Kind of you," he said, his hands not only icy but sweating.

She smiled.

He managed a few awkward questions. She grew up in East Tacoma. Her mother was from Puerto Rico. She mentioned her family, her studies, work. She looked right at him, not away.

He lost himself.

"Can I take you to dinner?" he said.

"What?" she replied.

"Sorry," he said.

He's country. Pero muy guapo. She didn't dislike him. Very handsome. She had the spirit of a wild horse: stay away, or come near if you dare. Samantha Valeria Arrarás knew she wasn't what people thought of when they thought of Americans. Puerto Rican from her mother, Ugandan from her father, along with Swedish and British. She'd let go of her father's surname and reclaimed her mother's. She loved her mother.

John's hands flushed with sweat again. He waved at her and turned to go and she smiled, and he was astonished at how much her smile delighted him. Down the hall, when she couldn't see, he slapped his hands together, covered his mouth and muffled a whoop. She hadn't even said yes.

Still, he felt as if the top of his head was on fire.

THE RING was like a small star in his pocket. Through the elevator doors from her floor, the third, going to his, the seventh, he was afraid. The first time on a saddle bronc was no different: exhilaration and horror. Glad he'd had the buck rein his dad bought for him secondhand, worn in and comfortable, if blackened. Single thick rope, awkward, tricky as a rattlesnake. The odor of sweat and rosin. He'd lost grip when the horse went rump high straight out of the chute, launching him headfirst into the dirt. Still, the buck rein was the only help; tiny saddle and his own balance no good to him at all. Bruised shoulder, and dirt in the nose and teeth for a week. Not a natural by any means but he could work. It took seven rodeos to complete his first real ride and when it came, it unhooked him good.

Digging spurs, arm high, horse a force of nature below, and John a dazzling dream above. The classic event of rodeo, skill and finesse over straight strength. He'd held the whole eight seconds, bounced and landed on his feet full of spit and fire. Cheer from the small-town crowd. Town called Rosebud, dustbowl, eastern Montana. Fatherless Child was her name, eleven-hundred-pound fighter he never saw again. Still loved that horse. Loved all the horses he'd rode. Metal chute, knees high-rails above the shoulders. The crowd, the gate pullers, the pickup men. Grit in the glove, horse's back hard as stone; muscle it down ready. Thick heat of body and breath from the animal. Knees up, spurs down, chute gate flung wide and animal and man sprung out clean and tight and wild. Tossed on a string, close to tetherless, horse like white lightning, free hand touching sky, punching, pulling, power in the hand of fear, and fear in the gut, and below fear tenderness, and deeper down, down deep love.

OFF THE ELEVATOR, John walked the hall and saw the men in their cubicles and was convinced that every man in the whole fortified world wanted an answer to the solitude, an answer that might help him set his world aright.

He knew their progenitors had come from almost everywhere, ranging near and far before they ended up in Seattle. Encompassed by water, they lived among rainforest. Be it a life of poverty or near limitless resources, the surroundings were only a faint reckoning of things far greater. Money, in one sense, was easy: limit your debt, increase your gains. Whoever did that had a real chance of bettering their circumstances.

But life and mystery were uncontainable.

Even if he never got to know the people who entered his door as fully as he wanted to, still he told himself he loved them. Their kindness and complexity, their deep and abiding failures, their eccentricities. The Queen City was theirs to claim. Because of Samantha, his vision enhanced like blown glass, it seemed he could love everything. His desk was L-shaped. His chair modern, leather-bound in gray with chrome legs and black wheels. Rolling from one side of the desk to the other, completing tasks with linearity and speed, he started to find everyone beautiful, like works of art, like something sacred he should give his life for. He remembered van Gogh, having read his letters to Theo in graduate school. The words stood in his mind now as if written in light:

The greatest work of art is to love someone.

Yes, he thought, it's true, even if he knew he himself would be hard to handle, his depressions like swollen rivers hard to cross. His job was rare in that he had access to the messiness of people's financial lives, things they preferred to keep hidden, credit scores and accumulated debt, how far short they were of 20 percent down, the years of burden that lay ahead, decisions fueled by health or illness, new opportunity or end of life, the hope of extraordinary success along with the possibilities of loss, total loss, bankruptcy and the inestimable harms that came with lack. His studies in philosophy helped him more than he thought they would. Gadamer's notion that time is fluid, it pauses and goes backward. Time marches on. Bakhtin's quest to find oneself in the beloved. Emmanuel Levinas and the beauty of the face. Love without reward, being of ultimate value.

Unknowingly we will ourselves to succeed or die, he thought. Before leaving at a decent hour this time, he stood. Out the window was a sky gray as stone. He looked at the back of his hands, rough instruments. Here in the Northwest or back home, blackbirds flew from tree to tree and down to standing pools or out over fallow fields looking for corn and wheat. They probed the bases of aquatic plants with their bills, plying them for insects. They ate ragweed and cocklebur, native sunflower and waste grains. They rose into the air wheeling at speed, diving, rising upward, banking low over ranch land or high over the hills of the city.

Below them men and women owed all, and owned nothing.

He turned back to his desk and placed his hands on the wood, feeling the hard surface again. At separate times, with no knowledge of each other, people came to him for loans at National American Bank on the corner of Westlake and Terry in downtown Seattle. As ardently as he did for himself, he feared for them and hoped for them.

He secured the best rates he could for them.

JOHN COULD give Samantha his whole life—he knew he could.

He repeated a line his mom had given him from one of her favorite poets: I who have died am alive again—thank you—for everything which is natural, which is infinite, which is yes.

But it's hard to stop dark thoughts, he reckoned, especially how the mind so quickly condemns. He needed courage for what he was about to do. He paused for a moment and stared at his screensaver, a panorama of mountains in Glacier National Park shouldering the blue of Hidden Lake. He wanted to make a life with Samantha. He felt severe anxiety. In a single rush he sat down and sent an email. Two days later came a phone call, followed by a meeting in the fifth-floor lounge. A shared lunch at week's end and the following week the first real date at Anthony's Homeport on Lake Washington.

"I never get tired of blue sky," she said. The day met the city in brilliant and deepening hues. She asked of his schooling, his interests, religion, work, his dreams. His family. She scared him, very much. But he felt joy in her presence. He asked of her mother's family, her father's. He wondered about her straightened black hair, the line of her eyebrows. She wasn't all numbers, he was glad, and told her so, intrigued with her upbringing. Her laughter. Her sense of joy. For her, he reminded her of some form of old European dignity. She loved his background in English literature, business, and philosophy. She'd dated a number of men. He didn't come on too strong. He let her move.

"You're handsome," she said. "I love your face."

He blushed. "You're kind."

He loved her face too but was too timid to say so.

It came out that she had a brother in prison. For something he'd not intended, she said, but couldn't manage to control. Her nuclear family was entirely shattered by it, her mother and father having come apart at the seams when she was fifteen, the rift between them wider and more silent since.

When the meal ended, they held hands for a moment at the table, smiling at each other as he paid the bill against her protest.

Leaving, they walked arm in arm.

A FEW MONTHS IN, she put him on the spot.

They were at Anthony's again, at a window table in a building that jutted over the water.

"You ready for me?" she said.

"I think so," he said.

He looked at his shoes, his grandfather's shoes. His grandfather's suicide like a fatal wound in John's own chest. During college he had to take a year off, returning to his parents after the onslaught of initial assignments tunneled him to such depressed thought he couldn't complete tasks.

He found it hard to get traction when he returned. Horses helped. What was the line-up he'd drawn in Reno back when he rode broncs for a living? It wasn't the animals with menacing names like Hell's Fire or Kitchen-of-the-Damned or Homicidal Tendencies that got you, it was the playful-named ones like Honey-Do or Conjunction Junction. Hell's Fire and HT were nothing. Honey-Do nearly broke his neck.

He and Samantha ate, staring at the water or each other.

With rough stock even the mean ones he loved, but he wasn't dumb; you could get kicked in the head by something you loved, and often it took a lot to avoid it. On the circuit you had to be careful but with abandon. Super vigilant, half-crazed. Everything so large-scale at the big rodeos—Kansas City, Laredo, Cheyenne, Denver, Sacramento. No more eleven-hundred-pounders, it was thirteen or more, fifteen hundred sometimes, horse blowing snot in the chute, white-eyed, fast, and powerful, with leaps that rivaled a gymnast. Roads, long black lines gray at the edges, hard driving, hard riding. He'd broken thirty bones, fingers and other hand bones, plus ribs; punctured his lung; he'd cracked a collarbone too, fractured his right scapula, and in a rodeo in Miles City broken his jawbone. His face wired up, he ate through a straw for more than a month.

His legs stretched toward Samantha, he looked at the shoes again. The first day he tried them on he'd found a sheen of dried blood on the shell of the left one. He was eighteen, just weeks after his grandfather's funeral. Back then it took no energy, his mind didn't dwell; he'd licked his thumb and removed the stain. His grandpa had only been sixty-five years old. Before he died, his parents said John was a lot like him. They didn't say that anymore. John had worn the shoes for an hour or two, then put them back in Grandma and Grandpa's closet. But now he thought darkly of his grandfather without wanting to. Tough old man who hardly spoke. Real down, ending it on a Sunday, body laid out behind the barn, head slung back and to the side. Dressed as if he was going to church. John remembered the slender barrel of the .270 flat on the grass. Then Grandma years later, but not violent, noble, or regal, even with Grandpa still a big hole in everything.

As a child, John had often wanted to die.

He never knew where the thoughts came from.

He looked at Samantha. His eyes were teary. He didn't want to admit how self-doubt moved like a dark spirit in him. His parents knew and walked the edges of it, trying to separate him from his feelings. Be ready, John's dad always told him, and John knew Samantha would challenge him the same way a bronc made a man reach, spur from the shoulder down, drop-swing motion, shoulder to ribwork, untempered, but rhythmic like a drum.

Alone in the high country he'd stop and lay his head on his horse's neck, Black, or Charlie, the two his dad still kept for him back home, Black an Arabian-cross, high in the legs and narrow face, and Charlie an old palomino quarter-horse. The sweet grass smell of the coat, breathing in, exhaling—it brought him back from any distance.

She stared at him. She was smiling. "You really think you're ready for me?"

He nodded his head and smiled back. "I believe I am."

SEATTLE, THE SUN hidden. John hadn't slept much.

He was in his office at 7:40 a.m. when he answered her call.

"Let's meet on the fifth floor again," she said.

"Sure," he said.

When he greeted her in the lounge he kissed her cheek and she smiled.

He thought her face looked pained.

"What's wrong?" he said.

"Nothing," she replied. "I just like seeing you."

Something's wrong, he thought.

He tried to look at her without looking away. "Are you okay?" he said.

"Fine," she said. She sat with one leg crossed over the other in a gray A-line skirt, darker gray tights, and black spool heels. She wore a light-plum turtleneck, her trim upper body forward some, her hands in her lap.

She touched his arm.

Her hand is so streamlined, he thought, like a swift or mountain swallow.

He took her fingers in his and started sweating. He tried to let go but she held on.

They were falling in love.

"Are you scared?" she asked.

"Down to my boots," he said.

IN DECEMBER he met her mother at their home in East Tacoma, and by February he set a surprise trip and they boarded the Amtrak Empire Builder at the King Street Station in Seattle and went by train through Spokane and deep into Montana along the Highline. He'd been dreaming of rodeo, big horses, sorrels and grays, blacks, massive crossbred pintos, paints, big rough stock from Texas, and him hat in hand and arm flying as he countered the arch-kicks and cut the leans. "In fact, bronco is Spanish for 'rough' or 'rude,'" he told her, "and it means warmbloods. A cross between draft horses and hotbloods like Arabians or thoroughbreds. Breeding was started in the 1930s by Feek Tooke in Ekalaka, Montana, and today you can see the results at every National Pro Rodeo."

She looked amused, enjoying his foray into Spanish.

When they arrived at the station it was after sundown and cold. His mother and father greeted them and they drove together into the fields for miles. Snow made the land pale white in the moonlight. He could see Samantha's presence blessed his parents. John looked out the window, trying to calm himself. He pictured pearl button shirts, three of them in a plastic container among the battle wares he'd carried on the road, the big canvas bag, the halter and halter strap, flank strap, buck rein, dulled spurs with rolling rowels, padded leather riding vest, bronc saddle in the floor space of the passenger side (lightweight, no horn), brushed Stetson (black, felt) atop his head and beside him on the bench a simple straw cowboy hat, black-banded, twelve bucks at K-Mart. No helmet—never liked helmets. He'd been on his own then.

His father, Jack, pale and still strikingly broad-chested, turned the sedan into the long two-track drive, the road flat and freshly plowed. He'd given John the buck rein with love in the giving. John saw the house in the distance, spare, with two outbuildings, and beyond, the long snowy plain that bordered the Rocky Mountain Front.

Not a few weeks back, John had called and asked if he could use Grandpa's two-person open carriage, and at that request his father had brushed it up and set it with runners for winter. Pamela, John's mother, went further; she adorned the sleigh with ribbons and bows and small delicate bells, silvery, starlike. Her Czech-Moravian sensibilities were uncommonly attuned to joy and family, and she loved the new lightness she saw in him. His father, German mixed with some Cheyenne, often said it had been his great delight to marry her. "We read together and ranch together," he told Samantha, "laugh together and dance together."

In the dark of morning his father drew the carriage to the front door of the ranch house leading a large gray work horse named Felicity, a family favorite, utterly gentle. John was in the old twin bed, the night still formless around him. Samantha was in the guest room, a room set west toward broad fields of snow and the expanse of two thousand acres John's father owned. John hadn't heard his dad go out, it was the familiar sounds that woke him: a few barks from the two blue heelers, followed by the tamp of hooves on fresh snow and the easy breath of the horse. He heard the glide of runners on new wax, the shimmer of bells. The smell of bacon and coffee brought them to the kitchen. Samantha was effervescent and unaware. In Seattle she'd deep conditioned her hair with hot oil, wanting it right for this trip. Montana air was dry, but it gave a fine luster and made her happy. She'd worn a black satin sleep cap and rose early to let the glow come up. She used the flat iron. Her hair was just as she liked. She felt beautiful at the breakfast table.

After breakfast, John bundled her himself.

"How nice of you," she said, "thank you."

Then he lifted her in his arms and carried her out the front door to the sleigh. When she saw it she gasped, and buried her face in John's coat. Her tears quieted him, and he drove her two miles in the half-dark to Elk Creek, cold air crisp and high in their lungs, snow covering the land to the east on a blue-white arc to the end of vision. From a rise of land they watched the sun emerge and fire the world and John held her hand and asked her to marry him.

BACK IN SEATTLE, though she said she considered herself a virgin and would keep it that way until marriage, they were moving in a stepwise physical progression: hold hands, embrace, kiss, kiss longer. *Catholic*, he thought.

His desire for her ascended like blackbirds on the wind.

He felt awkward in his body unless he was breaking horses, or being broken.

He'd thought himself inept with women, but months passed and she still found him charming, and this made him happy. She'd said she wanted a year to plan the wedding.

A weekday evening on Elliott Bay they ate oysters on the half-shell at Ivar's on Pier 54. She took his hands in hers and drew him close. She looked into his eyes. Her own eyes brimmed with tears. She kissed his lips.

She had a secret she needed him to know.

She couldn't tell him.

"Yes?" he asked.

He touched the corners of her eyes, smoothing her tears.

"It's nothing," she said.

"Okay," he said.

He took her at her word.

JOHN HAD limited knowledge of women. The woman's body was new to him, all his life having been unaccustomed to being with a woman he might date, love, or marry. Samantha was a secret, her soul something to which he was beholden, but of which he was largely ignorant. He and she spoke tentatively of life and the future, and likely because they weren't having any they avoided talk of sex.

Over Korean takeout she looked at him, content.

"I love the Seattle rainforest," she said. "I don't know fauna, but I know flora: blue-eyed grass, western iris, Peregrine thistle, and white-flowered hawkweed. Sea milkwort and mountain heliotrope, sticky currant, crowberry, dark woods violet, and coast black gooseberry."

Just last week she'd entered the lush density of the city's Pacific corridor, filled of black beach and rainforest, the water of a darker hue than usual. Buildings and boat life down along Dock Street, architecture springing up among the hills or out of caverns and swales of leafy overgrowth. She'd noticed a massive rake of coast rhododendrons in the dim light off the highway just past the long bridge.

"Yesterday I saw something miraculous," she said. "Flashing yellow in the dark, a willow goldfinch flying from a cluster of blooms. Rhododendron macrophyllum, the home of night beauty."

He imagined orcas gliding in the deep water north of Seattle.

"Te amaré por siempre," she said.

He lifted his eyebrows.

She didn't mind translating. "I will love you forever."

"Your turn," she said.

"Te amaré por siempre," he said. The words sounded like collisions. She grinned at his attempt, and his face reddened and they both laughed.

At night, alone, John was degrading himself to her image, using fantasy, trying to think only of her. When he felt unable to resist he used porn, in which case he could not think of Samantha, or he could only think of her head on someone else's body.

AT NIGHT, ALONE, Samantha spent time looking for facts. Her apartment viewed a brick wall north, and south beyond stacked public housing, a thin body of water. Her tía Sofía, an activist in Puerto Rico, got her started on it and the reading, inevitably, took her back home. She loved hearing her voice, and called her often.

"Beginning in the 1930s the U.S. sterilized Puerto Rican women, using them as guinea pigs," Sofía said from San Juan. "America enacts ongoing colonization of all Puerto Rican people to this day. Puerto Ricans still can't vote for the president or for those who serve in Congress though every Puerto Rican has to obey U.S. laws, pay U.S. taxes, and watch exorbitant percentages of our country's gross national product skimmed by U.S. interests.

"In La Operacion, known to U.S. government officials as FDR's Operation Bootstrap, Puerto Rican women were pushed toward sterilization in order to 'industrialize' the country. Eugenics as U.S.-imposed genocide began in 1936 and the percentage of sterile Puerto Rican women reached 39 percent by 1981. Keep reading," she said. "Don't forget your blood."

She wouldn't forget. She kept reading.

Puerto Rico, a protectorate of the United States, was used as a practice ground for bombing missions from 1948 to 2003, generating some of the highest cancer rates in the world due to radiation. Twenty-six thousand bombs were dropped on the Puerto Rican island Vieques in 1998 alone. A step closer, the U.S. not only infected Puerto Ricans with cancer due to the radiation caused by bombing as well as the radiation experiments the government conducted on Puerto Rican prisoners, but infected Puerto Ricans directly when Dr. Cornelius Rhoads, sponsored by the Rockefeller Institute, intentionally injected several Puerto Rican citizens with cancer cells in the name of science. He was an established physician, funded by the establishment.

Predictably, thirteen of his patients died, and he spoke of them as if they were vermin. Then he appeared on the cover of *Time* magazine.

America gave hatred.

Her Puerto Rican blood gave courage.

She thought her family a difficult mix of nations. Her father's father escaped Idi Amin's reign of terror, emigrated to England, and married a Brit

Swede woman. Her father married her Puerto Rican mother and she loved Puerto Rico because she loved her mother. She thought it justice to favor the heart of her mother, especially since her father had abandoned them. She needed sleep, but her mind wasn't still. She kept wondering how much of John's Whiteness, or hers for that matter, retained the blood of murderers like Rhoads.

SAMANTHA AND JOHN started to favor the open work space on the twenty-second floor for the view of the city and the Olympics. His sandwich was buttered bread, turkey and mustard. She ate rice with stir-fried cucumbers, carrots, and celery. "I like the high country for food," he said. "Deer or elk. Antelope on the plains. Wild turkeys in the cottonwoods when they roost, or in the fields where they feed. Pheasants, sage hens, grouse. These are my family's mainstays, plus beef and chickens. When you came home with me it was steak and chicken, but the wild meat is the best."

"Really?" she said, amused. She knew no hunters, and found it incredulous, but attractive in a way she couldn't name.

"I don't think you'd like it much," he said.

Like seeing a kingfisher in the trees along Mystic Lake her smile disarmed him. He needed to take her to Mystic too. Watching her he remembered the scent of his mom's cinnamon rolls carried from the oven to the oak table. He knew it to be a man's image of home and felt guilty.

"What about your family?" he asked.

"First and foremost, dessert," she said. "Preferably my mom's cinnamon rolls."

He laughed brightly. "Go on!"

"I love my mom's touch—Puerto Rican, definitely flavorful: roasted pork with yellow rice and gandules, deep-fried plátanos, shellfish, lobster, mussels, scallops, oysters, shrimp, crab, all in sauces to die for. Plus pernil, which is marinated pork shoulder. Basically, a lot of seafood and pork, or chicken—her asopao soup is heavenly. I think you'd love it all."

"I'm sure I would," he said.

"I'm sure I'd love your wild food too," she offered.

"I don't know," he said.

"Try me," she said.

"I will," he said.

"Good," she winked. "When?"

"When?"

"Yes, when should we go?"

"You mean go home to cook wild meat, or to hunt?"

"Both," she said.

He thought about it some.

"Guns and knife work," he said. "We shoot and clean the animal."

"And?" she said.

"All very bloody, skinning and quartering, using the bone saw, taking the meat and hide, skull and horns."

"Definitely sounds wild," she said. She leaned forward and touched his arm. "Let's go."

"Oh . . . okay," he said. "I think I can take you. Let me call my dad."

She chuckled. "You need to ask his permission?"

"No," he said, his cheeks pink. "He's just a better hunter. He'll know where to go. He'll prepare our gear."

"Your dad's a sweetheart," she said.

"You can wear my mom's boots and wool pants, down jacket if it's cold."

"This is thrilling," Samantha said, taking his hands.

"I hope so." He grimaced.

Her arms were strong, he thought, the muscles slender like filament or copper wire. He'd said yes to taking her hunting in Montana.

Thinking of how she might respond made him ill.

On his way back to his own workspace John happened to ride the elevator with the leader of the entire world holdings of National American Bank, owner-CEO Roark Rosenbaum Freeman. John recognized him but was shocked when the man put out his left hand to John. "Call me Roark," he said loudly, the handshake awkward, and John noticed the man's disfigured right hand hanging at his side.

"Tractor accident," Roark said.

They were alone, descending.

"Roar with a K," the man said. "Picked you out of the pile because you're from Montana."

John was surprised. He was unaware Roark knew anything about him.

IN EARLY FALL John and Samantha drove the pass below Glacier along Highway 2 through Browning and then south on Route 89 toward Valier as the sun went down behind the Elk River Gorge and the light lay low over the fields, the trees thick and many-hued along the river. The next day they helped his parents feed cattle, and that evening they enjoyed a meal of fried antelope and walleye along with sweetcorn and sweet tea. After sundown they turned the house lights off and talked by the fire pit off the back stoop, the circle of stone ablaze with tamarack. The blue heelers, thick chested, slept with their noses on their paws before the fire. In a simple chaise lawn chair, she lay with her back to his chest. The heavens were so bright she sighed and tipped her head back, a feeling of absolute joy in her as if her body were illumined.

She thought of Puerto Rico and the moon over the ocean.

She felt blessed beyond measure.

Holding her shoulders, he watched the sweep of her neck and the line of her jaw and thought of swans in the eddies of the Marias. He smelled night in the forest, cool and enclosed. He couldn't remember when he'd ever been so happy. He'd made dinner with his father. With white linen napkins folded over the left arm, they'd served the women. His mother and Samantha had spent the evening smiling and laughing.

"Early day tomorrow," his father said before he rose and went back into the house. John's mother went with him.

"Thank you for everything," Samantha said.

"Our pleasure, Samantha," Pamela said. "We're so glad you're here."

"A gift," his father said at the door.

So it was only him and her now in the black evening with the constellations like hoarfrost on the window of God. She leaned further back and he drew her close. "U.S. 89 is a Canada to Mexico highway," he said, "ending at Flagstaff, Arizona on the southern end." He cradled her in his arms and kissed her, a rich satisfying inhalation in which he heard a sound from her breathing that broke him with its tenderness. When their lips parted she held his face and he held her to his chest and they kissed until she lay her arm on his and set her head into the nook under his jaw. They were silent before they rose and he put out the fire. They held hands into the house where she prepared for sleep and went to the guest room again. He lingered in the kitchen watching her form in the dark before she turned down the lamp.

"Good night," she said.

"Good night," he echoed. Still watching her he whispered an old line of poetry, "the sight of the stars makes me dream." He moved through the house to his room, dreaming of her and the good their future might hold. He didn't feel any of the compression that normally afflicted his mind. He closed his eyes and slept like a bear.

For her part she was at peace. She remembered the birds he'd shown her that morning south among the vertical shoots of the cattails. She moved out from herself as she slept, ranging airborne from the marshes then ascending into the sky with speed, her body a flock of red-winged blackbirds moving as if tethered to her pulse.

NEAR four in the morning, John's father woke John and then Samantha. He made toast and eggs and they were in the truck by four thirty. The blue heelers watched them mournfully from the yard. On the window rack behind Samantha's head, the rifles were dark-barreled and sleek as they drove a dirt road into the mountains under the shadow of night, the sky obscure and unknowable. The dash lights lit their faces. His father answered every inquiry, his voice generous. Already he loved her for blessing his son.

"Tell me about these guns, Jack," she said, curious.

"Old family guns," he said, nodding over his shoulder. "Bought the .243 in 1972. The .22, for birds, is even older."

"Birds?" she asked.

"Yes," he said, "the birds are good eating. My favorite are grouse and pheasant. Sage hen is great too."

She craned her neck at the rifles before facing the road again, taking John's arm in hers. Though she was still in the main terrified of the idea of sex knowing what she knew, she saw in John something she wanted—kindness cloaked his power, and he carried an innocence toward her and his mother. She'd need to tell him of her life and family, sooner rather than later. She gripped his arm. The road curved, lifting toward the mountains. Clouds hovered over the ground in the predawn light, the rock by turns black or tinted faintly blue where sheer cliffs cut sharply upward.

"Impressive country," his father said.

"Astounding," she whispered. Her family had been urban, from East Tacoma's industrial flats. They did one weekend to Snoqualmie and Leavenworth when she was young, and a handful of trips back to Puerto Rico. The Catedral de Nuestra Señora de Guadalupe in Ponce. The Plaza las Delicias. But this was a different land. Colossal from every vista.

All her life she'd been leery of guns, but for John and Jack they seemed so natural.

"What happens with a rifle?" she asked.

"The mechanism?" John's father asked.

"Sure," she said.

"Well, the hammer hits the casing on the back of the bullet shell. The shell houses the gunpowder, and the strike causes a spark that ignites the powder. The explosion sends the bullet at high speed through the barrel and out to the target.

"Look at the stock on the .22," he said.

John pointed it out.

"Worn and darkened," Jack said. "Good feel of the wood in the hand. True line from the gun to the bird. No shotgun, no pellets spraying the animal. Just a single entry and exit. The bird is left intact, and no need to pick the metal bearings from the meat like you would with a shotgun. Pretty much ready for the frying pan once you clean and dress it and cut around the bullet hole. I've owned that gun since my second year in college. Gift from my father."

DRAWING HER CLOSER, John thought of his grandfather. He'd suicided with a rifle much larger than a .22. The burn hole under the chin, the exit wound like bedlam at the back of the head. His dad sold the gun at auction to get rid of it, but the gunmetal blue of the barrel still appeared in John's mind. No pushing ugly down, it stood up against beauty whether you wanted it to or not. He stared to the sky and the slow movement of the clouds over the far ridge, a soothing the land underwent from above.

He kissed Samantha on the temple. She smelled like wintergreen.

She looked at him. His family wasn't like hers, she thought. The Senders were more solitary, and distant from their own relatives. Distant relatives: the term likely came from northern Europe, she thought, not warm weather countries like her mother's Puerto Rico. In her family, everyone was close, you took care of everyone, you dropped everything and loved them whatever the cost. You helped them reach heaven. His family was loving too, but quieter, more private. Her mom's family had machismo and matriarchy but no stiffness: mom and dad, sisters and brothers, and everybody else could claim the same love, same food, same house, even the same bed. Everything swam the same muddy water. Every plate everyone else's, every door open to everyone. Except when they hated someone. Her mom had cousins in Puerto Rico as close as a sister, aunties she called mom like her own mother. Others she never spoke to. Bitter as the grave. But family was yours and you were theirs, no matter how peripheral, be they blood relative or not. Her family partied more, danced more, ate more, or ate more crazily, she thought, more sauce, more spice. They lived on top of each other. They lived in circles. Of course they had their jailbirds too, not just her brother, but a flock of men young and old, and one drug-ridden grandpa back in Puerto Rico.

She admired the orderly feel of John's family.

Attention to detail. Undeviating.

"The bird ends up fried or in a stew with potatoes, carrots, and celery," John's father offered. "For bigger animals, the Remington .243 there. Among big animal rifles, a lighter one, which I like, with a wide-angle Redfield fourplex scope for a two to seven power-variable." Her mind worked for translation. The words were alien to her. "Bullet travels twenty-nine hundred to three thousand feet per second. Dinners of elk or deer steak, elk or deer hamburger, summer sausage along with excellent elk or deer jerky. Antelope.

"We shoot at four power," he said. Samantha was tucked into his son, her face pleasant as she watched the rim of light in the east. "The mind experiences a reverse echo. The animal drops before you hear the report."

"How big are they?" she asked.

"Very big," he said. "Seven hundred to a thousand pounds for a bull elk. The cows or females run about five hundred to seven hundred pounds. With the bulls, unless it's a trophy animal we sell the hide and rack to a fur buyer. Just the hide with cows. An elk hide goes for fifteen or twenty dollars, and for bulls the complete skull and rack, raw, uncleaned, and frozen, goes for sixty or seventy dollars depending on size. The ivory teeth of a mature bull sell for forty dollars a pair, the ivories of a mature cow are ten dollars a pair. The molars aren't good for anything but chewing cud."

"You harvest the teeth?" she asked.

"People make jewelry of it," John said.

"Just the ivories," Jack continued, pointing to his own eye teeth. "Also called buglers or whistlers. They threaten other animals with their ivories, they don't bugle with them."

"Strange they're made of ivory," she said.

"Yep," he said, "just like a walrus or an elephant, but smaller and enclosed in the mouth." The plain unique ways God made women, men, and animals, he thought. "They polish up cream-colored or white if they're not too old. Scentless. People make necklaces and bracelets, or embed them in watches or rings or some fool thing or another."

THEY RODE in silence then, much of the land to the west still dark, light rising from below the world. They drove among immense mountainscapes, the road a steady incline of peaks and sky. John loved his father's kinship with wilderness; his father knew trees and plant life, wildflowers and seemingly every animal, badgers, bobcats, mountain lion, lynx, bighorns, deer, elk and antelope, coyote and wolf and wolverine, ferrets, porcupines, water snakes and rattle snakes, toads, frogs, turtles, even the mountain salamander John found under a rock in a rainstorm, black-bodied with a bright spine, yellow-striped from head to tail. But he knew birds most: meadowlarks, mountain swallows and swiffts, bald and golden eagles, nighthawks and red-tails, magpie, crow, yellow-headed and red-winged blackbirds, sandhill cranes, herons, mountain blue jays.

"The state of Montana holds a hundred mountain ranges," John said. "Many at eight to twelve thousand feet."

She touched his face. He kept talking. In her experience most men either talked too much or couldn't talk at all. They lectured others or spoke nonsense or kept silent. No words for feelings, as if the soul was also silent. But get a good man in his element and he was a river of sound.

"All of Pennsylvania and much of the Eastern Seaboard can fit inside Montana," he continued. "Blue-capped tree swallows. Gray owls. Goldfinches. The mountain lion leaps as high as fifteen feet and as far as forty.

"You should have seen my dad's uncle Billy's two-room shack. He was a trapper. Generally went by horseback, even though he lived right there in Choteau. Grandpa said he was decent with people when he was young but he suffered too much. His only wife died in childbirth and so did the child. He never married again. Dad took me to visit often. Old place with thin walls but he had a potbellied cast iron woodstove that heated the place like an inferno. Dried animal hides on boards leaning against the walls. A rough-cut table. Rattlesnake rattles in a small pile on the surface. A wooden three-legged stool. Hunting knife with a horn handle stuck into the cutting board. In the corner on the floor, small- and medium-sized steel traps. An old rifle up against the door."

"Lived like one of the wild creatures," Jack said.

"He did," John echoed. "I loved walking the trap line with him. Sad he's gone now. Died of a heart attack."

"Wish I could have met him," Samantha said.

"Me too."

"He would have liked you, Samantha," Jack said.

Samantha smiled.

"John, what was it like growing up with your dad?"

"That old coot?" John said and the men laughed. "In general, very good. Hard work. A lot of love. Tough. Humble. Happy. Taught me everything I know of rodeo and mountains, rivers and streams. Life. Family."

"I didn't teach you a thing about rodeo." Jack said. "That gift came from above."

John hooted. "Didn't feel like it, with all the broken bones."

His dad snorted. "Nothing true ever came easy. Plus it was your mom, not me, who taught you about family."

"See what I mean?" John nodded to Samantha.

"I do," she said.

"Almost there," John's father said. "Just over this rise."

THEY WALKED with near empty packs up through the trees where the sun filtered geometrically through wide-bole pines. The wet scent of the earth was thick though there was no rain. Unseasonably warm, the snow lay in the sharp cradles of rock thousands of feet above them. Unearthly, and more of an internal harmony than John remembered, elk bugles broke the air. He and his father in cowboy boots and old dark felt cowboy hats, Samantha in the hiking boots his mother let her borrow and a navy blue knit hat. Jack carried high-powered binoculars centered at his chest in a cross-harness.

"Sounds otherworldly," Samantha said.

"Among the great wonders," John's father replied.

They followed Jack's quick soft pace up through the trees skirting a meadow until he motioned them silently to the ground where they removed the packs. He set his hat in the grass. John did the same. Jack resituated the binoculars to his back. They all crept forward, chest to the earth, scrub grass and hard dirt beneath them, keeping their heads low, John slightly in the lead. He held the rifle flat to the ground, the barrel facing forward and away.

His father put a finger to his mouth, hushing them as he pointed over the lip down a gradual draw beside a rock overhang where Samantha made out the bodies of big animals, their breath rising pale through a mist where the great horns mingled. Eight bull elk fed on the grass near the river, their heads dipped to the ground or uplifted as they stood still or moved forward. The furthest one tipped his head back and she heard a high ghostly clarion. She was flat to the ground near John's left shoulder, between him and his father. The sound chilled her spine and tears came to her eyes.

John looked through the scope. The shot was a good distance, about three hundred yards. No wind here, but some on the land below. A slight bend to the willows. He placed the crosshairs just behind and above the shoulder of the bull in the middle. The shoulder was enormous. The animal a six-by-seven with a thick dark horn and silvered tines back-bent and alight. The giant crown swept up and out more than six feet in circumference. The elk would be a thousand pounds or larger. For a moment John wondered how Samantha felt about all this. He hoped she felt okay. The day would go red with the bone saw and knifework. He put it from his mind and steadied his breathing, holding the cross behind and a little above the animal's shoulder. He filled his chest with air, breathed out slowly and let the bullet ride. The bull collapsed from the chest downward, the horns tipping sideways into the ground.

The report echoed off the mountain walls.

"Very fine," his father said.

The other bulls trotted downriver and paused a few hundred yards on where they stood alert for a time until they calmed and dipped their heads again, eating.

John and his father and Samantha stood.

"Good bullet position," his father said.

John nodded once in recognition.

Samantha exhaled.

John looked at the tears on her face.

"I'm sorry," he said.

"No," she said. "I'm good."

"You sure?" he asked.

"Yes."

His father went to one knee, resituated the glasses to his chest, lifted them and peered down the draw. The other bulls were on the move again, into a stand of trees farther on.

"It's so final," she said.

In the crisp air, clouds of breath rose over her.

"Yes," Jack said, "Yes it is."

WITH HIS FATHER and Samantha, on the descent from Black Pine Ridge down to where the elk lay, John thought of the people whose loans he processed. They came from everywhere. He wanted to be less concerned with his life. He knew almost nothing about them, but considering how people encompassed the world and how only a few generations back his family had also immigrated in the hope of something more, they meant something to him.

And he loved them.

Just last week in the office, John had been daydreaming, looking out the window as he'd placed his thumb behind his earlobe and brushed the smoothness there. The feeling of being lost accompanied self-soothing, a self-loathing that went back to his childhood when he'd touched his chest under his shirt over fear of impending doom. He thought of it as the shade of his grandfather, a stone door hiding his father's anger, a glass one protecting his mother's intensities.

He believed in love but fear was not easily dislodged. What would he and she make of the world? When they emerged on the flat below, they walked with his father among spears of timothy grass. The sun had burned off the mist and the river shone pewter in the light, sweeping away from them along the plain.

"North Fork of the Teton," John said. He motioned with his nose to the mountains. "Crooked Mountain, and behind it, Hurricane."

He watched her as she walked next to him.

He loved her more than anything.

"QUICK IN THE field, son," Jack said.

Samantha questioned John with her eyes.

"Bears," he said. "Shouldn't be more than fifty or sixty minutes to dress it, then five or ten to load the packs. Do you smell the bear musk?" He waved his hand toward the tree line, the air heavy with it.

"I don't think so," she said.

John's father tagged the animal, attaching the tag with a zip tie. On a cylindrical sharpening tool that looked like a dark pencil Jack sharpened the hunting knife, a slender seven-inch blade with a bone handle. He opened the elk's lips and made four quick cuts in the gums with the knife. Then he asked John for the pliers and proceeded to remove each eye tooth with a slow downward motion. He handed the teeth and pliers to John, and commenced the larger work. They splayed the elk on its back as Jack straddled the lower body. Facing the blade away from him, he gripped the handle in both hands and cut from the base of the pelvic bone up through the ribcage, vigorously jerking the blade through the skin where the ribs met, and up through the sternum to the neck. This opened the animal and left the body cage wide. John helped keep the body splayed. Samantha agreed to hold the front foreleg. John recognized his father's secrets, especially how he used the knife to open the body at the ribcage and sternum. Most men made it a bloodbath, hacking the body with an axe. The more restrained movement, with a knife, was precise, as it should be.

Steam rose from the opening, the entrails and inner organs intact in willowy sacks, and hot. Jack was careful not to open the guts. Samantha felt a little lightheaded but fine overall. Jack had rolled his sleeves above his elbows. His hands and forearms were covered in blood. The work had much greater speed than she imagined. After about ten minutes, with a simple nod John and his father traded positions midstride and John rolled up his sleeves, sharpened the knife again and kept at the elk skin, cutting along the white fat of the hide where it met the marbled muscle of the body.

All she did was hold the hoof, or more like the wrist, she thought, but she felt good even if it was all so foreign and shocking. She'd taken record of things John mentioned back in Seattle. Wilderness in winter. Rock formations bound by snow.

A man found frozen to death on a fence line.

A woman pierced through the eye by the tine horn of a bull moose.

Jawbone of a lynx.

Beak of a crow.

The scent of tree sap. Grasses and wet rock and scat. He'd mentioned the sweetness of lupine and a wildflower called sticky shooting star, along with lady slipper, paintbrush, and wood lily. Mountains blackened by spruce and fir, white bark pine and lodge pole. Small birds flitted among the brush along the river.

He's lovely, she thought. His world is lovely.

John's father used the legs to tip the body as John drew the hide away from the ribcage with clean swipes of the knife, doing the same on the other side as his father tipped the animal back. The skin peeled from the body singularly. John pulled out the entrails, scattering them in the bunch grass between the animal and the river. His arms were hand to elbow in blood. He'd cut around the base above each hoof, digging the knife under the skin, flattening the blade to lift the hide away so it could be peeled back from the hooves to keep the hide whole.

Especially gruesome, John thought, sawing bone. The spine needed to be cut in order to remove the head. He used the knife first, passing it through the neck and windpipe to make room. Then he employed the bone saw vigorously to the spine until the head broke free. After that he quartered the animal, cutting through shoulder and hip joints before he sawed off each of the hooves and threw them toward the entrails. He took the edibles: the thighs, tenderloins, backstraps, neck and shoulder roasts and the scrap meat for the grind pile. Carefully caping the animal, he and his father took the hide from the upper body, the area from the lower chest behind the forelegs in a circle across the back in front of the hind legs and up through the shoulders, neck, and head. They leaned the elk to one side again to cut into the hide from the lower back to the base of the horns. Head, horns, and cape would be packed out in one piece.

"How are you doing?" he asked Sam.

"Good," she said. "The elk gives all doesn't he."

"Everything," John said.

"The remnants will feed bears, wolves, and hawks," his father added, "as well as coyotes, crows and other scavengers. Magpies, insects, maggots. The body is picked clean." He nodded to the open rib cage and body cavity.

She was surprised the blood had no smell to her, but could be so easily detected by other animals.

"The bones go white and dry from exposure to sun, wind, rain, and snow. Even these will be eaten down by porcupines. Walk the same path a year later you'll find the body disassembled, the bones fanned out and largely gone." John kept at the knifework, his arms moving swiftly as his father placed the quarters and other essentials in black garbage bags, tying the top in a quick knot.

GRACE EXISTED in the plain mercies between people, Samantha thought. She and her mother. John. John's mother and father. Her and John. A smile. A generous word. A touch. Lifelong commitments in a single glance.

All three packs were lined up on the ground now and loaded, larger and thicker than he expected. His father lifted and positioned the cape and head, tying it to the upper frame of John's pack. "The more traditional style is the European mount," John said, "the one I favor. For the European, the horns and whole skull are needed but no cape. The skull is bleached white by placing it in a bucket of maggots first then setting it on the roof for the sun to dry and whiten it further. Some people boil it to get it clean. The horns are then painted brown before skull and horns are set to a wood backdrop. The look is stark and skeletal. Ethereal. Beautiful."

HE COULDN'T BELIEVE she was here with him, and love so utterly unique in every human heart.

BY THE TIME all was bagged and ready, the blood on the back of John and Jack's hands had dried to a crimson sheen. Jack took a water bottle and an old blue towel from the side of his pack. He poured water over John's hands and arms and John pushed the blood down until the skin came pale again. His father gave him the towel but the blood and animal fat under the nails and in the nail beds wouldn't be clean until he was home. He mirrored the process with his father and when they looked at Samantha she raised her hands, which were pristine, and they chuckled.

John and his father offered the water to her and she drank and returned it and the men drank the water down. John stuffed the towel and empty water bottle back in his pack before he kneeled and his father hoisted the load onto John's back. The head of the elk was wrapped in canvas and strapped to the pack, the head facing downward, the wide spread of the horns and tines arcing upward like wings. John stood and helped lift the other pack to his father's back as his father kneeled. His father stood and lifted Samantha's pack in his right hand and she approached and angled into it.

They set off up the draw under a sky aglow in the east.

The first uphill climb was like digging stairs from a pit. They paused for rest multiple times and when they topped the ridge they put their hands on their knees and took in air as if their lives were hollow reeds. "Tough one," Jack said as he motioned down the draw. "Hard-bitten." The walk was steady as they crossed the meadow, the horns balanced over John's gait, the tines like great spikes sent up from the top of his back.

"No bear sign," Jack said.

"Good," John said. "But I still smell bear."

"Yep," Jack said.

Midway to the vehicle Samantha noticed the sun had tilted. The two men veered right and sat together on a ledge of rock half buried in the earth. She stood in front of them. The men put their hats down on the stone. Their hair wet and blackened, they leaned back against their packs, slipping their arms free. John was careful with the elk rack. They stretched their hands overhead before letting their arms drop slack to their sides. Samantha removed her pack, stepped onto the ledge and sat down cross-legged between them.

Jack reached into an outer pocket in his pack and pulled out three plastic freezer bags: a sandwich, a Snickers bar, and a Coke in each. "Never much for water over lunch," he said. "Coca-Cola being one of the finer pleasures." The sandwiches were buttered bread, sliced elk sausage, and pepper jack cheese. They sat together and ate, admiring the Front, clouds billowing downward over a distant mountain as if falling from a rock pool. The day was warm. In July, Jack had seen a brood of dust-blue butterflies shimmering on the groundcover. Nothing now. The men sighed almost in unison. They ate like wolves.

On the ride home she told herself she'd tell John everything.

They donned the packs again and kept a strong pace considering the weight, making it to the truck before dusk and home by dinner. They spent less than an hour in the garage, the three of them with John's mom, cutting the elk meat into steaks they wrapped in butcher paper, marked and put in the freezer. They cleaned up and came to the table. With fine conversation over the day's events they had white wine with a meal of fried and breaded rainbow trout, well-seasoned, and red potatoes under rosemary butter.

Holding Samantha's hand, John sat back in his chair.

He loved the smell of home.

IN THE MORNING John and his mom took Samantha pheasant hunting while his dad used a horse and the blue heelers to move the cattle to the upper field. They rode in Pamela's truck three across with Pamela driving, Samantha in the middle, John on the passenger side. With the .22 angled between his legs, barrel to the floorboard, they drove dirt roads midmorning with the sun flared on the Front, the long cliff-face a thrilling glory above the plains. The washboard road jolted them even with the slow pace they took hugging the shoulder. They looked for birds in the fields and barrow pits.

After breakfast, just behind the house, John had taught her rudimentary shooting with the smaller rifle. She shot at a paper plate set against the hillside. The exhilaration, strangely, settled her after all they'd done the day before. She eyed the land to the west. "The only place in America where bears still come down from the mountains to their fens on the plains," Pamela said. "One of the world's Magnificent Seven wildlife areas. Uplifts of rock many miles long, the most famous being the Chinese Wall just north of our home, up on the traditional Blackfeet lands near the Badger-Two Medicine area. Also, Castle Reef, near here. The Rocky Mountain Front is North America's most prominent site of mountain forming. The Blackfeet called it the Backbone of the World."

The truck crept to a halt where three male pheasants strutted the edge of a fallow field. They looked British, Samantha thought. Red facemasks, iridescent green necks and white-ringed throats, the gold chest plumage and long black-striped tail feathers also brinded brown. Suited in formal attire, they carried themselves with pomp and circumstance.

Pamela turned off the engine.

"Perfect," John said. "Let's switch places, Samantha. Slide over me."

She did and he rolled the window down, checking the safety and setting the rifle out as he spoke her through the progression. "Hug it to your shoulder. Look through the scope. Do you see the bird? Close your off-eye."

"Okay," she said.

"Lean in," he directed her. He had his arms around her shoulders, his hands on her forearms, shaping her. "Are you comfortable? The body should be comfortable."

"I am," she whispered. "I see the bird."

He released her. “Place the crosshairs on the upper chest, just below the white ring. Let your breathing come easy. Use your thumb to undo the safety.”

She heard ticking from the truck. A slight wind among the grasses.

“When you’re ready, take a nice slow breath and hold it, then let it out and squeeze the trigger, keeping your eye on the chest.” His voice was deep.

When she fired, she saw a puff of dirt rise in front of the lead bird. The pheasants skittered in different directions but didn’t fly. She kept the rifle butt firm on the inner curve of her shoulder.

“They’re well fed,” he said. He took the gun, popped the casing with the bolt action and loaded the chamber again. “Give it a moment, then try again.”

“You were close,” Pamela said. “This time you’re good.”

Samantha chose the second bird now where he halted, facing her forty yards away. She breathed in and held her breath and when she exhaled and squeezed the trigger the bird fell sideways in the scope and lay still with one wing open a little above the body. From the small cylindrical housing above the trigger came a whiff of smoke.

“That’s it!” he said.

“Very nice,” his mother said. “Well done.”

Samantha’s lips trembled. Her heart was high in her chest.

“May I?” John said and thumbed the safety and she pressed the stock into his hand and slid under it and over his lap as he moved to the door again. He cleared the casing. The other two birds were thirty yards upfield now and he dispatched them in two shots not five seconds apart.

They walked to the field together and he lifted her bird first and rung its neck. The bones made an audible snap. He did the same with the other two before he took a small jack knife from his jeans pocket, meticulously cut and pealed back the skin, removing each body from its feathers as if from a jacket. “Comes off easy when the body’s hot,” he said. “Much harder if you let it get cold.” He cut from the ribcage down then, opening the birds and throwing the innards into the dirt at his feet, letting the blood empty from the body cavity. He made two quick incisions on either side of the joint above the feet and snapped them off at the natural bend. His mom pulled a black plastic bag from her coat pocket and he placed the birds in, their bodies clean and glossy. They walked back to the truck where he opened the door and placed the bag on the floorboard before taking out a bottle of water, pouring water over his hands and rubbing them together. He wiped his hands on the grass and on the front of his jeans and they all got back in the truck.

Samantha felt queasy.

"You're a natural," John said to her.

SAMANTHA AND JOHN set the table with crystal glasses, bluebird china, and silver. Pamela placed two simple pewter candle sticks with white tapers in the middle. "I'd love to have you cook with me," she said, and they helped her at the kitchen counter, cutting the pheasant filets and coating them in a mix of egg yolk, ground almonds, and light flour. They fried the birds with butter and olive oil and a spoonful of wine and let the filets burn some to seal the juices before they lowered the heat for finishing. They blackened asparagus spears the same way, and prepared potato puree with honey butter.

Samantha felt fine now, having prepared the food with John and his mother.

His father came in from the fields. He cleaned up in the washroom and came out to greet them. "Splendid," he said, admiring the table as he lit the candles and they all sat down together.

"To Samantha and John," his mother beamed, lifting her glass. "May your love be full, and your life a joy forever."

Her favorite Riesling looked perfect in the fluted glasses.

"For good health and kindness," said his father. "And to friendship!"

"Thank you," Samantha said through tears.

They touched glasses and drank to each other.

IN THE MORNING John and Samantha hugged Pamela and Jack, John's mother kissing Samantha's cheek, his father drawing them all into a bear hug so they leaned in and their heads met. "Be safe," he said, his voice breaking. They held each other before John and Samantha went to the car.

Pamela waved goodbye. Jack walked toward the fields.

John and Samantha drove west to Glacier and skirted the southern line of the park down through the Mission Range. They'd borrowed an old pair of his father's binoculars and stopped on occasion, eyeing big hawks on the fence lines, a coyote loping in the distance, a yellow-headed blackbird at the tip of a cattail. "Yellow is capable of charming God," she whispered.

As they crossed the border at Post Falls and drove through the foothills around Spokane, then the high desert after Ritzville, they spoke of nothing grave: what made for great music, a Willie Nelson duet with a woman named Grace, two different turkey hunts with his father that had some humor to them, the exact day and time she knew she loved him, the exact day and time he knew he loved her, how to whistle, her shoe size, her waist size, an encounter in the high country when he'd seen an eagle crouched over a deer carcass. He encircled her wrist with his thumb and forefinger, delighting in her happiness.

Going up Snoqualmie Pass his mind turned back toward work life. Lending. Borrowing. He didn't notice her quietness.

She was convincing herself to face him. She felt strong enough but wasn't sure he could bear what she had to say. She'd waited too long, she feared, much longer than she should have. After Snoqualmie and past Mount Vernon, over the long bridge on the highway into Seattle, she said, "Remember when I told you my brother was in jail?"

"Yes," he said.

"He—" she hesitated. "Remember how you told me about your Uncle Hibbie who did time in the Montana State Penitentiary for writing too many bad checks?"

John nodded.

"My brother, London, was in prison for more than that," she said.

"Oh?" he said and glanced at her.

Her voice caught. She cleared her throat. "For quite a bit more," she said.

Her face went taut. He silenced himself.

"Will you pull over please?" she asked.

"Here?" he said. They drove through the I-5 corridor downtown.

"Please," she said, and he moved the truck to the shoulder, coming to a halt as cars roared past.

"He was convicted of rape," she said.

"My God," John said, staring at her face.

"He raped me."

"My God!" he shouted.

"I know. I should have told you."

"My God," he said, quieter.

She put her head down.

"I'm sorry," he said. "Please go on. How old were you?"

"The bad stuff started when London was twenty and still living at home. From when I was twelve to when I was fourteen. When he was arrested, it sort of wiped out my mother and father. I think my father blamed himself. He was always a self-critical man. He left soon after London's arrest and I haven't seen him in the years since. My brother went to prison, served his time, and got out. We've lost him now and my mom and I don't know where he is."

"Oh," John said. Not knowing what to say, his face was hot. He pressed his earlobe between his thumb and forefinger.

"My God," he said again. Tears spilled from his eyes. He touched her arm, then wiped his face on his sleeve. "I don't . . ."

"You don't need to say or do anything," she said. "I just need you to know."

He took her face in his hands and they stared at one another and wept. He held her to his chest. Then he held her face again. "I do," he said. "I do need to say something. I need to do something." He shook his head. "I need to find him."

"No you don't," she said.

"Yes," he said, "I do," his chest heaving, dark thought compressing his mind and ticking upward. He put his hands in his lap. She watched him. "Where do you think he is?" he asked.

"During the trial he was held in King County Jail. Then they moved him to the penitentiary in Walla Walla. When he got out they put him in a halfway house in Seattle. Then he was on the streets. Then we lost him."

"I need to kill him," he said. His words felt like someone else's, like barbed arrows shot from his mouth. He pressed his hands into the wheel, pushed the brake to the floor.

"No," she said. "You don't." She wouldn't be the woman the statistics told her to be. She'd been sexually abused. It was heinous even to speak of. Her brother, and by his absence, her father, had taken her innocence. That, they could never replace. She'd done the work to regain herself, she felt sure now. More and more since they'd lost London, her faith had taken on the texture of reality to her. Like her mother Alma Victoria's faith, and her beloved grandmother Alma Valencia.

John didn't understand. She would need him to understand.

She placed her hand over his. "Look at me, John."

When he turned to her he broke again and she didn't take her eyes from him. His arms shook as she kept her hand on his and placed her other hand on his shoulder.

"I don't want you to think this way," she said. "In fact, I forbid you."

A semi blew past, rattling the windows.

He looked away. "I can't agree to that," he said. He had gasoline on his hands. He smelled the pungent benzene fetor of it.

"You'll have to," she said, still holding him, pressing her hand to his chest. "I'm living my life. Wherever London is, he needs to live his. You and I need to live ours."

"How?" he said. His look was severe.

"Breathe," she said.

"This is too much," he said, looking away from her.

Watching him now as he turned away, she thought perhaps she should have waited longer. She put her hand on the back of his head.

"It's too much," he said.

"Nothing is too much." She touched him gently.

His neck felt thick. He'd thought her a virgin like him and now it mattered in an evil way. He hated his thoughts.

"I don't know what to do," he said.

"Some things are beyond knowing," she said. "Life is life. Death is death. Sometimes life is like death. We weather it or we don't. If we let it be, death can be like sleep. Then we wake. After London went to prison, after he was there for some years, I began to change."

He let go of the wheel and faced her again.

"I stopped cutting, stopped covering my face behind my bangs. Stopped being suicidal. Stopped courting alcohol, drugs, misery. Applied myself in school. Found two great mentors. Went to college. Found one of the top counselors in the city who has spent her career working with rape victims. Found women like me who wanted to live."

She'd taken a pilgrimage with her mentors through religious sites in Spain where in a dim lit corner of one of the recesses of the Basilica at Montserrat north of Barcelona she'd seen a young woman enter, hooded, with her head bowed. The woman approached a great black crucifix, reached upward and held the feet of Christ. Weeping quietly, she kissed Christ's feet. Samantha didn't fully know her own will to love, or even believe. When she was younger she might have said "none" if asked on a government form if she believed. She'd never say none again. Now she saw forgiveness and atonement as hidden powers below everything.

He looked in the rearview mirror, then at her. Her eyes glistened with the hardness of jade. She was alive and well. Nothing was important to him anymore. Nothing of his past. Nothing he'd made of himself. Not the horses he'd ridden. Not the money he'd made or positions he'd held. Only her. Her friendship and what his mother would call Samantha's immortal self. Herself, her beloved person connected to him.

They were in his truck, a beat-up Ford, parked on the shoulder of the freeway downtown. The heights of industry ascended above them. Vehicles tunneled forward at great speed. "You're everything to me," he said.

"Te amo de pies a cabeza," she whispered.

He turned, questioning her.

"I love you completely," she said.

"I love you too," he said, as he put the truck in drive, held her hand, and checked the rearview mirror, accelerating on the shoulder before he entered the lanes.

"We're alive," he said. He felt so bereft for her.

She drew his hand to her face.
"Thank you for telling me," he said.
"Thank you for listening."

THEY TOOK the exit south into the city along the water past the stadiums, passing through the Pioneer-Skid Row district. When they stopped at her apartment, he walked her to her door on the third floor. They kissed one another with feeling before they parted, and he drove back north through the city to his own solitary room.

They slept little that night, aware of the knowledge between them.

He doubted his readiness for what lay ahead.

She didn't know how he'd respond.

Her body then had seemed to her a blank void. Herons like signatories flying low over gray water. But the soul could heal the body. Her mother had brought her back from dark submersion. She felt safe with John. There was wilderness within her not unlike the high mountain terraces he'd known. She wanted to preserve that wilderness together.

THE NEXT DAY, a Sunday, she called and he met her for coffee in a shop called Pearl overlooking the Sound a short walk from her apartment, a place brimming with activity and honeycombed with private alcoves. At a leather chair halfway through the room he recognized Gabriel Kennedy Reed, a man he'd written a loan for. John remembered his wife, Angelica, beautiful, buxom, kind. He nodded and Gabriel smiled.

When Samantha and John sat down at a table facing the water, she took his hand.

"How are you?" she asked.

"How are you?" he said, staring at her.

"Not good," she said. "Wondering if you want the ring back."

His hands started to sweat.

"I don't want the ring back," he said.

Her friend Mary told her those she loved had given her a box full of darkness. She had eaten the dark hours. It took her years to understand that this, too, was a gift.

"I'll need help to go where we're going," he said.

He needed to go home again where his mother would have something important to say. She'd be a touchstone to him and Samantha.

"You'll walk this road with me?" she said.

"Yes," he said.

She loved his voice, and how he kept his eyes steady on hers.

"Eres el amor de mi alma," she said.

"Tell me," he said.

"You are the love of my soul."

"Dear Samantha," he said, "you are the love of my soul."

"I'll have to go home," he said.

"When?"

"Soon."

"Why?"

"I can't be wanting to kill your brother. I need to see my mom and dad and go to the mountains to sort things out."

She believed him.

"I understand," she said.

"I called my boss this morning. Didn't tell him anything, just said it was serious and I asked for another week, and he said fine."

John took both her hands in his now. He wasn't sweating anymore.

"May I have your permission to tell my parents?"

"Yes," she said.

"They will be respectful," he promised.

"I know," she said. She wanted them to know.

FOR SAMANTHA and her mother, life had been a pinwheel of daggers both before and after her brother went to prison. But what had once consumed Samantha became something she'd lived through. Something she'd forgiven, and let go of in burning ceremonies and long meditations, in America, in Puerto Rico, in Spain, and by living her own life.

After John left for Montana she drove to a meeting she knew in the basement of the Lutheran church on Union Street. The mentors she knew now, especially the older ones, were sisters to her. They were not defined by what they'd suffered. The hell they'd gone through was unspeakable. But they'd endured. They were women of every color, every class. They were open. Keeping secrets beckoned the landslide. As children or grown women, men demeaned, degraded, cursed, or loathed them. Kicked them. Beat them. Burned holes in their bodies. Molested and raped them. Over the years handed them off to an uncle, a son. They'd whipped them and thrown bricks or bottles at them. They'd held them over cliffs or out the windows of speeding cars. Subjugated or imprisoned them. Hated them.

"Sex abuse is base and ugly," said Selah, a Black woman with tight curls. "Soul murder. But still we rise."

To Samantha the women in the room were estuaries. They contained darkness and set life in motion. They greeted one another and named their wounds, cried together, laughed together.

She tried to speak at least once per meeting. Her sponsor Julianne, a woman half Eritrean half White, always adorned in gold, shaped like a leaf, finely tapered, almost demanded it of her, saying voice is power. Samantha waited her turn. When it came, she said, "Intimacy means responsibility. I told my fiancé about how my brother abused me."

An older British American woman with short black hair looked up.

"I want to trust more," Samantha said, "fear less."

"Be fearless," the woman said. "Fearless."

What healed all wounds wasn't time but people.

Many of the women loved and married women, and many loved and married men. In general they were thoughtful, not judgmental or critical. Not perfect, but damn good. Be they rough or bold, gentle or quiet, the softness of their beauty, their eyes and voices, changed Samantha. No one's life required the presence of men, especially bad men. But contrary to their original experience, some of the women she knew nurtured or found good men and these men the women loved and received, gave to, made love to, befriended, and believed in. The women were veterans of ancient wars. She hoped her mother felt all the love Samantha felt, her mother's childhood in Puerto Rico also fraught but in different ways.

JOHN DROVE through Choteau past two in the morning and sped southwest on the dirt road that led to the ranch. When John laid his head on the pillow a single thought met him before he drifted toward sleep: she'd taken in stride every wild place he'd brought her to, but when she'd given him something even more fierce he'd faltered. He'd talk to his mother in the morning, listen, then work the fields with his father. The following day he'd ride to the high plateau, come down again and go to Samantha.

He'd give her an honorable man.

The great sorrows were like death, she'd said, and death like sleep. And he slept.

HE WOKE in pitch darkness with a distinct memory of Roark Freeman's face.

He had a hard time going back to sleep.

ROARK, ON THE other hand, slept like a baby. When he'd left the twenty-second floor and taken the elevator to the top floor earlier that day, he entered his office and motioned to his secretary who closed the door behind him.

He sat down, lifting his disfigured hand to peruse the bent wrist and loose fingers.

"Mongoloid," their father had said of his brother in a haze of smoke over the combine. "Half-wit." The body caught like an anvil in the machine. His father's silver cropped hair, his look unwavering.

They'd stared at one another over the warp of the engine gears, the division of life from limb. There was nothing more to say.

"Wrap that hand, son, we'll see the doc in Miles City."

He wasn't sure his father knew. Certainly he suspected, but Roark never let on.

He opened a leather moleskin address book he'd owned for many years. What was objectivism but a new way. Not some blithering idiocy over the less fortunate. He went to the entry for his own name. Below it he'd drawn a triangle and blacked it in. On each of the vertices he'd written in all-caps the word ME. The advance of reason, individualism, and free-market capitalism. A shoving off of governmental coercion and slack humanity in order to secure healthy rational self-interest, independence, productiveness, pride.

Roark fired nonworkers with venom.

The kind of drunk he hung on himself like a feedbag at the company parties and the way his hands handled the women made his VPs question his appetites. He thought of the VPs as ragdolls, a little stiffer than the rest, but similarly cow-eyed and incapable of amplitude. They didn't have a father like his either, he thought.

His father had made a fortune in copper and ranching, and started Roark with a lump sum of a few million. Roark surpassed his father thirty years ago by managing his and other people's money and property, especially their more profligate leanings. With over five thousand bank locations, and unnumbered high-value properties, he saw himself as the greatest developer in America.

When he built the tallest building in the world, the world would think so too.

Billions begat billions.

He hid his money in holes the government had a hard time finding.
He couldn't remember his mother's face.
Because of his father he knew he'd never marry.
He sometimes wondered if his father killed her.

IN THE MORNING at the kitchen table John told them Samantha's brother raped her when she was young. The house was dark but for the bright overhead light in the kitchen.

"She deserves as much love as there is in this world," his mother said immediately, her face ashen.

The room was quiet.

"She's paid a heavy price," his father said.

"I don't know that I'm capable of giving her the love she deserves," John said.

Pamela watched her son and felt the terror. There were things only she and Jack knew, events from her own childhood best kept close. A husband, yes. A good husband. But not a son. She knew now she'd need to tell her son and Samantha too.

"Her whole family has suffered," his father said. "Wouldn't wish it on anyone." He and Pamela exchanged glances. Jack rose and paused for a moment, facing John. "You've come home to go to the mountains, but work with me today first."

"I will," John nodded as his father grabbed a coat and went outside.

His mom took his hand. "Stay here first," she said. "John, I want you to love her forever, and I want you to love her family." She looked to the window and then back to him. "But if you can't be the one to give her love, you need to release her right now."

"I want to love Samantha, but I don't know that I'm strong enough."

"No one knows until we step forward."

She placed her hand on John's arm. He teared up.

He bowed his head and she touched his hair.

"We love you," she said.

"I've never been with anyone," he said. "I'm afraid, now more than ever."

"I imagine so," his mother said. "You're modest like your grandmother. Generous, and honest."

The light came from the bay window.

In the high meadows the weather was clear but a few thousand feet farther into the Rocky Mountain wilderness, snow crowned the continent. He thought of Stevens. Among twenty snowy mountains the only thing moving was the eye of a blackbird, and he remembered, back in the city people moved at different speeds in different spaces, their bodies circumscribing orbits unique and transitory. There the birds were seen from afar, or flew overhead, or darted among the masses.

"Don't expect her to be someone other than who she is," his mother said.

"I don't know what to expect," John said.

She nodded to the window where the world was darkly forested on the first bench to the north. "Expect love," she said. "She's stronger than you think."

"She's stronger than anyone I know," John said.

"Your dad's a good man, John, and I love him. You are made like him. He'll love me to the grave, and after, as I'll love him. If marriage is to be uncommon, as I believe it should be, it will require every bit of you. All of you, and all of Samantha."

She looked closely at John.

John doubted himself.

"Samantha and I need you," John said.

"We're right here," she said, "your dad and me."

THE THREE OF THEM went about the day then, but at night Pamela informed her husband she'd be telling Samantha and John everything. He drew near and leaned over her, softly kissing her temple and her cheekbone and then her lips.

EARLY MORNING, John took mount on the Palomino, cantering the animal out the front gate and down through the fields toward the Rocky Mountain Front. Behind the saddle, at rest on the horse's rump he'd tied a bedroll comprised of a sleeping bag, his fly rod, a light tent, cooking utensils, pheasant, deer steak, and butter in butcher paper on ice, and a bag of flour along with salt and pepper. He wore his beaten black cowboy hat with the rolled rims. The rifle was in the scabbard. Following a game trail, he made his way up the draw just north of Ptarmigan Pass.

He'd come to the mountain to listen.

He was on a ridge in the sky above the land. He could barely fathom how much he still wanted to kill a man. He'd been unable to tell his mom and dad, though likely they reasoned as much. Dwelling on it his heart felt hollow and high in his chest. Wisps of steam rose from Charlie's shoulders. John dismounted and unloaded his wares, removed the bridle and saddle and clucked once, saying, "Eat." Charlie shook his mane and moved a length away bending his head to the grass and John hand-brushed the sweat from Charlie's coat until the horse was dry and happy.

John took his time setting up camp near a rock outcropping that rose overhead. Good windbreak. Rock bordered with pine, opening on a field of shin-high grasses. From this height the west was laid open before him for fifty miles or more, the river valley far below skirted by stone, vaulted with sky. The faint smell of grizzly was in the air, a dank musk he'd known from a boy. Still it never failed to elicit fear, and that's healthy, he reckoned: fear. Better to taste it than push it away.

HE STAKED the tent on the lee side of a tree bole in the flat between the roots. He refilled his canteen from a nearby stream, the south bound rivulet of Ferret Creek that would join the Lynx Basin tributary east of the confluence at Cut Bank and Two Medicine and meet the Marias and eventually the Missouri, a nation later falling into the Gulf of Mexico to reach the Atlantic through the Florida Straits between the U.S. and Cuba. He gathered kindling and dry wood and a few stones. He set the stones at an angle and built a banked fire over which he cooked cuts of pheasant and deer steak. He'd shaken the meat in the bag of flour with salt and pepper. The meal fulfilled in him something he couldn't name and when he was done he leaned back with his head on his saddle viewing the sky flare in the west. He lay there welcoming the oncoming night and how it subdued his spirit, blending him with the dark. As the fire glow burned down he was at rest.

His horse was near but it was the color and brightness of the dark, manifold with stars, that gave him a feeling of intimacy. People bear what must be borne, Samantha had shown him as much. He wanted to be worthy of her. That's why his grandfather's suicide shook him, it symbolized a gun set in the mouth of intimacy. The family hadn't fully regained equilibrium even over a spate of years.

The moon a scythe behind a single cloud in the southeast, he remembered his bar fighting days in Great Falls. A man could be beaten and torn but never know the inner life a woman carried as a matter of course. More lines his mother memorized with him came to him. The night was uncommonly warm. He remained where he was. We only live, only suspire, he thought, love crafting of each person a shirt of flame.

His breathing deepened and he drifted off.

THE NIGHT was broken once by the call of a wolf, and he woke, his upper body cold. He entered the tent and slept to sunrise. High in a tree fifty yards from camp he'd cached the food along with the pan, plate, and utensils he'd washed in the creek. Now he walked to the creek again, knelt and washed his face, and took a long draught of water, the chill invigorating. He rose and eyed the horizon where a line of limestone stood swept with light.

Samantha, he thought. The garment of praise.

He walked among the trees beside the creek bed.

In a kind of shared sisterhood, she and his mother were fiercely loyal.

Sisterhood was a universe of its own, he thought, a thing he loved and admired.

What allowed people to come through suffering and find new life?

HE CUT SOUTH descending away from the creek toward the camp again. He'd check the cache and set up his fly rod before taking Charlie to Battleground Lake, a mile west, where he knew the big brook trout would feed on any fly he dropped on the surface. Clean the guts in a single sweep after the knife mark. Push the detritus down the spine with index finger and thumb, into a bouquet of clean water.

Through the last stand of jack pine and some aspen he saw Charlie swishing his tail, his ears alert and movements jittery. Strange swells of wind on the plateau, more readily picked up by a horse, scenting not only bear but lynx or bobcat, maybe a mountain lion. He walked to the horse and spoke kindly to him and the animal settled some. "Go ahead," he said as Charlie ate. "We've got a good ride ahead."

He rubbed Charlie's shoulder and drew his hand down the horse's back and scratched the rump before he went to observe the cache. He felt the wind on his chest, a breeze pleasant and laced with honeysuckle and woods' rose. Among a few larch and bull pine he felt the rope and stared up into the tree where the cache appeared undisturbed. The smell of bear musk thickened the air, and when he turned he was smote by a force that leveled him to the ground and nearly knocked him senseless.

Book 2

> We do not want riches, we want peace and love.
>
> —Red Cloud

AURORA AND ELIAS

IN SEATTLE, a half mile down First Avenue toward the water, in another high rise, Elias American Horse placed his hands on his desk, bracing for what was to come.

He felt sure he'd lost his wife, Aurora, not physically, but in her affections, and the thought of it thorned him to the point of panic.

Before he got to Seattle he'd borrowed his grandfather's beaded drum beater. He'd placed it on the corner of his desk at Northwest Farm and Ranch. Now all he could do was stare at it and try to overcome what felt like violence inside.

He was Oglala Lakota Sioux, part Assiniboine. On the Fort Peck reservation most were Dakota or Assiniboine/Nakoda, but his family had moved from South Dakota to Montana and mixed before he was born and he was happy for it, having a huge family. Of one reservation but three nations, Oglala Lakota on his dad's side, Nakoda from his grandmother, and the third what his uncle Clayton called "these United States." Slim with high shoulders, a fine-boned face and hard eyes, he was a runner, a former high school All-American with Montana records in the mile and two-mile. He hadn't been in shape for far too long. He felt weak not strong. From his pants pocket he drew two long smooth rattles taken from the tails of rattlesnakes and set them on either side of the drum beater in order to remind him work, and women, were like singing, like pealing wild riffs from a high vocal front the same way a man cut calves from the herd for branding. He was no singer—he was a drummer that blended his voice with the higher voices. The hard beats that sounded from the drum came like blood, the thrumming and singing from his brothers wholly untamed. His brothers came from everywhere. The group in Seattle had singers from seven nations.

Aurora had been steadily undoing him. No, he countered, he'd been wrecking her in the same ways or worse. Normally he was a hard worker, having learned from his mother and her wiry life just what hard work meant. But work was work, and love was something else; he couldn't fathom how the two came together. He still took pleasure in Aurora, her bold front-forward posture, the scent of her skin, her face and collarbones, a woman made like rivers and boulders. She had a great job. He led men in the farm insurance industry. She was a damn good nurse.

When it came to love, they devastated each other.

IN LATE FALL, despite everything, they'd taken a loan out from John Sender for a townhouse along the belt loop in Green Lake. They entered his office and as Sender shook their hands, smiling, Aurora had smiled back at him and kissed him in a faux-European way on both cheeks. The man had blushed. His face was bony. Judging from the photo framed on his desk, of two young daughters and a beautiful woman, he was older than Elias, though Elias thought he looked young. Two low-grade industrial chairs with blue cushions were set across the gulf of his desk. He motioned them to sit as he moved behind the desk and sat across from them in a leather high-backed office chair. The positioning was not favorable to Elias and Aurora, but their finances were and the loan was processed without a hitch. Sender set black gel pens before them and pushed forward and regathered their signed papers with uncommon speed, collating the stacks crosswise on either side of his forearms. It was impersonal but they had Montana in common and it put them at ease.

They all carried advanced degrees. They were also country in their sensibilities.

John was smooth, adept at what he did.

"You're fast," Elias said.

"Rodeo," Sender responded as he moved. The papers were unending. He'd warned them the signing would be near an hour long.

"Me too," Elias said.

Aurora's face brightened, making John smile at her.

Elias chose not to take it personally.

"What event?" Sender asked.

"Team roping."

"I've seen some great ropers," Sender said. "Night train from the chute. Hands quick as a birdwing."

"We were decent," Elias said. He thought he and Sender might be friends.

"Better than decent I bet," John said, looking at him.

"How about you?" Elias said.

"Broncs."

"Bareback or saddle?" Elias asked.

"Saddle. Not tough enough for bareback."

"Bone-breakers either way," Elias said.

John nodded. "I reckon we've both got those."

"Sure do." Elias lifted his hands, two fingers askew on the left one. He glanced at John's face. His face had been through the battle.

"Not rodeo," John said, motioning with a pen toward his jaw, his smile and tone self-effacing. "Northwest Montana." As he slid more papers their way, Aurora brushed his wrist with her palm. Elias stared at her. Her hands, John thought, not indelicate but strong, were likely hands Elias loved holding. He shifted topic, and kept his arms clear of her.

"What brought you to Seattle, Mr. and Mrs. American Horse?"

"Jobs," Elias said.

On the way out, they passed Roark Freeman in the lobby and when Roark saw them he stopped John and stepped close to Elias, almost standing over him.

"Did our man get you what you wanted?"

"He did." Elias said, nodding at John.

Roark looked Aurora up and down, rubbing his bad hand on the side of his pants.

"And you, did we give you what you need?" he asked.

Aurora didn't answer, still staring at John.

John told him they were from Montana, and Roark smiled and said he was too, from out near Jordan, north of Miles City. John remembered how Roark bragged about being raised in a Victorian castle on land bought with old copper and cattle money. A very remote place, John thought, nowhere near civilization. A house of odd construction. Seeing how he stood even closer now, imposing his frame over the couple, John turned and walked them out the front door.

They thanked him and crossed the street.

As they walked up the sidewalk Aurora told Elias she thought John smelled like peppermint.

"I fancied that White boy," she said.

It made Elias sick, hearing this.

"His boss was something ugly," she said.

Elias went back to work, and so did she.

In the world, he thought, you had to be wary of every dream and nation.
He wasn't afraid to fight, and he wasn't afraid of the White boy or his boss.
He was afraid of himself.
He wasn't sure Aurora loved him anymore.

JOHN WENT BACK to his office still worried about Roark. Alone or in pairs, among the many for whom John processed loans were not only Elias and Aurora American Horse but also Phillip McBane, Gabriel Kennedy Reed and his wife, Angelica, and Juan Carlos de la Cruz.

Like John, Elias, Phil, Gabriel, and Juan Carlos all hailed from Montana.

He'd found this out in the small talk that came with signing. He imagined their ancestors arrived from different places, known and unknown, like his ancestors, finding circuitous routes to the Treasure State.

Notably, each of the men was born, like him, in Great Falls, Montana.

A decent-sized Montana town, it belonged to the nation in unique but also predictable ways. An unknown serendipity united them all, being born in the Catholic-owned Columbus Hospital, named for the one who falsely claimed to have found America. Born in Great Falls, a city named not just for the roiling river but also for the nation's mortal capacity. City of flat surface streets, no tall buildings, and limited industry, touched to the long plains that ran from northern Montana to middle America. City of the falls of one of the great American rivers, the great falls of the Missouri, a five-waterfall progression Meriwether Lewis and William Clark took thirty-one arduous days to portage in 1805. A city the city planners—White, sincere, blind to the backs that were broken to make America—discussed with long effort what to call, agreeing in 1883 to name it Great Falls.

Great Falls, the Electric City, was perched on five electric dams, one for each waterfall. For John it was a simple fascination, his place of birth, the land around the city both flat and hilly, the city itself housing a vast net of power lines and the effluvium of small factories that made the red-winged blackbirds go quiet. With undaunted will to see a western mecca built on hydroelectric power, generation after generation the planners continued to plan. City of government agencies, city of Malmstrom Air Force Base, city of nuclear capability, nuclear silos dotting the plains north with underground caverns housing the devil's wound.

TOWARD EVENING, Elias American Horse moved from his stupor to tie up some loose ends on two large insurance claims. When he came home from work to find Aurora already there, he was grateful he didn't have to wonder if she was out wandering again.

He was no angel, he reminded himself.

With the townhouse dark they sat on the couch together, watching the lights of the city laid out on hills inlaid with black water.

"I've seen the most beautiful deaths," she told him, "and the most unlikely second chances."

"Tell me," he said. His desire to love made him listen. Everyone said she was a great nurse. Stronger than most docs, and hard-headed, immovable. He loved her fine body, muscled and thick-thighed, strong and slender in the arms and neck. When she spoke he usually stonewalled her.

"A year ago, an eleven-year-old boy rolled an ATV," she said. "When the ambulance came and they brought him to the operating table, his brain was half out of his skull, most of his bones broken. His internal organs were all crushed."

Elias lay his head on her lap. "Keep going," he said as she stroked his hair.

"The neurosurgeon said their son would die. The intensivists believed he had no chance. 'We need to do this operation,' the neurosurgeon told the family, 'or the swelling will herniate the brain stem before we can stabilize him.' The boy made it through the operation and we induced a coma for six weeks. When we woke him, there was nothing. Twelve more weeks passed. The family kept holding on. LifeCenter Northwest came in to have them sign away the organs. We all thought the family should just let him go. They said no, and a day later the boy moved his thumb. Three months later the boy was walking and talking. Every single doc said he'd die. He's more alive than ever."

Elias smiled deeply. "That's a great story."

"He's alive and walking through his family's house tonight," she said, "he's singing. He didn't love to sing before. He loves to sing now."

"He's singing a new song," Elias said, gazing at her Aurora's face.

"What if I were Crow when you married me?" she said. "What if my last name had been Pretty Horse?"

He laughed. He didn't imagine he would've married a Crow woman.

His wife was a good trash talker, able to shift her mind and his in a moment. A fiery one, he thought, but joking is how she courts me even now that we're married. Another dumb old word, courting. But one his uncle Clayton said with deep satisfaction. Elias called him "Uncle" like he called plenty of old men on the rez, but Clayton was his true uncle, his father's brother, and Clayton had loved him as far back as Elias could remember.

Aurora's auntie Julia had married a Crow man.

"If I was Crow," she giggled, "I'd love my own name and keep it too. Then I'd be Aurora Pretty American Horse. Because it's funny," she said, "and fantastic."

"You mean Pretty Horse-American Horse," he said.

"Or Pretty-American," she said, laughing.

"Pretty enough," he said, "but not American enough, enit."

They both laughed.

ELIAS THOUGHT everything of her, but he thought nothing of the Catholic God her mother claimed. When he considered God he called God Wakan Tanka or Great Spirit. He didn't forgo his traditional roots, he just didn't pay them as much attention as he used to. He liked being a city boy, scaling mountains of metal and glass.

Based in Seattle for a few years now, his accounts ranged from Washington to Montana. He did it because he was good at it. In reality he couldn't care less about the remote spaces of the Fort Peck rez in Montana where he was raised. He loved his people. He did not love the government-fed concentration camp they were on.

He liked concrete and steel.

He liked girders set deep into the ground.

He wasn't a rez boy anymore.

He was urban.

So was Aurora.

He admitted his faithful stretches were becoming rare, but to him, though he had no direct evidence, her exploits felt too powerful and too abundant, her reprisals falling on him like a rockslide. They grew up together. Her full name Aurora Borealis Runsabove. Aurora Borealis American Horse was her name now. When he asked her to marry him she told him she wanted a hyphenated last name back then too and they both howled. Aurora Borealis Runsabove-American Horse.

"Jokes," she said. "Longest name in United States history, enit. Nah, I'm going American Horse."

Her decision pleased him so much he realized he was probably a chauvinist pig.

She wanted a cat or dog or both. He wouldn't allow it.

She worked in one of the most important hospitals for children in the world.

He didn't tell her enough how proud he was of her.

SHE'D BEEN HIRED in the Neonatal Intensive Care Unit at Seattle Children's just north of Lake Washington. Bold in nightlife, supremely talented in the White work world, she was not afraid to use her voice when needed. She believed she understood families. They got crazy, or went crazy, when their child's life was threatened. The bodies grew hot or cold and smelled differently.

In school she'd discovered she was made to serve babies but the baleful nature of the job could be difficult. Earlier that week a baby died on her, weighing only two pounds seven ounces, a baby girl named Luciana. Aurora comforted the family, calming them by being present in the room when needed, waiting outside when not needed. But the death of a child was inconsolable. Always. Nothing answers loss. No one knows what comes after dying, but she wanted to leave each baby with a prayer of love on her lips. No one knew she did this, not even Elias. But this baby died before she'd had a chance to pray. With the family, she'd done the fingerprints and footprints of their dead child. It always helped the grieving. The family was Italian American, thick-set, and they loved each other very much. The grandmother wailed. The child's mother was silent.

When they went home she walked them down the hall, and down the escalator to the front door. She walked them out the hospital entrance and saw a blackbird flicker into the air from a nearby tree. She stood with her arms wrapped around her as the family entered the parking garage stairwell. They looked so pitiful. When they were gone she thought she'd just go back to work. Instead she slipped into the nearest cleaning closet and closed the door. Sitting on the floor in a darkness mingled with the smell of antibacterials, she wept into the cup of her hands.

Emerging sometime later, she completed her tasks.

When the shift was over she cleaned up, showered, and put on her makeup in the staff bathroom. She applied primer and a light powder foundation, concealer for the gray beneath her eyes, no blush. She used her fingers instead of a beauty blender. She applied liquid eyeliner and blacked her eyelashes. She chose wine-colored lipstick, outlining her lips with a dark purple pencil. With a few brush strokes her hair looked lustrous. She stared at herself in the mirror. Don't collapse, she told herself. Walk out this door and be someone else for the evening.

BEING MARRIED, Aurora thought if people were married for any length of time they wore a tough face. A grimace at how it happened to them like everyone. Friendship no longer present, humor gone, sex no longer easy. Anger all-encompassing.

Even together they lived apart.

She and Elias had learned ways to forget each other.

He roamed and fantasized. He glazed his eyes with porn.

She opened up to those who were formerly strangers.

Spoke to them. She wasn't afraid to acknowledge others.

She wasn't afraid to sleep with them either.

SHE TOOK the Mercer exit into downtown, paid exorbitantly for the valet service at the Pacific Tower, and rode the elevator up to the Mt. Rainier Lounge. The young bodies mixed with the old and brought dusk tragically alive. She watched the rim of the world ignite at sundown, a sky of crimson, the water a blue veil below the Olympic crown. At the Pacific Tower the alpha men always turned tongue, flirting with her like she was their own. The most ignorant called her Indian Princess or Pocahontas. Some talked love trash like they owned her or wanted to.

The world was nefarious, she thought, and skin arresting. House and home. The beauty Creator gave you, a robe of peace not a coat of shame. She could stereotype men as well as they stereotyped her. In fact, she owned them, she thought, a truth confirmed in how she held the room. Here or in SixSeven at the Edgewater, or the bar at the Needle (she didn't care how gauche it was), she knew what it meant to make men want. They silently passed her notes saying they'd give anything. Some proudly fat, others middling and thick, some skinny and light-footed. One flashed gold rings and green bills in her face, cackling behind eyes like holes in the skull. In most men she found more death than life. She usually wasn't afraid; the rez a repository of death even more harrowing. She gave as much as she took, her own eyes doors on an abyss she'd never found the bottom of.

Men too dominant ruined things. From a child she never liked being ruined. She wanted men tame or at least one down to her. There was something to the sense of being in control. Comparing men to other men to their face while in bed increased voltage. Like a tongue on a battery. The difference between mediocre and great was imagination. Bodies were gentle or invigorating, harboring intense feeling, cajoling, pouting, smiling.

Almost none were listeners, she thought.

She never took money. She wasn't a tramp. Plus she didn't need it. She made good money. She made sure they paid for the room and it had to be nice, preferably a glass house in a glass skyscraper. She liked open sight lines. Sometimes to be funny, she left money for them. Five bucks. Fifty on occasion, or a hundred, so the man would actually feel himself the hooker he wanted her to be.

In her purse: pepper spray and the silver revolver her father gave her, a snub-nosed .38 Special with mother-of-pearl handle inlays and fleur-de-lis engraved on the barrel. Pepper spray put a man down but didn't kill him. The non-White indigenous body was a pleasure bordered on violence from the beginning of time. As a nurse she knew the reality of Native femicide, here in the Emerald City, back on her reservation, and throughout the Americas, the female body in pain, the body erased or disappeared. Like her Mojave friend Natalie, she wanted to disappear, not into violence but into love, into church and darkness. In the moonslick night, her hand under the beloved's shirt, no longer visible.

When it was over she could love the morning again, especially outside hotels like the W on Fourth Ave where the water appeared downhill as a wedge of color through the Seneca window to the west. When she emerged, sometimes she saw passenger planes high overhead setting diagonal jet streams between the skyscrapers. With men she favored dancers because they walked like Salukis. Deep-chested and long legged, slender, tensile.

She didn't let Elias know anything of what she did.

"Nakodas are the best lovers," she told him, and he used to smile.

AS A MATTER of fact, she told herself she still loved Elias at least a little because no one loved like him. He had her ultimate body type, an athlete with a poetic mind, and a great dancer himself, but country style, who always seemed to smell like autumn and the necks of horses. Plus he had some Nakoda in him. When she wasn't too defensive she admitted their friendship had healed her many times over. The distances he'd run for her. He knew many of the most grave things about her and still loved her. But he was unfaithful. A handsome man, secreted like a vein of gold, was hard to keep to yourself. He tended to tell her everything in his own time, even if it hurt. His fall back was confession. Hers was solitude, and then escape. She could live with this shared weakness.

But it made her love him less.

Other than Elias's body type, she also adored women. She preferred elegant and lean, and not just angular but rounded. Women were so different from men. Softer. Less hairy. Scented with mint or lilac or honey crisp like apples or apple pie.

She couldn't abide body odor.

But with women, mostly she couldn't stand the clinging.

"Just live," she told them.

"Stop hanging on. I'm already gone."

A little high, or in the afterglow of intimacy they looked at her as if into deep space. "I won't save you," she said. "Save yourself."

Men were rarely more than one-timers.

Women tried to make her their permanent home.

She left them like their fathers had.

She also loved Elias because he smelled good. Very good. Better than other men or women. And he danced so well, his hand to the small of her back just above the double rise of her glutes in with the piping her back muscles made. Jitterbug champion from a long line of them, his grandpa and uncle great dancers too. Plus he could fancy dance like a whirlwind.

She didn't know why she needed to break him.

Likely because she hated him as much as she loved him, she thought.

Just as she loved and hated herself.

She took another sip of vodka and stared out at the flock of men on the seventieth floor of the Rainier Lounge. She felt warm and easy. They glittered tonight. She couldn't think of Elias now or she'd fall to pieces. Over the drum he sang with his brothers like something born of the hurricane. No matter how much of his own feminine he embraced, he was a man, and she loved his manhood. She drained the final thumb of liquor, the liquid hot in the back of her throat. The burn entered her chest and she liked the game. She felt a tingle along her spine, the hairs on the back of her neck raise. Men beckoned her, their heads hard and resplendent, their eyes like black glass, naming her, making her want. She'd had her share of mis-want.

So many on her reservation were poor, she thought. Drunk or poor, or both.

She'd gone hungry. She'd known severe deprivation.

But in every room there was an angel or two, and they usually weren't the rich ones. Truly she believed there were angels. People or perhaps animals made of spirit, flesh, and bone, and they'd saved her more than once. They carried good medicine. They were holy. She hated the old traditional teachings but she couldn't totally discard them. True, she hadn't been hungry in years. Here in the city she was sated. But if she got hungry again she'd return home. For her grandmother's touch. Then her hunger would be a spiritual hunger. For blessing, or prayer. For ceremony.

She questioned why the good angels couldn't be more differentiated from the killing angels? Her father was good now. Distant or slack, and pretty much gone when she was a child, he'd sobered up. He was one of her angels now. She didn't know when she'd see him again. Even in his binge years, he'd taught her something. She carried the .38 Special at all times. He still asked her about it. "Keeps you strong," he said. "Plus you're better than me at hitting the bullseye." They practiced plenty when she was young and she loved how it fit neatly in her handbag beneath the mace. Pearl grip, silver body, two-inch barrel, stout recoil. She kept it loaded.

When her father got sober her mother left. She didn't doubt it had something to do with self-hate. In her heart of hearts, Aurora claimed to be different.

She stared longer than she needed to at one man or another.

They held her gaze, finding her exotic, she thought.

Without having to call the rising forth she rose from her chair.

She shut men off with a glance or simply "No."

She startled them with "Yes" or "now."

Men were electric doors, opening and closing. With those she took to bed she had her many horses of desire. Tonight she needed to leap across the sky and forget death. She wore a black lace cocktail dress by Carolina Herrera. Half-sleeve. No slip. She could braid her own hair exquisitely, something her mother taught her, and she and her sisters had practiced incessantly. Dutch braid or French, lace, waterfall, rope or fishtail. Diagonal or straight, reversed or upside-down, four-strand, milkmaid, tailing to a bun or chignon. A woman's hair was her secret shield. Tonight, she had her hair down. Velvet high heels by Gianvito Rossi, thin string roman lacing to the knee. The Chanel handbag tonight over the Fendi. Her name never hurt her either. Men loved foreign. Even if she was actually Native. She walked to a man at the corner of the bar who looked a little Cree but upon closer inspection was likely a White Middle Eastern mix. Perhaps from Jordan, she thought, with a White parent.

"What's your name?" she said and smiled.

"Mohammad," he said with kindness in his voice. "And yours?"

"Aurora," she said. His scent was high and airy, clean, distinctive.

She took him by the arm. He followed her out the door.

"WHAT ARE YOU?" she asked when she was done.

She'd chosen Chiante, one of her favorite boutique hotels.

He lay on his side, staring at her, touching his fingers to her forearm.

A fine linen sheet draped one of her legs.

"American," he said.

"I know," she said. "And?"

If her friends at home saw her they'd call her apple.

Red on the outside. White on the inside.

He smiled.

She touched his chest. "I mean before that."

He thought about it. "Nothing," he said.

He doesn't know himself, she thought.

"How about you?" he asked.

"Never mind," she said.

SOME TIME BEFORE DAWN she slipped into bed beside Elias, crossing herself again as she stared at the ceiling. She thought of her mother and tears came to her eyes. Nakoda, Catholic, and having lived only a half-life, trying to die years before the day came. Aurora turned to her side and pressed her back into Elias's chest, matching her legs to his, wrapping his arms around her.

"Bless you," he said in the darkness.

She couldn't tell if he was asleep or awake.

"O ma key ya nah," she said. Help me please.

She heard his breathing go smooth.

She fell asleep in his arms.

ELIAS HAD SUFFERED two deaths in his family during his first year in high school at Wolf Point, both cousins. They'd been close to him nearly from birth, children of his uncles' families. Paulina American Horse took a cocktail of her mother's prescriptions—muscle relaxants, Thorazine, and Zoloft. She fell asleep and stopped her heart. Griffith Dogchild, drunk, drove his brother's motorcycle into the concrete wall of the bridge at Deer Creek at two in the morning after a kegger on the Missouri River. The land like a wrinkled old blanket. The bike a column of flame when it struck.

Elias saw his father drag his mother down a flight of stairs by her hair, breaking her sternum, dislocating her right shoulder. To counter the undercurrent Elias ran stoic all through high school then went to Fort Peck Community College and on to a scholarship at Montana State where he graduated with honors and a bachelor's degree in agribusiness and public relations. He vowed to escape. Get away from the insanity and make some big money. Make a life.

He landed an internship with Montana Feed and Co., a ranch supply operation in Billings, and when they hired him on it took him nearly no time to increase the company's market range from Montana to Wyoming and North and South Dakota. At age twenty-four, a head-hunter tagged him for a lead manager position at Northwest Farm and Ranch in Seattle. He considered his wife, Aurora, a better person than him, stronger, more capable. He'd told himself he'd always go where she called, her body a fire that made him burn like he was fuel. But inevitably she had followed him. Wolf Point. Bozeman.

They manipulated and fought each other.

They loved. They repaired.

She had not wanted to move to Seattle.

They moved anyway.

With three miscarriages in the first four years together Aurora had fallen to back-bedroom depression for a time while he ascended as an amateur runner, a drummer, an agricultural business executive. But in Seattle she'd dug herself out and after a bachelor's of science in nursing, specializing in neonatal intensive care, she'd earned a master's in public health, along with post-grad certificates in infant mortality and lung efficiency.

For his part, Elias completed a PhD in sustainable wheat rotation, rising like a rocket through the corporate air.

BACK IN WOLF POINT for a weekend, Elias retrieved his grandmother's beaded coin purse to place on his desk with his grandfather's drum beater and the elk's eye teeth. When he returned to Seattle he continued in the townhouse with Aurora, refusing to take a loan on a bigger place though they had the salary to do so. Instead, as he was promoted at work and his earning power increased, he purchased rentals and flipped houses, hoarding the money.

With regard to finances, Aurora hated him for trying to control her.

Her voice had grown more piercing. His, more thick and self-satisfied.

ON HIS WAY home from work again, he called her wondering whether he was a fool and they should really let each other go. He didn't know if he could. Maybe she wanted out for good.

He hoped she'd still give them a chance.

He wanted to whisper in her ear. Pidamayaye. Pidamayay. I am grateful to you. Thank you. But his tongue couldn't seem to move the words.

After seven years in Seattle now Aurora was so distant. He felt convinced she'd already had three affairs, two with Muckleshoot men they'd met at the casino, the last with a Coeur D'Alene woman she came across at the farmers' market in Ballard. They couldn't be honest with each other, but their bodies knew. When she came home late she kept saying either she'd had to take the night shift or she was out with friends. For his part he'd lied to her more times than he cared to count, breaking every promise he'd made in their quiet Catholic wedding. A simple unfortunate progression—(a) tell her you're going out to get some milk, (b) slip into the black overhang of one slick White joint or another, (c) talk sweet and get a White girl drunk, (d) speak one of his languages to her: "Haw muchkay"; "Hello female friend" (e) get drunk yourself and follow her home, her open hand waving him on.

MEN WORKED ON borrowed time, Elias thought.
Little in the way of wisdom.

THE NEXT DAY when Aurora stopped by his office crying, Elias came around his desk. They sat face to face in mission-style chairs with brown leather flats on the seat. He noticed the mahogany grain of his desk, the expanse like a small ocean, swirl and counter-swirl running over the surface. Her freshness filled the room.

When she was like this it broke him completely.

"Cante waste nape ciyuzapo," he said. I greet you from my heart.

Her eyes told him thank you.

She didn't talk. He was silent too.

She wore scrubs. To him, she was as beautiful as ever.

He pressed his forehead to hers.

They interlaced their fingers in each other's hair.

HE TOOK her to Eduardo's sweet-scented kitchen on Queen Anne.

Seated at a round oak table painted red they were quiet until the meal was over. They held hands then, watching the people go by.

"Are we losing each other?" he asked.

When she bull-rushed him he only got more angry.

"Are we?" she said. She wasn't crying anymore.

"I don't know," he said.

"I hope not," she said. She reached and touched his face.

He leaned his face into her hand. "Pidamayaye," he said.

"Thank you," she echoed.

He had his liaisons. She had hers. But he wasn't about to fully open that chest, knowing the power of disloyalty. He got a pale rage even thinking of her with others. If he had to hear her spell it out, it would blossom to blood-red. There was a space between the stomach and the breastbone for scarcity. Disquiet lived there too.

He held her hands in his and rested his head on her shoulder and she leaned into him. We're broken like our relatives, he thought. Ironic how their families were generally conservative, Republican, promilitary, homophobic patriots. Closed-minded, but liberal in nearly every sexual practice. Or perhaps not so liberal as unfaithful. Like him.

He couldn't bear that liberation. Not anymore. As he read of traditional ways or listened to real Oglala Lakota elders online or on the tribal podcasts, he felt a gaping expanse inside. A genocidal hole, he called it, for nothing could staunch the wound that hole made. He'd tried to drug it over, sex it down, drink it away. The elders said you needed to love through it, and holding Aurora, he knew this to be true. There had to be loyal people somewhere. But he and Aurora were lost. He'd been a rez dog. Not uncommonly, because of his own poor character, he'd had sex with others solely for retaliation, repaying Aurora for her disaffection. But he'd never been faithful.

There wasn't a soul he knew on the Fort Peck Rez who'd been faithful either. Or even among the many Lakota, Nakoda, or Dakota families scattered over Montana and the Dakotas. He knew those families, and even if he felt moved to be graceful, and even if he wanted to listen, he found it unlikely his friends' parents had been any different from him. He had to concede most families were flawed, those of traditional ways or the Catholic faith or otherwise.

The parents were just older, he thought, and sometimes wiser.

He'd try again, he told himself, kissing Aurora's head.

But faithfulness, or wisdom for that matter, didn't grow on trees, even if now that she and he were urban with great jobs, money seemed to.

TO THEM BOTH America smelled like loneliness. And yet people of all races intermarried and lived together. They lived and died, rose and slept, made love, made meals, celebrated, danced and had children.

They did this every day.

His rez was no different. Sioux married Sioux, Sioux married Cheyenne, Blackfeet, Crow and White. Everyone married everyone.

From tribes who'd formerly killed each other.

People risked everything for love.

FOR AURORA'S PART, in the months that followed she noticed his goodwill, but she didn't trust him. He wasn't trustable. No man was. She didn't put much faith in his new beginnings, even if she was happy to love on him some. Here in Seattle they'd grown up together, so much more than back home. But he didn't command her. No one did. She went her own way, and as her mother taught her, she was ready. If a man weighed on you too much, drop him. She'd loved Elias a long time. But if it came to it, she knew she'd do what needed doing.

For now, she'd go ahead and get close and keep her distance at the same time.

When the cinch got too tight, which almost always happened during one of his traditionalist Oglala kicks, she needed to take off for a night or two to loosen him up again. She was Nakoda. And Nakodas weren't dumb, she laughed to herself. She felt it whenever he coiled his ideas around her like snakes. She liked the city, the hum of it, the sequin of skyscrapers and grit of bridges, the viaduct, stadiums, and rivers of cars. She also loved the home country, and she was good with a gun. Knife too, with how her grandfather taught her to clean and dress wild game. She knew Elias knew this, and that it both frightened and excited him: the throngs of buildings, electricity and steel, the array of mountains, sky, and plains that grew within her chest.

He just needed to stop being so preachy if he wanted to keep her around.

MEANWHILE, A SUBTLE escalation was occurring during her work in the intensive care unit in which she was of two bodies and two minds. For days her stomach had felt ill, churning much of the shift. She tried to move through it, unfocused and in pain, feeling a grief she didn't want to own. The baby who'd died was not her first. There had been so many, but the last one, Luciana, had put her over the edge. Every day she washed up and donned her scrubs, inserted IVs, checked tubes, touched the hands, arms, and shoulders of desperate people. Families taking their babies home or sending them to heaven. Women and men of every color. Here where their child could be swept away in a heartbeat no one was stoic. Almost no one without faith.

The thrum of life, then silence. Sorrow was infinite.

She was made for this job, she told herself. She'd known pain her whole life.

When death knocked, she woke, prepared to ferry children from this world to the next. Off the elevator from the garage to level six and neonatal intensive care, a Wednesday in October she entered the hall in light blue scrubs with a flower pattern blouse. She and all her nurse sisters were good with families, great with babies. No male nurses in the core, she thought, sadly, male contact comfort equally paramount for sustaining life. Perhaps more paramount, the absence so defeating as life went on.

She went into the unit face-masked, her eyes smiling as she nodded to her fellow nurses on point: Sela Sinjaya, Alice Jones, and Juanita Zamora whose shift was just ending. They smiled back and Aurora commenced checking the babies in the incubators, each one intubated and wired to cardiorespiratory and blood pressure monitors, temperature probes, pulse oximeters, and her least favorite, endotracheal tubes, the apparatus strung down their tiny throats, connecting the babies to mechanical ventilators.

Away from work she still drank at night, needing to be numb, but here on level six at the Seattle Children's NICU she was sharp as one of her uncles' hunting blades. She served babies of even the earliest gestation, the toughest cases in the world. The neonatal docs, women and men, were professional, linear-minded, and big-hearted. Each giraffe omnibed incubator cost forty thousand dollars. Even the panda warmers for normal delivery rooms, open topped, with radiant heat, were twenty thousand. But in the NICU the babies had giraffe beds, close-topped, blanketed, the room darkened, and any micro-preemies, twenty-two or twenty-three or twenty-four weeks old, became million-dollar babies with the machines that kept them alive. Age of viability had gone from twenty-four weeks to twenty-two in recent years. Even the twenty-two-week babies somehow survived. Their bodies weighed just over a pound. They were translucent, the skin undeveloped. She applied Aquaphor as a kind of second skin. Swaddling and nesting were the favorite words her mouth knew. Being sure not to overstimulate, she gave touch pressure to calm them, to womb them. They slept on sheepskins in the tightly rolled nests she made of blankets, also womblike—arms to their face, hands to their mouth, knees midline. Their mothers were referred to in terms of gravida and para, such as G5, P2, meaning five pregnancies, two live children, three miscarried, aborted, or still born. As nurses, they never called the preemies by their first name, only their last: "baby girl Mwangi" or "baby boy Hanson." Except for Luciana, she kept to this requirement, her intellect and bodily presence a unique combination of rez sensibility, scientific acumen, sometimes adrenaline, and love above all. Always she followed the three Cs of her training: composed, caring, and in control every minute of the shift.

Families needed confident nurses.

"You make such beautiful beds," the other nurses said, "so crisp and tidy, such beautiful nests." She blushed and her chest felt hot, but she relished their praise. She went through the shift change listening, then started two new intravenous lines, maintained the others, managed the ventilators, and assessed the vital signs of each of her babies. She cross-checked the babies Alice and Sela monitored as they cross-checked hers. She touched in with each family, comforting mothers young and old, directing a husband to hold his wife and speak kindly to her. He responded willingly, opening his arms, encasing his beloved. He wrapped his wife like a shawl. Aurora's command changed his anger and he cried now when he held his wife and whispered good words to her.

She used the baby warmers more than warranted, loving the response the babies' intricate bodies made, the touch of her hands giving them more life than any of the machines. The babies' lips were shaped like the wings of butterflies. Their small fists clutched the tips of her pinkie finger as if lifting the world into existence. Their arms were smaller than her index finger. The eyes peered out, more aware than people imagined.

She touched morbidity.

She fought mortality.

Shifts were good hard work and she enjoyed the movement of her frame through the rooms, attending deliveries, weighing and measuring babies. The babies' names were sacred. She never revealed them to anyone outside work. The Great Mystery knew them. Heaven knew them. As far as she was from Nakoda tradition, she always asked her father to pray for them. He didn't need their names, he said. Wakan Tanka named them.

She taped the tiny light of the pulse oximeter to a new baby's hand, measuring the amount of oxygen in the baby's blood through the skin. She made sure the oxygen saturation monitor read right before she checked the mechanical ventilators again, watching the fast puffs delivered to each small chest, their chests no bigger than the palm of her hand. She had one baby on extracorporeal membrane oxygenation, blood from the baby's veins pumped through an artificial lung where oxygen was added and carbon dioxide removed before the blood was returned to the body.

She massaged them near constantly, and as soon as medically possible taught her families to do the same. Skin-to-skin contact with the mother in the earliest moments was sometimes the difference between death and life. Between thriving and a disease called *marasmus*—a wasting away of the fat and muscle the body breaks down to make energy. Such a gradual deterioration was markedly steep in the NICU. The life is in the blood, she recalled, a strange but verifiable truth. The body a living sacrament just as the nuns on the reservation had said, though she'd foreclosed on the idea when she was young.

At the end of her shift, she washed up and changed her clothes in the nurses' lavatory. When she stared at her face and put on a little eyeliner, she noticed she'd forgotten her nausea a little on that shift. The answer struck her then. She was pregnant.

She backed against the wall, away from the mirror. She didn't want to be pregnant. She breathed in and out, three quick breaths, then took her bag and went down the hall to the pharmacy where she bought a pregnancy test. Entering the nearest bathroom, she sat on the toilet and peed. Three more quick breaths.

She pulled up her clothes and stood in front of the mirror waiting.

She registered a positive pregnancy test, vomited in the sink, washed up again and went to her car, her body's dread a terrible anchor. She'd recently tested herself for STDs; she wasn't stupid, she tested every six months, and but for a few bouts of human papillomavirus, she was good. What she hadn't bargained for with all her precautions was bringing new life to the world, the choice, and the weight of not knowing who the father might be.

She asked for two days off, figured her missed periods at two, not uncommon for her but never with nausea, and got her blood taken for DNA testing. She knew the DNA nurses.

"Can you get his semen?" Simone asked. "Then I can quick route the results."

That night she met Elias in their bed and went into the bathroom after to swab what she needed from his life essence. If it wasn't him it could be anyone. She didn't want it to be anyone.

The next day she waited on a call from Simone.

The angst left her when Simone told her Elias was the father.

She returned to him that night, and when he slept she held his head to her chest so warmly she thought she could love him again, loyally. She couldn't of course, sleeping the next night with a Kenyan American man who looked like an arrow.

But her heart wasn't in it and as the weeks passed, she tried to wean herself off other men. Still she was unsuccessful. During the day she had no control over her tongue. She tore his flesh with the hooks of her mouth, and he either ignored her or broke her wide with his own viciousness. But she pulled him to her at night when she made it home, gripping his shoulders as she drew her naked chest to his back. His hair smelled clean. They turned to each other. Held each other.

He touched her like he knew her again, gentling himself, letting her touch him like he was known. If they could live only in the dark, she thought, they might survive.

THE DRUG-ADDICTED BABIES and the HIV-infected babies took the most out of her.

Bloodline a malignant too wary source of illness and ill will.

Was she different? She liked to think so. She'd done a line of coke on occasion, popped pills, or weeded her way to calmness. She wasn't addicted and since becoming a nurse, when random testing came in she stopped doing drugs. It wasn't drugs; for her it was emotion, rage, hypervigilance, injury the hydrant she couldn't turn off. She was a destroyer. Anyone who got close enough told her that. She destroyed people. Or they thought she did. No, she admitted, she did, even if they misread her. Like anyone, she wanted to love and be loved. She thought of abortion but felt too sick at heart to consider it a real option. She hated even the idea of drinking now that she was pregnant. She'd seen others and America herself as the source of her displacement, but carrying life changed her. She found her old troubles useless compared to the future of her child.

She watched her body embrace necessary uselessness.

Uncommonly useful to the life of another.

ELIAS ACCEPTED she still slept around.

He didn't know she was pregnant or that he was the father.

He'd been talking by phone weekly with his uncle Clayton again. Quiet, modest, respected, good with people and horses. Especially good with the young. Elias was happy to be in touch. The conversations were changing him. Clayton prayed and sang over him at the end of each phone call. Elias felt it, his uncle making him better despite the arc Elias's life had taken in recent years into greater financial and work success but further from spirit. Further into self. More ambition. Less love.

He had a lot of transformation ahead, which he knew meant he had many losses to face, and much suffering. His uncle was preparing him for this. Elias had been getting up earlier in recent months, going to bed earlier too. Aurora had seemed to soften some, though they still fought like enemies. He couldn't yet get himself to entirely stop seeing other women, though he'd curbed his appetite substantially. He tried to affirm himself, even if last night when she left the house he'd called one common to him, a White girl named Melissa from South Seattle. They didn't know each other's last names—Melissa preferred it that way. They met in her apartment, neatly modern if located in the junkyard part of town. She was built like a house of angles, her arms and body, her face and temples, her cheekbones, the ridge and sides of her nose, all planes, her shoulder blades like metal plates, the double-column of her muscular calves, her pelvic crown, and arms like works of art. She'd been an Olympian in rowing. Even her heart, though, was pointed. He didn't know her at all, and she didn't know him. They met and serviced one another without speaking and went their way. He could tell after the act she didn't like the sleeping part, with him or perhaps anyone, and so he always left.

He returned home in the early morning before Aurora. In bed alone, he stared into the blackness. He never minded the dark when he was in the wilderness. The mountains that topped the continent. In the city the dark was a hangman's noose.

The sun would be up in two hours.

So would he, the day's demands a horse he rode morning to night. He fell asleep in a cold sweat dreaming he rode herd on unruly steers. When one broke free he followed it and leaped from his horse to the steer's back. There were no heifers. He pulled the steer's head, nose over neck, and set it to the ground. Another one broke free and he mounted his horse and tracked that one too, pulling it to the ground. The cycle repeated itself in endless recursion as each grounded steer got up and entered the herd again as others split off. He just kept jumping cattle until his clothes went ragged and his hips ached. He never got ahead of it.

A WEEK LATER, after midnight, cold wind blowing east from the Sound, Elias came home from work and kept his coat on as he flipped the switch for the gas fireplace. Sitting in a leather chair he drank bourbon and thought of Aurora sleeping down the hall. Her face lit by the city, her body shrouded in Egyptian cotton. She was home tonight—he'd seen her coat on the counter. What I need, he thought, what there is no replacing in the wide world is a good woman. In his best moments he saw her this way. I know a good woman. Nothing like her. Nothing on this earth. In the place beyond, maybe. Creator knows.

He wondered if women thought the same about men. A good woman lacked the self-absorption of men. She understood beauty and power, wearing them like the wind. As the wings of an eagle lift the eagle without apology. He couldn't think of anything to match a good woman. A mountain lion perhaps. A song. But nothing truly captured her essence.

He rose, walked down the hall to the bedroom. Kneeling at the bedside he touched Aurora's head, drawing the hair back from her face. She didn't wake. Her breathing was quiet. Without her humor and affection he'd be lost. He'd always known loss, father-loss in abundance, and before the sober days, a certain mother-loss too. Aurora made him feel everything and he was a better man for being with her. Her being so alive. Even with the disparagement she imprinted on him he had wolf hunger for the love she gave. The others wanted a good woman too. Her friends, her lovers.

Before, like a tilted person he'd said they could have her but that was only when the smallness of his understanding equaled the smallness of his heart. He countered it by wanting to kill them all. He'd been coldhearted and bullheaded, listless with regard to the vagaries of love.

But now he wanted only her.

So many astonishing things, mountains and rivers and skies, land and horses, lights, cities, streams of vehicles on night highways, ships like ghost work in the fog along the coast. Countless things are beautiful, but there was nothing he'd found that had ever come close to approaching her shape or countenance. Nothing in this world, nothing in the next. He couldn't picture the Great Spirit blind to her beauty. The Great Spirit was above and below her and within her. Creator praised her. Thinking of it, he felt joy.

Even if she could make him bone weary with shame.

What he had no say in or power over was her gravity. Her wit and laughter, her quickness of mind. Her spirit so fiercely its own. As a young man he'd admired her far before Uncle gave him the nod to speak to her. Her silhouette in the distance was something. But it was nothing compared to the real woman, her life here with him, now, despite all. Thinking of her leaving him made him want to drown himself in alcohol. She was not his and never had been. No one thought like her, danced like her, sang like her.

No one partied like her either.

Dusk to dawn.

He wished he could wave his hand and secure the future.

See them hand in hand walking in the fields of forgiveness.

He needed to make peace.

He leaned closer and kissed her shoulder. "No one like you, Aurora," he whispered. "None like you." He rose and stripped to his underwear, got in bed, and lay with her, touching the back of her head before he put his hands to his side and let his head rest on the pillow.

"Elias Make Peace," he whispered. "Elias Make Peace American Horse."

But when he fell asleep he dreamed of war.

THE NEXT NIGHT, she didn't come home. He slept alone, and early the next morning entered the flow of cars in the I-5 corridor.

Work had been a rapid climb. At the start of the year the C-suite of Northwest Farm and Ranch designated him for executive leadership development. He'd worked hard for the company, moving from financial specialist to credit officer to relationship manager to running the crop insurance delivery team. In the next step he'd join the operating committee that managed the bank nationwide.

A fast-tracker, they called him.

He felt flattered. He was good with people, great with numbers.

As National EVP of Insurance, only a month away, his salary would jump $180,000 immediately, approaching $500,000 a year.

But in the past three years he'd been falling apart.

At the end of the day he returned to the house. She hadn't returned his messages. She'd left again and hadn't come back. He slept restlessly and in the pitch black he rose from bed and showered. For work he preferred khaki pants and a long-sleeve white Oxford. Meeting with high-powered clients, he wore fitted western suits and a bone-color Stetson, with gray leather cowboy boots, the stitching on the toe in white thread. With women at night he preferred fine-lined Armani and a black shirt, the shoes black velvet loafers by Ferragamo.

Today he wore a western suit.

HE ENJOYED contradictions. He'd given in a year ago and borrowed the money for the house she wanted.

After the day's work he was back at the kitchen table in wan light. His body hurt again, anxiety pressing the bones of his chest. These days, he was nearly always in pain.

The house was an iconic craftsman on Queen Anne hill, two blocks off the main drive. A view of water from the back deck and the upper bedroom. Their bedroom. The period details were remarkable. The loan was a whale. "Jumbo," John Sender called it, the White guy with a face chiseled in granite who was becoming his friend. In the signing meeting she'd tried to hit on him again and John rebuffed her like John Wayne. Normally, White boys were all the same to him, no matter their physical differences. They put themselves over you even if they were beneath you. But he and John had both rodeoed to some success and John was humble enough. They'd even spent some good time together, outside the bank, and it made Elias happy.

He had to laugh, he and John bound by fate.

He and Aurora sent bags of money back home. Still they had more than enough.

He'd been so agitated buying this big bus of a house, but he had to admit it was gorgeous. "Fastidiously preserved and updated," the realtor said. The house smelled faintly of pipe smoke, but the sell points were substantial. A large, covered, rocking-chair front porch. Hammered metal work in copper and bronze throughout. Gourmet kitchen. Flood-lighted rooms. A low-pitched roof with deep eaves and exposed rafters. Built-in cabinetry. Two large fireplaces. Distinctive dormers, and three wide-set upper porches for "spending time outdoors."

"Ha," he laughed. Outdoors. Considering the Beartooth Range, the porches were paltry. Montana's southern border boasted Two Oceans Plateau. Hellroaring Plateau. The Beartooth Highway among the great wonders of the world. High alpine ridges and sheer rock walls, granite peaks, deep-cut gorges, lakes arranged like blue plates among the mountains.

Outdoors was relative.

The house had interior tiles by noted American artist and potter Ernest Allan Batchelder. But the house depressed Elias. He'd be a VP soon, he told himself. In his suit he fell asleep in the chair by the fire, woke at 4:40 a.m., got up and started pacing. At 5:32, seated in a kitchen chair as he held his chest, the front door opened, and Aurora walked in. She glanced at him and tears came to his eyes. She nodded and walked down the hall to their bedroom where she kicked off her heels and slipped under the covers with her clothes on.

Oun she la yo, he thought, watching her body retreat to the bedroom. He opened his hands on the table, pushed himself up, and went to the bedside.

"Have compassion on me," he whispered, kneeling.

Almost before he said the words, she was asleep.

He put his face to hers for a long while, the bridge of his nose pressed gently to her cheekbone, before he rose and walked back to the kitchen.

EARLIER THAT NIGHT she'd done something that made her very glad.

At Club Contour, a nightclub near the waterfront, she saw John Sender's CEO alone at the bar. She approached and sat beside him. The grinding strobe made the light false. She didn't think he recognized her. He looked at her wickedly and she told herself she'd teach him a lesson. She found it easy to lure him, purchasing three vodkas for him in succession, easier still to convince him to pay for the presidential suite on the top floor of the Four Seasons over the water. She touched his shoulder, flattered him, witnessed the fool banalities he shouted over the music: "Wedlock is like wearing concrete boots to sea. Any other extended coupling is equally reckless. Gratuitous. All societal or governmental intervention allows unproductive people to leech the hard-earned wealth of those who keep the economy strong." He motioned with his thumb to the crowd behind them. "The parasites feed on the heroes. They would feed unchecked until the hero is dead but it's better for the parasites to starve if society is to achieve what it is meant to achieve."

"And what is society meant to achieve?" she asked, angling toward him.

He focused on her chest. "The good of the hero. His fulfillment and ascent."

He looked at his watch. His eyes were glassy. He thought of his great ambition, specifically the building that dominated the skyline of his dreams. He thought of the Native woman in front of him and found he wanted her.

When his father had driven him to Miles City the blood from his hand seeped into the floorboard, a stain he'd been tasked to remove for years. The stain was not removable, his father finally admitted, enraged. The watch Roark wore was his father's, the face of it flashing on occasion in the lamplight. Aurora placed her hand on his arm, then lowered his hand to the curve of her hip.

99 Union Street. Three thousand dollars a night. She had the number in her phone. He nodded, she made the call. At the desk he gave a false name and paid like money meant nothing. He wanted bondage and she said yes but when he struck her head she drew her hand from her purse and maced him in the face.

He howled and went to the floor, crying worse than a child.

She kept her distance, cursing him.

She left five dollars on the counter like he was a common whore.

CONTRARY TO AURORA'S intuition Roark had recognized her from the start, remembering not only her look, a body he found animalistic, but the name John gave him their first meeting in the lobby after Sender secured her and her husband's loan. After she'd gone he raised himself, called the desk, shouted at the receptionist for milk and did not tip the worker who brought it to him.

Over the black granite sink in the bathroom he poured the milk in his eyes.

"Aurora," he said into the mirror, his eyes fueled and raw.

"Aurora American Horse."

HE'D PAID for the hotel with a credit card lifted from a lesser rival a day earlier at a high-level meeting of ten bank CEOs detailing new restrictions from the Federal Reserve.

When his face calmed, he slept.

In the early morning, he showered, dressed, pocketed the five dollars, wiped the credit card with a towel, used a napkin to place it in a trash bin three blocks from the hotel, and walked briskly to work.

At five in the morning, no one saw him enter the building.

In his office he thumbed the pages of his address book. Nothing electronic, and therefore no trace. On the computer he looked in Sender's portfolio for the most recent address of Aurora American Horse. After writing AAH on the back page of the address book in black pen, he darkened a small triangle in the upper right corner. The lower right corner contained another black triangle but no name, a prostitute from South Seattle. He pressed his left forefinger over both triangles. Then he turned to the A section, to ARC—American Rationalist Convergence—a nationalist group whose western region he secretly led and funded.

He wasn't worried about Aurora. In due time, he thought.

He put the phone on speaker for the monthly meeting directed at his C-level strategy team.

ELIAS'S ABSENTEE father had taken him to the Beartooths as a boy.

Some of the only love he remembered him capable of.

I should get back there, he told himself.

In the house alone he found it difficult to overcome the way his mind consumed him. He'd lost his lust for money. His wife was a kind of darkness unknown to him. He placed his hands on his thighs, wiped his eyes on the shoulders of his shirt, stood and stared out the window. The sky was impenetrable.

Sitting down again, he ran his hands through his hair. He'd be servicing two gigantic accounts today, worth millions more than his own home, ranches east and west of the Cascades. One on the slope of the Olympics and one far away from Seattle, in Montana near Bozeman in the Bridger Mountains. He'd been to Bozeman for college, for cross-country and also some hunting. Felled his first bull elk at fifteen outside Gardiner; the ivory teeth still mixed with the others in the medicine pouch on his desk, the leather-wrapped hollow turtle shell Uncle gave him. The shell came from the body of a painted turtle hatchling Elias found dead near Dry Creek. Clayton, with his old, gnarled hands, had boiled it to remove the meat and used soap and water to make it shine. Clayton had also made the leather purse of whitetail hide to house it in.

"Put all those ivories in," Clayton had said. "All of them from your five kills, and the longest rattlesnake rattle you have."

Elias did what Clayton asked.

"Here, this blackbird feather too."

Elias placed the feather, no longer than his little finger, in the turtle shell and drew the strings tight, tying the soft leather in a bow.

"Thank you, Uncle."

"For flight," Clayton told him.

The rattle Elias put inside had twelve segments ending in a round button and was nearly three inches long. That snake had been close to five feet with a light gray-brown body, a distinct black-cloud back pattern flattening to rings toward the tail, and a cream-white underbelly. Some rattlesnakes were olive or gray-green. This one had the coloring of dust. He counted it a blessing to come upon the remains, a golden eagle lifting off from the snake in a swale on the plain toward Wolf Point, plying the air in the distance like an oared ship. Elias was hunting mule deer. The snake's body open and raw after the eagle's gorging. Chewed to its depths at the neck and along the belly. He'd removed the rattle with his knife, put it in his pocket and blessed the snake and the ground and sky, the eagle too. It was the week of his grandmother's seventy-first birthday.

He thought of his mother and grandma again.

He was thirty-three now.

The image of the snake torn open in sparse grass made him think of a small rattler that took a shot at him in the Beartooths back in college when Elias rounded a rock outcropping. It was a ninety-degree day, the snake piping like a snare drum, but apparently short-sighted. The relief Elias felt at not being bit had flooded his veins. His heart felt like smoke.

After edging around the snake he'd crossed the rock bridge south of the massive talus at Goatsbeard Lake where he summitted a sawtooth he didn't know. He was alone, as he liked to be, the sun near enough to touch and surprisingly warm even at a pinnacle that topped eleven thousand feet. He stepped down into a gorge on the ascent and traversed a couloir below the pinnacle. He accessed the summit by slipping into a five-foot crack in the south wall and notching upward for half an hour before he emerged on a knuckled spar just below the top. At the highest point he sat down with his knees in his arms and beheld heaven and earth, the sight lines revealing nearly the entire Absaroka-Beartooth Wilderness on a fifty-mile axis. East to west, canyons fell to valleys that trickled snowmelt into East Rosebud Creek, a tributary of the Stillwater that met the Yellowstone on its way to Billings, the Missouri, the Dakotas, and middle America.

He was too urbanized now, he told himself.

Aurora needed to be strong against him, he thought; he felt her posturing.

They didn't have any pets. She hated him for refusing her that.

Made of concrete, wire, and glass. He'd forgotten sinew, flesh, and bone.

When he rose from the kitchen table he vowed to get back to Montana.

AURORA GONE AGAIN, the following Friday he flew late night to Billings and spent the next day early in the Beartooths, reaching that same knuckled spar and granite vista by noon. Looking out he exhaled and felt his body go slack. In love I am beholden to you, Aurora, for what is greater than me. A vision such as this, granite peaks and silver water, stripped him to the bone. He remembered Aurora kissing him and wept.

When she kissed him, he fell into nothing and rose into everything.

He spent Saturday night at the Pollard Hotel in Red Lodge in a large corner room that reminded him of cattle barons and copper kings. He ordered room service and ate the best ribeye he'd had in years, the fat and blackened cut flawless and smelling so much like home he almost cried again. He'd rented a gold Camaro, sleek in its lines with a wide wheelbase, the engine throaty and responsive. Sunday morning at a hundred miles an hour he drove from the base to the height of Montana, from Red Lodge all the way to Fort Peck. He visited his mother and grandmother and kissed their faces and made them a simple lunch of grilled-cheese sandwiches and tomato soup. In the afternoon he rode the fields with Clayton, surveying the Herefords, eating a dinner of fresh cucumbers and sirloin tip steak Clayton grilled for him before he fell asleep on Clayton's couch. In the morning he drove to Billings in the predawn black for the return flight to Seattle where he took the light rail and was back in his office by noon on Monday.

He repeated this pattern or one like it every two weeks for a couple of months. He slept with fewer women, drank fewer drinks, and listened to Clayton. He visited his mother and grandmother. He worked on loving Aurora more.

The one he'd always loved best.

She came and went at her leisure. She said she loved the Emerald City.

He liked it less and less.

They touched one another mainly in passing, and though they spoke soft words in the night the distress was palpable between them.

BECAUSE OF THIS, his will for life suffered, the dark-mindedness abating only slightly in December of that year when he joined his uncle for the sixteen-day memorial ride from South Dakota to Minnesota in honor of the Dakota 38 + 2.

Due to Lincoln's fatal decree, thirty-eight Dakota warriors were hanged on a single scaffold in Mankato, Minnesota in 1862. The largest mass execution in United States history.

Days later, two more were hanged.

Before the ride Elias made a long sweat with his uncle, absorbing the searing stone-heat from the steam, then dipping himself in the frigid waters of Two Tails Creek where Clayton had broken the ice.

HIS HORSE was a large black Appaloosa named Gameboy his uncle let him ride. A good horse. If you didn't have your own horse sometimes you had to ride a bitter old nag that would rather bite you than be rode. Gameboy was steady and approachable. Elias was grateful.

They went through winter, cutting the wind with their faces.

Twenty men befriended him, the most memorable being those who rode near his uncle. Elias loved them for how different they were than his work world. For their laughter or quietness, their humility and brotherhood. They were his father's age or older, or somewhat younger: Melichi Four Bear, Pelter Jones, Owen Gray Bear, Fat Smith, Hubert Iron Cloud.

Clayton told him the truth he'd known but avoided. Clayton wasn't like the rest of America, deaf to a past and oblivious to a present the Dakota, Lakota, and Nakoda would never displace.

He and Aurora were still married, Elias thought, but barely.

MORE AND MORE people were afraid of marriage and yet were still attracted to the idea of beautiful union. Some didn't want marriage, but some, like him, wanted it more than ever, or maybe he only wanted something to fill how hollow he'd become.

Single people were no more satisfied than those who coupled.

Very few people lived like perfect fires, intimate and alive.

He wished he and Aurora could be given that life.

THE HOUSE kept weighing on Elias.

"It'll be easy," John had said, "your credit is stellar."

Elias liked John. He felt calm in his presence, even if the house kept feeling as if stones were being cairned over his body one by one until he couldn't breathe.

"How's Aurora?" John had asked in the pre-loan meeting without her.

"Decent, I guess," Elias said.

"You and I should get a beer after this," John said.

"We should," Elias answered.

Hell of a thing, friendship with this White boy in the city.

He had to laugh at himself.

"How about the Seattle Rodeo Club?" John said. "At Picket's Sports Bar we gather to watch Professional Rodeo Cowboys Association events. Picket's on Third Avenue downtown. Tonight, it's the National Finals Rodeo. Top fifteen headers and heelers in team roping going for the prize money."

"Yeah," Elias said, "that'd be a real good battle."

When he texted Aurora saying he and John might get a beer, she said, "Sounds fun, I want to go too." He said no and didn't tell her the location.

When he and John walked in the door at Picket's, John's friends waved to them from a table in the near corner facing the big screen. When Elias approached, John introduced him saying something about Elias being a team roper and they each got up, cupped Elias's hand like an athlete, and pulled him to their chests.

"So glad you're here, Elias. Thanks for coming."

"Nice to meet you, man."

"Team roping. Beautiful, brother."

Elias took the chair next to John and the night was basic. Not all White boys, gratefully, at least two other non-whites, and one he couldn't make out. Faces joyful or slack, facing the glow of the screen that made their bodies ledges of shadow and light. His guard went down with each successive beer. John bought more than most. Elias pitched in. At the end of the evening John asked what he'd thought of the team roping.

"Very quick," Elias said. His hands moved with recollection. The body remembered the power of big animals.

"Yes," John said. "Never made it to that level with saddle broncs, but always wished I'd given it a good five more years just to see."

"More broken bones?" Elias asked.

"Sure," John said, smiling. "How about you?"

Elias pictured the great Native ropers he'd known. He knew six men who were better than the ones he'd witnessed tonight. He'd battled many of them with some success through the years.

"No," he said. "I needed to get out and make some money. Feed my family."

"Well you've done well there," John said.

"I don't know," Elias answered, thinking of Aurora.

"You and your wife have a nice connection," John said.

Elias eyed him to see if he was optimistic, opportunistic, or stupid.

"How about you, John, are you still in love?"

John's face turned red. "Yes I am."

Elias thought he should love Aurora better then, seeing John's hope.

From there, the friendship flourished. He and John called each other more often, getting together over beer or pool, sometimes coffee, the occasional lunch. The juxtaposition of White cowboy and Lakota, or rather cowboy and cowboy, a fraught history they both acknowledged.

ON THE WAY to Mankato the ride was hard and the soreness took some days leaving his body. As he rode, he thought of his family. He wasn't sure he could cleanly trace it but he associated himself with American Horse the Elder more than the Younger. The Elder, born in 1820 and mortally wounded in the Battle of Slim Buttes in September 1876, was one of the legendary shirt-wearers, duty bound to lead warriors in peacetime and in war. Said to be wise and generous in all dealings, he was also commanding. American Horse the Elder's cousin Red Cloud and fellow Lakota Crazy Horse were his lifelong friends. American Horse the Elder was the son of Old Smoke, leader of the Smoke People also called the Bad Faces or Iteschica. His auntie Walks As She Thinks was Red Cloud's mother. American Horse fought in Red Cloud's War and helped kill Custer and his men at the Battle of the Greasy Grass after Sitting Bull's dream in which White men were thrown into the Oglala camp from the sky. American Horse was captured under White vengeance at Slim Buttes, where he was shot in the gut and held his intestines in his hands to keep them from spilling out. He clenched a stick in his mouth and kept silent, handed his gun to the White commander, and sat by the fire where his wife tried to stem the bleeding with her shawl.

He refused the treatment offered by the commander's surgeon.

American Horse died in the night.

Before he died he said, "It is always the friendly ones who are struck."

After he died, White soldiers scalped him.

THINKING OF THE PAST, Elias American Horse rode with a rift in his mind. During the Indian Wars of the 1800s there were four shirt-wearers, including his forebear American Horse the Elder.

Crazy Horse, Young Man Afraid, and Sword were the other three.

Each was given a shirt made from the hides of bighorn sheep, decorated with feathers, quill work, and the scalps they'd won in battle. The tribe directed the shirt-wearers to care for widows, orphans, and those who had little. The four were chosen because they were greathearted, ferocious in battle, and the tribe knew they would do their duty with a good spirit.

There were soldier chiefs who filled White bodies with arrows or attacked close in and hammered the skulls with stone hammers. There were women warriors who set axes into White men's chests, and took scalps. Afterward, they mutilated the enemy together, using knives to slit open the body cavity, the chest, arms, and thighs.

He asked Aurora why she always carried her dad's pistol.

"Look around you," she said.

ON HORSEBACK from South Dakota to Minnesota in the dead of winter, he wondered where all the wise men had gone. Where were the shirt-wearers? Yes, some men became medicine men, or monks, or priests, but like all men, they wrestled with their own evil. He imagined some overcame, though he knew none who had except perhaps Clayton. And maybe that rez priest named Joe. Others were overcome. He knew plenty of those.

In America, men became almost useless. As we age, perhaps we live in the space between, he thought. His grandmother had been moved by Father Joe's modesty. Joe lived his last fifty years on the rez, serving and giving, and though Joe was tough as hell, he didn't make many enemies and he helped many enemies become friends again. He gave deference to people and God. Like a thumb scraper, Elias thought, always useful. When Joe died, Elias's grandmother said at his funeral, "He would have been the right husband for me."

Most men knew little or nothing of spiritual life, Elias thought.

Some became new age gurus.

New age gurus were generally dumb shits.

But some men were truly wise and maybe each man knew at least one of these, Elias thought, and whether or not he availed himself of this wisdom likely determined everything.

THE SKY PALE, the wind a blade across white plains, Elias rode next to Clayton. Lakota men, women, and children were mown down and butchered at Wounded Knee Creek. Buried in a single mass grave after a blizzard, their bodies frozen, limbs askew. The others had starved to death on the reservations afterward, mothers and fathers watching their children die, and dying with them. Even so, Elias's own father and grandfather volunteered for military service, and served America with distinction.

Both his grandfather and his father loved America, and didn't express hate.

But sometimes he couldn't stomach history.

It was the united part of United States that baffled him.

Not only him but Leonard Peltier, he thought, and Annie Mae Pictou Aquash, the highest-ranking woman in the American Indian Movement who was taken to a far corner of the Pine Ridge Reservation where she was killed by a gunshot wound to the back of the head. When her decomposing body was finally found, the coroner "failed" to find the bullet hole in her skull, and the FBI severed both of her hands and sent them to Washington DC, supposedly for identification purposes, before they buried her as a Jane Doe. The Lakota do not forget this was an act of war. Her Mi'kmaq and Lakota defenders, women and men, Elias thought, still walked the earth.

For millennia his relatives called themselves Lakota, Dakota, or Nakoda, meaning "friend" or "ally." Prayer was the center. Prayer, the center of family. Prayer, the center of life. In the Oglala Lakota nation, one of the seven major Očhéthi Šakówiŋ nations of the Seven Fires Council, Lakota was preferred over Sioux as Sioux was a misnomer given by the Ojibwe meaning "little snakes."

The Dakota 38 were hanged under the orders of President Abraham "no-middle-name" Lincoln. The hangings followed the U.S.-Dakota War, which came at a time when the Dakota people faced the shrinking of their territory, their land smaller and smaller until the U.S. government had it whittled down from many millions of acres to a tract less than ten miles long. The people did not have hunting privileges beyond that sliver of land. They were never given the money the government promised, and had no store credit with the traders.

Trapped, starving, increasingly hostile, the Dakota seethed against the

White leaders, none of whom had the foresight to turn the tide from rage to food.

History could burn the heart to ash, Elias thought.

In fact, when the Dakota decried the U.S. government's late payments and tried to ward off starvation, a White trader named Andrew Myrick who had general stores at the Yellow Medicine and Redwood agencies imitated Marie Antoinette, saying "Let them eat grass."

The Dakota starved.

There was an uprising.

Dakota warriors killed White people.

Myrick was found dead on the plain, his mouth stuffed with grass.

The U.S. military retaliated, imprisoning a thousand Dakota men, women, and children.

Thirty-eight Dakota men were singled out to be hanged by mass execution, and later, two more. Each one like me, Elias thought, each with a mother who held them and sang to them, a father who kissed them and blessed them, a family who prayed over them. All my relations.

The Dakota 38 were hanged on a square upraised scaffold. Men with their chests to the sun, they walked in a single-file line, and died there, hanged by the throat until the windpipe collapsed and no air entered the lungs. Lightburn on the edge of the world.

Lincoln ordered the mass execution the same week he signed the Emancipation Proclamation. The Dakota men swung in disproportionate light, centrifugal and blown back into the sidereal amplitude of their making.

The day was December 26, 1862. The day after Christmas.

Often as they rode, Clayton reached out and put his hand on Elias's forearm, comforting him, giving him strength. When Clayton did so, Elias put his hand over Clayton's, returning the grace he was given.

AURORA WONDERED how she'd become what she'd become.
Angry most of the time. Untrue to Elias, and so cold to him.
Still beautiful, yes.
But at this rate, she reasoned, not for long.

IN THE YEAR BEFORE the long ride, Uncle Clayton had made Elias promise to read everyone from Momaday to Silko to Welch to Harjo, from Erdrich to Deloria to their own vivid new stars M. L. Smoker and Layli Long Soldier. Elias didn't mind at all, the practice of getting to know something deeply just like the practice he'd followed in completing the PhD, and now that he was on the ride, the facts he'd learned ran in his mind: Sixty-six of one hundred Lakota women and men on the Pine Ridge rez were alcoholic; one of every four children born into fetal alcohol syndrome; life expectancy for adult Lakotas extremely low; the unemployment rate at 80 percent; the suicide rate four times the national average.

In June, Timothy Black Elk hung himself.

Clayton said Timothy worked with middle school students in math and reading.

From April to September, Pine Ridge had eleven suicides.

Native peoples, those of mixed race, those of mixed gender or sex, the traditionalists, the no-faiths, the Native Christians, the Native anti-Christians and atheists Elias had come to know in Seattle were all fallible deities trapped in the mind of America where non-Whiteness was not allowed.

Without being White, they wanted to live White anyway. A mythology of inevitability, he thought, dominance by any color a holocaust of mind and spirit. This is where being disappeared. He thought this way to avoid his own covert complicity.

He'd tried to run Aurora the same way, only with traditional Lakota thinking.

He needed to listen to her.

More than ever, he desired to love and grow old with her.

IN THE MORNING, three mornings before they were to arrive in Mankato, Minnesota, Clayton read to the men over breakfast. Elias put his nose in the collar of his coat, listening. The day would be long and frigid. He was already cold.

"On Saturday, December 19, 2009, U.S. President Barack Obama signed the Congressional Resolution of Apology to Native Peoples of the United States," Clayton said. "No tribal leaders or official representatives were invited to witness or receive the apology on behalf of tribal nations. President Obama never read the apology aloud, publicly—although, for the record, Senator Sam Brownback five months later read the apology to a gathering of five tribal leaders. There are over five hundred and sixty federally recognized tribes in the United States. The apology was hidden in an unrelated piece of legislation called the 2010 Department of Defense Appropriations Act.

"The U.S. government does not know how to ask forgiveness," Clayton said. "But we can guide them. The motto of this ride is forgive everyone everything. The purpose of this commemorative ride is healing and so let us remind ourselves as Očhéthi Šakówiŋ, as Oglala Lakota, Dakota, and Nakoda, through healing comes greater life."

When the talk ended and they went out to saddle the horses for the day, Elias walked close to Clayton. He put his arm around him as they walked, and kissed the old man on the cheek. Elias had assumed life was calling him to figure things out, but here he found he simply needed to give himself away.

"Let me prepare the horses today," he said.

"Thank you," Clayton chuckled, "but no thanks. I haven't trusted your city-boy instincts for a long time. No use starting today."

"Okay," Elias smiled. "I'll be the helper again."

"Good," Clayton said. "Remember that story I told you about your auntie. She saved a hundred Lakotas, Nakodas, and Dakotas at that rehab center after she got sober. She did it by listening and caring. Same thing you need to do with Aurora. Listen."

"I'm trying, Uncle," Elias said.

"Try harder," Clayton said. "And thank you. I needed that kiss today, for strength."

"You're welcome, Uncle."

As they prepared the horses, Elias thought: I am an enrolled member of the Oglala Tribe. A citizen of the Oglala Lakota Nation. Descendant of American Horse the Elder, and all his relations, Crazy Horse, Red Cloud, and Sword. I'm also a citizen of the Assiniboine Nation, Nakoda through my grandmother and Aurora.

And I'm a citizen of the United States.

Presidents can be cowards, he thought.

Elias had often been a coward himself.

But he hated cowardice, and thinking of Aurora again, he prayed for courage.

ON THE FINAL day of the ride he thought of Wounded Knee.

Wounded Knee was a bone he picked with America. Elders, women, and children slaughtered and left on open ground in late winter, the men with them. Old secrets near Wounded Knee Creek. Chankpe Opi Wakpala.

The Dakota execution in Mankato was the rot beneath the bone.

Other than the thirty-eight plus two, the thousand who'd been imprisoned were released but they had no more land and so they scattered to the west and many of them ended up dead too. Winter had no mercy. The hangings came near thirty years before Wounded Knee, like something cold touched to the lips. A gun or knife. The way a dog gnawed a bone clean. He'd eat that bone if he could. Ingest it and let it fortify him, even with its putrefaction. Meat and gristle, sinew, cartilage and the knot at the joint, the calcium of the bone, and inside, the marrow.

A few months before the ride, Montana grass fires ranged the expanse of the state, burning fifty thousand acres. Smoke covered British Columbia, Montana, and four adjoining states in ash, stopping visibility at five hundred feet. Hands in the fields wore kerchiefs over the nose and mouth. The air was charcoal on the tongue and took a long time clearing. At dusk and dawn, fulminant bitter suns. At night, blood moons. The fires were so far from him here as he rode through sleet and ice in the slanted winds of South Dakota. But his mouth still tasted of ash.

The killings were grotesque. In Mankato the bodies jumped on the rope in one disjointed motion. Before the hangings, from the pens in which they were held, each man relayed a blessing to his loved ones, and sent small mementos, his pipe or a little tobacco, some beadwork, a lock of hair. A White man, Captain William J. Duley, whose wife, Laura, was captured, and three of whose children—Willie, ten, Bell, four, and Francis, six months—were killed by the Dakota in the Sioux Uprising, swung the axe that cut the rope and clean-dropped the foot plank below all thirty-eight men at once. This happened on Mankato's main street with a large crowd gathered and people standing on rooftops for a better view. The bodies struggled, then hung slack for public witness, head and hair unnaturally tilted above torso, limbs like reeds sifted by wind.

At Wounded Knee, slant arms were frozen in place, faces drawn, eyes askance as the spirit lifted away. They were taken in wooden lorries to a mass grave. He couldn't erase the picture of a mouth frozen open, a wedge of dirt laid over it, filling the mouth, covering the body, the way into death or back toward life forsaken. No laughter in the trumpet of the throat, or tears in the eyes. Just silence as he rode. A lip of rock, perhaps a cliff face signifying the grave.

Thinking this way, he stepped into darkness.

Far below was an immeasurable abyss.

Aurora told him she didn't want to think of any of it, not Wounded Knee, not the Dakota 38 or the two, not any of his goddamned dwelling in the past. She blamed him for their loss of love. But he dreamed these things, and he needed to tell her his dreams. Before he left for South Dakota to join Clayton for the sixteen-day ride to Mankato, she'd put her fingers in her ears as he spoke. He'd crossed the line and shaken her shoulders but it was like shaking a bucket of rusted nails, the whole tangle solid with nothing breaking loose.

He'd shouted and she'd clenched her fists. "Will you please shut the F up?!"

She didn't like to cuss and so she said F instead, and somehow that decency brought him to his senses. He lowered his hands.

"Get the F away from me!" she said.

The feeling of her containment destroyed him, and he fled the house. Like too many men, he'd physically harmed her, shaking her, a porcelain bank he couldn't empty.

He wasn't well. He needed to get well.

On the final day, Clayton rode with him, eyeing the distance and a gray mark on the horizon that was Mankato. Clayton's body was a slab of granite that weathered every storm. His heart though, was soft. I'm too hard, Elias thought. I need to be softer. But that wasn't right. I need to be both, he thought, watching Clayton's face below the black line of the Stetson he'd tilted forward into the wind, his dark eyes almost hidden above the scarf that covered his nose, mouth, and jaw. Those eyes had seen everything, Elias thought, and still looked out on the world with clarity. At least whenever he wasn't half-insane about women or what children were his or not.

IN MANKATO Elias stood by his horse among the other horses. He wanted to be quiet and out of the way. He wanted to shut his mouth as Aurora had directed him. The ride was terribly cold each day, and he hadn't warmed yet. His body felt tight, the limbs heavy in the sockets. He heard the proceedings and the White mayor of Mankato droning loudly, declaring "a year of forgiveness and understanding." Elias put his head down. It was not good to be alone, he thought, and just then an old woman appeared. She was smudging the horses, wafting sweetgrass smoke over the bodies. He leaned his face into the coat of his horse, at the sweep in front of the shoulder on the neck. He held the mane in his right hand. The scent of the coat was good to him. The old woman approached and smudged him and lifted smoke into his face like he was one of the horses and they both laughed. He kept his head down and she touched his lips and he spoke, saying, "Thank you, grandmother. Thank you."

He held her hand and lifted his face and she smiled at him, her grin toothless, the mouth pursed. "Let me tell you the names of thirty-nine of the forty executed Dakota," she said. "I never learnt the fortieth. Bless him and all his relations. Just as you are blessed, my son. Some were full Dakota, others Dakota and White. Listen:

"Ta he do ne cha. One Who Forbids His House," she said, bowing her head and lifting her free hand as she went on.

"Plan doo ta. Red Otter.

"Wy a tah ta wa. His People.

"Hin hau shoon ko yag ma ne. One Who Walks Clothed In An Owl's Tail.

"Ma za bom doo. Iron Blower.

"Wak pa doo ta. Red Leaf.

"Wa he hua.

"Sua ma ne. Sounding Walker.

"Ta tay me ma. Round Wind.

"Rda in yan ka. Rattling Runner."

With her thumb this time, she touched his forehead.

"Doo wau sa. The Singer.

"Ha pau. Second Child Of A Son.

"Shoon ka ska. White Dog.

"Toon kau e cha tag ma ne. One Who Walks By His Grandfather.

"E tay doo tay. Red Face.

"Am da cha. Broken To Pieces.

"Hay pe pau. Third Child Of A Son.

"Mah pe o ke na jui. Stands On The Clouds.

"Harry Milord.

"Chas kay dau. First Born Of A Son.

"Baptiste Campbell.

"Ta ta ka gay. Wind Maker.

"Hay pin kpa. The Tips Of The Horn.

"Hypolite Auge.

"Ka pay shue. One Who Does Not Flee."

Was she naming him? he wondered.

"Wa kau tau ka. Great Spirit.

"Toon kau ko yag e na jui. One Who Stands Clothed With His Grandfather.

"Wa ka ta e na jui. One Who Stands On The Earth.

"Pa za koo tay ma ne. One Who Walks Prepared To Shoot.

"Ta tay hde dau. Wind Comes Home.

"Wa she choon. Frenchman.

"A c cha ga. To Grow Upon.

"Ho tan in koo. Voice That Appears Coming.

"Khay tan hoon ka. The Parent Hawk.

"Chau ka had. Near The Wood.

"Had hin hday. To Make A Rattling Voice."

She placed her hand on his chest.

"O ya tay a kee. The Coming People.

"Ma hoo way ma. He Comes For Me.

"Wa kin yan wa. Little Thunder."

When she finished, she went on to the other horses and he watched her go. He leaned his face into the neck of his horse again. The sweetgrass and smudging and her abundant naming changed the taste in his mouth and he felt a little better for it.

Mankato wasn't much. Another White town. They stood among single-

or two- or three-story buildings downtown. Block structures made of brick, old-west windowpanes and flat roofs. A wide sidewalk on a two-lane street. No boardwalk. Blue Earth County. He thought of Aurora in Seattle. He needed to love her in her landscape, not his, with magnitude.

He needed to stop trying to coerce her, and just love her.

THE AIRPLANE hummed loudly, a lightweight hopper with dual propellers and a low ceiling. There were maybe thirty people with him, flying over the Rockies. Watching the others, Elias's head felt heavy but he couldn't sleep. In his waking dream, the old woman accompanied him. Her smudging and sweetgrass. Smoke and the color of smoke. Before Elias boarded the plane, he and Clayton had hugged each other and wept on each other's necks. He remembered the microphone at the ceremony and this or that White man's loud voice, and then Joe Kicking Horse saying softly he made the ride because he and his whole family wanted to speak a message of forgiveness and remembrance and love.

Do any of us know the suffering of others? There are so few ways, he thought, to truly know someone. Touch. A hand in your hand. The trace of a loved one's fingers on your arm.

He was going home to Aurora. His chest ached.

His whole life from that day in Mankato on, he remained faithful to her.

But on a Sunday in Seattle, a week after his return, she left him.

HE REALIZED she was gone when he looked in her closet.

In Aurora's own waking dream, driving across the Montana highline, he called to her, saying, "Doe key ya lay hey? Where are you going?" and she answered, saying, "Wah gnee ktya. I'm going home."

On the highline near the Canada-Montana border, white grasses stood windswept to the horizon. From a swale just south of Wolf Point, a stripe of blackbirds bolted heavenward pursued in predatory flight. Raucous, chaotic, they amplified their voices, rising from where they built their nests, low among shoots of vegetation in wet barrow pits along the dirt roads. Their clutches were set near the surface of the water below the cattails, bulrushes, and sedges. She imagined the fledgling chicks hinging their beaks wide. The adult blackbirds would return and drop food into the pink dark openings.

Truthfully, she felt she knew nothing of Elias's dreams or hers.

She had a braid of sweetgrass and a mahogany crucifix she held close as she drove. She didn't like holding these things, but pregnant, and worried, she thought she should. Before she left Elias, she'd kissed the lips of Christ, then put the crucifix in her pocket. Love is forever, she thought. The sweetgrass braid had been his, but she knew he'd want her to have it.

JOHN SENDER called from his office in the National American Bank building, asking if Elias wanted to purchase a half-floor suite high up in The Towers, a jet-set seventy-seven-story dual skyscraper near Capitol Hill. "Good appreciation," John said, "good returns."

"Yes," Elias said. Money didn't matter anymore. Not the getting, not the keeping.

He left the Queen Ann house empty.

Went to sleep on the razor's edge of postmodernity.

John serviced the loan.

ON THE TOP FLOOR of the bank building, in the corner office, Roark locked his door so he could stream videos of women with women, women with men in positions of compromise and abject burden. He told himself he was a purist. The bodies were White. He thought of Aurora and wondered how he'd let himself desire her, the shame like an axe in his chest.

He hadn't killed much since his brother. He wasn't afraid to take life, just hadn't had the urge for a while, until now. He thought he should practice before performing what needed to be done. He knew whores, despised them, had killed one in her teens more than ten years ago, the girl with her own black triangle in the back of his book. He knew where and how. Aurora Avenue North. Pacific Highway South. The leeches no one knew or cared about. Native or Black. Poor White. He wanted what he wanted. He and his father, he thought, and reckoned there are monsters born in the world to human parents. But countering himself he thought of racehorse theory: He had better blood, better genes. Evil came from those who wanted handouts because they were not smart enough or strong enough to succeed. The weak believed monsters came into being in the form of the strong, but it's not true. We who are unafraid to be violent lay claim to life, he thought, and life is our providence.

Let the leeches be placed on dry land. Salted. Burned.

They couldn't own or master anything, for they were unhuman.

And he was not inhuman, he told himself, but humane.

THOUGH SEPARATED by a thousand miles now, Aurora was loyal to Elias.
Her mother had died young, as had Elias's father.
Blood was a haunting bond.
The depths could not be fathomed.

AFTER AURORA had been gone for a long time, she remembered Elias differently. She remembered especially her three miscarriages in Seattle and Elias caring for her. He'd cared for her as a good man would, but the sorrow had been bottomless.

Only Elias had seen her laid bare.

She missed him terribly.

The new pregnancy forced her to face herself. She did not want to think of it but she knew she must. He was different and she was different since she'd left.

Normally she easily dismissed him.

Living with her grandma in a two-room shack, she needed to get herself together. She thought of divorcing him, thought of him receiving papers with the Washington State seal on them, him embittered and wary of life, women, fatherhood. Even without knowing she was pregnant, and after yelling at her, he'd gone on the ride with a new countenance, quieter, more of a listener. She didn't want to hurt him anymore.

In the three weeks he was away on the ride, she'd made plans with her sister to go to her grandma's in the pregnancy's third trimester. He still didn't know she brought new life, and she didn't want him coming to Montana for her or the baby. She'd driven across Washington and the Idaho panhandle and deep into Montana to stay at her grandma's house, remote northeast of Wolf Point where no one visited but hawks and mule deer. The baby was not enough to bind them—there were deeper requirements.

Elias didn't have that higher sense yet, she thought.

Neither did she.

But she felt it building like the aroma of timothy grass in the morning. She'd left Seattle. When it was time, she'd have the baby with her grandma and her sister by her side. She'd trashed Elias for his traditional ways, his urban holy, but now that he'd fashioned himself a rider in honor of the Dakota 38 + 2, she missed him. Carrying his child, she couldn't bear the thought of her people suffering.

One walked in fear or faced life with a certain soldier mentality.

Her fingers felt numb.

Her grandmother quietly snored in bed beside her.

FROM WOMEN, MEN RECEIVED life and breath, she thought.

From men, men gathered death.

She said a prayer for Elias and the baby before falling asleep herself.

PRESIDENT LINCOLN had them hung the day after Christmas.

The Dakota 38, and later the two.

Elias's mother mixed her Catholicism with her Lakota.

If he recalled it right, Aurora's grandmother did the same.

"Blessed be Wakan Tanka," Elias's mother said. "Have pity on us, Creator. Go with my son." She said this over the phone, blessing him when she heard he'd be riding. He could see her in her plush velvet recliner, raising her hand up. When he asked her what she knew of the 38 plus 2, she said through tears, "All I need to know. Strength and dignity are their clothing. They smile at the future. They run. They fly. Go, help bring them rest."

He liked her more and more. She had a common sense to her that was not White. But she loved White people as much as she loved her own people, and she loved her people as much as anyone he knew.

The ride had ended up opening a crevice in him.

Shortly after Aurora left him, he fell apart.

He'd thought she would come back.

He stopped calling Clayton, went back to drinking. She'd gone home. Another month passed, and another. He sank to self-pity. Four months. All her media went dark. She didn't call. She didn't answer his calls.

Her family kept her privacy. "She's thirty-three," they told him, "a grown woman."

"And so are you," they said. "Grow up."

Instead, he spiraled.

After they hung up on him, he placed both hands on a square of Jack Daniel's Single Barrel Select, lifted it to his lips, and downed half the bottle.

As for Aurora, though she missed him, life had led them away from each other. Elias stewed on sadness, on how she'd gone to a place beyond his reach. He didn't know what to do.

Some years passed.

Book 3

Love . . . is like nature, but in reverse; first it fruits, then it flowers, then it seems to wither, then it goes deep, deep down into its burrow, where no one sees it, where it is lost from sight, and ultimately people die with that secret buried inside their souls.

—Edna O'Brien

PHILLIP AND ALBERTA

PHILLIP MCBANE, military dropout, White as potato flesh, flipped marriages like a shift cook flipped pancakes.

Until he met Alberta Amah.

In a low-income housing unit, naked in her bed, waiting for her to emerge from the bathroom so they could go again, he raised the whiskey bottle to his mouth and let the slow burn torch his throat, preparing himself for ecstasy.

She emerged from the bathroom, took the bottle and tipped it back. What shocked her a couple months into living with him, specifically when she held him close, was that he was loyal to her, and she was loyal to him. She had not experienced this before, how a man and a woman could love one another without anguish. When she felt hurt, she cut out the heart of the men before him by giving her body to others. Generally, men spiked hard then, even if they'd been wild a hundred times to her ten.

She loosened her robe, let it fall, and got in bed with him now, late morning, the apartment complex a step below poverty in the public housing projects of South Seattle, east of the old Yesler Terrace. The city was cloaked in a bank of fog below a dark gray sky. He didn't care if she showered so she just dabbed herself with some powder and perfume. They were fine if they smelled a little rank. The apartment had no view but concrete and wire and she knew when she walked if she rounded the corner and went north a few miles the water would not be visible there either.

In the sunshine Seattle's beauty made it one of the great cities of the world. It was also one of the Whitest, despite its liberal heartstrings. Whiter than Wichita, her friends told her. Today was the eighty-second day in a row without sun. Since coming to Seattle she'd lived through knots of gloom that lasted seventy-three, sixty-eight, and now eighty-two days. There had been additional stretches of ten and twenty days without light. Before, when the world went blank like this, she felt blind, more dead than alive. Depression a mean sister hounding her to hate herself. Two sons left behind leaving a hole in her. Her daughter Amanda famished for love. No money or mobility.

Rain didn't matter anymore now that Phil was here.

She thrilled to his presence. Sure they were often if not always either drunk or high or both. They nurtured numbness but he was good to her. He didn't hate her even if Amanda hadn't completely warmed to him yet.

Alberta pulled Phil close in their bed, pressing her forehead to his. "Why do you love me so much?" he asked her.

He's a sweet thing, she thought. Her sweet thing.

Amanda was in the main room with the coloring books.

Alberta echoed him, "Why do you love me so much?"

"Because you're a fox! Best woman I've ever known."

His words made her happy. She kissed his neck.

"What about your mother?"

"She was a tramp," he said.

"And other women?"

"They're not you. They never loved me like you do." He was telling the truth. He could get past her looks because she worked like a tidal wave, drowning him with just the kind of affection he needed. He reached and held her hand. "Why do you love me so much?" he said again.

She rolled over him and bracing her arms on the bed, kissed him with wet full-bodied kisses. She wasn't sure, but she thought he cried then, and it made her want to cry too. She'd never really been loved by a man. She'd never been loved, she thought.

She could lay with him and sleep the day away.

He didn't grow tired of her.

She didn't hate him.

IN HER ARMS he was surprised and he wasn't surprised how much she'd fallen for him. She despised her body, except with him, likely disliked her life too, he thought, except with him. All he had to do was be nice to her. Say kind things. Touch her.

She'd had some atrocious men, and this benefited him because he wasn't bad in the same ways. Plus, because she was big, she loved skinny, and he was skinny, except for how the weight collected in his jowls and the small pot belly perched like a mound of dough above his pelvis.

She also loved beer and mary jane. He'd done it all from marijuana to white horse, from acid to speed to coke, but he preferred poppies. She wasn't into poppies like he was but he was sure he could convince her. Poppy's Big Fat Poppies was his online opium supplier. The bulky pods spilled their seeds and he made a stew of it and the stew dissolved into his system and slicked his mind like oil. Thankfully, she wasn't laced too tight. She smiled. She laughed. She could get that big body in a groove he absolutely loved.

She called him Phillip, like no one did, and he let her. When he was high it sounded like "Will up." He never had much will but he liked someone acting like he did, and she acted like he did.

She told him he'd make it, and make it big.

At what, she couldn't say.

When she fell asleep again he got up and went to the kitchen and spent the early afternoon brewing and when he drank the bowl down he gagged three times but when it submerged him he felt glorious. His body went slack and dreamy and alive. He believed in God then and didn't fear death. But it didn't last and on the low side he felt humiliated. He got back in bed and clung to her body like a dog to a stranger's leg. He wanted her to kiss him and receive his kisses. He kissed her but she didn't wake.

Staring at her face, touching himself, he fell asleep too.

THEY WOKE late afternoon to Amanda crying. Alberta yelled at her and went back to sleep. Phil went in and patted Amanda's arm until she calmed. She was old enough. He didn't know why she needed to cry.

"Are you hungry?" he asked.

"Yes," she said.

He fixed her an English muffin with butter and grape jelly and gave her a glass of expired milk.

When Alberta woke, Phil brought her to the kitchen. Tonight, he'd teach her how to make opium tea so he didn't have to do all the work.

"I don't like opium," Alberta said.

"You will," he said, showing his teeth.

She wrinkled her face.

"That's cute," he said.

"What?" she said.

"Your face."

She laughed. He was a charmer. She loved how he charmed her. She'd do anything for him. Previously it never worked out, but Phil had outlasted most and she liked to play the dream to the end. She didn't like her mind trying to sabotage her.

"Show me," she said.

He kissed her, sloppy, the way she liked to be kissed.

"Thank you," she said.

She tasted like pork and onions.

"Thank you!" he exclaimed, and started talking like his tongue rode a hamster wheel. "It's a racket, a big nationwide racket, and that's good, that's why it's so cheap, twenty bucks a month, two hundred forty a year, and we're golden you and me together, walking on air like birds!"

"Two hundred forty?" she said.

"Two hundred forty each," he said. "That's four hundred eighty. Hardly a dent in the welfare flow, and it's for our own welfare! I love being high, don't you? And on the man's dime, not mine. Not yours. We can flop around this place all day, loving each other up and down like rabbits, making the bed our burrow and eating chips, brownies, cookies, candy bars, scratching our itch!"

He threw a leg in the air and shook it like Elvis.

She giggled. He sounded crazy. He looked crazy.

She wanted crazy love.

They'd been under the same roof a couple of months now.

When he was high he called her his Black Russian.

"Five parts vodka, two parts coffee liqueur," he said. "You make me drunk!"

The words rolled from his tongue like water.

"You make me drunk too!" she shouted. "But I'm not Russian. I'm Bulgarian and Nigerian, and all American."

"Whatever," he teased.

African American, she thought, in the most real way. He had a love that knew no borders and she let him run with it to see what tunnel it led to. In the naturalization process she'd memorized the Oath of Allegiance because her mom asked her to, and because she'd been so excited to be American. She wasn't so excited anymore.

"But I like it when you call me Black Russian," she said.

She kept his dream alive.

"I'm glad you do," Phil said ecstatically. "You hear me, gorgeous? My pretty Berta! Are you my Black Russian?"

"Yes I am!" she said.

He often called her Berta, which she loved, but once, when angry, he'd added an h and called her Bertha, which she deplored. She knew it was a fat woman's name. It happened a couple of weeks back on the day she collected her welfare check. She came in the door elated and a moment later when they were together in the tight bathroom just after having sex he called her Bertha and she slapped his face so solidly he stopped talking and wept outright, dismayed she'd used what he called "domestic violence" and on him "of all people." The one, he said, "who loved her better than anyone."

She agreed she shouldn't have and apologized repeatedly through her own snotty tears that tasted a little like lemon on her lips.

He hadn't held it against her, she credited him that.

ALBERTA AMAH had been married twice before, and Phil McBane was hitched three times, all five marriages relatively short and somewhat to very violent. He'd had a brief stint in jail. She hadn't held a decent job in a long time. They got married anyway. Most of the kids from their previous marriages they didn't see, except her oldest daughter Amanda whom they had in their possession. She was ten years old.

"I want a ring," Alberta said over the economy-sized bag of Doritos she shared with Phil while watching a reality show about NBA wives.

"I'll get you one," he said.

They'd known each other just over six months and he knew she was the best he'd ever had: lavish in their lovemaking, not a pain in the ass all the time.

He proceeded to work construction under the table for three months to avoid wage garnishing. He put it all to a ring she found just right, despite its modest size. He couldn't do better than her. She was a keeper.

WHEN ASKED, Phil's family said they were White mongrel, mostly Irish, with some French, one aunt had mentioned. Still, he was a shade more olive than most cracker White boys, especially in late summer, and it had been suggested by his friends, and the occasional stranger, he might be "Native American or Indian or mixed" to which he routinely said no, until when he was thirty he'd swabbed his lineage because his grandma paid for it to double-check her own. In his own mind he'd always been White but now he found his genetic admixture was also roughly 5 percent from the Americas (places like Central and South America), and 5 percent Pacific Islander. To make ends meet he cleaned motels, drove truck for small grocery stores, and tried to buy and sell through garage sales and pawn shops.

He wondered if he could get a better job by acting like he was Latino.

Really he had no clue what he was except a chameleon.

Especially when it made sense.

ALBERTA LOVED PHIL. She'd started school again, taking a class at Shoreline Community College because she wanted to be a counselor. With the right schooling, she could work her way toward a job helping people as a Registered Chemical Dependency Counselor. Even the sound of it thrilled her: RCDC. Like ACDC. She was eating paint chips at night when Phil slept, the ingestion something like pain being swallowed and escaping the body backward, a distinct if somewhat unpleasant feeling. She used her nails at the base of the walls behind the appliances, or behind furniture. She had to get on her hands and knees to dislodge the small flakes and put them in her mouth. At the back of her throat she liked the buildup of foreign bodies, an echo aggravation, almost unbearable until the swallowing. The aftertaste hellish. Painting her nails with kerosene and clear gloss helped, but it burned the nailbeds.

Back in Vegas she'd gotten pregnant and nearly flunked high school. Her mother had come to America as a refugee. But here in Seattle she'd been maintaining an A in her first course, a fantastically weird one called Abnormal Psychology. She found she loved the birds in Seattle and often watched them while she studied. The pigeons congregating on the rooftops, sweeping from roof to roof or down to the street where they pecked the sidewalks for food, searching like anxious old men. She liked the gulls in their tantrums over the water or adrift on a slow glide between the buildings, and how blackbirds whirled from ground to sky. She also treasured how even a used textbook emitted a fresh ink smell from the spine near the centerline. With a clear sky the light reflected from the Sound upward through the streets and touched the shadows of the city. A city illumined by water. Alberta was chunkier than she wanted to be, by all counts a large woman. She looked quite a bit more Black than White but she was White too, she thought. Either way, she loved it when she saw herself as gorgeous in the right light.

An uncle had molested her as a child in Nigeria. Before he went to prison. Before he got out and committed suicide when she was thirteen. Life had been extreme: detachment and need, appetite and survival.

In America, though she was far below the poverty line she felt rich. But with she and Phil drunk and high so often she knew she needed to change.

She needed to be clean if she wanted to get her Associate Arts degree. She hadn't succeeded in being clean. She wondered why some people are so cursed and others so blessed. She'd felt blessed before. It wasn't money she wanted, but happiness. She just wanted to be a part of lovely things.

She wondered if Phil truly wanted her.

He had soft qualities she admired.

Before him she thought she preferred stronger men.

Now she just hoped she'd be enough for him.

WOMEN AND MEN never knew the loading of X chromosome they carried nor the extent of the Y, she thought. Some declared, "I am woman!"; others, "I am man!"; still others, "Both!"; and a few said, "I don't know what I am."

Some bore a blend they concealed, telling no one.

Sometimes their bodies agreed with them, she thought, but God alone knew them.

PHIL MCBANE'S FOREBEARS, from his paternal line, came from Ireland. His great-great-grandfather McAllister McBane boarded a steamer called the Margaret in 1874 from Dublin to New York City and went south knowing the old plantation owners needed cheap labor. He walked much of his way to South Carolina and landed on an old farm where the head master lived alone in a dilapidated antebellum house with three pillars extending to a peaked roof.

The master who hired him was George Huntington. His operation was as much drunkenness as tobacco and as he sat in his parlor vociferating over his loss of slaves and how he'd loved them and hadn't much harmed them, McAllister McBane agreed with him.

George Huntington spouted nonsense, the house odiferous of the old man's wigs and unwashed clothes. Throughout the near country former slaves decried his claims, remembering the family of five he hung just after emancipation and how not a few had died in his care, how he'd maimed many, blaming them for the maiming.

MCBANE DIDN'T mind how Huntington carried on.

He's old. Let him prattle.

Plus the man named him overseer.

"Seventy-nine years!" Huntington shouted, "and it's come to this."

"To what?" McAllister asked, having fetched and stacked wood in the kitchen for the cookstove.

"Bastard Lincoln!" the master yelled from the parlor. "Not worth the spit on my shoe. If he had one slave he'd have never got rid of him, and I wouldn't be rid of mine now either." He licked two fingers, crossed one leg over the other and rubbed the toe of his riding boot, shining it with the cuff of his shirt. He wore a black velvet overcoat and tails, threadbare at the elbows, split-seamed and dull, stained irreparably on one shoulder.

"Not even the spit?" McAllister called.

"Not the shite on the sole of my boot!" Huntington yelled.

"Not even the shite?!" McAllister volleyed.

"Not even the shite!" Huntington confirmed.

BEFORE A YEAR'S time the master and McAllister were knit close. McAllister rode the remaining free Black people, two old men and their older sister, until the place turned a profit. He was less than fair in paying wages, and ugly in his demands. Rough when the work occasioned roughness. He called them One, Two, and Three.

"No names," he said. "Don't care to know you."

Their names were Methuselah, Roman, and Fanny. Their surname Bettencourt. They'd survived the killing years. They knew each other's mannerisms, picked at each other some, and laughed together. Sang the old songs. Loved God and family with eternal confidence. Pitied the White man his bedevilment.

McAllister saw to the scanty crops, and though McAllister was a quick study and Huntington thought him a genius, the three could only cultivate and harvest ten acres and that meant working the body near to death to make the field produce. Tobacco finicky as a man's affections, requiring his best wisdom and meanest temperament. A third of the year involved the time from seed up to when they prized the cured leaves into hogshead barrels. The infernal plant grew best in uncultivated soil so the rest of the year he devoted to land clearing. Preparation of seedbeds meant long days of clearing, burning, and hoeing. Seeds were sown before April and mixed with sand for more equal distribution. They raked the beds then, covering the plants with pine boughs to keep a healthy grow. They shinned the seedlings to a palm-length apart and transplanted in May, him and them each preparing five hundred knee-high hills for cultivation per day. He hated the back breaking and to relieve his emotions he screamed at his charges.

After hilling they waited for rain, sometimes replanting so the plants took better as the hills became ready cultivators. They primed the growers, removing the leaves closest to the ground and topped them as well, cutting bunch growth from the head. At maturity of color, texture, and pliancy, they harvested six-foot to nine-foot plants by taking a sharp knife to the base, putting the tobacco to the sticks for curing before striking it to the barn floor to let it sweat, the reek producing something near to the feeling of inebriation. At last they spun, rolled, and packed it in the hogsheads, a thousand pounds of tobacco to each barrel, then carted it to port, where it was sold and shipped to England.

Old work, outdated but effective.

The plantation was a sliver of what it had been.

Still, under McAllister McBane it turned a profit, the Huntington labels proclaiming:

Life is a smoke!—If this be true,
Tobacco will thy life renew;
Then fear not Death, nor killing care
Whilst we have best South Carolina here!

MCALLISTER COULDN'T stomach slave work but it needed to be done so every time he joined them in the soil he also cussed them in a language so tasteless and incomplete the veins crawled at his temple. He loathed getting in with them, preferring his view from the sun glare of the saddle, head wrapped in wet cloth beneath a wide-brimmed hat. Nights when the drink filled his gullet and tainted his brain he was wont to hate himself, but days he convinced himself he was born to lord it over others, especially the likes of these. His hatred grew. In April of the first year during the hilling he merely cursed them. Year two he face-slapped them more than once. Year three when their stooped frames slowed in high heat he jumped from the horse and almost beat the oldest brother to death.

The old woman bug-eyed him.

That night he couldn't sleep.

AFTER THE BEATING, Methuselah, Roman, and Fanny Bettencourt rarely looked at McBane.

In his dreams he saw their faces plainly, each with a vacancy that covered malignity, a fury in which they led him at knifepoint into the fields where the two brothers pushed him face first to the ground, sat on his back and neck, and the sister stuffed dirt in his mouth, prying his teeth open with a stick and packing his throat so he gagged and writhed and went still.

As the season wore on, McBane's dreams came more frequent and he knew he wouldn't outlive them unless he removed himself north.

On a morning filled with sun he striped the three very badly with his riding whip and fled without saying goodbye to Huntington.

He'd stolen the horse, provisions, and a good cache of Huntington's money.

THE DAYS were liquor days, and men drank hard. Going north McAllister McBane wasted Huntington's cash on drink and gambling and women. He wandered for a few years, living on odd jobs and squalor. He wasn't a good-looking man and as he aged and consumed he looked like a red-haired mole, fattened, florid-faced and balding. Dead poor he went west, passing through the Appalachian expanse and made it to Missouri and finally Oklahoma where he worked for an Indian Agent filing papers and tending the man's horses before riding out drunk, a little richer for the pilfer, his saddle bags set with some of the Agent's hard currency and silver dinnerware. McBane sold the silver in Madison, Wisconsin, crossed into Minnesota Territory and drifted north through the Fond du Lac Indian reservation where he debauched himself with an Anishinaabe woman behind the town trading post and continued on, his head in a haze of rye. Riding back east and further north near the southern tip of Lake Superior, the blue arm of the lake in shadow over miles of shoreline, his nose ran with snot and his eyes watered. Surprising himself, in the elemental beauty of that landscape he acknowledged God.

He went south again, further south as if by homing instinct, arriving at the rail station in St. Paul where he attained work servicing the trains in their stops before the long trek west. He worked machine and track for ten years, fathering five children he never claimed. At age forty-two he married a dull-headed wife, a former whore with three teeth, impregnating her with twins—spindly, lop-haired boys whom McAllister detested on sight.

During his forty-ninth year, McAllister McBane was severed in two at the chest when he slipped on a railway coupling. He fell between the cars where the draft gear met the draw gear just as the train billowed from the station. His cleaved body, jostled back in place by the undertaker, was delivered in a closed-top pine box to the graveyard where no one but his wife attended the burial. A noticeable stench in the air.

Across town his torch-haired sons were catching frogs at Thistle Creek.

PHILLIP MCBANE, two generations removed from McAllister, had unruly hair three times as long as the frog-enamored twins but equally coppery in texture and tone. One of the twins ended up in Montana doing road work and marrying a former Hutterite woman from the Birch Creek colony near Valier. He moved her to Great Falls and they had three sons, one of which became Phil's father.

Phil's father was such a consistent wastrel, Phil lived in his presence only twice as a boy. What he remembered was the bruising. The man had early onset gray hair, and he struck with a hammer fist. Unafraid to brawl he was often jailed for disorderly conduct. At home a good slapping made Phil's bones ring. Phil slept on the floor near the trailer wall behind the old Naugahyde couch to avoid him. The man had killed Phil's dog in a rage. A mutt Phil had loved.

Phil thought he himself had suffered less than the dog, and felt relief and sorrow about it his whole life. He never forgot his father kicking the animal like a football into the wall, and how Phil had held the limp body to his chest behind the couch until the dog huffed suddenly and yelped, leaping into a dead run through the small living room and kitchen, around the metal card table where they ate dinner. Three laps with its butt down, back legs churning a little cockeyed until the dog stopped, sniffed the air once, and fell dead on the linoleum in front of the oven.

Phil's mother slept most days, depressed and jobless.

"Get yourself together, boy," she told him when he was thirteen. "I got nothing for you." His father long gone. Men didn't like her, and she didn't like them. Phil thought she liked him at least a little, or had some care for him based on the simple hope that he'd be okay.

The girl across the tracks and up two blocks, eighteen to his thirteen, liked him a lot, even if he knew she liked others too. Her name was LaVonne. When they got naked he did what she told him to. He felt dirty but he laughed more than he ever did in the trailer, plus he felt light and better than he did at home, even if he never really knew what her directions meant and was never sure if anything happened between them but a lot of gaping and rubbing. In the second summer of this she moved, and the way she kissed him goodbye on the side of the house where her parents couldn't see made him shake.

In high school his acne turned his face red and bumpy, neck to hairline. It scared him how ugly he became. He avoided mirrors. He wanted a woman, any woman, more than he wanted anything. Preferably an older woman who could teach him all he didn't know. He realized he knew almost nothing. Back then he masturbated compulsively, deviant in his porn preferences. He was angry at his mother, apathetic and doped up as she was, but more devoted to her than most boys were to theirs.

Like his buddies, then to now, he kept his worst fears to himself and often thought of death. There was a president in the White House who was White. Before him the president was Black. A pandemic came and wasted millions and the White one seemed to beckon an age of victimhood and enragement in the same speech. Every speech like the one before.

Phil knew next to nothing of these things.

WHENEVER HE was high as the sky above Mount Rainier, lolling in the arms of Alberta, Phillip McBane didn't fear anything.

HE ALSO DIDN'T move much. He ate junk food. Slept. Tried to make Alberta serve him.

Schemed ways to make money.

Rarely made any.

PHIL HAD NEVER known anything other than poverty.

His wife Alberta, the former refugee, had known poverty multiple times more poor than him.

ALBERTA loved her married name. Alberta McBane. She loved Phil.
He made her feel American. Easy how he filled her heart with love.
She was confused before she met him.
Now he drugged her to sweet sense.
She started to feel she didn't care if she went back to school again.

SHE WAS an ample woman and she knew certain men loved ample women.
For her part, she loved thin little White men.
She also loved America even if America didn't love her.
At the start Phil told himself he could take her or leave her.
In the end he couldn't go a day without her.

PHIL DIDN'T KNOW what to borrow, or from whom. He felt fine stealing from his former wives or from the government. He paid no child support and no taxes. Long before Alberta, when he'd needed his own place and a former army buddy gave him the loan officer John Sender's number, Phil had put it in his phone for future reference.

BACK THEN, angry again, holed up in a different friend's trailer, Phil borrowed his friend's car, until he was arrested on the edge of the Safeway parking lot in North Seattle. His third wife, Opal, was asleep when he took some of passed-out Lenny's crystal meth, the keys to the rusted-out Honda along with five dollars, and walked out the door crazed, alive. His friends called him Phil, or Philage, or Philward to be funny. His mother called his friends turds. He hated the way her lips formed the word. Five blocks later two policemen put their fists to his face and struck him down like a rabid animal, then beat him on the paved sidewalk at the edge of the parking lot where people gathered, gawking. He remembered now how his mind took flight, rocketing upward. I'm seeking, he'd thought. I'm striving. I'm in it with all my heart. He shouted in their faces. They told him to shut his mouth, then rose and holstered their batons, put him in the squad car and drove off, adrenaline like black sand slowing in their blue, translucent veins.

HE'D BEEN released from Seattle county jail in nearly no time. In a dirty T-shirt and jeans without knees, hollow look and wide-set eyes, he'd called John Sender, and gone in to take a loan for his own singlewide trailer. Opal had sat next to him, cosigning, telling John how dumb Phil was for getting thrown in jail.

Then or now, Phil didn't love her at all.

"The amortization schedule on this one is pretty simple," John told Phil. "Not much down, and not much to pay each month."

"Amer tie schedule?" Phil asked.

"It's the payments, dummy," Opal said.

Phil ignored her, mesmerized by the scars on John's face.

John wondered how people made it. Phil, like he and Elias, men birthed by history. "Keep up on the payments and she'll be yours in no time," he said. "Just ten years." John couldn't justify how a box of paper like a singlewide could take ten years to pay off, but he knew people needed a home, and owning your own meant something.

ROARK SAW John that day in a conference meeting on the twenty-second floor.

He didn't speak to John but knew he'd been rising, securing larger loans at a stronger pace than the rest, accepting how Roark fleeced him without regard. What abuse Roark knew as a boy now he subsumed in healthy egoism; he simply told himself to forget childhood. He first knew his father's pride in him on the drive to Miles City to fix his hand. What he'd felt then surprised him with its power.

He went to his desk and viewed the water, the skyline south. Running the fingers of his good hand through his hair, he felt the upraised lines crosshatched on the back of his head. His father despised government, despised people, the underlings, and specifically moochers, beggars, users. The races below, along with the White poor. In Montana it was Indians, his father loathed them and so did he. Not just Aurora. All of them. Elsewhere, it was every crack family on welfare. Border-crossers. Illegals. Freeloaders. Every fool who followed the other fools. Homeless. Mentally ill. Poor. Criminal. Middle class. People of all shades. Hookers. Gays. Natives. They made him sick. Anyone unable to make good on investment, whose herd-need pushed their ill-preparedness on those who oiled the nation's greatness.

In bed with women he was instinctual and passionless.

"If you believe in angels," he said as their eyes blurred, "believe in devils too."

PHIL LIVED only a short while in the trailer he bought with the loan from John Sender. It sat empty once he left Opal to move into Alberta's concrete-bricked flat, a step up from the thin walls of the trailer.

He didn't hate his previous wife. He just didn't like her anymore.

Opal complained a lot and had a vicious tongue.

Alberta was much nicer, and she was interesting.

BEFORE HE EVER met Alberta, Phil got through high school on sleep and weed, and entered the military half by force through his father's friend, Bodie, who said it would clean up his life. Phil ended up in boot camp in Columbus, Georgia. A complainer, lazy, waifish, and stubborn. A year later he was in Iraq, afraid and useless.

In an accident behind the Forward Operating Base in which a welding spark landed in his left eye, nearly blinding him, he was sent home on a medical discharge. He couldn't forget though, his own sergeant, a giant Black man from North Carolina, standing over him, as Phil, eye-patched and slack shouldered, packed his bag. "Dishonorable," the sergeant said. "You know, and I know." Phil turned to him but averted his gaze. "You're lower than the shit on my boot," the sergeant said. "We're lucky and you're lucky. Lucky you didn't get any of us killed. Lucky you're still breathing. Someone would have died from your stupidity. Get stateside, fool."

Phil's face had bloomed red. His eye had pulsed for over an hour.

When he returned home, the eye ended up marbled and doglike.

WHEN PHIL was twenty-seven, the same man who'd helped sign Phil up for Iraq told him his alcoholic father was dead.

"Passed in the night," Bodie said.

They were seated at a card table in the box kitchen of Bodie's trailer. Phil sat opposite Bodie, the balding, purple-nosed friend of his father. Reluctantly, Phil had come when Bodie called.

"Grotesque, how he died," Bodie said. "You want to know how it went down?"

"Not really," Phil said.

Bodie grimaced.

"Sure, go ahead," Phil said.

"Terrible," Bodie said. "Died in his bed."

Bodie's chin trembled.

Tough to lose a friend, I guess, Phil thought. "How old was he?"

Every lost father in the world was Phil's father.

"Only forty-three, and to die that way." Bodie's voice hitched.

"What way?"

"Throat collapsed as he slept. He drowned in his own blood."

Phil nodded. He didn't feel anything.

"Will you go to the funeral?" Bodie asked. "Pay your respects?"

"No," Phil said.

"Why not?" Bodie looked at him cockeyed.

"Because I never knew him," Phil said.

"Who gives a shit," Bodie said. "He was your father."

"I do," Phil said. "We never knew each other."

"He loved you," Bodie said.

"How do you know?" Phil asked.

Bodie looked confused.

"I don't hate him, or love him," Phil said. "I don't feel anything."

"I guess," Bodie said. "But pay your respects."

"I don't even know what that means," Phil said, his head growing hot. "If you want me to look at his body, no. Hold his hand, no. Kiss his forehead, hell no. He abandoned me. He deserves nothing. I won't be going to his funeral."

Bodie's shoulders slumped. His nose bloomed like a carnation. "He might have no one there."

"He's dead," Phil said plainly. "You'll be there for him."

Phil left then. Another gray Seattle day.

PHIL TRIED university and failed.

He tried community college and failed.

He tried vocational-technical school and failed.

He tried jobs he didn't keep.

He worked cleaning tables at the Bozworth off Twelfth Street. The place was low-budget and shifts were consistent enough, a decent Americana restaurant. Vinyl chairs upholstered white and chrome-rimmed. Fifties lamps. A bar with black swivel stools. The checkerboard tile floor shone like a cue ball and got slippery as a hog as the shifts wore on. He loved the corn dogs and chicken fried steak.

He was fired when they took a random pee sample and he was positive for marijuana with a strain of Auntie Emma: from the fat cigarettes he called Buddha or A-bomb. He hadn't pegged the Bozworth for being so highbrow.

Good for them. The previous week he'd stolen seventy-nine dollars from the till.

He'd met Alberta three days later in an unfamiliar apartment that acted as an amateur meth house on weekends. She was mighty ugly, he'd thought then. He didn't really like her face. Then again, he thought his own image was more like an albino hippo's face. When she sidled up to him on the couch and lay next to him stroking his chin with her fingers he was moved, and rather than the awkwardness so common to his bodily responses, with her he felt somewhat confident.

Kindness. He liked her kindness. She was hefty. He didn't mind hefty, and when he kissed her he found she was not just a good kisser but an exquisite one.

He fell in love with her kisses.

SHE TOLD him she loved tiny White men.

He looked like bologna and smelled like it too. She loved bologna.

He was her ticket, the ladder to take her higher, and he fit her fancy to perfection.

In America she could eat all the bologna, mayo, and cheese sandwiches she wanted. In Nigeria, food had been scarce. Her mom was an engineer in Bulgaria but in Nigeria the men wouldn't hire her. Her mother's last name, Ivanov, meant God's grace.

At the close, Alberta's mother left her Nigerian husband, married a second one, and left him too, taking all the kids of both families in secret at night. Alberta hated that journey. She and three of her siblings were bitten by scorpions. They had no food or water. But people helped them with medical care and provisions and when they finally made it to Mubi in northern Nigeria a Muslim family cared for them. They remained in hiding from Alberta's mother's husbands for three years before being granted permission to immigrate to Las Vegas, Nevada. Alberta finished high school there and left her mom, ten siblings, and her two youngest kids, making her way north and west, working fast food and living on food stamps.

She loved Pepsi, chips, and cake.

She inhaled hamburgers.

She was big in Nigeria. She was bigger in America.

In Las Vegas she was hot all the time.

In Seattle the rain cooled her down.

She'd taken only Amanda with her.

Phil was her prize, and she worried he'd hate her daughter, but from the first moments, Phil touched Amanda's hair and smiled on her. And to Amanda's credit she'd eventually taken to him, less wary than she normally was with Alberta's men, dead-eyed as they often were, and violent.

Phil was not especially violent, and Alberta could put a twinkle in his eye. She tried to bring that look to his face as much as possible, along with the sweet little dimple on the right side that came with it, melting her. She smothered him with kisses, laughed at his jokes, and gave her robust body to him as fully as she knew how, which turned out to be plenty for him in the beginning.

For a time she experienced the greatest love she'd ever known.

She desired him inside and out. His soft reddish-pink body, and his wavy, kinked red hair. He wasn't gorgeous. His face was odd. But his eyes, even the cloudy one, and his smile could place her and him on a rocket ship. She felt exciting. She thought less often of her skin troubles and the eczema sores that seemed not so visible on her thighs and calves. She thought less of her failures, how she'd left her other children, the life she'd left behind. Her sores didn't itch as much, she scratched them less, and one had to look closer, she thought, to see them now.

Her practice of eating paint chips even seemed to lessen some.

His frame, the bones smaller but muscles more taut than hers, enchanted her. Their contrasting tones and skeletal structures, eyes, nose, and chin, cheekbones, neckline, and skin, their very bodies, were like works of art in counterpoint.

"What nationality are you?" she asked.

"I'm an Irish bastard," he said, and they laughed.

In the beginning she had invited him over more often, and on an evening with the TV blaring and them slouched shoulder to shoulder on the couch, the weight of her inevitably leaning him toward her, she'd spoken in a hushed tone that got his attention.

"Why don't you go ahead and come live with me?"

"I'd be happy to," he said.

In the small apartment, a hole rented for the price of a mansion, Amanda was in her own room. The child was quiet, lost to one of the Disney movies she loved. So Alberta had gone ahead and removed her own clothes and pulled down Phil's gray sweats and sat on him right there until it was done, Phil grinning the whole time. She loved him. She kissed him slowly, with feeling. In love the body is wounded, she thought, and in its place the soul becomes one with the beloved, overcoming everything.

When they kissed, their kisses were all-consuming.

She stood and went to the kitchen then and came back with a glass of water they shared. Looking at him, watching him drink, she felt like one of the angels in God's paradise. She cuddled him close on the couch, holding his head to her chest until he slept.

They married a month later.

ALBERTA AND PHIL didn't talk much about their own family histories. Alberta consciously tried to forget the death days her mother heroically saved her from in Nigeria, and knew nothing of the meanness her mother had faced in Bulgaria. Phil, mainly unconscious of his family's past, couldn't conjure memory of his generational line. Phil's forgotten memories were bound to Ireland. Alberta's to Africa and Europe. He'd heard once and then promptly forgot about the Irish famine. For two generations the McBane family had forgotten and so McAllister McBane the one-time overseer and ten-time charlatan disappeared from memory along with an even more obscure McBane named Franklin who was a soldier in St. Patrick's Battalion during the Mexican-American War.

Alberta had a Christian grandmother she didn't know from Bulgaria who talked of Turkish Muslims with such hatred she sounded murderous. She had a Muslim grandmother from Nigeria she didn't know who spoke of Christians in the same way. The two grandmothers never met each other. They were both dead now. Members of Alberta's generational family were among the inheritors who survived the Batak Massacre of 1876 when more than five thousand of the seven thousand inhabitants of the Christian Bulgarian town of Batak were raped, slaughtered, beheaded, and burned alive by Turkish Muslims of the Ottoman Empire. Members of Alberta's generational family were also among the Nigerian Muslim herdsmen who survived a pitched battle in which Christian farmers used machetes to attack, kill, and butcher Muslims. As recent as 2011, videos depicting Nigerian Christian Berom tribesmen eating the flesh of a Nigerian Muslim Fulani man they had killed and cooked were circulated widely, inciting further violence.

Their histories shrouded, Phil and Alberta didn't fight each other initially but put their energy into the life they made. They lived in the present, for each other, to get by, to get ahead, to get high.

What is pain, she thought, but discomfort from illness or injury, torment, agony.

She was free now of the agony she'd known as a child.

Phil tried not to think of pain until he felt some.

Then he put his pain on opium.

"ALRIGHTY THEN," he said, assessing the status of his drug habit. They were happily married now, he told himself. "Might as well be in this together, Berta. Let's do this! We order the poppy bulbs online. There's a million and two sites under home decorations, then dried flower arrangements, bulbs, seeds, and finally poppies—but no need for all that." His skin was slack below his eyes, the sockets rimmed out. A waft of mold entered her nostrils. Old bread on the table. Old dinners in the sink. "Poppy's Big Fat Poppies are the best. Just go to his site, place the monthly order, and Poppy takes care of us. The bulbs come straight from Afghanistan. Already dried. Only dry thing in Seattle."

He grinned. A cheesy grin.

She grinned too.

THEY PROCEEDED to make opium like their own two-person cartel, but supplying only themselves, no one else. Opium tea, he called it.

To her it was a dirty soup that tasted like an infected wound.

What came after though made the sacrifice worth any price.

ALBERTA MCBANE kept thinking her life would get better.

She had Phillip.

She disliked their continual drug use, but tried not to think of it too much.

BY THEIR SECOND anniversary they found themselves chewing their nails, hovering around the mailbox whenever a new supply of pods was set to be delivered. They thanked the mailman, a spry pepper-headed White man, and carried their boxes of poppies back to the apartment where they immediately heated the water. They cracked the crowns over a blender and watched the seeds grow to a black mound that made them salivate. "*Chemical-free dried poppy seeds!*" the label proclaimed. Their noses sniffing the air, they put the lid on the blender and mixed the seeds to smithereens. Crack, mound, repeat. Add scalding water. Low-blend then for just less than a minute. Storm front on the way. They smacked their lips waiting for rain.

They forgot to feed Amanda. She fended for herself, emerging from her TV cocoon to take whatever munchies they splayed on the kitchen table.

"Seattle Rain," they called it, their own private brew. They strained the mix through the silk backing of a pair of her panties into two big plastic bowls from the dollar store. This weeded out what didn't blend. They added lime juice to cut the wicked taste. Standing in the kitchen watching the gray day through a narrow window over the sink, they drank a few bowls each, shooting whiskey beforehand to deaden the taste buds.

The flat was full of cats.

They went to bed together and stared into each other's faces until the transcendence made them levitate, making love, glistening. Amanda could be heard somewhere in the distance asking for something they couldn't name. They didn't answer. They floated away.

The cats peed all over.

They bought "extra-extra-large giganthiums" by the case. Big Poppy provided financing, and just as Phil said, the monthly price provided enough high for nearly unlimited sky-walking. Before long the taste resulted in automatic gag reflex and they fought to get it down. They succeeded because the reward was great, the high so distinctively high. There was a putrescence beneath everything, but they loved each other's bodies with euphoric fixity. They were constellations in a limitless sky. Works of divine imagination. Every curve and angle, each window an orifice on the sensual.

She'd had some Milton in high school from a good teacher whose last name she couldn't remember. But she'd never forgotten the story of *Paradise*

Lost. She hadn't read it, but she remembered a scramble of lines from nearly nowhere: Gratitude bestows reverence, allowing us to encounter everyday epiphanies, those transcendent moments of awe that change forever how we experience life and the world.

They were breathed into existence by the breath of God, Alberta thought.

And when they fell, she thought, they fell as Satan fell.

They lived in opposition to their children, the one they housed, the others they abandoned. They borrowed against themselves and time, against insensibility and stupefaction. They got high with strangers and lovers, they unzipped and zoomed with each other and unknown others. They were dizzy and chilled. Their skin was sallow. They passed out. They slipped in and out of comas. They could barely breathe. They lived, Phil told her, in the glorious twilight of their lives.

Born in the same year, they were thirty-three years old.

The year of crucifixion, she thought.

The year of resurrection.

She knew nothing of the Bible, and very little of the Quran, just that those who are faithful and do good will enter into paradise.

She wanted to be faithful and good.

Staring into Phil's dull eyes, she believed they'd enter paradise together.

JOHN SENDER heard Phillip McBane was turned into collections for defaulting on his payments.

After a few months, collections reported they couldn't find him.

The trailer went to foreclosure.

ROARK BOUGHT another new car, drove the coast north with a White whore he purchased on the edge of town. The blow job in the dark was marginally satisfying. He was sure she'd been a welfare baby. He beat her and retrieved his money, leaving her by the roadside. As he maneuvered the vehicle south again, he watched the world brighten. In the distant lights of Seattle he envisioned his building dwarfing the cityscape.

ALBERTA AND PHIL remained tied to each other.

Mornings the sun was a needle.

Midday the stupor hadn't left them.

Night they brewed and strained, brewed and strained.

Three of their friends stopped breathing but Alberta and Phil stayed in the land of the living. They chewed an abundance of ex-lax to counter constipation. They drank gallons of water to combat cottonmouth.

They drew the shades. Locked the doors.

They didn't mind being oily, smelly, and dirty for days.

They retrieved their supply like labradors.

Normally they saw neither dusk nor dawn.

When they woke they scratched each other's skin like rodents infested with fleas. They made each other bleed. They were hungry. They were insatiable. They ate junk food. They opened boxes of poppies. Their mouths went dry. Their mouths watered. Their mouths went dry again.

They kept collecting welfare.

Increasingly they were filled with dismay. Phil wanted to kill himself, but didn't tell Alberta. Alberta wanted to take Amanda and get to her mother's house. Her mother was living in Oregon now. Alberta's other children were with her sister in Vegas.

Or somewhere.

She and Phil had not hit rock bottom.

They agreed to stop.

After fulfilling one last order and drinking the last seed dry, against all odds, they quit.

THE SEX was better.

Before she met Phil, Alberta was impregnated five times by three different men and had five abortions. The children she brought to term were born of two additional men whom she married and divorced. For Phil, when he totaled the women he'd been with before Alberta, three he was married to, and many he'd simply slept with, as far as he knew the abortions numbered about sixteen.

They hardly spoke of such things.

During the opium haze Phil impregnated Alberta.

Alberta didn't tell him she was pregnant.

She didn't tell him she got an abortion either.

ALBERTA WAS BEGINNING to discover how often she let Amanda down.

She couldn't let herself think about her sons.

Inevitably, she thought, most women joined themselves to bad men.

Phil wasn't like that, she told herself.

She turned the blade on herself. There were mothers who were absent, who discarded their own, and there were mothers who were present but who deeply wronged their children. There were mothers who couldn't function, couldn't parent, couldn't hold gainful employment, couldn't go a day without a man, couldn't rise above anything.

She was all of these and it made her cry.

THE FIRST DAYS sober, Alberta contemplated cutting off her legs.

Phil pounded his head into the door jamb when his skin crawled.

He harmed himself to forget the burning in his brain.

Alberta pulled out the hair at her temples.

They felt as if their bodies had been struck by a train and the bones would never stop aching. They ate more ex-lax to relieve the pressure from their bowels. They puked incessantly. He hunted for a clean washcloth. He dampened it and wrung out the excess water, folded it neatly and placed it on her forehead. The truth met them there.

They loved each other.

That's why they wanted to be sober. And for Amanda.

That's why they loved each other.

PHIL MCBANE sometimes wondered if insanity wasn't just a step away.
Two weeks into his sobriety he fell off the wagon.
He tried not to admit what knocked on the door of his awareness.
He told himself to keep his hand from the handle.

WHEN PHIL was a boy, his father slept with a shotgun in his bed. When he wasn't home, which was almost always, he slept with the next-door neighbor and lied about it and everyone agreed to let him lie even though the neighbor was Helen, Phil's mother's best friend.

No longer sober, Phil brought home three roses from the corner 7-Eleven for his wife Alberta. He was hoping to make up for the night before when Alberta caught him sexually abusing Amanda. She'd found him standing over the girl while she slept, his pants down. He wasn't even that high. When Alberta walked into the room she'd slapped him so hard he hit the floor and Amanda woke up crying.

"Get out," Alberta had said.

"No," Phil said, and rose up and punched her, then watched as she clutched at her neck like she couldn't breathe.

That was yesterday.

Roses calm a woman, he thought, help her think straight.

The flowers stooped in a drinking glass on the kitchen counter.

Today, tired of everything, Alberta drank a beer and picked out a steak knife from the drawer next to the fridge. Jobless to avoid his wages being garnished, back on opium again, he'd tried to convince her of the great need to renew their opium den. They could charge an entrance fee. His friend, Bones, a large man, almost mute, not a good man in Alberta's opinion, had been staying with them. He was passed out on the couch. She heard Phil's breathing, heavy down the hall. It was late and dark and he was nude, sleeping on top of the bed. She set the beer down on the kitchen table, walked the necessary distance, raised the blade high in her right hand and drove it into the center of his stomach. In the mayhem that followed she took Amanda and left, telling herself she'd never be back. When I truly love, Alberta thought, I find beauty everywhere. Phil wasn't charming anymore. Yes, he'd been nice once upon a time, but now she needed to save her child and herself from men like him.

She tried not to think of the sons she'd forsaken.

She tried to think only of Amanda.

AS IT WENT, Phil went to the emergency room, then returned to the apartment. He didn't tell the doctor anything. Three days passed before he took the bandage off so he could itch the gash directly. He was high on a bundle of weed and the speed Bones gave him to get over the loss of Alberta. Hard to believe she'd knifed him in the stomach while he slept, waking him to what he recognized as her thick head, skin folds and sweat lines on her neck while the blood pooled on the flat below the arched bones of his ribcage. She'd stood over him and said calmly, "Take that." He'd pushed the heel of his hand into the wound and called 911 while she took the car and Amanda and went to Oregon to be with her mother.

He didn't blame her.

Now, lying on the couch with his shirt off, itching the wine-colored threads on the gash above his enflamed belly button, the birth knot blue black and hard as a marble, he still loved her. Bones was passed out on the floor in front of him. Phil felt sane as he rose and knelt down, taking money from Bones's front right pants pocket, stealing what was likely Bones's last twenty bucks. Then he took Bones's car. He wanted a box of raspberry-filled powder donuts from Safeway. He didn't want to walk five blocks, what could be wrong with that? But after a few minutes on the road his mind went blank and he drove the vehicle onto the sidewalk, smashing into the corner of the building.

IN HIS TRUCK driving nowhere, kneading his hands on the wheel, Elias American Horse witnessed the incredulous: the hood of a car buried into the hard edge of a Safeway supermarket.

He didn't give it a second glance before he was back worrying over the loss of Aurora.

MINUS THE CAR CRASH the event was a near-exact repeat of what Phil had done a few years earlier. He put his head on the wheel and sat there half-asleep until the cops came. Smoke entered his lungs, followed by the taste of oil. When he saw their blue uniforms, he felt electrified. He got out of the car and raising his hands, spoke in what he thought was a dignified voice before he jumped them and got himself beaten to submission again. From the ground, through the lattice work of trees, he saw a merle of blackbirds dart upward and bank north, the light on their wings flashing silver. As he watched they mingled in quick wind and flew back south through a procession of skyscrapers, people, and cars.

AT THE ARRAIGNMENT, in an orange jumpsuit Phil was led into the courtroom and seated in the aisle directly right of where he entered, manacled at the wrists, chained at the ankles. Since he'd been jailed he discovered he both hated and loved God. But no big deal, he told himself, God likely hated and loved him too. To counter the endorphin withdrawals they had him on methadone first, before weaning him to pink suboxone pills embossed with a tiny dagger/crucifix on one side and N8 on the other. He was the last of fourteen criminals to be arraigned that day. In spite of everything, he thought melodramatically, I will rise again. I will take up my heart, which I let go of in all my emptiness, and I will keep going.

Alberta was seated in the first row behind the defendants' table.

She wouldn't look at him.

Even now he loved her.

Her youngest brother had come from Vegas to sit beside her, a fledgling bodybuilder in a tank top and Jheri curl. Phil saw her lips pursed like wrinkled metal, her eyes like plugs in the flesh of her face. He sat for two hours. He didn't love her, he told himself. She wanted him put away. He should hate her. He stood when he was told. A guard walked him to the table and when Phil passed in front of his wife he raised his hands, shackled, to touch her arm if she'd let him. She rose and spit in his face, calling him a bastard.

Her brother pulled her back.

The judge told her to sit down.

Phil had little awareness of what was to come. Despite it all he still hoped things might work out better for him and her.

Unbidden the future commenced tracking him like a hound.

He'd be surprised at how his life would end.

He'd be equally surprised at the scope of love's dominion.

Book 4

I know for sure that love saves me and that it is here to save us all.

—Maya Angelou

GABRIEL AND ANGELICA

GABRIEL KENNEDY REED borrowed his father's love of music.

He led worship in Seattle for college students.

He and Angelica had been married seven years, living in Seattle four of those. They had three daughters. He sang for God despite what he knew to be his innumerable shortcomings, even as he borrowed his wife's good favor. She was awake, but with her eyes closed in bed next to him. When he reached to touch her she turned her back.

He wasn't a rich man by any means, but they were a little more secure now.

This week he'd be taking her to see John Sender at the National American Bank on Westlake Ave, the loan officer one of their friends recommended. For the first time, Gabriel felt sure they'd be able to get a loan on a place of their own.

FULL-TIME Christian worker and lead vocalist with a fast-growing ministry for undergrads at the University of Washington, Gabriel was a poor student in high school. He grew up in Great Falls, Gabriel Jefferson, half-Black, both scapegoat and curiosity. His Black father, being military, told him to get over it. His White mother, seldom present, often jailed, never noticed. When Gabriel was young he borrowed his best friend's class notes and proceeded to fail his freshman year in high school twice. He might have had a learning disability but his father said God is in control and refused the school counselor's desire to get Gabriel professional help. The school, being redneck, didn't force the issue, and Gabriel, having suffered his mother's absence since he was three, did not go against his father's wishes.

At seventeen he flunked out of school, never passing ninth grade. At eighteen he discovered massage parlors and hand jobs. At twenty he was a delivery man for a food services company that shipped candy throughout the Northwest. On his third overnight trip, on a stop just outside Boise, he lost his virginity to a small-town prostitute who was pale and thick-boned. Her skin was cold. She didn't speak. She kept her face to the wall. He hated himself. At twenty-one he got his GED and went to Birmingham for a national Campus Crusade conference called Infinite God.

He stayed, worked construction, met Angelica Kennedy Reed in the choir at Hopewell A.M.E. Church, and fell in love. He loved their physical differences: him being thin, light-skinned, and high boned, her being big, dark, and beautiful. She had huge brothers. She played piano like music was in her blood and played organ like it was God's own instrument. She graduated not only summa cum laude but co-valedictorian in mathematics at the University of Alabama Birmingham, with a double major in women's studies. Angelica called herself a Black Christian womanist, more womanist than feminist, meaning more purple than lavender, more Black-woman-centered, against White patriarchal ignorance, White women's racism, and the sexism of Black and other men. Afrocentric. Grown. Loving other women, and strong in the spirit, the struggle. Aligned with nature, Creation, people, God.

God as life and love, creativity and joy.

She loved Blackness. She loved men and women, and centered women's lives.

She hadn't gotten to the part yet where she loved herself.

Gabriel found Birmingham humid but not awful, lush with trees, crisscrossed by highways. A lot more White than he'd imagined, but a lot more Black than Montana. Angelica loved math. She adored the stars. In her arms he felt wholly himself for perhaps the first time. The smell of her skin reminded him of cherry blossoms. They often drove the hour to Tuscaloosa and walked along the Black Warrior River holding hands. Previous to dating her, he'd dated many, but secretly he'd also paid for more than one-hundred hand jobs and had sex with twenty-seven prostitutes. He vowed to stop. He was successful until the night after he and Angelica were engaged when he left his apartment in south Birmingham, walked ten blocks to Sal's Therapeutic Massage and was masturbated by a young Korean woman of indiscriminate age who said her name was Louise.

THE NEXT DAY Gabriel told Angelica everything, and she left him.

Three days later she called and said she'd still marry him but he had to go to counseling. He agreed and for three months they went twice weekly to see their pastor, a scholarly Black man named Clamenta C. Everman, tall and broad-shouldered with a narrow face. In their wedding ceremony Gabriel sang a ballad to her and Angelica cried. On their wedding night Gabriel cried. He felt like a virgin again. It took him three years to get a one-year Bible degree from Melchior Christian, a small private college in south Birmingham. Angelica read his textbooks aloud and every night he taped her voice, stream of mercy, and listened and relistened until he knew the material. She loved novels, loved reading in general, and told him it was nothing, she liked reading to him. He was accepted for a position with Campus Crusade and successfully raised the required 90 percent of his support goal (a salary of fifty-five thousand per year comprised of family, friends, and strangers giving monthly or one-time gifts). He reported to headquarters in San Bernardino, California, with Angelica for eight weeks of training after which he was assigned to the University of Washington to lead worship, his powerful tenor voice an essential gift. Not rich, but nearly debtless, two used cars bought with cash, a loan with no points was easy and when they walked away from John Sender's office arm in arm, they walked away happy.

For his part, John Sender admired seeing couples love each other, and wondered at how physical some were compared to others. Gabriel and Angelica, like people whose boat went down in a storm, clung to each other as if to the last cane of wood on the ocean: the skin of the forearms blended, fingers entangled or lifted to touch a shoulder or the softness at the back of the neck. Though his work took a steep ascent he never refused work on the margins of the economy. Watching these two, he was grateful for how Samantha didn't mind his personal shyness.

Inversely, Gabriel witnessed John's habits too. Precise and high-minded, a rodeo man Gabriel discovered when he asked about Montana, John being well-dressed but unembellished, detailed, focused. The side of his face a strange arrangement. His wife and two girls framed behind him. When the hour was done John flinched when Angelica reached to hold his hands, thanking him. Gabriel thought John tall and out of sorts in the dull halls of a bank building, and questioned how much John himself had borrowed, thinking it next to nothing due to the stiff crease of his pants and the gray line where his lips met.

Angelica also noticed John.

"You look like you love someone too," she said, holding Gabriel's arm.

He blushed. "Yes ma'am. I certainly I do." He touched the frame of the photo.

"Well God bless you."

"Thank you," John said. He smiled and raised two fingers and a thumb to his head, tipping an imaginary hat.

"You know what they say," she said. "The greatest of these is love."

John thought Angelica and Samantha might make great friends.

"You should loosen that tie," Gabriel said.

"You're fine just the way you are," Angelica countered, patting John's hand.

"How about you?" John said to her. "You two look positively blissful."

Angelica laughed and gripped Gabriel's arm.

"I hope so," she said.

"What does it take?" John asked.

"Time," she said, "and smarts. A whole lot of heart, and God, so much help from God. A little luck too." She smiled.

"The one you've got," Gabriel said, motioning to John's picture of his wife and kids, "just sweep her into your arms and give her a kiss she won't forget." He held Angelica's face in both hands and kissed her.

"Hush now, Gabriel," she said. "Let him be. He's got his own ways. He doesn't need yours."

Gabriel smiled. "Oh, I think he does."

John smiled too. "I might," he said. "Her name's Samantha."

Were there any truly good men? Angelica wondered. She believed all were made by God, not just the good ones, and all were worthy of love because of that design, that intention. But had she met one, personally, who was not a continual cheater? For the moment she left John free of judgment. She squeezed Gabriel's arm again and thought of her father. Though she saw her father as if he wore a halo, he'd had his trysts, and she knew her mother had been consistently disloyal. Maybe people weren't meant to be faithful. Maybe only God was faithful.

The death of Christ was proof, she thought, looking at Gabriel, then John.

The death of God, the feminine soul of God.

Dazzling, beyond comprehension.

She glanced at the stack of papers they'd signed. The house would be a home. She took John's hands again, enfolding them in her own.

He didn't flinch this time.

"The soul of Christ be with you, John, and God bless your love."

ROARK BELIEVED Christians the antithesis of virtue.

The altruists, and moralists, the ugly little collectivists, lemmings diving from the cliff to their deaths. Nothing healthy or objective about them.

God was the decline of civilization.

A MONTH LATER, on the day they moved into the new house, Gabriel had sex with a co-ed at the girl's apartment in the late afternoon.

On the way home from the university that night, he got a speeding ticket. Though he'd never been to jail, he constantly feared either being arrested and imprisoned, or killed for no reason. When he was accosted or detained by the police in Montana, Alabama, or Seattle, he felt afraid, and angry enough to eat concrete.

In their bed that night, normally Angelica drew near.

"I'm too small," he'd say.

"You're just right," she'd tell him.

But tonight, her back was turned again. She could intuit his lechery, the need evident in his desire for her to comfort him.

Every one of her brothers had been jailed at one time or another.

"Cop stopped me on the way home tonight," he whispered.

She didn't respond.

ROARK'S ASSISTANT told him John had exceeded all annual goals again, mainly through selling more upper-end houses and bridging to commercial holdings. Some waterfront. Some downtown. Some both.

Roark invited Sender to his office for the first time.

As John entered, again he noticed Roark's deformity.

"Tractor accident," Roark repeated.

"How?" John asked.

"Not worth repeating, sit down."

Roark stared at him for a long time, eyeing him as if John were made of gold.

"I want you to triple your numbers this year."

As in all things Roark was thinking of himself and the skyscraper, him looking over his kingdom. He'd make it touch the heavens.

"Fine," John said.

Roark noted John's square jaw. The sharp angle of the nose. The scarred jawline. This one could be a blue chip, this Sender. Good with money. Sharp. Unafraid. He'd need to take him under his wing a little more.

That evening as John left the office his stride to the bar for rodeo night quickened. He'd spent time with Roark. Personally.

Elias American Horse had arrived before him.

"Do you remember my boss?" John asked when they were seated.

"The big White boy?" Elias asked. "Like a white whale," he chuckled. "Aurora didn't like him."

John brooded. That big White boy is why you have a house, he thought.

Elias fixed his eyes on John's face. A dark motive passed between them.

Changing the subject, John asked him, "Do you still love Aurora?"

"I do," Elias said nakedly. "I don't think I'm good at it though. I mean, she deserves more." He wiped his eyes with the back of his hand. "Never mind. I mean, I don't know." He couldn't tell John everything.

John put his arm around Elias. "More beer for my brother here," he signaled a waitress. After a couple more tall ones the two were laughing together, singing a Hank Williams jingle from *Moanin' the Blues* that accompanied the steer wrestling highlights on the big screen. When they walked out into the night Elias paused before they took separate directions. He put his hand on John's shoulder, then tapped John's chest three times with his fist. "Means more to me than you know, John, this brotherhood."

"Thank you," John said, loose now, embracing him. "Thank you, brother."

GABRIEL TOLD himself no one understood a woman.
No one except the Lord of heaven.
He tried to forget the bone-gnawing in his conscience.
But women sinned too, he reasoned. Women could be as bad as anyone.

ANGELICA REMEMBERED early in the marriage how much she wanted him to be a reader, a thinker. She wanted him to know all she knew, but he was mostly uninterested. She'd turned her body away from him. Now she felt him staring at her back. Their kids wild all day, asleep now. She couldn't abide idiot men but she couldn't abide the man-hating crowd either. She turned to face him. His eyes were lonesome. His hand on her arm. In college she'd gone to women's movement events at the Sorbonne in Paris, at the University of the Western Cape in South Africa, in Prague at Charles University, and in the coastal city of Karachi, Pakistan where she wore a pashmina to cover her face when she visited the shrines. She read all of Zora Neale Hurston, Lucille Clifton, Angela Davis, Toni Morrison, bell hooks, Judith Butler, Audre Lorde, and her most beloved, Alice Walker. She memorized the speeches of Sojourner Truth. She'd tattooed a column of cursive names in black ink into the skin over her left shoulder blade, black on black and lightly visible, speaking through to her heart: Coretta, Corazon, Ellen, Benazir, Tawakkol, Sojourner, Shirley, Mary, Audre, Toni, Alice: presidents, poets, and prime ministers, freedom fighters, writers, representatives, Nobel Prize winners, activists, opera singers.

Mainly due to Audre's honesty and power, she didn't fear darkness anymore, not night or dusk, not the earliest or celestial dark, not the dark within. She recalled how Lorde reclaimed darkness for good: "These places of possibility within ourselves are dark because they are ancient and hidden: they have survived and grown strong through that darkness. Within these deep places, each one of us holds an incredible reserve of creativity and power, of unexamined and unrecorded emotion and feeling. The woman's place of power within each of us is neither White nor surface; it is dark, it is ancient, and it is deep."

Men feared that darkness and therefore favored conquest.

Men borrowed things they refused to repay.

The debt was financial, Angelica thought. The debt was moral and spiritual.

Now White men killed innocents in grade schools and high schools, through police brutality or insanity, in movie theaters and churches and bars or from hotel rooms where they placed automatic weapons in windows and opened fire. White feared Black. Such action, murderous, infectious, was racial, gendered, economic, sexual. It was the prison industrial complex in the open, not just behind razor wire.

She thought the ultimate choice would be self-transcendence.

Identification with the beloved through crucifixion.

Self-sacrifice toward ultimate love rather than ego-gratification toward cruelty.

Here, facing Gabriel, she still felt lost.

But when she touched Gabriel's face, she believed.

By embodying love, she thought, one is truly alive.

She knew Gabriel betrayed her.

The truth scared her. The truth gave her life.

SHE DIDN'T blame God. She blamed human culpability, collective history. All the trauma, harm, and hate human beings hold in their hands. She cried some as Gabriel kissed her lips. He lay back and she heard his breath deepen into sleep. She believed in toughness, forgiveness the sinew and muscle of a body that wore the raiment of glory.

They had a job to do.

But Gabriel was so reckless.

No, stop calling him out, she told herself, only God understands us.

Her and Gabriel's job was merely love. Love alone.

Him, her three daughters. They all needed her. But loyalty being the lesser part of need, his disloyalty proliferated. He often had little or no understanding of what moved her, but she felt she could teach him one day if he had the inclination.

Most of the women she knew had been violated by men of every irreligious or religious persuasion. Her husband's own penchants were not new, but simply the contemporary expression of an oversexualized patriarchy spanning the millennia.

SHE KNEW the lengths people went to inhabit the body of evil were infinite.
Evil requested of heaven to sift people like wheat.
People were sifted.
Some were evil personified.
Women and men were atomic, nuclear, incendiary.
Men were especially violent.
They did almost all the killing of women and other men.
Women were derisive and scornful, hating with ferocious hatred.
Some were more drawn to violent men than nonviolent men.
Some to unfaithful men more than faithful men.
Some to women of every persuasion too.
Men were frail. Women were frail.
Strength awaited those who listened and believed.

LIKEWISE SHE understood Christian men were some of the worst men in the world, but they were also some of the finest. Muslim and Buddhist men too, Jewish, Confucian, Hindu, atheist, agnostic, all were the best and worst.

He was asleep now.

Men were swingers, she thought. They were lonely masturbators. They wanted a glamorous woman or a hard-bodied man, even if pickings were slim. Most men were homely. Fattened up. Their hairlines receded, though he was trim with a nice hairline. Men didn't really know what they believed and didn't seem to care. Their bellies pendulous, they birthed nations.

Too readily they trusted their instincts.

Too many of them didn't read books, she thought, and neither did the president.

As they aged they lost love.

Gabriel was no different, even if touched with the voice of God she knew he spent too much of his life teetering between mediocre and hell-bent.

Responsibility separated wheat from chaff.

By fate men were chaff, she thought, by destiny, wheat.

AFTER THE FINAL escrow signing, Gabriel emerged from John's office beaming. Angelica beamed too. She was lovely, John thought. Radiant like the sculptures of Rodin. Their credit rating was sound so they'd borrowed enough to own a split-level rancher east of downtown.

A Black man from Montana and his Black wife. A rare pairing, he thought.

Gabriel, Phil, Elias, and me, he thought, men left to our own devices.

The loan was in her name.

"In case of death or foolishness," she'd said, and Gabriel had signed it all to her.

GABRIEL MIMICKED the vocal intonations of the gospel greats.

In monthly phone calls home to Montana, he'd tried unsuccessfully to challenge his father, his father being more baritone than bass, harsh of mouth, and seemingly all-knowing.

GABRIEL ALSO tried to think of monogamously loving Angelica.

His mind felt impossibly tangled when he did.

HE'D CONVINCED HIMSELF every man took advantage of those around him, borrowing things both common and strange, things cold like cash, or things more ultimate, like charisma and concern, or below these, and more virile—more core—anger, distance, deviance.

GABRIEL HAD no interest in the lawn so the yard grew feral, odored of dust flower and weedy undergrowth. He borrowed time, evenings, to read his father's Bible. Passages about Christ humbling himself, about the Son of God not considering equality with God a thing to be grasped, but humbling himself, taking the form of a man. Angelica, no green thumb herself, was now a part-time floor manager for Nordstrom's in women's shoes. She still played a mean piano and her original organ stylings for which his tenor was so suited and to which the students flocked.

She seemed to have changed her frigidity over his most recent infractions.

"I still like you," she told him over a dinner of flank steak and greens.

Not for long, Gabriel thought, and it made him sad.

He felt edgy in the head and wanted sex, but not with her.

OF LATE, GABRIEL found himself in the Birmingham of his mind, no longer attuned to the ear of sound but to a bass beat roar that rose direct from the streets he'd given witness to in the name of God back in Alabama, the young men he'd sung to on the West Side in the hoods of Pratt City, Smithfield, and Titusville, or in the dirt between the projects at Cooper Green or Loveman Village. He looked on those families as if to say you are my brother, my mother, my friend. But staring back at him was an alien sense. No one wants God anymore, he thought. They want indifference, or nothing. They want pride. When they watched him, be they a young gangster from Avondale half a nation away, or a barista in a coffee shop right here, they seemed to say: "You are my enemy."

Certainly, Angelica tried to instill more faith in him, care for loved ones and strangers, even rapture in sisterhood, brotherhood. The Beloved Community, she told him, echoing Coretta and Martin Luther King Jr., likening that community to the house of God.

Last night, he'd white-knuckled it through to first light.

But now he was at his favorite coffee shop, Pearl on First Avenue South, wondering where that server had gone. He'd been here most of the afternoon, watching her hips.

He hoped she was still here for him to tip her.

I'm a hypocrite, he thought. My father was a hypocrite too. In the morning Gabriel had memorized a few verses from Hosea before leaving for the coffee shop. Words like "prophecy," like "judgment from the throne of God." They made him think of what Angelica said of Toni Morrison or Marilynne Robinson. If those two were God he'd be sentenced to death, but then she said she thought him just as likely to be resuscitated by their wrath and sent forth to become a better man. *Gilead is a city of wicked people, stained with footprints of blood*. For the word "Gilead" he substituted "America." *As marauders lie in ambush for a victim, so do bands of priests; they murder on the road to Shechem, carrying out their wicked schemes*. But who are the priests? he wondered. *After two days he will revive us; on the third day he will restore us, that we may live in his presence. Come, let us return to the Lord. He has torn us to pieces but he will heal us; he has injured us but he will bind up our wounds.*

He didn't know what the words meant anymore.

In the past few hours he'd looked at the frame of forty or fifty women, seven or eight men. In fact, he'd never really known his father, despite the education his father had given him in music and people. His father always had an uncanny knack for liaisons with undesirable women. Gabriel likened that generational wound to a revolving door with handprints that could never be cleaned.

I should get home, he thought, as he finished his coffee. The light was going down. But home was heartache, and fortification, and here in public he could almost stay in his own skin, perhaps hold it together for another day.

My name is Gabriel, he told himself, angel of mercy.

His life was meant for love and reconciliation, but he was a failure at both.

Leaving the coffee shop he parked his car less than twenty minutes on and walked through the University of Washington campus in response to a digital billboard advertising a lecture on race in America. He stood before the lecture hall staring because his wife was always telling him to go to these things, read the books she read, change what needed changing.

"You need to be a radical Black feminist," she'd said, and she wasn't joking.

He sometimes told her to shut up.

"I'm a man," he'd said.

"And I'm a woman," she said. "You need to be a Black feminist."

"I disagree," he told her.

"Everyone should be a feminist," she said.

"I don't want to hear any more woman-speak," he'd said loudly.

He sounded like a redneck even to himself.

Standing before the hall he decided to go in. He sat down. Heard the people breathing. They were full of energy over a lecture on Black families lynched in the Jim Crow South. The knowledge disgraced him and called him somewhere ugly. The incidents occurred as late as the 1950s. The crowd, generally of color with a few Whites sprinkled in, sparsely populated the medium-sized lecture. For Gabriel, the event was extremely uncomfortable. The presenter, an incandescent mixed-race woman, gave a survey of southern lynching, eventually focusing on The Hanging Bridge in Clarke County Mississippi near the small town of Shubata where Whites lynched

Blacks and dumped the bodies in the Chickasawhay River. She was from Mississippi, half-Black half-White she said, a lawyer who was also a clinical psychologist. She believed in prison abolition. He was from Mississippi too, at least his Grandma Lu and family. His blood. She linked forgiveness to atonement and reparations. For her, forgiveness was health, whether true atonement and reparations ever came.

She positioned forgiveness at the heart of Black culture. She quoted MLK. "We must develop and maintain the capacity to forgive. He who is devoid of the power to forgive is devoid of the power to love." She quoted Charles Johnson. "How do we portray the racial, cultural, gender, and class Other? It's very important that we make this attempt given our goal of truly becoming a multicultural society."

Nonsense, Gabriel thought. He felt the crowd grinding their jaws with what he thought of as soul-excoriation over the hanged families, the pictures gaudy and grainy on a forty-foot screen. Black bodies disappeared and lynched, White bodies made more visible, shouting in ecstasy, brushing shoulders with the dead, a thigh or knee, a shinbone, a jawbone odd-angled above them. White faces with evil in their eyes.

"Lynchburg. There are nine towns in America named Lynchburg," she said.

"Can a country truly grieve?" the speaker questioned. She was so earnest. "Can we rename ourselves? Reimagine love for each other? Envision love?"

Gabriel wasn't sure. He didn't think so.

But he was sure he was attracted to this woman.

"Lincoln," she continued, "the so-called White champion, racist as he was, had a giant's soul. But along with emancipation came a complexity of leverage and vengeance. From 1877 to 1950 there were four thousand lynchings in the Jim Crow South. Trees. Bridges. Ropes looped over the nearest overhang."

Her voice is liquid, he thought. Likely she can sing.

Her voice made him wonder if instead of being a music pastor he should have chosen a different path. He wanted to run into the darkness beyond the warehouses and never stop running.

After the lecture he introduced himself and she looked on him with graceful eyes. He went with her and a small group to an eatery along the water and they all talked and drank into the night. To close the evening she drew him away to her hotel, and how they met each other naked and unashamed was among the most gratifying encounters he'd had in recent memory.

In the dark of morning when he returned home and lay with Angelica his heart recognized her and he cried. She came awake for a moment, kissing him. He moved his body closer to Angelica and felt the heat of her and kissed her cheek once wondering at death and why he had any right to live before he fell asleep.

The dream that came to him then was odd. Angelica presented a conundrum to his soul. I lead churches, he said quietly to her in the dream, but I know how to lose my faith. Yes, she answered and touched his forehead with her ring finger, making the sign of the cross. What about the history of lynching in America, she whispered. He started to weep. Quiet, she said. I don't care about her. It's safe to say all four thousand lynchings were performed by Christians, the southern kind. She put her hand on his jaw, gently. We are the church it's true, but we're not responsible for the lunatic fringes of our religion. But lynching? How could any sane Christian . . .

He slept fitfully. When he woke he fled the house.

BACK AT PEARL, a few blocks south of Pioneer Square, where the windows looked out on the Sound, he tried to work on music. The Needle was just north, a reminder of outer space. He admitted he liked this city built up from the water, disjointed with flat topped substructures jutting above alleyways, short square buildings set into the rise of streets, skyscrapers balanced on hills. Cars teemed through the lattice work, and people walked with rain on their faces and dullness in their eyes. Unlike what he'd witnessed in Alabama, no one seemed to be too happy, and few were full-blooded hick like the Montana he knew.

He worked out chord progressions with a number-two pencil on the guitar charts he'd spread on the table.

"Straight black, no sugar?"

He looked up to see the server again. Her cleavage startled him. She was bouncy, high-hipped, and confident. She smelled like almonds.

"Sugar," he said, nodding at the bell of her lower body as she walked away.

MEN WERE SINNERS, Angelica reminded herself, and when evil consumed them they found anguish irreversible. When she walked out of the Starbucks near the house, a large White man ogled her. She sighed and walked on, but anger came.

Tedious, she thought.

I'd like to slap that White man's mammy-wanting look off his face.

Men need moral lives, she reasoned. At the bottom, when morality was stamped out, a seeping of the moral marrow of the bones resulted in three inevitable compulsions: killing oneself, killing others, or both.

Gabriel was a decent human being, and she was by no means enslaved to him.

He's just empty, she told herself.

Evil was a betrayal of love. Men betrayed with a kiss.

Women betrayed with disdain, she thought, casting men into the outer dark.

FROM AS FAR back as Gabriel could remember he sang a scale like no one else.

His father had bought him records, vinyl being greatly preferred to digital, feeling it was his duty to educate his son in the vocal dynamics of the gospel legends ranging from the Blind Boys of Alabama to Albertina Walker, from Sister Rosetta Tharpe to the Queen of Gospel, Mahalia Jackson. A natural with lead and harmonies, music rang in him like the melody of water.

A retired Air Force captain, Gabriel's father had been stationed in Great Falls most of his life. A man who loved snow, he was one of the few Black airmen who, after retiring, still called Montana home. Gabriel's mother, on the other hand, was a one-night stand for which Gabriel's father felt remorse. Her name was Kimberly Withers, a girl raised by bigots from out past Geraldine, a small town east of Great Falls. Gabriel's father thought Kimberly danced like a wild creature and sang uncommonly well for being a White girl. She was dark ginger and Welsh. They shared both faith and faithlessness, but they never married. Gabriel's father gained custody at age three when Kimberly was arrested in a meth house three blocks south of C. M. Russell High School.

Gabriel, light-skinned, grew up in the wake of his mother's self-harming ways, her undue mercy toward God and men, her lazy Susan from women's prison to halfway houses to the street and back again. In this way Gabriel grew into manhood in the unfiltered world of his father lording it over women, his father's God-fearing worship of military precision and uncommon affinity for Miles Davis and Ray Charles, his endless mutterings over jet fuel, oxygen, altitude, and wind shear.

IN SCHOOL it's true Gabriel was far below average. But in music he was a vocal prodigy. When his father took him to Mississippi at age seventeen, Gabriel's Grandma Lu looked at him cockeyed.

"Lawd," she said, "White as milk."

"Should've seen his mama," his father said. "Wait 'til you hear him sing."

THINKING OF KIMBERLY'S BODY Gabriel's father had a rabid combination of love and ownership. He was a patriot, a student of history who saw history as something both then and now. Power was not given but taken.

In Montana, Black was either abomination or fascination.

She was as thirsty for love as anyone he'd ever known.

IN THE AUTUMN of a good year, Gabriel Jefferson had fallen in love with Angelica Kennedy Reed. With nostalgic glow, he remembered.

He'd thought her gorgeous, so dark she looked luminous.

She'd made him want to be true.

They'd met over a piano in Birmingham when they were both twenty-one, and a year later, married. They took the name she suggested: Kennedy Reed. He didn't care about his name too much, plus he liked the new rhythm. Majestic on the piano but quiet-hearted on a stage, not a vocalist, not even a choir member, her hands built cathedrals of sound through which he sent his high tenor like an arrow driven from Orion's bow: Take My Hand Precious Lord, I Surrender All, It Is Well With My Soul, His Eye Is On The Sparrow, We Shall Overcome. At Hopewell A.M.E. Church off Forty-Fourth Street in north Birmingham the first two years of their marriage, the people responded to his soaring aerials and rare incantations but it was the ornate soul of the piano she played that made them weep.

The third year of their marriage they'd moved to Seattle for his Campus Crusade job leading worship at the University of Washington. He discipled a cornucopia of students, and sang like a songbird every Thursday night for the event the Crusade leaders called Hunger. Angelica had what seemed to him a dauntless spirit, formed friends easily, and played piano or Hammond organ with such force the students filled the auditorium and spilled out into the street.

The good days, he thought, lying to himself.

ANGELICA COULD HARDLY BELIEVE Obama had been president of the United States of America. The rare president led like a philosopher-king. The common president did not. All presidents had faults, some more than others. All went down in history, many ignominiously. A handful put a terrible wound of infamy on the nation.

Few among them left the nation better for their relationship with her.

BY AND LARGE the men of the nation were of mixed race, she thought. From the Latin *miscere* and *genus*: to mix kind.

MOST NIGHTS ANGELICA couldn't sleep. Her intuition told her she no longer mattered to Gabriel. She was anxious and depressed, but when he lay beside her, her mind attuned itself to great things. The bonds we share lend themselves to fracture but we were born for fusion. It wasn't that she couldn't sing. She just preferred playing piano and organ, and she was shy when it came to singing. She'd been reading *Atomic Physics* by Max Born. For her, anything intelligent ameliorated Gabriel's infidelities. Fission disrupts and alters kinetic stability. Fusion coheres, generating subatomic unity. Her linear mind served her well not just in music but in studies of rhetoric, logic, philosophy, and the mathematical perfection of complex equations. After Running Start she'd finished the math and women's studies degrees at the University of Alabama Birmingham as one of the university's seven valedictorians. A plaque commemorating this hung above Gabriel's desk at the Crusade office off Fortieth Street and Eastlake. He loved to brag about her. When she'd finished at UAB she thought she might apply to graduate school for a PhD in astrophysics.

Here in Seattle, three daughters later, she was thinking of it again.

ANGELICA LOVED telescopes.

She loved the vertical expanse of planets and stars.

Normal matter—human beings, planets, stars, and all the visible parts of the universe—was only 1 percent of the whole. Dark matter was about 80 percent. Dark energy about 19 percent. Everything was imprinted with darkness and light. Black bodies astounding and foreign. Supernovas. The dark inside galaxies and super galaxies. The dark surrounding asteroids. Radio lobes. Energy jets powered by the accretion disk of supermassive black holes and flung free under black hole material consumption: the jets, from end to end, measuring larger than any galaxy. Lyman Alpha blobs, one blob two hundred million light years wide inside the Aquarius constellation. The Boötes Void, a span two hundred fifty million light years across. The Shapley supercluster, a collection of galaxies four hundred million light years long. Quasars, or quasi-stellar radio sources a billion times more massive than the sun, also referred to as extremely luminous active galactic nuclei powered by black holes. The huge, large quasar group or the Huge-LQG, with seventy-three confirmed quasars, an expanse so large it would take four billion years to traverse. These, and the infinite scaffolding of galaxies surrounded by dark matter, a web fathomless in size.

The solar system captivated her: the Milky Way, a large barred spiral galaxy almost two million human years across. A hundred thousand light years. Angelica thought of the Milky Way as feminine, containing more than a hundred thousand million stars.

God is all, she thought, and we're nothing.

Or we're a part of everything.

MEN WERE evil. Men were good. But some wore goodness like an invisible garment, and these were the angels of men. Some shoved their fists into everything, making humanity a lie, making intimacy evil.

When she powered up the television in the living room the news kept cycling the president's gibberish and as she listened her throat went raw, the muscles of her back knotted up and she felt as if she'd been kicked by a horse.

Women were evil too, she reasoned, but in different ways.

Still, since men held power, she believed God would hold them responsible for the ways it was wielded.

Too often they were bombastic and bellicose.

Their families hateful and lonely.

But she reckoned her own life too was less than what it could be.

SHE TRUSTED IN God, for to believe in God was not just the feeling but the hope that there is a God. Not a dead one but a living one urging us with irresistible force toward more loving.

Though she loved her father and mother, she had painful habits they wouldn't ken. Her wigs for example. The patchy skin below them. Under stress, from a child she'd torn out her hair by the roots. She disliked her body. She hated how she'd harmed her hair. But she had a comely mind and a strong soul, and that was enough. Still, her hair bothered her. It was the crown God gave her, but it couldn't be healed.

Women fought for the right to control their bodies. Women fought for the right to choice and the right to life. By White men southern bred, Black women were harmed, raped, and killed. Slaveholder religion came straight from the devil's mouth. God was on the Black woman's side, she knew that much. It wasn't God who raped people. People raped people. In fact, when she considered the crucifixion and the vulnerability of the human body, she knew God was raped too, united with people in their misery, incarnated, and in fact one with all who suffer. Straight, gay, trans, or bi, women suffered severely either after marrying or not marrying, after having children or aborting, or simply after what seemed to be the common experience of love followed by the death of love. Women religious and nonreligious. Many irreligious. Some so good they shined. Most blessed with a natural empathy she found uncommon in men. In love as in parenting, as a woman aged, if the sum of her relational storehouse was isolation her discomfort increased.

Her mom felt that way to her. Her mother too was uncontrollably unfaithful.

Angelica believed a life of either taking liberties or having liberties taken from you in America ruined what it meant to be married. Marriage meant to love and serve. To worship the beloved with one's body and soul and all one's possessions. A troth, in the old language. Faith and fidelity pledged in solemn agreement. A betrothal.

Despite the growing evidence of her circumstances, the remote feel of Gabriel's body and her own grave foreboding, alone in bed again she repeated her father's mantra.

Love endures, love never fails.

GABRIEL WAS KNOWN to enter the vocal practice rooms at the U after midnight. There he could be solitary, unbothered. During the day the vocalists and other musicians peopled the soundproof cells like bees in a hive. At night there were only a handful of music students, set like porcelain figures in their isolate glass enclosures, and he ignored them.

They ignored him too.

With just his voice and a piano, after earlier disgracing himself again to the point of weeping, his spirit brooded before it rose, lifting him straight to God.

TO ANGELICA men were like birds, light of wing or fierce of eye. Predatory or docile. Powerful and impressive or small and light as air. Her husband's voice adorned her music as a lily in the field. Whenever they united there was such tenderness to him. Some years ago, on a journey taken with his father high into the Beartooth Mountains on the road from Absarokee west of Billings, she'd seen red-winged blackbirds in significant numbers. Nearly no Black people in that whole big state. Blackbird singing in the dead of night. She'd felt scared. She'd never seen such wilderness, and those birds were like the kisses of God at the roadside. Red and gold at the shoulder, and black in flight, like the flicker of an eyelash. Though she knew birds were unclean, she imagined the scent of them like sunlight and honey. Take these broken wings and learn to fly.

Into the light of a dark black night.

Her husband did not yet know how to fly.

They'd fly together when he did.

GABRIEL STILL hoped in marriage. Even as abject as he felt now, he could resurrect himself knowing Angelica still loved him. But he knew if she truly considered his real self, her love for him would die. His infidelities were real infidelities. Against her, their daughters, himself. Against her mother and father and her whole Alabama family.

Also against God.

Sometimes he thought God was hateful.

On such days he hated God.

But when he pictured Angelica bearing his disgraces, he felt unutterable sorrow.

Tonight, despite everything, she made a request. "Come to me, Gabriel. Sing." Her face looked tired as she lay on the couch, a floral pillow beneath her head, her body making a deep impression in the cushions. Her eyes were closed. "Gabriel, sing over me." He felt unworthy but her voice was an exhalation so he walked to her and stood beside her, reaching down, placing his hand on her forehead. Keeping her eyes closed she let her own hand come to rest on his thigh. He thought perhaps she didn't want to look at him. She's just tired, he told himself and for a moment he was enraptured, looking into her face, beholding the curve of her cheekbones, the way her jaw met her neckline.

She called him sweet man and he went to his knees and moved his hand from her head to her chest, just below her collarbones where the swell started in earnest. He began to sing, humming at first. You are my home, he thought, my sanctuary. He sang one of the old, old spirituals, letting the tune enter the air generously to ward off desolation. The lyrics moved him, taking him back to when people had uncommon hardiness, and he realized he was nothing, but still wanted to be something. God or not. He hummed the melody over her, slowing the melody down.

"Oh I love that one," she said. "Keep on. Bring it to where my soul can feel it." He loved her southern talk. He didn't know why but every time she spoke that way he felt released and his spirit knew rest. The song was All God's Chillun Got Wings.

He brought it up from where it had been, and set it down into her body, deep into her Alabama sensibilities. "I got shoes, you got shoes. All o' God's chillun got shoes." His voice ascended. "When I get to heaven I'm gonna put on my shoes. I'm gonna walk all over God's heaven." He rounded the turn, pressing his hand firmly on her chest and she said quietly, "Yes."

She didn't open her eyes. Her body was full of peace.

The barriers between them fell away. What is done in love is well done. Poetry surrounds us everywhere. For a moment he thought his voice went forth as if made by God for God, and when he sang like this, always he verged on tears. He'd trained himself to stay there and let the emotion fill the room. "Yes, my sweet man," she said, and he touched her and gave the words to her. "I got a harp, you got a harp. All o' God's chillun got a harp." He tilted his head back and opened his throat. "When I get to heaven I'm gonna take up my harp. I'm gonna play all over God's heaven."

"Bring it low now," she said, and he placed both hands on the ascension below her collarbones. "I got-a wings, you got-a wings. All o' God's chillun got-a wings." He felt her body rise. "When I get to heaven I'm gonna put on my wings. Heaven, heaven. Ev'rybody talkin' 'bout heaven ain't goin' there. I'm gonna fly all over God's heaven."

When the silence came he lay his head on her chest and they breathed together. Before long, she was asleep. He knew she didn't sleep well. He didn't sleep well either. But when he sang to her like this she slept like a child in the arms of her father. He kissed the nook of her chest just below the neckline, the skin tasting faintly of salt. He lifted his head.

"I have no harp and no shoes," he whispered. "I have no wings."

IN THOSE DAYS men kept secrets women didn't want to hear.

GABRIEL'S father raised him but never wanted him.

IN OTHER countries other colors, in every country a single subatomic architecture. Angelica had been reading more atomic physics, along with astrophysics and the nature of nuclear warfare, reminding her of the world's history of genocide. Blood upon blood back to the beginning. Who believed in justice anymore? She did. It wasn't hard to see the similarities between the atomic structure of the heavens and the subatomic unities in human DNA.

She knew the treatment her ancestors received at the hands of American White primogenitors. A woman enslaved, raped repeatedly. Separated from husband and child. A runaway. The same woman's mouth mutilated. Her body branded, whipped at the post until she miscarried. Her front right tooth broken from her mouth, to mark her. A heavy iron collar with three inward spikes bolted around her neck. Whipped further on multiple occasions publicly, not an inch of her back free of laceration. Her hands broken, and feet maimed. She lived through all this. She wanted freedom. Using a field shovel her master murdered her by blunt force trauma to the head. He gloated over the killing and commanded his other slaves to bury her.

She was one woman. She was every Black woman taken from Africa to America, the Caribbean, and South America from 1525 to 1866, 12.5 million Black people, half or more the bodies of women. Angelica knew about black body radiance in the stars: an idealized physical body in the stellar superfluity that absorbs all incident electromagnetic radiation, regardless of frequency or angle of incidence. A woman's body could be that powerful, carrying the dark of the galactic expanse to a place of utter illumination. Black women absorbed rape, iron shackles about the neck, wrists, and feet, whippings, hangings, quarterings, and nearly every form of murder. Piercings and dislocations, dismemberments. Death after death.

A perfect black body absorbed all incoming radiation and didn't emit any. A Black woman absorbed every darkness, her soul ecstatic in light. This is how she made sense of the senseless. Fission was the splitting known to humankind from the beginning. For the second time in U.S. history non-White births surpassed White births. Fusion knitted everything from the human heart to the ends of the known universe.

We are made of fusion, Angelica thought.

We are pure light.

SOME OF US are dreamers, she thought.

SOME ARE THE dream deferred.

AMERICA TRIED to love her, she thought. At the kitchen table she stared out the window, then looked at the two books on the nightstand near the recliner. One by Chimamanda Ngozi Adichie, another by Anthony Doerr. Novels helped her see others more fully. A deep pleasure when the children slept. After a great one her spirit felt love healing everything. Reading, she was a bird in heaven or a butterfly tilting through air.

Light, she thought, the omega point of everything unknown.

Jesus a golden boat on a long, dark river.

Last week Gabriel met her in bed and touched his face to her shoulder. Drifting, he caressed her jaw with his hand. When his body quieted, she placed his hand in hers and kissed the underside of his wrist.

As for men in pain, she thought, these men, brothers known or unknown, on their own or in droves, placed their fingers in one another's wounds to dig out lead, to stop blood and suture lacerations. They were harmed by blunt injury, by piercing, by burning. They spoke the future into the ears of their children before dying.

They wept on their sons' and daughters' necks.

Even the best of men couldn't seem to maintain or advance love. Everywhere she looked in the outside world if they were afire with love, well-married, hopeful, or even adequately matched in the beginning, they ended up separated, divorced, or at the least ill suited. She went to the recliner and kept the TV on as she read. The sound decreased her loneliness unless it was the president speaking. The president shocked people. He spoke of women and minorities, immigrants and refugees, he spoke of Muslims, abortionists, and Mexicans. He called them drug addicts, criminals, rapists. He was the president of the United States. He said he'd grab women by their private parts. He didn't read books. He didn't believe in books. He said he believed in God. He held the Bible upside down. He won the election.

Thinking of him, she knew most women of color felt acute psychological, physiological, moral, and spiritual travail. Many White men couldn't care less, many White women too, especially the Christians. In fact more than half the nation worshipped his backbone, and the thought made her shudder. Daily living accumulated toward decency, mediocrity, or horror—showing the nature of love between people. She wasn't exempt. The bad love amassed, and the result was beyond imagining. Notably, of men who committed suicide in America, seven of ten were White, aged forty-five to sixty-five. Nearly seventy of them suicided every day. Most often, they too were Christians. Some didn't believe in anything. Why did they hang themselves, overdose or slit their wrists, drive cars over embankments, or place guns under their chins? She couldn't say, other than they carried the guilt of history and the shame of the women they'd hated, the women who hated them. Black men escaped fate even less. Black men of any age died sooner than other races, many by murder. In epidemic numbers they entered the school to prison pipeline, after which for the most part they didn't return.

Native men were the least visible of all men. Native women even less visible.

Men of every race had heart disease and died of it readily.

Still, men were born not just violently but tenderly, she thought. Contact comfort kept them alive, love made them thrive. Brotherhood begat brotherhood. Sisterhood an infinite wellspring. However rare, she still believed men and women needed to love one another.

She did her part-time work for Nordstrom's but for the most part she disliked the corporate world. Excepting the people, that world would be made of nothing but metal, glass, and technology. But then again, but for the people, the nasty ones she either had to avoid or try to delicately confront, it might be solely made of love.

Out the kitchen window in the dark she stared through her telescopes. The rain and cloud cover often occluded visibility but she was patient. For better light-gathering and greater resolving power, the aperture size was the most important. She used the ten-inch canon-shaped scope on low power to view faint star formations like diffuse nebulae, and the smaller four-inch scope with no more than medium-high power for brighter things like the moon and planets. With the small one, because it had good optics, she could see Saturn's rings and the principal cloud belts on Jupiter, but for deep sky objects such as galaxies and star clusters the larger aperture was needed. Their shapes appeared to her eye as a precise and complicated choreography: the Butterfly, Swan, and Barbell nebulae; the Sagittarius or Delle Caustiche star cloud; and M99 of the Virgo Cluster, the exquisite spiral galaxy known as St. Catherine's Wheel. M99 with three times the star formation activity of an average galaxy of its size was named for St. Catherine of Alexandria, Egypt, the virgin martyr who died in 305 AD. Beheaded when her touch broke the torture wheel.

Her favorite of all though was the Horsehead Nebula called Barnard 33, a dark nebula located south of the star Alnitak in the Orion constellation, farthest east on Orion's Belt and part of the much larger Orion molecular cloud complex. She liked the cloud formation because it was dark but embedded with stars. She liked it because in deep space, dark was not dark, but light. She renamed it because she wanted to. Instead of calling it the Horsehead Nebula, or Barnard 33, she called it Bright Horse.

IN AMERICA Angelica found a certain internecine racism kills us all. Men sometimes spoke as if the world was right, though wrong followed them as soon as they woke up. Men were Black and White and of mixed blood, blind to inequality in houses and cars, in poker games over felt tables, under the smoke of cigars in front yards, or blunts on back stoops. She remembered her brothers this way, smoke inhaled and breathed forth from the mouth and nose like purple haze from the centers of industry. Men died young. Their hearts gave out. They died old. Their bones and minds grew mealy or cancerous. They died of hard work or street life. They deserted their own. Their women supported them. They discarded their women and children. Their children adored and hated them.

Men were shadows and portraits. Empires of light and clay.

Whoever experienced intimacy thrived.

At 2 a.m. Gabriel wasn't home yet. Angelica went to bed anyway.

WHEN GABRIEL arrived, Angelica came fully awake and told him there are traces of diverse races in our DNA. There are also traces of the stars.

With her mind, he thought, she could earn a PhD in anything.

Likely he was the only thing stopping her.

"Don't let me hold you back," he said.

"You don't," she lied, whisking his words away with her hand.

"Want to know what harmony is?" she asked.

She wanted a new reality.

She believed in pipedreams.

"In our DNA," she said, "we're all one."

She pictured John, the White man who worked in home loans, a man she knew little of but who seemed kind. She thought of her and Gabriel's children and John's children. What tapestry made America, she wondered, what beauty?

She'd didn't mind speaking kindly to Gabriel even when he slipped into bed late.

She went to sleep cradling his arm to her chest.

THE NEXT DAY, Gabriel doubted life. He set five dollars under his coffee cup at Pearl, smiled at the woman who'd served him, and walked out the door toward Garden Street. Just past Fifty-First he turned left toward the water and home.

For two years, since the birth of his third child, his wife, Angelica, was taking a deep dive into outer space. In their neighborhood of close set thin-walled houses, quiet Angelica, night owl, played piano almost exclusively not at home but at the U now in order to please their neighbors—Vietnamese, Black, White, Chinese—who reported their children needed sleep. She slept in most days, worked at Nordstrom's only two nights a week, kept her Bible close, worshipped novels, watched the news like an acolyte, ate more, and looked robustly curved from every angle.

He still loved her lips.

But he preferred her lighter.

"You're too thin," she said as much to him as to herself, but he found the words off-putting. He was angular with a nice build. Not thin. She didn't like herself. How could she? he thought. Laced with public gentleness her private circumstances made her a fortress. He likened her covert self-derision to a hornet's nest.

She likened it to a much-needed lie.

SHE ADMITTED she even thought of her hair dishonestly, a wig the Whites knew nothing of. As a teenage girl she'd pulled more than half of it out. Now, married to him, she'd succeeded in yanking nearly all the rest. The release it gave her helped her hate him less. Hate herself more. She couldn't find work in her true field. She didn't yet have the higher degrees. In astrophysics the opportunities were very male. She didn't blame anyone—she blamed the system. At her lowest she blamed Gabriel. America was monolithic. She and Gabriel didn't know which African country their families came from, Gabriel's family having been enslaved in South Carolina originally, Angelica's in Georgia before they ended up in Mississippi and Alabama respectively: all other records lost. She immersed herself in the work of womanist and feminist thinkers, and therefore at her best she didn't blame Gabriel. Feminist movement was certainly capable of high critique toward the masculine. Whether or not it was capable of critique toward itself, and therefore capable of loving the masculine, was a question she asked herself.

If there was one thing that soothed her most it was hats. She always wore hats in Alabama, not because of her hair problem but because she loved them. She continued the habit in Seattle, growing it to what she deemed a healthy addiction. She might have near a hundred now. Debt was optional, she thought. How much does Gabriel owe me? Sun hats and panamas, cloches, berets, conductor's hats, top hats, bowlers. She had every color of the rainbow, and over twenty different styles. The double delight of a wig and hat covering her bald spots was like a concealer that made you look good and kept people away from truly knowing your face. In Seattle, due to the coolness and the rain, it was easier than Birmingham. She could cover the hats in a plastic bonnet when needed outside, and generally her head didn't sweat. She had felt hats and wool hats, velvet, canvas, and silk, but above all she favored days when the sun was big and she could wear her church hats. She had emerald hats for the Emerald City. In light chiffon or organza, wide brimmed with an embellished bow, they were towering and dramatic and coveted, at least in the South.

She hid herself well.

But always, she thought, her faults were transparent.

God knew.

GABRIEL KNEW TOO. Trichotillomania. He remembered how appalled he was when he read the description: hair-pulling disorder involving recurrent irresistible urges to pull the hair from your scalp, eyebrows, and other parts of the body, being unable to stop.

Like a compulsive thumb-sucker. She wore jaunty hats southern style and believed he liked her that way. She even wore hats in bed sometimes.

Most often he hated her for it. The patchy bald spots repulsed him. He, as much as her, wanted her to keep them covered at all times so he and anyone else wouldn't have to abide the unpleasantness. But hats in bed? She's no prize no matter her organ playing, her dazzling mind or how she oozes sweetness, he thought. She's a troubled, disordered thing.

A week later when he walked in the door early, strode through the house, and saw her in the easy chair before the TV again, her wig slightly off kilter under a thick knit black stocking cap, the kids' clothes and playthings scattered through the rooms, he shouted, "Get up!"

She wasn't afraid of him. But she hated him fighting her.

Unconscious to him he'd borrowed his father's rage.

SHE DIDN'T look up. She was watching the president again.

Violet glow at the window. The president looked so White he was pink. A few miles away the Sound darkened, tunneling toward nightfall.

"I need to go out again," Gabriel said.

"How long?" she asked, staring at the flat screen.

"Not long," he said, approaching her.

Absently she reached toward Gabriel's pantleg.

"I'm sorry," he said, "for yelling."

"I know," she replied.

To him she felt like mud, immovable.

The president prattled incoherently, his wide mouth a red gash.

"I'll be back," Gabriel said.

She knew enough of him to know he used her to excuse himself.

"Okay," she said. "See you when you get back."

IN TIME TO HIS STEPS through the living room and down the hall to the front door she went through the names in her head—Calvin, Joe Barry, Chuck and Ronnie, southern men, family and friends who'd died when she was young, who died today, Bobby Jones and Franklin, Elward, Babo, Hightop, Methusalah. As the door closed behind her husband she thought of their women. Their wives and daughters. Their lovers. She cried a little but felt all right, considering. Unbeknownst to him, the kids were with an undergrad named Julia, spending the night to give Angelica and Gabriel a break. She'd had some rum and a half tablet of Valium and she was high, but not dangerously so. The president was a door that could not be opened. She was in the dark, as were all her American sisters and brothers. Blood of my blood: black, red, white, and blue.

She considered Gabriel's women.

His hand jobs and hookups. Alex, Alyssa, Abigail. They couldn't keep from texting him. His Beatrices, his Beetlejuices, or Beelzebubs. Hair peroxided, dyed to garish neons. Carlyssa or Carlotta. Cara. Cushaya. Cashunta. Legs like pins beneath a bubble ass or precipitous breasts. They mashed makeup on their faces as if to prove something to the world.

IN AMERICA, Gabriel believed if you were to be a man, you borrowed boldness, a kind of ownership, and urgency.

For sex, he'd always had nothing but urgency.

MEN WERE not aware how much their women knew them.

Angelica laughed aloud as she cried. We borrow dignity, or we borrow disgrace.

The night was dark now. She entered the kitchen again, sat down, and gazed longingly toward heaven through the bigger telescope. She thought of knives and shotguns, the birthright of her father and brothers, perhaps herself. Really, she knew none of Gabriel's women or their names. She would never see their hands and feet, their faces. Their bodies. She merely smelled the after-effect when he returned and lay with her sleeping in the half-light before dawn. His face was beautiful. She'd kiss him tenderly when he returned, listen to his breathing, notice the glow of his skin and how his chest rose and fell as if beckoning her.

She loved her mother's relationship with God. She'd lived a loose, unfaithful life in the church, like Gabriel, but when she wasn't awash in guilt or anxiety, she was very good. She wasn't domineering, ignorant, or overly rigid; she understood the dread of God, the holiness. She no longer held such contempt for men. She'd loved Angelica's father. Slept close to him. Held his hand to her heart when he died. Immortality. Her mother claimed they could trace their Blackness to the cradle of the world. A Black Adam and Black Eve who lived somewhere north of the Tigris River at the beginning of time. Genesis. Angelica didn't know about that but enjoyed thinking her people helped originate the world.

She didn't care what Gabriel might be carrying. She'd parsed it countless times. If she and he died of disease, they died together—his dreams and hers no different from the atomic fusion of the stellar extravagances, the dreams of God. Skin to skin, she could imagine Gabriel a true man again, and she a true woman. She could dream, and see him as a blackbird, red at the shoulder blades with bright gold wing bars. The body radiant black. Yes, we are fractured, she thought, but there is fusion in the wing of a blackbird. She wanted to believe after death, if God so willed, she and Gabriel would find each other more lovely than before.

You are my friend, she thought. You are my beloved. You are the one my soul loves.

IN THOSE DAYS Gabriel was nothing to fight for, but women fought for him. Two tramps in the alleys behind Key Arena. Shiona and Lulabell. Because he paid double. Two housewives from a Bible study he'd spoken at a year back in May. Girls with big butts and slack hair. Mona and Kristie. Emotionally, he gave more than they'd ever had. He told himself he always gave more.

He hated himself for what he gave.

He hated himself for what he took.

EACH WOMAN who found Gabriel attractive had been raped in one way or another.

They were partners or significant others or wives.

They were princesses and prostitutes and from childhood to the present they'd been groped, invaded, fondled, penetrated against their will, wrecked, trashed, and left behind. They were straight or not straight. Gay, bi, cis, or trans. He attracted all.

Each person, in insight and without limit, their own being.

Each one ascending or descending as free will or fate demanded.

AT A TINY juke joint in west Seattle, Gabriel sat next to a woman and asked her name.

Her name was Aurora American Horse.

She turned a cold eye to him and looked away.

He found her face captivating.

THE SAME NIGHT in one of the gay bars near Capitol Hill, Gabriel spoke with a man named Juan Carlos over vodka and Coke. He sensed the man feeling him out with his questions but Gabriel wasn't drawn to him so they moved in separate directions.

GABRIEL STILL wasn't home, and this time she was up after 3 a.m.

Just after staring into the central disc duality of Andromeda, a scintilla of words met Angelica unbeckoned. Like her grandmother Jesse, she had a knack for pinpointing location and as she lifted her Bible she found what she purposed, passages that marked her mind, consoling her: *As far as the east is from the west so far has God removed our transgressions from us. For God remembers how we are formed. God remembers we are but dust, and our days are like grass.*

She pictured Gabriel, his head laid back on a thatch of bunch grass in the basin that spread east to west below Great Falls. *We flourish like flowers in the field. The wind blows over them and they are gone, and their place remembers them no more.*

HER LIFE, the lives of others, each was a galaxy. Thick and starry from the core to the wings. Wrapped by swirling light that was miraculous when viewed from a distance even while the heat at the center could be annihilating. She valued grounding, and balance. She valued gestation that birthed creatures of body and mind capable of immense gravity and abundant flight, and this was never far for her from the Christian conception of God as love.

Witnessing the stars, she understood there is but one freedom, freedom of will, which meant freedom to love. Responsibility to the other, the stranger, even the enemy, as beloved. People who both loved and hated God were equally responsible. She weighed 260 pounds if she was honest. I'm smaller than my two sisters though, she reminded herself. She knew, being older, they'd been abused more than her growing up. They loved her. She loved them. They lived together back in Alabama now and laughed a ton, supporting each other like arches in a cathedral. Considering her mother and father despite all the infidelities, Angelica asserted love was the mystery below all mysteries, that science and art are love's sisters, and that an artist, an astronomer, a woman or man, a failure, is infinitely loved, unworthy, and infused with grace.

WHEN GABRIEL came home past four she was in bed. She drew back the covers and welcomed him. When his breathing grew calm, her body moved over him like something elemental, like the earth itself. Like mud. Or blood. She was his heaven, a host of stars clustered in the darkness a million light years away. Her bosom was something he loved. She put her chest on his chest. He either feigned sleep or was asleep, she thought. But his body rose beneath her. "The Lord merely spoke and created the heavens," she said. "He breathed the word and all the stars were born." Gabriel's body went taut for a moment. She kissed his lips. His lips tasted like apple wine. "Yes, Angel," he said. "You are my beloved." The tone of his voice awakened her soul.

After, she lay on her side and curled him into her, kissing the back of his head.

"We all come from the wound," she whispered.

From the living room the television glow lit the hallway.

The president spoke without ceasing.

IN HIS DREAMS Gabriel walked with Angelica at dusk along the water where the city passed behind them and he knew his place in the world.

HE'D TAKEN money from his father three times in four years to help with hospital costs for the three daughters born to him and Angelica: Ruth, Hagar, Tamar. The Crusade ministry at the University of Washington was filled with Holy Spirit fire. On the news pandemic loomed in Asia. America fumbled to respond. Though Gabriel couldn't stop his sexual compulsions, his voice, agile, upraised, still drew in close to one thousand students every Tuesday night. Sweat engulfed him, his neck glistened.

A voice so holy, people wept.

"Warm me up, honey bear," Angelica said on a Tuesday afternoon in early spring.

"Cool me down, honey blossom," he answered, despite his sins, a language of passion they'd shared at the start and lost along the way. The words returned to them like a blessing and made them move closer until their lips met. The kids were with a student again. Angelica was so all-encompassing he felt taken into the depths of her, as if she'd drawn him into God's creation. He'd been too hard on her. Below her skin, within her, he was no longer gone. He was home.

For Gabriel marriage was part and parcel of serving as a minister of God, but faithfulness was an eternal war. He viewed sexual monogamy as impossible, a misconception of former leaner times, of men incapable of wooing women—even if he wished for Angelica's sake, for her beauty of heart and the measure of what he knew to be her nature, he could treat her right. That night after leading the students in praise he borrowed twenty dollars from his director thinking he'd use it to take a couple of new converts for a burger and a coke. He reasoned he'd been doing better recently. When the students said they couldn't go, Gabriel drove to the city center, parked his car and went walking. He entered an adult bookstore and watched a peep show for five dollars. Outside, a block further on he spoke to a young woman, walked into an alley, and paid her fifteen dollars to give him a blow job.

Angelica would be prophetic, he thought, like God's best Hosea, and bear with fortitude his doglike inclinations, his serial screwing of what, beyond her, entranced him. His ineptitude came out on occasion in hatred for her.

That night in her bed he wept again.

But he didn't change.

WE FLEE, ANGELICA thought, until we hear the soul of Christ whisper in our ear.

Come close. Don't be afraid.

I love you forever.

WEEKS PASSED. A White woman approached her after a Crusade function saying, "How come I never see you in cornrows?"

Because you're ignorant, Angelica thought.

"Because I don't really care for them," she said, smiling.

"Oh," the White girl said with a surprised look. "I'm jealous. I think they'd look great on you."

"I prefer full hair," Angelica said, touching at her wig.

"You've got such nice thick hair," the other said. "Mine's so thin and stringy."

"Where you from?" Angelica asked.

"Here," she said. "My mom's Filipina. My dad's from Norway. Got his hair though, and mostly his skin."

Angelica studied her closely. She'd made a woman of color White.

Just last week a blue-black woman from Rainier Beach by way of the Sudan talked to her about cornrows too and she thought nothing of it, just told the girl she'd had enough of those when she was young.

Judge less. Love more.

She pictured an organ's midrange and high notes in her hands, the subterranean base notes entering her body through her feet, elongated tremors of sound building to a resonance that made her strong and responsive and beholden to unseen glories. We're not mechanical, she thought, we're not the question and we're certainly not the answer.

She wanted to give people song, not silence them.

AT NIGHT she thought the nature of love was simply hydrogen and oxygen. Light and breath. The binding material in our DNA, the bonding material at the center of high magnitude stars. It came to her again what her grandmother said, that God is light and in him is no darkness.

Her philosophy with regard to Gabriel: She was he and he was she. Light exists in the essence of a manifold universe, in atomic and subatomic properties, in the light of his eyes meeting hers, the way his hands held her hips with purpose, and peace, and how she enveloped him in a fire limitless and momentary, here then gone. Ever returning. He was made of her. She was made of him. One.

THE WRINKLE of tension Gabriel bore as a person of faith, living falsely, standing up in front of the crowd and singing his God-songs while leading a double life, became a wide-open rift that harmed his mind. Sure he and Angelica had a house but it just meant more debt. And everything else was debt too: credit cards and cars, clothing, food, gas, insurance, heat, electricity, and even something as daily as coffee—the monthly bills were upside down. Her hats. His behaviors.

I should love my children better. Ruminating on how distant and harsh he could be, how the girls needed Angelica just to counter his unfriendly absences, he believed they'd be better off without him, especially with him feeling something sinister to existence. Angelica should just leave him, he thought.

She'd never leave him, he countered.

She believed in marriage.

He believed in it too, but the wages of sin were relentless.

Death.

He wasn't strong enough to shake his fists at God.

EVENTUALLY, LIKE ANY good family, they used credit cards to take the kids to Disneyland.

When they got there, it wasn't what he imagined. Crowded, too many lines, and too hot. They should have waited two more years, to avoid so much crying. In the mass of people, he noticed Angelica's body and even her presence grew bigger while his dwindled.

On the second day, just past noon, a small White man who looked like a body builder propositioned him while he sat on a bench watching Angelica and the girls wait in line to talk to Mickey. Something about a sex club off Pico Boulevard in Santa Monica. Gabriel took the guy's number and when Angelica returned, he lied telling her he had an emergency phone call with his Crusade director. He left, staying away all afternoon and all night, not returning her calls. On the drive back in the dark of LA's freeways, he dissembled, crying from where Pico met the I-10 East, through downtown Los Angeles to the I-5 South. In the final stretch, he believed it would be better for everyone if he drove the car into a concrete wall or an oncoming car.

BACK HOME ON A SATURDAY after a Crusade event, Gabriel ran into John Sender as the loan officer materialized on the front steps of the Pacific Northwest Ballet. John's face glowed like one who'd experienced irrevocable beauty.

"Hello, Gabriel!" he said, "Good to see . . ." and before the words ended Gabriel pulled him into an awkward embrace, holding him close, speaking into his ear.

"Do you still love your wife, John?"

"I do," John said, trying to separate as Gabriel drew him closer.

"Does she love you?" Gabriel asked.

"I believe she does."

"Good," Gabriel said. "Never let her go."

As Samantha emerged from the doors behind him, Gabriel released John and moved hurriedly down the street.

The horizon appeared slanted over Gabriel's head.

Almost birdlike, John thought, how we move. Like birds in sevenfold synchronization the human world is interconnected by flight, he reckoned, not into sky but loneliness, and self-sabotage, and the darker mysteries of life and love.

IN THE MORNING at work Roark called John into his office again.

"You know, John, I'd like to mentor you."

John was flattered.

"The first problem is you're a moocher," Roark said.

"Come again?"

Roark stood with his back to him, looking out over the lower buildings, the span of water over the Sound to the Olympics.

Roark waived his hand. "You're a moocher. See those mountains. Are they subject to anyone? No, they're not. That's me, John, an Olympian of commerce. You, on the other hand, continually enslave yourself. I, however, will not be enslaved."

John sat erect in a black leather chair with no arms.

He felt a tick developing at the corner of his left eye.

"A second-hander. A boot-licker. You don't achieve enough because you're not hungry enough. You're not hungry enough because you mooched off your parents. You let them feed you, clothe you, change your diapers, give you things like money for school, a roof over your head. You're likely still a baby financially. I can change that. They should have left you out in the cold. You'd be hungrier."

"I'm plenty hungry," John said.

"Shut up, John. You're here to listen to me."

Roark paced the room. A broad window ran the length of the office and met the right angle of another window. Roark normally kept the shade panels up and wore sunglasses. The room was cool despite the sun's power just below the zenith.

"My level is not your level," Roark said. "You'll pay me hand over fist, but you'll get where you want to go. Retire early. Go back to the ranch. Am I right?"

"Sure," John said, figuring Roark had him slated for higher rank, more reimbursement, greater stock options. The heavy lifting it all entailed.

"All right then. You need to adopt a more inflexibly self-righteous stance. Sit up." Roark didn't face him, just leaned a shoulder against the window looking away, his malformed hand indiscreet at his side. "Independence and integrity," Roark continued. "Conformists are leeches, parasites, the bottom dwellers of the social order. Weak-kneed. Weak-minded money grubbers. They cry and whine and take handouts any chance they get. But I live free. The noble soul reveres itself. I don't want for anything. If that means cruelty so be it. The supreme individualist rises. The collectivist sucks the teat of history. The truth is most people prefer humiliation at the hands of a superior man. They prefer being subdued rather than achieving their own life."

John decided he wouldn't judge the kind of crazy coming at him.

Roark smiled, his teeth horsey.

John decided he'd add fuel to the fire and see where it went.

"You're at the top," he said, opening his hand to the room.

"I am," Roark gloated.

John didn't need to bow to him, he just needed to do the work. Make the deals. Let Roark do the preening.

Roark came close, not six inches from John's face, took his sunglasses off and stared at John's scars then into John's eyes. "I don't think you have it in you, John. You're a little shit of a man."

"More of a man than you are," John said, eye to eye.

"Nope," Roark laughed. "But good spunk."

Roark turned to the window again. "As for me, I'll never retire. The word disgusts me."

John recognized in Roark some fear at John's physical presence.

"For me sex is plentiful." Roark roamed the room again, rubbing his lame hand on the outside seam of his pants. "Free of consequence, and rough. Money and other extravagance comes to those who take. Not the pretense of intellectualism, but actual intelligence. Not rats fearing God or the so-called law, but militant atheism over altruism. The consecration of achievement. I'll show you a moral economy of inequality that is the just result of those who live superior to the vermin around them, in mind, economics, and especially integrity to their own vision."

"Oblige me," John said.

Roark laughed again.

"I will," he said, "or rather, I'll oblige myself."

Over lunch brought in by Roark's assistant the mentoring went directly to whale potentiality, big data, and the proper use of adjustable-rate arms to afford greatest profitability across the major National American Bank accounts in the region, from Amazon to Microsoft, from Facebook/Instagram to contracts with the U.S. government. As John left Roark's office in the early afternoon he felt more tainted than he wanted to admit.

A foulness to Roark from the secretion of ill-scented sweat.

John wondered what Elias would think of all this.

THAT NIGHT Roark traveled Pacific Highway South after 1 a.m., picked up a middle-aged woman who said she'd be Indian for him, took her to the Seven Gables Motel, made her paint her whole face with red lipstick, beat her with his stone right hand until she passed out, and humiliated himself into her limp body.

THE SAME NIGHT as Gabriel wandered, Angelica told herself she didn't like wine. She drank it anyway for how it calmed the nerves.

As the children slept Angelica moved to the back wall of the kitchen, sat in the chair near the window, eyed her telescopes, got up again, paced more. Structural equations—capitalistic, industrial, warlike—informed America, she thought, linking choice to fate. People needed choice. She wished to live a day in her life again, when choice had been more important than she knew.

AGGRAVATED, she sat down to her computer hoping to get in a social media fight with one of her sorority sisters. She knew it was just an excuse to exhibit anger since she couldn't seem to do so with Gabriel, who'd earned it tenfold.

"Across race, economic status, religion, and location, be it rural or urban, even accounting for population increases, babies come to term or don't," Angelica posted. "If they progress they progress and good for them, but the number of those who are aborted currently exceeds all the plagues of history."

At 3:03 a.m. Eastern, one of her sisters, Kayla, was still up. Angelica had never been good friends with Kayla.

"You don't know what the hell you're talking about," Kayla posted back. "So shut your mouth!"

"As a matter of fact I do," Angelica wrote.

"You need to shut your mouth, bitch!" came the reply.

Angelica didn't post anymore. She'd likely delete this flurry sometime before morning when more of her sisters would materialize, but for now she let the words sit and burn her insides. She hated Kayla. No, she hated the statistics. They came from the Centers for Disease Control, the Guttmacher Institute, the World Health Organization, all three of which the National Right to Life Committee used to make their own report, including the 3 percent possible uncounted error from Guttmacher.

Sixty million abortions in the United States since 1972.

One and a half billion worldwide.

Scientists saw it and said it was good.

But by and large, Angelica knew many women kept the decision very private.

She knew because she kept hers to herself too.

Gabriel didn't know. Her family didn't know. Her sorority sisters didn't know.

On that count, she couldn't bring herself to talk to God about it either.

SOME WOMEN seemed to relish the choice, she thought, but many grew despondent.

She knew she did.

Was it breath of our breath or an afterthought?

"Why do women get depressed so much?" Gabriel had asked her when he'd come home after counseling two coeds. "Why are they so anxious and depressed?"

"Because," she said. "Life can be so depressing."

"But men don't do that," he said. He was staring at the television and talking aimlessly, sitting cross-legged on the couch.

"Yes they do," she answered. "They just go silent and kill themselves."

He hated it when she talked like that.

He'll never understand, she thought.

Released from the burden of having to care for another mouth, another body, a body they might not want, she believed women were torn between the sense of having claimed an ancient freedom combined with an equally ancient responsibility. They celebrated. They mourned. They said they were at peace and tried not to think of it once it was done or they picked the scab incessantly. Some women lived and loved well. Others suicided. It wasn't just men.

Kayla kept sending curse-laden posts into the thread.

Angelica didn't answer.

Staring at the screen she thought of Janice and Jade, Janice her close friend from South Carolina, Jade from New York. She cried some. Poured herself another glass of wine. Kayla had been a year ahead of them, Angelica remembered, and not too bright. Angelica, Janice, and Jade had pledged Zeta Phi Beta with twenty others in their class at UAB, blue and white and black elegance, so much music and dance and laughter. So much serving the community together. They'd remained close over the years though their lives took different tracks. Angelica knew Jan and Jade each had at least three abortions, maybe more. They were high-quality women, women she loved and respected. Most of her other Zeta Phi Beta sisters were not opposed to abortion either, some out of deeply pursued philosophical and political positions. Some because they forgot to take their birth control. A few because they didn't believe in IUDs, opposing the idea of a foreign metal object in their uterus. To their great benefit, and to hers, they'd all been able to put off parenthood, even after years of sexuality, according to their own desires.

Throughout history women had died or risked death, faced beatings, enslavement, and countless humiliations to secure this freedom. A great freedom, personally, Angelica reasoned, and to the sisterhood of Black women an essential increase in gender equity. Yet she felt in her own life and the lives of others, suffering kept assuming a new more compromised body that perhaps nothing could fully heal. She didn't blame history, or her sisters who seemed to be more detached. In most ways she was one with them, and still wanted to be equal to the upward arc they'd attained. She didn't judge them, or at least tried not to. But she often felt they judged her. She was a pro-life feminist. A Black womanist pro-life feminist. When she put her views up, some of her sisters vehemently disagreed. Not usually as aggressively as Kayla, but certainly in ways meant to humiliate her. She kept thinking about the guilt of her own decision to abort before she met Gabriel. She couldn't get past it, how below her dislike of their choices was her own cowardice at how she didn't seem to have the will to claim her own life. She'd been too ashamed to tell her dad she was pregnant. It would have been rough with her brothers and sisters, and with her mom too, but ungodly terrible with her father. He'd have tried to make her go to term and let the baby be taken by the family, or worse, by strangers. But giving her baby up was like a sickness in her mind, a deeper, more abiding ugliness she never even let herself consider. She pictured the child growing, living with others, even if it was her own people, knowing she'd given her away, knowing the child would believe she didn't want her. This was unbearable.

She'd found the work of Dorothy E. Roberts her junior year in college. Magna cum laude at Yale. Graduate of Harvard Law. Distinguished professor. Fulbright Fellow. Black women of power existed at every level of American society, though with how little attention they were given nationally, Angelica wondered where they were until UAB changed all that. Yes the numbers were indicative of systemic White dominance, but now she knew where to look and Dorothy E., constitutional law expert, made her want to rise into the sky, carry light, and keep ascending.

America has always been against reproductive freedom for Black women, Dorothy said—from the Middle Passage to fertile slave mandates to prosecuting women for their conduct during pregnancy, from welfare restrictions based on fabrications about welfare mothers getting pregnant just to get a welfare check to high tech reproduction that benefited primarily White middle-class or above couples at the same time that Black women's childbearing was being deterred through unjust prosecution. On up to the Eugenics movement designed to coerce poor Black women into being sterilized, extending overt manipulation of Black freedoms, the use of Norplant and other contraceptives in population control all the way into the 1960s and '70s and continued through reprehensible political movement until now.

Angelica looked to the window and shook her head. The fantasy of dominance is the fantasy of power. She loved Dorothy and loved her appeal to justice through new laws made to procure and fortify constitutional rights toward authentic equity and inclusion, and to defend and protect the absolute right of Black women to make their own decisions about their reproductive lives. Even more, she loved Dorothy's prophetic vision of Black women's wombs. Black wombs are seen as a threat to society, Dorothy revealed, and therefore society tries to atrophy or deaden them. Criminalizing Black pregnant women, America criminalizes Black motherhood. But Black women keep their wombs alive and vital through intelligence and freedom to choose what they will.

She held burdens Gabriel knew nothing of.

"I don't think we can make it," she told him the last time he walked out the door.

"Only God knows," he said coldly.

She pictured him out prowling, driving her mad, driving himself to the grave.

She blessed the children that came through him, through her.

SIMMERING IN HER CHAIR, she wanted to be all womanist, all feminist, calling both women and men to the communal heart and mind of a Divine endowment. Replacing anger with discernment was her birthright. From Sojourner Truth to Ida B. Wells all the way to Kimberlé Williams Crenshaw and Patricia Hill Collins. From Mary Church Terrell and bell hooks to her beloved Dorothy E. Roberts, even to Judith Jarvis Thompson's elegant conceptions of the unconscious famous-violinist, people seeds, and the ever-expanding child, and Judith's demonstration that the fetus's or anyone else's right to life does not invalidate the pregnant woman's right to her own body.

Even a White experimental novelist from Italy, Italo Calvino, could be seen as graceful when considering his impassioned defense of a woman's right to own and care for her own body through abortion, rather than be humiliated and continually made subservient by the over-masculinized hegemonic world. If Dorothy and Italo met, Angelica wondered, would they get along after Dorothy deconstructed him or would he fight the deconstruction? Would her constitutional law destroy his invisible cities, or might they be mutually boundless in a way unforeseen?

Almost unconditionally, Angelica believed in and affirmed choice.

But she also thought about all the women she knew who never recovered. Perhaps their ongoing depression was a compound issue of structural patriarchy, parental abandonment, and lack of love. Alcoholism, illness, addiction. But some of it, she felt sure, was specifically and painfully due to the hauntings lost children made.

Some of her friends in Seattle or back in Alabama broke down whenever they thought of their abortions. Others hardened themselves. A few of those women believed in nothing, and she wondered if that might not be the better route for her too. If she brought it to mind when she held her own daughters, she wept. Below joy, sorrow like a bone break. She both feared and loved the angel of abortion, and thought this angel different and somehow more fearsome than other angels. Like angels who guarded prostitutes and drug addicts, abused children or widows, cancer victims and victims of famine, she believed the angel of abortion had unique power or perhaps even greater power than the angel of death. She sensed that power when she walked through a store and saw a baby carriage, a mother or father pushing a child. She pictured her own aborted child she'd named Carolyne walking toward her in a yellow dress. Angelica couldn't tell how old she was. Always the image put her beside herself. She wanted to leave everything then, Gabriel, her girls, and drive north into Canada and forget God altogether.

No one understands me, she thought. Except perhaps my own blood sisters.

OR MAYBE GOD does understand me.

Or God doesn't exist.

She put her hand on the computer screen for a moment.

She didn't want to make demands of anyone. She wanted all her sisters, blood or otherwise, not only to be loved but to be loving. Any sister suppressed by the onslaught of misogyny from antiquity to now should feel free to abort. There's no other way out but through mutual reliance and communal determination. But she wasn't sure her own logic could sustain her.

She wanted all to have abundant life: women and children, as well as fetuses and embryos, female or male. Her worldly colleagues hated her for this. But she was who she was. Besides, whether worldwide abortion numbers were at 1.5 billion or zero, none of us can understand ourselves, she reasoned, let alone someone else.

Calvino, like so many public intellectuals, was an avowed atheist. She questioned anyone who claimed they could name the existence or nonexistence of God. Atheists and priests were fools, morally ruined, having borrowed against ego to secure their small kingdoms. They killed in the name of science or abused in the name of religion. She was convinced people abandoned one another in the same ways they abandoned God.

But she also knew some priests and atheists who were among the loveliest, most wise practitioners of truth and beauty on earth. Each an infinity unto themselves.

Who knew?

No one, she affirmed. Not Italo, and not her. Not even Dorothy, though Dorothy, like her, loved the soul of Christ. She'd read somewhere Dorothy's favorite quote was "I can do all things through Christ who strengthens me." There is only one human race, Dorothy's parents taught her: White or Black genes didn't exist, the lie of racial purity a political invention built to further the demands of those who engineered supremacy. In fact, Dorothy's parents had married across race. Her Black mother studied for a PhD in anthropology. Her White father conducted anthropological research on approximately five hundred interracial couples in Chicago for four decades from 1937 to 1967. But in the end the promise of interracial marriage was just that: marriage, replete with destructive tendencies, born of the hope for something more than oneself.

Calvino believed only people who bring a child into the world to be affectionately welcomed, cared for, and loved should be allowed the choice to have children. Better to abort rather than inflict more vulnerability on the child and the world. Well, no one can predict or ensure hate, Angelica thought, let alone love, and to act like it was possible to predetermine who can love a child before facing the onslaught of life that makes breathing bearable or unbearable was pure foolishness. She was ready to love now.

When she last went home to Alabama, she'd been asked to counsel a sixty-three-year-old woman named Jessie Mae Washington from her home church who'd had a botched abortion as a teenager. All Angelica could offer was prayer, and prayer wasn't enough. The Guttmacher Institute reported the abortion rates for Black women as almost five times that for White women.

Beyond that, worldwide the epidemic of female infanticide, female slavery, and femicide burdened all. Looking into the stars it enraged her as much as it frightened her. Earlier, before Gabriel left for the night, Angelica had been in the recliner. Then she'd gone to lying on the floor because it made her back feel better. Then she walked down the hall before returning to sit next to the kitchen window where she dismissed her own reflection by shaking her head. She rose and drifted back to the hall to check on her daughters.

In sleep each child's breathing was full.

She touched their lips with the back of her fingers.

She wondered why she kept holding so tightly to her need to shape the marriage into something decent. She kept devoting herself to impossible things. She put her head in her hands. When would Gabriel become who she thought he was meant to be. She needed to give up, for her sake and the sake of her children. When she envisioned getting a PhD, she felt on the verge of realizing herself, but acknowledged the pursuit itself might just break him. She didn't want to break him. Why am I attracted to a man who treats me so poorly? Why do I stay with him?

Why do I want to pull out my hair?

Another year, thirty-three. No longer young.

I should hate him more. Hate myself less.

What will happen to my children?

AND YET, FOR all their failures, people still sought love.

Not merely disillusionment or desperation, they practiced listening, and quietness, the ability to give and receive kindness. Even she and Gabriel could sometimes follow the urge that sent them in the evening walking with each other, or brought them to the table, a deck of cards, a conversation, songs they shared, whispers. Greetings at the door, goodbyes.

They danced together.

They carried the stars their eyes beheld, the hopes that bore them up.

Compulsion, fear, disaster, desire.

As far as she could tell, people tried everything, but still failed, and before love died they looked fiercely at the future and borrowed the illusion of love's permanence, and oh how she had leaned in, and oh how he had unfurled a willing heart, and all of us, she thought, will never forget how once our kiss was the beloved's bright dream.

GABRIEL WAS LOST to her and she wasn't sure she cared anymore. If she didn't have Ruth, Hagar, and Tamar, she didn't know if she'd still be here. To make it through the night she told herself she needed to stop her morbid thoughts.

She went to the living room, sat in the armchair, and stared at the TV, muting the sound so she could think. She lifted her journal from the bookstand by the chair and started reading her notes on a talk she'd heard by the poet Robin Coste Lewis on the Black virgin, the Mother of God. The Holy Black virgin mother of the world. "Christianity in the form of the Black virgin smiled at me," Robin said, "stroked my cheek. Told me to stand up." Churches had protected the Holy Black virgin through the centuries, churches in Viet Nam, Palestine, Tobago, Mexico, Poland, Italy, Spain . . . people guarded her with their lives, offering her refuge, war after war after war. The notes gave Angelica peace. The Messiah is not White. "Culture is my project," Robin said. "Race is a pathology. Not you and me or us and them but the world as an intimate. There are no *others*. Let's start with and end with my deepest shame and then we can go from there. We are lost together. We are loss. The personal is political. I can tell you anything if it means we can maintain intimacy. Desire is what makes us alive. Your demons knock on your bones. Learn how to be still with yourself. Embodiment means everything. I am a body. I touch your body. Pain and limitation. Age and mortality. A lush land of pleasure. Be still."

Angelica had suffered to bring Gabriel to greater knowledge but in reality she believed this was God's task. When Gabriel was seeking, he saw her or other women as the princess in the clouds but below it all was his own lack of seeing women clearly, with modesty. She was guilty of making of him a prince too; she kept sending him out to vanquish the foes but he kept coming back having had sex with them. Until he saw clearly, he couldn't be well. Same as her.

She removed her wig and let her hands move over the skin of her head, feeling the small bumps of inflammation at the base of her skull. She used her thumb and forefinger to worry a small patch of hair behind her right ear. Pulling the roots free, she felt pain and relief. His gaze, dominant, uncaring, disloyal, replicated the White gaze, she thought. Hers, submissive, over-caring, over-faithful, mirrored female martyrdom, bitterness, and contempt for the masculine. She wanted the new abundance signifying subatomic unities at the center of the universe, darkly stellar in capacity, housing light, multicolored, multi-oriented, female and male, reconciled.

The Anima Christi. The feminine soul of God.

God can bring us to life from a living death, she thought.

"The masculine projects all of its fears into the female body," Robin said. And the feminine projects all of its fears into the male heart, Angelica reasoned. She turned the page of her journal and found a photo in the crease. She lifted the photo, kissing it gently. It was Gabriel singing, but the bottom half was torn away below the waist, an act she'd committed angrily some time ago. Had she envisioned herself more powerful she might have started graduate school a long time ago. Less powerful, she might have ruined herself with hatred. His upper body was fully expressed, hands raised, face shining with sweat, his mouth turned upward. His eyes closed in a kind of blessing.

He'd be singing somewhere, his song sent forth to people and God. "Blackbird, blackbird singing the blues all day right outside my door. Blackbird, blackbird why do you sit and say pack up all my care and woe, here I go singing low? Bye, bye, blackbird."

The body receives trauma, she thought, a nexus of fusion capable of ultimate restoration, and atomically speaking, resurrection. Hydrogen powers the stars and our DNA, and its most common form entails one electron orbiting one proton. A photon or quantum of light is created when a hydrogen atom absorbs other photons, thus destroying those that are absorbed, and then emitting, in turn, more photons. More light, she thought. And God is light, and God is love. After each of these "excitations," the electron recedes in energy, emitting photons along the way. If a photon with sufficiently large energy is absorbed, this can even unbind an electron from its nucleus, a process called ionization. These crippled hydrogen atoms, no longer able to absorb or emit light, then manage to capture a free electron back into a bound energy level. They are only resurrected in this way, thus creating infinite light.

With all creation we are eternally dying, she thought, but extravagantly and irrevocably we are eternally resurrecting. For human fracture is fission, but love is fusion; fusion being of a scale exponentially more powerful. Millions of birds die every day but we never see it, she thought. They like privacy in this holy, fatal moment. He didn't deserve her hatred. But she didn't deserve his either. Without forgiveness and love, how can anyone bear living? She missed her family back home and felt like a fool for ever having left. She placed the days ordained for her in the hands of the Almighty. We find ourselves by coming home, she thought, a true home, one we grow up in or one we never had, and there is a dawning when love reflects back to us what we are meant to be, the yes, the why. The body absorbs darkness and emanates light. Only God knows what lies in the darkness, she thought, and light dwells with him.

She didn't know where she and Gabriel would end up.

She hoped it might be in one another's arms.

Book 5

To love is to undress our names . . . to turn desire into love, to embrace, finally what always evades us, what is beyond, but what is always there—the unspoken, the spirit, the soul.

El mundo nace cuando dos se besan.
The world is born when two people kiss.

—Octavio Paz

JUAN CARLOS, MARY IRENE, AND PAULO

JUAN CARLOS DE LA CRUZ too hailed from Montana and asked John Sender for help with a home loan.

Juan Carlos believed he still loved his wife, Mary Irene, but he wasn't sure anymore. Seated in a leather chair in his study, he stared at her photo, a prized photo he kept close, one she'd given him of her dancing. He pressed it to his lips before he spoke a line from Shakespeare, "Let me enfold thee, and hold thee to my heart." He remembered then the line was from *Mac-Beth*, about brotherhood, foretelling a frightful end.

RECENTLY RELOCATED from Oklahoma to Seattle, Juan Carlos came from one of the oldest Mexican families in Montana. He purchased a bare three-room condominium in the Ballard District for him and Mary Irene, a woman of mixed Japanese and Polish descent.

He understood money and real estate.

He was talented and sometimes awkward around men. He hated his father.

JUAN CARLOS DE LA CRUZ's family had arrived in America having traversed the old Wolf Pass south of Nogales before the vicious border years, before Eisenhower's Operation Wetback, and even before the harried tensions of the late nineteenth century. They'd gone back and forth in the old days, his earliest descendants having ties to the Mexico that came before the new America, before 1848 and the Mexican-American War when Texas, New Mexico, Arizona, California, Nevada, Utah, half of Colorado, the Oklahoma panhandle, and a sliver of Wyoming were claimed for the "united" states. Finally, it was a great-great-grandpa who traveled from Mexico to Montana in the massive cattle drives of the 1860s, settling just east of the continental divide.

Circa 1849, Emiliano Victoriano de la Cruz was born in a village near what would later be called Plano Oriente in what is now the northern Mexican state of Sonora. Plano Oriente became Cajente when the South Pacific Railroad established a station there in 1912 and eventually became the larger Ciudad Obregón. But the village was mud huts and dust in the 1860s and with a late outbreak of smallpox, at thirteen Emiliano lost both parents, all six of his sisters, and three of his brothers. He and the two youngest brothers remained. The two were absorbed into other families but he was old enough. He moved north, finding work as a feeder for a cattle operation south of Nogales, becoming a horse handler at fourteen, a wrangler at fifteen. At seventeen he was made a vaquero for a large cattle drive outfitted by a Texas operation, moving a few thousand head of longhorn from Nogales to the Montana Territory in 1866. Hired in a single look by a tall White man named Nelson Branch, Emiliano smiled when Branch promised in broken Spanish three horses, a daily meal, and pay at the end of the drive. On the journey through the pass from Nogales into Arizona, Emiliano stocked a large cloth bag with black walnuts, soaking the shells in water along the trail before he knife-hulled them and shelled them with a stone to prepare for curing. When the walnut meat was ready he gave handfuls to the White man, the meat wafting like rich soil, and the two became friends. Branch called Emiliano, Leo, favoring him, ultimately treating him near to a son.

They started in the cool of February and arrived in Montana in the high heat of August. Working in shifts as they moved, their band consisted of

Branch and eleven cowboys, a horse wrangler for the remuda, a cook, chuck-wagon and oxen. The group of eight Mexicans and six Texans made good time, herding north in daylight, watching at night against theft or stampede. They kept the animals in order and well fed over the Bozeman trail, losing only a handful to river crossings, arriving two weeks early in Montana, at Deer Lodge, formerly the seasonal settlement called Spanish Fork. Here half the cattle would be fattened and loaded at the railhead for Chicago and points east, the other half kept on large tracts of unsettled grassland, the Montana open range claimed by a Colorado cattle king named Conrad Kohrs who owned fifty-thousand head across Montana, Wyoming, and Alberta in Canada.

Branch was paid well for the condition of the stock and the promptness, and on a bend of the Hellgate River east of Deer Lodge he gave all but Emiliano their stake and the crew dispersed. He treated Emiliano to a beef-steak at a rich man's saloon in town, paid him twice what he'd paid the others and asked him to stay on and help run Kohr's operation west of Deer Lodge.

They worked for Kohr, purchased neighboring ranches with their earnings, and ran cattle. Staying alone together in a single room cabin they saw Kohr's cattle and their own through two winters before they determined not to live together and ordered brides from the east in separate telegraphs posted on the same day in the spring of 1869, both brides arriving a month apart in late summer and turning out sturdy, hard-working, and capable of not a little love.

Nelson Branch and Emiliano Victoriano de la Cruz's ranches border each other in the Deer Lodge valley of southwest Montana to this day.

BORN TO ONE of Emiliano's many descendants, his family citified and living in Great Falls, Juan Carlos de la Cruz came bawling into the world in the birthing wing at Columbus Hospital, measuring fifteen inches, weighing eight pounds and eleven ounces. A few years later, the family moved to Billings where his father sold small houses among the blocks off Montana Avenue, graduating to higher homes on the rimrocks and the far west end, eventually owning a good-sized real estate company featuring commercial, residential, and legacy holdings by the time Juan Carlos entered ninth grade. The family lived in a remodeled craftsman in the old money neighborhoods a few blocks from downtown.

Juan Carlos had six brothers.

JUAN CARLOS WAS A STAR at Billings Senior High, lettering not in basketball, football, or track but in theater, a star whose command on stage transfixed his drama classmates and attracted the elderly in droves. Being brown, his father Mexican American, his mother a White Dane, he drew his doses of old Montana racism, especially from the so-called jocks, but he was fluid and gregarious and navigated conflict uncommonly well. He played leading man Tom Wingfield in Tennessee Williams's *The Glass Menagerie* as a sophomore, as well as Sky Masterson in *Guys and Dolls* as a junior, but it was his gravitas, assured masculinity, and violent passion as Stanley in *A Streetcar Named Desire* his senior year that made women approach him in strange ways.

His father was workaholic, distant, bullish, and a hidden incestuous pedophile. His father was also the engine that fueled him and made him blaze like an industrial fire. Onstage he felt made of molten raw materials at high heat. His father called his mother meager and weepy. Dumb bunny or pussy. Juan Carlos hated this because he loved her, even if her emotion was blunted and lacked range. His father raped Juan Carlos from age eight to eleven, and because of it Juan Carlos was largely silent in the home, only speaking openly when in the company of his best friends or when he bloomed onstage in theater camps and school plays. When he began flourishing in high school, he found himself not so much afraid as angry. His father never went to a single play, citing work as necessary to supply his mother's indulgences, calling Juan Carlos babyface or pussy like his mother when Juan Carlos asked him to attend.

It was following these exchanges that Juan Carlos first contemplated killing his father. At the after parties, Juan Carlos got drunk and loud and always fled past midnight, driving the old white '74 Impala to the oil refinery south of town along the muddy flow of the Yellowstone. On the curb outside the car he eyed the tip of the flare stack where the torch fires burned. They were atmospheric and miragelike, discharge gasses dispersing incessantly above the flames. The odors a miasma of consequence.

Like him, the flare stack wept with rage.

JUAN CARLOS'S MOTHER went with him to the National Unified Auditions in Los Angeles where he was accepted to five top-tier universities for theater, choosing Oklahoma City University for the intensity of the instructors, the fact that the school produced seventy-seven plays a year, the mix of actors, dancers, and singers, and the placement percentages on Broadway or the big regional theaters in Chicago, San Francisco, and Seattle.

College was much harder than he expected and near the middle of his second year, having earned no roles, not even ensemble, he contemplated suicide. The name of his father resounded in his head. Jorge. Heavy handed. His father's misplaced touch, in his father's eyes a deadness belying the force with which he did harm. He pictured him in front of the ornate ofrenda in the front room, food and water, photos, flowers, candles, champagne. Dia de Muertos. His father's fraud life: praying, calling on the souls of the dead in the living room at sundown, obliterating his sons after dark. Juan Carlos didn't call his mother, thinking his failings too much for her. He drank and smoked dope and imagined scenes in which he cursed his father and slapped his father's face before cleaving him at the neck with a shovel or impaling him through the teeth.

Juan Carlos didn't return for Christmas that year, and after Christmas break two graces met him: First, he earned the role of Magaldi in a student-directed production of *Evita*, and second, one of the dancers, a nice looking girl named Mary Irene, spoke kindly to him.

"Where are you from?" she asked.

"Montana," he said, "and you?"

"Jersey," she said.

He loved her accent. Her skin.

She smelled like cinnamon.

She asked for his name. He asked for hers.

"Your voice has such presence," she told him. "I'm never cast as a singer. My vocal coach says I'm too scared to project."

"Is that why you're a dancer?" he asked. He noticed the sweep of her body, her long legs and back-bent shoulders.

"Maybe," she said. "I want to be a singer, but dancing I feel alive. When you act and sing, I see it in you. You're completely alive."

They were down the hall from the green room, seated next to each other among the leftover set and hand props from shows that dated back decades. He sat on a wooden box next to a pale blue rocking horse while she sat in a vintage chrome kitchen chair patterned with orange and white daisies. They'd both be on in five. Up in the high ceiling, tattered posters clung to the rafters. A set of deer antlers hung from the pipes.

"I don't know if I'm alive," he said. "I appreciate the compliment though."

"You want to get a drink after?" she asked.

"Sure," he said.

They waited a moment before walking to the wings.

Entering the light, they felt lithe and magnificent as panthers.

THE NEXT DAY in a class called Vocal Production for the Actor the professor placed her hand on Mary Irene's stomach to be sure she breathed correctly and wasn't tense. A thin French Canadian woman in her late thirties with a flintlike face, she asked Mary Irene to crouch and say a few words while releasing the neck, head down, spinal ridge open.

"What should I say?" Mary Irene asked.

"Your acting vision," the professor said. "Shake your head. Loosen your neck."

The other students looked on.

"Okay, stand again." She positioned another student near Mary Irene who read from a piece of paper, whispering Mary Irene's own words into her ear from behind. The acting vision came from a freefall writing experience in an earlier class session, about what Mary Irene believed, in acting and in life. A personal creed of sorts. The professor directed Mary Irene to speak it out to the class. She then moved Mary Irene's body, placing her hands on her stomach and back, saying loudly, "Engage the art!" She pressed her hands together, holding Mary Irene firmly. Most students, when their time came, trembled as they performed their vocal manifesto for the class. The body and voice shook. They cried. Mary Irene cried more than the others.

She was thinking of Juan Carlos.

The teacher asked her to put her hands to the floor with her legs straight, head down. She made a fist and pounded Mary Irene's lower back. "The sacrum is the seat of creativity. The source."

"Your true voice is lower, Mary Irene," she said. "Not so high. Don't hide yourself in a mousy little girl voice. Use your true voice. Reach down! Into the earth. Reach for the depths of the real voice, *your* real voice. Don't manipulate. Stop making higher sillier sounds. Give us your serious self. Breathe Mary Irene! Flow through the breath so when you go to the depths your voice doesn't get caught. Stand now. Talk through the tears. Now Mary! Speak! Let it move through you."

Mary Irene spoke. The voice boomed in her chest.

"Yes!" the woman said. "Keep on now. Go!"

"I believe in people," Mary Irene said boldly, her voice reaching out and over her classmates to the walls at the back of the rehearsal hall. "I believe in love. I want to be loved!" She wept, but the voice was bigger than any she'd ever known.

Her classmates wept with her.

"Speak through!" the teacher shouted. "Don't cut it off. The body wants freedom. The voice wants what it desires. You are an artist! You are a person! Let it move. This is you transcending yourself. This is art! This is life!"

Later when Mary Irene sat in her dorm room alone, she wrote down four additional lines, adding them to her acting vision:

I really want to be vulnerable even if it takes work.

I relish the work.

I love people.

I love my life.

Secretly, in her own mind, she added, I love Juan Carlos.

THE FOLLOWING DAY in a different class, this one with Juan Carlos called Movement for the Actor 1, the group practiced contact improvisation. The professor was a wiry, spiderlike White man with a nose like a nymph. He directed them to walk in a circle around the space of the rehearsal hall, then move toward each other, walking randomly among each other. "Use a soft focus, eyes averted," he said. "Do not make eye contact. Be aware of the space and the people around you but don't register specific detail."

They moved tentatively, as if approaching death. "Now make eye contact as you walk," the instructor said, and Mary Irene made eye contact, but felt a wall between her and the others. They looked mean. She kept wondering why they seemed so angry when she was trying to be really happy. Juan Carlos's face was stone. She avoided him.

They all dressed in black.

"Now make contact that is magnetized," the teacher announced, "so you're charged by the other person. But don't touch each other." They started to come together then, changing their bodies noticeably through facial expression or bodily cues, turning to gaze directly at someone or slowing down or shifting their head or arms in some way by how the other person affected them. "You're a hive of human bees," the teacher said calmly. "You're mindless animals feeding off one another's instincts." His monotone voice filled the room. "Now be so electrified you need to make physical contact."

Normally Mary Irene felt uncomfortable with this as she didn't know what to do. And now that Juan Carlos had seemed hateful to her, it was even worse. Do I touch someone's hand or shoulder? A chest or back? Should I kiss someone? What if someone tries to kiss me? Some people were malodorous, which revolted her. Some smelled neutral. What was she? Just then Juan swept into her from the side. Lightly holding her waist he lunged and she stepped into the crease of his hip and as he lifted her she forgot herself, her back arching, her arms reaching for the oval of fifth position. He smelled wonderful. The riverine aspect of the movement took her over and he let her down and she found herself pressing her wrist into someone's head, feeling an intimate pushback so that she let herself be moved, she and a stranger walking together into open floor space. A unified sense arced through her spine as if her form was aligned with wild creation, like the trumpet of a daffodil or the neck of a swan. She went to the ground where a female classmate rolled over her back, the two gathering, separating. So much was in the hands, the forearms, the back of the arm below the shoulder. From there it went to full body movement with whoever one encountered, a testing to see how comfortable the pairing, or how much weight you could hold, or how much of you they might encompass, descend with, or elevate. Some were stronger. Some lighter. Some unresponsive or listless.

She was lissome and nearly weightless, and her movement worked on others like gravity and transcendence. The movement became a dance fluid and free where people opened and grew aware of each other and trusted one another. "Now go beyond the two-person interaction," the teacher directed, "incorporate a group of people." And sometimes a girl would be lifted in the arms of four or five men and carried through the room, her body in flight. Everyone a poet, Mary Irene thought as she experienced the unity, everyone a painter. The body would be someone else's or hers, a white dove in the sky, and then she would be set down and another motion would follow as the group released and moved together again, flowing in rhythms strange and unknown and inviting.

When she emerged from class and walked the campus the previous two hours were a blur, her bodily memory imprinted with the most intricate details, accompanied by feelings of immense intimacy. Her senses heightened, it took another hour walking to calm down.

Juan Carlos had been good to her.

She hoped he experienced her as graceful, and good to him too.

JUAN CARLOS AND MARY IRENE dated through their college years. They knew nothing of the Oklahoma City bombing before attending the university but once they visited the memorial early in their dating they returned often, studying on the grass benches below the Survivor Tree. There was a strange displacement to how the tour they'd taken placed them in the building as if on the day of the bombing. The reflective journey through the site was curated not only with great respect for the dead but with uncommon hope and serenity.

Emerging, they felt great love.

After graduating together, they married and moved to Seattle where they lived together in the condominium for three years before imploding.

SHE WALKED out, saying he was abusive.

TELLING HER he never loved her, he didn't chase her.

IN THE FOLLOWING years they knew little of each other, their lifestyles or encounters, their hazards and deep troubles. They quit theater simultaneously to avoid seeing each other but when a director told Juan Carlos Mary Irene hadn't auditioned for months, Juan Carlos quietly crept back into the scene.

When fighting they'd said they didn't believe in marriage anymore and valued open relationships. But after they split they each entered a second marriage almost immediately, fast burns that ended nearly before they began. After that Juan Carlos launched himself into the drug and sex culture, surprised at his capacity to harm and be harmed, lusting for men and women and things titillating and peculiar.

AT TWENTY-SEVEN MARY IRENE was raped and didn't report it, not trusting a legal system run by men. Her rapist, whom she met at a party in the lavish Hotel Diamante downtown, impregnated her. She never saw him again. At work in broad daylight or in the quiet of her bed she cried on occasion. She wasn't close to her family, her mother a skinflint whose miserly emotions turned her away, her father so distant as to be nonexistent. She struggled considerably over the decision, finally deciding to have the child. She liked how her body responded, truly filling out for the first time, her hair healthy and thick with luster. She'd been so slender, light on her feet with an agility and flexibility akin to the great Russian dancers of the Mariinsky and Bolshoi Ballets. She touched her womb near constantly, speaking love. She imagined the scent of the child's breath like vanilla. The baby grew to the third trimester and died in her womb. In the two-year aftermath, Mary Irene tried to kill herself three times.

WHEN SHE AND Juan Carlos chanced upon each other, it was as completely different people. She saw him on a sidewalk in the business district below Capitol Hill. They embraced quickly, passionately, and the way their bodies met then was a healing to them both. She pressed her lips to his neck. He put his face in her hair, breathing her fragrance. In college they'd needed each other, her for what she sensed as strength, him merely to make her smile, to enjoy her smile, her friendship, and often her body.

Now they were more serious, less idealistic.

They were also more beautiful.

They married each other again and had a daughter named Ana Luz.

Mary never told Juan Carlos she'd been raped or carried another life.

The miracle of childbirth united them with untold force.

It seemed so long ago when they'd first fallen in love, gorgeously in her mind, and after college moving to Seattle for acting and dance. They'd starved. They were artists, beloved of audiences at Seattle Repertory Theatre, Spectrum Dance, and the alternative nonprofit Taproot Theatre. They'd worked hard, two and three jobs apiece. They were devoted to each other until they weren't. They'd broken apart and lost the dream, and in between they began "normal" working lives. Eventually they both quit the artist life. Returned to each other they worked smarter and more efficiently, moving up the corporate ladder: him in real estate, her as a manager at Boeing. During the early years of their marriage she climbed higher, but Juan Carlos was a climber too and soon his earnings skyrocketed. They hired a nanny.

They worked more hours and made more money.

They loved their daughter, but it was hard finding time for each other.

They sensed they were descending again.

They held it together for Ana Luz.

JUAN CARLOS BORROWED a purple marabou boa and a white silk scarf from Mary Irene's lingerie drawer. She preferred to call him Juan Carlos because she loved him and loved the sound of his two names on her lips.

His friends in Seattle, many of them White, called him Juan.

JUAN CARLOS, IN Versace suit and Gucci watch, secured a jumbo loan on a big house in the First Hill area east of downtown. The loan officer was John Sender again, the good-looking man with the hard face. Juan Carlos and Mary Irene met John on the ground floor of National American Bank, an open floor plan that looked onto the street and welcomed the masses, but John merely led them through the lobby, nodding to a teller near the front, and again nodding to a man in a desk near the back of the room before he whisked them up an elevator lined with black marble and stainless steel.

How do banks know, Mary Irene wondered, which accounts deserve special treatment? Juan Carlos knew they did a credit check aligned with an asset tabulation to assess current and future capital. He smiled to himself thinking how odd it was for him to have been a stage actor and Mary Irene a dancer, blind about business and with nearly no financial base, and now here they were in the corridors of power. As if reading Juan Carlos's mind, John ushered them into a conference room facing west on the seventeenth floor. The bank had cut a hole in the corner of the building to build this room, the architecture extending outward in a chevron beyond the previous edge. The sweep of it placed them cleanly in midair. Everything was glass, dark wood, black leather, chrome. When they sat down they both stared forward. The sun shone high. The ocean glowed cobalt from here to the Olympics. John smiled now. He knew Juan Carlos's money had become substantial. He hoped this loan would lead to more from Mr. de la Cruz, his colleagues and acquaintances.

Mary Irene and Juan Carlos loved their new home. At night the lights of Seattle along the water graced the front window like a sky not above but below and filled with a multitude of stars. She scented the house with lavender. Believing himself of high Spanish blood, he saw the city as his courtyard.

Mary Irene will be my queen, he thought, but within three months, determined to remove his wife's germs, he was knocking on a neighbor's door where a plump White woman loaned him a new pair of rubber gloves and some cleaning solution.

Returning home, Juan Carlos disinfected the toilet seat in the master bedroom.

He knew it to be insane. Thinking her dirty.

His mother and his true brothers, Ruben, Antonio, Alejandro, Esteban, Pedro, and Manuel, he was estranged from. From childhood to now his brothers had despised his tenderness. Wounded, he despised them back.

As he cleaned, he thought, "Our father ruined us all."

FOR INFRACTIONS as a boy Roark Rosenbaum Freeman's father had beaten his head, producing contusions, welts, and open wounds, a mess of minute ridges Roark hid beneath his hair as an adult.

His father had wanted his mother dead.

Roark would never know the truth of how she lived or died.

JOHN SENDER kept rising. If you work hard in America, he thought, if you have any discipline at all, it isn't hard to make money.

He was less aware just how hard making money proved to be for those who lived below him. He was fully aware his boss, Roark Freeman, lived high above and seemed to be increasing in power in converse relation to common sense. In their most recent get-together they met at a coffee shop in south Seattle. On the way in, John said hi to Gabriel Kennedy Reed seated near the window. John detected a weight of despair behind Gabriel's eyes.

Roark was already seated, wide arms up on the plush leather of a couch in the back. "Hurry up, John," he said, lowering his arms. "I don't like waiting. You need to be less concerned for those who aren't in your class. More concerned about me, more rational. The virtue of selfishness, John, that's what gets things done."

John's thoughts turned like the cylinder of a revolver in his mind. For all the man's focus on reason and rationality Roark's thinking was among the most obtuse he'd ever encountered. Towering self-centeredness hid the mind of a child.

"You're smart, John," he said when John was seated in front of him. "That's why you climb. Stop messing with the lower class. Have some veracity and uprightness. Get on top and stay there. Now apprise me of your current whale accounts."

John stared at Roark, perhaps too long.

"What are you looking at?"

"Nothing," John said.

Where before he'd thought Roark's hair unkempt but imperial, speckled white and black, now he found it lank, dirty gray in the light. In Montana, John thought, Roark's mind would be compared unfavorably to a rockpile. But here in the city no one questioned him. "The accounts are fine," John said.

Roark held forth, pounding his contorted hand on his thigh.

John had hoped time with Roark would be an unforeseen benefit.

More and more he disliked these meetings.

JUAN CARLOS'S FATHER, the small-time real estate magnate in Billings, Montana, not only raped his son but secretly kept women in other towns. His massive ego made him a giant but distant figure. When Juan Carlos was fourteen, his father brazenly disgraced the family in a short-lived affair with a nineteen-year-old high school dropout. In those days, Juan Carlos took his father's prized stiletto switchblade, a possession his father kept in Juan Carlos's mother's lingerie drawer—a blade given by Juan Carlos's father's father, the long-haul truck driver ten years dead who'd bragged about beating on women.

Juan Carlos's mother was from a town called Shepherd, twenty miles east of Billings. Her Danish White family never accepted her marriage to Juan Carlos's father and she birthed the six boys plus Juan Carlos to spite them. In sixth grade, Juan Carlos wore two pairs of tube socks to school, folding them down to form a thick band over his ankle. He slid the black handle of the blade into the slot between his ankle and his Achilles where it stayed firm and hidden under his pantleg and he could feel its rigid line and think of grabbing it if he needed to. He wore the socks when he slept too, the knife where he liked it, and he almost felt safe. The week his father's affair became public, Juan's mother bought him a pair of designer jeans by Armani Adolfo, and despite his pure hatred for his father, Juan Carlos borrowed his father's bravado.

WHAT PEOPLE borrowed varied. Money and drugs. Clothes and swagger. But all, when enraged, borrowed the landslide in their fathers' eyes, the sorrow their mothers harbored—and absence and violence entered the blood like a new deficit, impenetrable, monstrous, increasing.

When Juan Carlos returned home at 3 a.m. on a hot night in July, his wife sat up in bed. He was drunk, standing over her. Mary Irene, he thought, a weird name for any era. Irene her great-grandmother's name. They'd been married again nearly three years now. Their daughter Ana Luz was two years old. Mary Irene watched Juan Carlos remove the purple boa and white scarf near the armoire, fold them, kiss them, and place them neatly in his own underwear drawer. Physically, he was strong and fluid, she a light and supple woman. At thirty-three, perhaps more beautiful than she'd ever been. Those items were hers once. His cologne stunk like musk. In a quiet voice she said aloud what she'd been thinking for more than a year. "You're gay." She didn't have time for this. At Boeing her boss made her work sixty hours a week. She needed sleep. Juan Carlos turned, walked to the bed, and slapped her face so hard he left the imprint of his hand like a birthmark on her jaw.

AFTER SLAPPING his wife, Juan Carlos borrowed a bed to sleep on at his friend Paulo's house.

He was afraid he might kill her.

He called his mother and told her he was leaving Mary Irene.

"Juan Carlos," she said. "Go back to her right now. Your wife needs you. Mary Irene needs you."

"I won't," he said, and not wanting to hang up, he did.

That night Juan Carlos undid the knot and took the white silk scarf delicately from around his own neck, handed it to Paulo, watched Paulo tie the scarf tightly around Juan Carlos's left wrist and proceeded to be swept into his embrace. Paulo with a lean perfect chest. Born in Bogotá, Colombia. Fear in Juan Carlos's eyes, the heart felt immortal. The next evening at home again he lied to Mary Irene. There was no need to conceal anything anymore. It was Saturday night. He had never liked her sex. No, he remembered distinctly, he had liked it a great deal, even loved it. Tonight she demanded it. No, he decided, he'd never really loved her. She approached and tried to unbutton his jeans.

"No," he said, but she kept on. He wasn't going to slap her anymore. He put his hands on her and moved her away from him. She didn't cry.

"It's someone else," she said.

"Whatever," he said.

In the morning over breakfast she berated him. She'd gotten her boss to agree to the day off but a day was nothing. She was more tired than ever. Their daughter Ana Luz sat in the high chair. At the end of the argument Mary Irene said, "Admit it, Juan." Then she lifted the plastic table top from Ana Luz's high chair and threw it at him in a swift two-handed motion, bouncing it off the side of his head, making his hair look silly. He watched her pull Ana Luz from the chair and clutch her to her chest, the child screaming. His wife's face was blotchy. He rose, approached her, and tore Ana Luz from her arms. He left the house and took the baby with him to Mass at Our Lady of Fatima. When he returned home his wife was seated with her hands face down on the kitchen table.

His head felt bruised.

"I want a divorce," she said.
"Fine," he said.
She got the child. He got the house.

SHE STILL considered herself Mary Irene Higashi, though she'd married twice and taken his last name, de la Cruz. She was Shinto through her father, Roman Catholic through her mother. Japanese Polish or Polish Japanese. American. During World War II priests and civilians of both sides of her family were genocided: in Poland before the stone facade in Bydgoszcz's Old Market Square, and in Japan in the paper and timber homes of Nagasaki. She couldn't abide a man's disharmony. Still she told herself she loved men despite themselves. Her cold father. Her pugnacious husband.

A month before he left, mentioning the president to her, Juan Carlos had shouted, beating his words into the air like an eagle climbing before he put anger into their sex and she absorbed him and his emotion.

"Yes," she agreed, the president's wall was infuriating.

But what did Juan Carlos do about it? she questioned. What had he ever done?

She looked White; she could pass, though in World War II, the American branch of her family had been forced from their homes in Oregon into internment at Tule Lake just south of Klamath Falls in Northern California. Of Juan Carlos's Mexican American friends, usually outside the business world, sometimes in the drama community or in the meeting spots downtown, the undocumented had to be hypervigilant against deportation. They were in hiding everywhere they went. To her his ignoring them and the militarism they faced, the essentialism and hypocrite doctrines, the big White man's male gaze, was worse than him degrading her. He disgraced his own blood. He disgraced himself.

In those days she never fully recognized how her disapproval emasculated him, castrating the center of his existence. She was blind to it, though it had entombed her own sex daily and set him alight against her. Even so, his choices were his own, and for many of them, disingenuous, self-indulgent, he suffered.

When she was honest, she didn't love men anymore.

She wanted to like them, but who could like them? Their bones were too big, they were too hairy, and they often smelled bad. They spread their legs on airplanes. Took the armrest. Talked too much. They didn't know what a good father was, or a good husband.

She and Juan had attended a weekend at the Gottman Institute to work on it but now she knew even then he'd been undercutting the marriage. The facts were brutal. Eighty percent of more masculine-oriented people who divorced shared a single characteristic: They didn't receive the influence of the feminine. They stonewalled the beloved. Conversely, 80 percent of more feminine-oriented people who divorced held contempt for the masculine. They hated the beloved.

She still didn't think she hated him. But ask him, and he felt hated.

The passage between lies and the truth was harrowing.

She and he would split the money, the holdings, the child.

She had her mother's faith.

Of God the old refrain rang out, dark is his path on the wings of the storm.

JUAN CARLOS HAD a mind at odds with life.

He recognized this but tried to think positive anyway.

HIS FAMILY LINE rose from humble beginnings.
He had desperation in his blood.
He made money hand over fist.
He didn't want his marriage. He wanted Paulo.

THE CULT OF THE COUPLE existed but not everyone wanted coupleship, he reasoned.

Women and men loved other women, other men, other couples, other forms.

The demise of intimacy settled like a cancer in the bones.

But from the ashes, he thought, some found solace.

He doubted the verity of true affection, adoration, deep feeling, or a life completely devoted to another, but against all odds some rose anyway, he thought, their bodies transcendent in flame.

PAULO MEDICI, Juan Carlos's lover, never trusted Juan Carlos as much as Juan Carlos wanted him to.

They shared travel as a unifying function, building memories in Italy, Spain, and the long open valleys of Colombia below the mountains near Cali.

"I'm here," Juan Carlos whispered, but Paulo doubted.

Why should I trust him if he left Mary Irene for me?

Will Juan Carlos ever love me as I wish to be loved?

Regardless, Paulo told himself he'd love Juan Carlos with a love that couldn't be killed. Paulo was Colombian American, almost hairless, crisp and clean, and made of sincere gentleness rather than the conflictual spirit so common to his own family.

AS MUCH AS possible Juan Carlos chose not to think of Mary Irene. Instead, he tried to think only of their daughter, Ana Luz.

EVEN IN THE first year with Paulo, Juan Carlos was increasingly unfaithful and finally, he left Paulo. He moved then from the loose cocaine-induced trance of the bathrooms in Seattle's gay bar scene to seducing his own young college-aged bright boys and finally to an exotic sex flare with such a yearnful arc he felt shot from a gun. And depressed beyond reason. He overreached twice on speed and whiskey, vomiting all the contents of his stomach. After a year this way he told himself to calm down, and met Paulo again with a desire to be less self-centered, more loving, less prone to self-harm and more interested in living.

He wanted to see Paulo as the one he'd give himself to forever.

Holding hands, they stood on the rim of the Needle, secluded but surrounded by people. "Paulo. You know it's difficult for me to say this outright, but I want you to know I love you."

For Paulo the vibration of being visible to a single beloved but invisible to the strangers around them was like a chrysalis. He rose to where he floated over the city, above the low-hanging clouds, witnessing the sky without rain. Below him the clouds intermingled like smoke among the trees, a stillness through the curves and crests of urban sprawl.

He'd so wanted to hear those words from Juan Carlos, but he steadied himself. "You've been lying to yourself, Juan Carlos. I don't trust you. When you loved me back in the beginning I wanted to be your husband. I didn't want to be an acquaintance, or even a partner. I longed to be called your husband. Now I don't. I've had mine on the side too. I'm not above you. But I'm afraid."

"Of what?" Juan Carlos said, and quieter, "Of me?"

"Yes," Paulo said, "of you and me together." He took Juan Carlos's arm and placed it around his own shoulders. "We haven't proven ourselves." He felt so bastardized when people disrobed and discarded him. His puff-faced father, blank and unaware, hedonistic to a fault. The man's breath rancid with cigarette smoke. His unconscious mother. Hateful, and paradoxically trying to placate Paulo now when before she'd slaughtered him with her scapegoating and the fortune she'd paid to try to "fix" him. Her own husband as gay as Christmas.

"And should I be afraid of you?" Juan Carlos said.

He enfolded Paulo, holding him in a tight embrace.

"Certainly," Paulo said. "My lack of any real resistance is a problem, for you as much as me. You'll run me over again. I have no force. I'm like my mom. I lay down. You don't respect me. Then you leave me."

"I do respect you," Juan Carlos said.

"I don't know that we've ever really loved each other," Paulo said.

"But we'll try," Juan Carlos said. "I want to be with you. No one else."

He admitted to himself Mary Irene had loved him, and often very well.

"But lack of love wrecked your family, didn't it?" Paulo asked plaintively. "You left your wife. Deserted your daughter. She doesn't have a father anymore, Juan Carlos. She has an excuse for a gay man, a male tramp, drug-addicted, often depressed. Unknowable. You can't call that love."

"I don't," Juan Carlos said in a low voice.

"Thank you," Paulo said.

"You're too critical," Juan Carlos said.

Paulo started crying.

"I always make you cry," Juan Carlos said.

"I cry," Paulo said.

Juan Carlos kissed his tears and leaned in.

"I'm a failure," Juan Carlos said. "I know I am. A bastard to my wife, a fool to my daughter. I've hated my life. No fault of theirs. I'm terrible to live with. Mary Irene knows. You know. I know. I love my daughter. I hope you know that too."

"I do," Paulo said.

"But I can't go back," Juan Carlos said. "I'm not that man. I'm not sure Mary Irene will ever forgive me. But my daughter. I hope she will. I'd give anything for her."

"I believe you believe that," Paulo said, "but you don't show it. Your words are like bad air. You need some integrity. Or you'll suffocate us, and her."

"I'm afraid too, Paulo."

"I know," Paulo said. "But I want you to be decent. To me, but to Mary Irene and your daughter too."

"Mary Irene?"

"Yes," Paulo said.

Juan Carlos was silent.

"I can't, Paulo. You know that."

"You can," Paulo said, touching Juan Carlos's cheek.

"Though neither of us are in any condition to be married," Juan Carlos said, "I still want to marry you."

"I'll think about it," Paulo said.

From their vista on the Needle the city coursed beneath them for miles.

ROARK KNEW relatively nothing of Juan Carlos, Mary Irene, and Paulo. He pocketed percentages from the loans John Sender processed, but his mind was elsewhere.

He spent his days atop the skyscrapers of American capitalist ingenuity.

He spent evenings brewing vengeance for Aurora American Horse.

In between he led ARC's western region, working on ways to dismantle governmental control and the welfare state by sowing fear, anguish, and paranoia. Aurora's people should feel lucky to be alive, he thought, especially considering how they sucked America dry with their age-old government funding. To the victors go the spoils. If you were conquered, you shouldn't cry. Take it straight, or move to another country.

He'd received the names and numbers of the leaders of ARC's neo-Nazi cells implanted in the Seattle Police Department. The etymology of "Aryan" meant "noble," or "noble one," and he couldn't think of anyone more noble than him.

For a long time now, a singular image took precedence. Not just a skyscraper, but the heroic pattern, the blueprints of Frank Lloyd Wright's vision for the tallest skyscraper in the world. Sixty-five years ago such a vision had seemed fantastical. Today it was within reach. He'd call it Sky City. Roark owned large swaths of Seattle, Portland, San Francisco, LA, Chicago, New York. His holdings overseas kept pace. He'd be the primary stakeholder. In his waking dream he stood atop the structure in an office with no bend, no wind shear, no movement at all even on its top floor a mile above Seattle.

Arms crossed, he'd take a wide stance and behold the world below.

PAULO AND JUAN CARLOS made a pact to love each other again. Against wisdom. Against their own misgivings. The divorce from Mary Irene, after a long battle over belongings, money, properties, custody, and countless affronts to her personal dignity, was settled quickly with Juan Carlos's new mindset, and finalized shortly after his meeting with Paulo at the Space Needle.

On a nondescript day in September, Juan Carlos entered the elite condominium he'd leased for Paulo in Escala, the luxury tower in the downtown corridor on the corner of Fourth and Virginia.

"I ended it today," he said.

"Ended what?" Paulo asked.

"The divorce fight," Juan Carlos answered.

"How?" Paulo said, standing at the cutting board where he diced asparagus spears and swept the cuts into a sauce bowl of light butter and parmesan. The condo windows were wall to wall, floor to ceiling, showing the cityscape and the sky on a 270-degree radius. Belltown stepped into Seattle below, a work of art and industrial sightlines cascading through the shopping district down to Pike's Place along Pioneer Square and up through the foothills toward the branched fusion of the freeways.

"I gave her everything she asked for, and then more than she asked."

"Mary Irene?"

"Yes."

"So you gave Ana Luz all she'll ever need too?"

"Yes."

Paulo set the sauce pan down and walked to him. He kissed him. "You are the man I hoped you would be."

Juan Carlos stared at Paulo, feeling both surprise and elation. "We've just given away everything I had behind me," Juan Carlos said, "and a portion of what's to come."

"You've given away money," said Paulo. "But even better, you've increased love. Your heart is free."

Paulo went back to the kitchen and drew fluted crystal glasses from the cabinet, filling them with champagne.

"To Mary Irene," Paulo said.

"Yes," Juan Carlos agreed, "and to Ana Luz."

They touched glasses.

"Always," Paulo said.

When he and Paulo went to bed that night they listened to the live rendition of George Michael and Elton John's "Don't Let the Sun Go Down on Me" on repeat.

After turning the music off they held each other until they slept.

MARY IRENE HIGASHI knew little of Paulo and Juan Carlos's decision-making. She was grateful Juan Carlos had become responsive to the work of raising their daughter. Also, she was starting to overcome her past, the massive downdraft in her heart over the loss of Juan Carlos, and how she'd been raped by a stranger and lost the child, a boy she'd named Carlito. She loved knowing her daughter, Ana Luz, was Polish, Japanese, Mexican, Danish, and American. She asked heaven to love Carlito as she did, and asked Carlito to guide her and watch over her and Ana Luz.

She'd been teaching Ana Luz her Polish and Japanese roots.

She hoped Juan Carlos would impart wisdom from his Mexican legacy too.

What Mary Irene knew of her family came through her grandmothers. The way this arrived was in fragments of eventual coherence, the way birds emerge and return individually to the same tree before erupting together into the air. Her grandmother on her father's side had overwhelmed her from their first meeting when she was twelve. He'd brought her from Japan without English for what he termed "a better life." She'd been silent on most things, but on the war and Nagasaki she'd been sealed as if buried beneath a mountain. She had power nonetheless, great power, carried lament in her body always, and cycled between dark-hearted and protective. She seldom spoke, and never wept, though her father could break down just thinking of what his mother had endured. Through all this, he'd been very cold with Mary Irene, likely not meant to be a father, she thought. He knew little of fathering and lacked the desire to know. Before her grandmother died, just a year ago, she'd called Mary Irene home to New Jersey, asking her and her father to sit together at her bedside. As she spoke, Mary Irene's father translated saying she couldn't bear the past, but she wanted Mary Irene to know. Her father looked on, holding Mary Irene's hand along with his mother's, his face wet with tears. On the floor, Ana Luz fit wooden blocks of varied shapes into a board of like-made holes.

The world is about power, Mary Irene thought, when it should be about love.

The explosion in Nagasaki generated heat comparable to the interior of the sun. Temperatures in excess of six thousand degrees centigrade incinerated people and instantly ignited the air. Even a mile or two from the epicenter the bodies were charred, but closer to the flash point thermal radiation and penetrating nuclear radiation from gamma rays and neutrons resulted in vaporization.

MARY IRENE had been a dancer and when she was a dancer she'd given herself to beauty. Now she felt compelled to preserve her grandmother's legacy of survival. Mary Irene remembered how Juan Carlos touched the hair at the back of her neck and traced the line of her collarbones with his fingertips. If I'd have grasped life at its depths, she thought, I might have loved him more.

She didn't question the reality of evil, or the need for a response, but the cynical bitterness bent also wasn't for her. She believed good to be ever present, if elusive. Similarly, she held the grace of the dancer immortal. Her grandmother, too, had danced through fire.

Ana Luz climbed into her great-grandmother's bed and fell asleep in her arms.

AT LUNCH, in the downtown branch of the Seattle Public Library John Sender had gone to pick out two books his favorite business philosophy professor from Seattle U. had recommended to him in a recent email: Adam Smith's *The Wealth of Nations*, and Edward Gibbons's *The Decline and Fall of the Roman Empire*. He carried both books in his hand when he saw Mary Irene reading at a table near the southwest windows. He veered in her direction and she paused, looking up as he approached.

"I saw you and thought I'd come say hi," he said.

"Kind of you."

"I hope all is well with Juan Carlos and the house."

"Very well," she lied. She'd never been one to air faults.

"Good to hear. What are you reading?"

"A history of Nagasaki," she said plainly.

He didn't know what to make of that. "Oh, I'd better let you go then."

"Thank you," she said. "My great-grandmother came through it all."

She didn't know why she said that, and felt ashamed.

He smiled. He thought he shouldn't have. They shook hands.

He looked at his books, at her.

On the way to the door he thought, I don't know people.

JOHN'S MOST RECENT foray with Roark was an uncomfortable maneuver that ended up in John meeting him at a strip club, Roark drunk and pontificating his rationalist philosophy again.

"I'm an avenging angel," Roark said. "By the way, do you ever see Elias American Horse and that slut wife of his?"

The language shook John.

Bodies moved overhead in raw oblivion.

"What?" he yelled above the noise.

Roark hit John's chest with the heavy right hand.

"Do you ever see that slut Aurora American Horse?"

John didn't say anything. The man was a fool.

"Answer!" Roark said, gripping John's jaw in the vise of his good hand.

John slapped the hand down, saying, "Don't ever touch me again."

"That's better," Roark shouted, and cackled as he asked John for a five. "And what of your honey, Samantha? She's got good color."

"Careful," John warned, and took out his wallet.

The man was drunk.

He handed Roark the note.

"Your daughters have to be near old enough for the meat market by now."

Roark watched John's face and laughed harder as he placed the five in the back right line of the G-string arcing over the hip bone of a young White woman dancing on his lap. "That's what I like about myself, John," he said, "the purity of my ruthlessness." He gripped her rib. "They're all suckers. Losers. Users. The lesser-thans who want what only the great achieve."

"Don't," the woman said, trying to move his hand off her ribcage.

"Touch the hell I want!" he bellowed, shoving her forward. His eye hardened as she danced to another table. "Those who think they suffer disgust me. The so-called martyrs. The self-proclaimed victims. The Me-Too-ers. The Black Lifers. The essence of a true woman is hero worship—the desire to look up to a man. But not like you may think, John. Not dependence, obedience, or anything inferior. Rather, intense admiration. Adulation. The true woman wants a man with spine, John. Backbone. Better keep hold of your Samantha. She won't like your spineless hide forever. Hero worship is a demanding virtue: a woman has to be worthy of it, intellectually and morally. As a human being she has to be his equal, then the object of her worship is specifically his masculinity, not any human virtue she might lack."

John couldn't wait for the night to end.

"Get rid of the gloom and doom, John. I own ninety cars, why would I care about you? Me and the Centenary Edition Aston Martin Vanquish I rode in on. Only a hundred ever made. 6.0-Litre V12. Graduated Skyfall Silver finish. Solid sterling silver still plaques and wing badges. Obsidian black leather interior. Two Valkyries at home too, worth twenty times as much. You want to know the number? I'll tell you. The Valkyrie's are three million dollars each. 1160 horsepower hybrid naturally-aspirated V12 with F1 powertrain tech, each seat designed through 3D scanning specifically for my body shape, 0 to 60 from a standstill in 2.6 seconds, a.k.a. the AM-RB 001, a.k.a. the Nebula. Fastest street-legal car in the world but you wouldn't know anything about that because you're small change. In fact, last year when I was asked in a court of law to state my name and occupation I said, 'Roark Rosenbaum Freeman, the world's greatest businessman.' You might ask why I said that, John."

"Why?"

"Because I was under oath, John, that's why."

John wondered what kind of woman could marry Roark. Likely none, but he knew that line of reasoning to be false. The hero worshippers exist. He thought of Samantha who he considered his equal. He'd never want her to worship him, though he tended to desire to worship her.

He felt sick.

UNDER HIS NEW perhaps spiritual dispensation Juan Carlos de la Cruz's business boomed into the many millions. He secured deals on large scale multi-year economic development projects downtown and watched the money appear in the ether like a mantle of gold. Of real import to Paulo and himself, he became present to his daughter, Ana Luz. Available and steady. He had kind eyes, she told him.

He also, slowly, grew more graceful with Mary Irene.

She seemed to have forgiven him.

He'd gained some life. Still, he'd been severely harmed, and forgiveness or not, lifting himself out of the pit proved racking. The vacuum at the base of it could be bottomless.

He was back in his favorite leather chair, black with gold accents, set in the corner where the windows met. The ocean and rain were of one color, the city oblique and metallic. He had done well for quite some time, only having sex with Paulo, from tender and straightforward to uniquely flamboyant. On occasion they had tired mundane sex. He kept secret his ongoing partiality, from a boy, for pornographic bondage fantasy that escalated with the erosion of the goodness he felt in himself and the world around him. He knew Paulo held a punitive insight into this progression, tending to pepper Juan Carlos with condescension when discovered. In the months since they married they both gave their whole heart. They'd been open in this regard, Paulo almost invariably receiving Juan Carlos, the pitch and catch Juan Carlos imagined all couples went through. Not unlike the impossibility of getting Mary Irene to pitch some, she eventually had no engine, both her and Paulo preferred to be the passenger when it came to sex. Except during Mary Irene's last gasps when she'd thrown herself at him shamelessly. But by then he was already gone.

Under such conditions he shut himself off from the beloved.

And opened an underworld of excitement that now as he aged seemed to flash only for a moment before expiring. He generally pushed anyway, kept dying, kept dreading himself and all around him. Even masturbation became work. Inversely, with Mary Irene and Paulo, he'd been a nonstarter emotionally, basically from the outset. He could make the first jump; he had cables that hooked into them and brought most anything to life when he wanted to. His looks and voice, his stage play, his laughter a zest that gave delight, and though acting was his first in college, he hadn't lost his dancer's body that made his partners stare on occasion in awe at his nudity. He pushed relationships over the initial threshold with immediacy but when life settled in he seemed to go lifeless emotionally. The injury he inflicted on those he loved obliterated them.

Yes he'd done better with Ana Luz, openly caring for her now rather than numbly burning his allotment of relational currency in hate for Mary Irene. In turn, this had serendipitously increased his care for Paulo. But the reflection of Mary Irene in Paulo mesmerized him: the same people in different bodies. Or at least the same undertow.

In his right hand he rolled a glass of fine cognac.

Paulo was in bed.

It was night.

Juan got up to go. It was that simple. But first he walked to the kitchen and through it toward their bedroom, hearing the faint hum of forced air as the heater ticked on. He felt numb seeing the gloss of industrial light on the black hardwood floor, the modern white couches in the master bedroom and the small slant of chrome legs, the unused accoutrement of a drafting table like a blade in the corner of the room.

He placed his hands outspread on the bedroom window, meeting the glass with his face, staring into the necklace of light along the waterfront north. He missed Mary Irene, and he missed Paulo, questioning if such dualism was possible. Paulo was asleep behind him, breathing softly under the covers, dreamless and unknowing. Love is the invincible. But there was also death, entombing him from a child to now.

He walked to the master closet, dressed silently, and walked from the room, staring at Paulo's sleeping form. He entered the hall, pressed the down button, and emerged from the elevator on the ground floor.

He walked through the revolving door and crossed the street moving south.

A mist in the air covered him.

Paulo knew Juan Carlos's abuse, how he'd been abused, and how he abused. It wasn't a reach for either of them to think the whole world was abused. If anything, they'd both be hard-pressed to convince themselves otherwise.

Three blocks on, Juan Carlos picked up the pace, almost jogging. He felt heavy, but kept on until he entered the doors of The Gull at 2 a.m. near the water. The men hailed him as he entered and in a matter of minutes he was in the bathroom blowing a silver-haired Google executive. You couldn't avoid techno, better to give than to receive. Even the music jolted electronically. What happened to the days of punk when every song was anarchy? The music of self-hatred only goes so far though, he thought. Seattle. City of a million pulses of light. Twitch and counter twitch. Lyft. eBay. Even HBO, ESPN, and Hulu had a major presence. But these were tiny children compared to the behemoths: Microsoft, Amazon, Facebook, Google. When it was over Juan Carlos went out and took the arm of a young sleek-bodied graphic artist from Burien with lavender hair, leading him back to the bathroom.

The stalls were small private rooms and neatly kept, with French shuttered doors that locked. The speakers in the ceiling were loud. Juan Carlos didn't want to pitch anymore. He nearly forced the young man to take him, and so the man did, joyfully, leaving him with laughter and a smoke when it was done. Pulling his pants back up, Juan Carlos sat on the closed lid of the toilet with his face in his hands. He wasn't himself again for a long while and when he left the building he walked to the water wanting to kill himself.

At one point during the years his dad penetrated him Juan Carlos ate rat poison. Why couldn't a man just kill himself when he wanted to? He could, he reasoned, if he had the means. He kept walking until he passed below the Alaska Way Viaduct and stood in an open gap watching the piers. Seeing the blackened tar of the beams, the water in oily light, he found the night more alive and richly colored than the day. His skull felt dull from vodka and mushrooms. He had no gun or knife, nothing with enough force to split him from himself. He wanted to spill down through the asphalt and concrete into the earth and water. He had no will to climb and fly headfirst into the void. He wanted to die quietly. Even now, with the new disease thresholds, transmitted disease was like a monster in the dark, restrained but pacing. Rock 'n' roll culture, drug culture, gay culture for so long meant high-risk culture. Most often he'd thrown himself into high risk. He just wanted to be without pain. He didn't have his cell phone. He wouldn't leave a final message anyway.

His life of real estate deals and business intrigue, press and bottleneck, digital or face to face, ladder after ladder of ascent, covered him in chains.

Lack of love crushed him. He had no vigor to bear it up anymore.

He sat down and leaned his head against an enormous concrete pillar. His clothes were damp. The foundations of the Viaduct were dug nearly three hundred feet below ground where harder soil locked the girders in. Before long the Viaduct would disappear, the state's plan already ratified, but now the structure rose four stories overhead: a conduit ferrying people in machines of metal and light. The blank drone of cars intermittent but steady touched his mind and put him to sleep.

When he woke the road above teemed in the dark and he wondered at the passengers, their faces lit by dull green or red light. Encased in rain-covered glass they entered the city as if being delivered from death to greater death.

He walked north to the Alexis Hotel and took a cab home.

He took his shoes off in the elevator, moved slowly upward with his head pressed to the wall, walked the hall silently, thumb-coded the door and closed it softly behind him. Returning finally to the bedroom where Paulo slept he saw how his beloved lay like an angel in white, the sheets shrouding the torso, the face graceful and ablaze with sleep. He turned and entered the closet and hung up his clothes.

He put on silk pajamas and slid in beside Paulo without disturbance.

They faced one another, Paulo's hushed breathing a rhythm he needed. He leaned forward and kissed Paulo, tasting the almond oil from dinner. He lay back on his pillow, the pain like a hammer in his head.

He touched his hand to Paulo's hand.

IN THE MORNING, Juan Carlos didn't tell Paulo, and Paulo never asked.

They continued on as they had, with Paulo either feigning or unconsciously claiming ignorance, and Juan Carlos fearing the next slide would end them altogether.

He redoubled his efforts, trying wholeheartedly, as much as he'd given himself to anything in his life, and the effort did not go unnoticed.

"Why are you so nice?" Paulo asked from the kitchen a month later.

The lemon and shrimp Paulo cooked in the skillet drew Juan Carlos's eyes, the motion of Paulo's arm signifying a beauty he'd lost, reclaimed, still desired, and feared.

"Because I love you," Juan Carlos said, ashamed. He came near, putting his hand on Paulo's shoulder, then removing it before cutting the onion bulbs Paulo set out. To smile with the eyes and voice, Juan Carlos noted, even as the heart recoils, is to be unknown. He needed to tell Paulo everything: how he'd punished their love again.

But he didn't tell Paulo, he merely served more, hoping acts of love could overlay or replace secrets. He didn't want to admit how much disdain he held for their beloved relationship, and in effect, though it hurt Juan Carlos terribly, disdain for Paulo. He found himself at the same crossroads. Like a dog returns to its vomit. The crossroads was not Paulo or Mary Irene but himself.

"You're too good to me," Paulo said.

"It's you who's good," Juan Carlos said. "not me." He used the blade edge and swept the diced onion bulbs from the cutting board into his hand and into the skillet.

"You feel like heaven," Paulo said.

"Because I'm so happy with you, Paulo."

Out the window the city at dusk was magenta, white construction cranes like sentinels over great bodies of water, the streets black and wet with rain.

VERY FEW MADE beauty of turbulence, Juan Carlos told himself, except perhaps van Gogh, the painter he'd loved from a boy. In van Gogh, suffering and mystery were one. Suffering: to bear from below. Vincent was an angel of movement and light.

I need you now Vincent, Juan Carlos thought.

He'd painted God from the asylum, the starry night from insanity.

"Lift me from the dark," he whispered. "Help me."

The next day and the days thereafter, Juan Carlos propped up his love for Paulo further, meanwhile taking lunches on Capitol Hill in the Seattle Eagle or the Pony, Wildrose or Diesel. He didn't care if it was upscale or dive. He skulked into each one to relieve himself, knowing the effect was deadly.

For Paulo's birthday he surprised him with a Pharaoh Hound shipped from Malta.

"WHAT IS IT?" Paulo questioned.

"I'm getting old," Juan Carlos said. They were in bed after dinner.

Juan Carlos couldn't perform.

Paulo waved a hand. "You're not old. Just tired."

"Work is too much," Juan Carlos said, keeping his eyes from Paulo's.

"Maybe I'm too fat," Paulo said, though he was slender as a gazelle. "Maybe I'm not your type anymore."

Juan Carlos touched Paulo's jaw with his fingertips and stared into Paulo's face. "You're my type."

The Pharaoh Hound sat closemouthed on a velvet bed near the window, an ancient angularity in the body and face. Paulo lay his head on Juan Carlos's chest. "It's your job," Paulo said. "You're bringing in so much money you can stand to rest some." He sat up, gestured to the dog, the apartment, the windows, then touched his index finger to the Bvlgari Serpenti Tubogas Juan Carlos had given him, an eighteen-karat rose gold coil watch that went from forearm to wrist, ending in a crisp diamond shaped window. The watch cost fifty thousand dollars.

"Money is nothing," Juan Carlos said.

"Love is all," Paulo answered.

That night after Paulo slept, Juan Carlos left and didn't return.

EARLY EVENING the next day, Juan Carlos happened upon John Sender at the Elliot Bay Book Company. People milled among the books, he thought, unaware of life.

He and John spoke over a low-set table on the left side of the room.

"I didn't know you were a reader, Juan Carlos. How's Mary Irene?"

"She's good I think. We split awhile back."

"Sorry to hear that."

"And you? How have you been?"

"Seem to be holding up just fine," John said, "thanks for asking."

Juan Carlos didn't want small talk. "What do you do for fun around here, John?"

Sender squinted.

When he didn't answer, Juan Carlos pressed forward. "What do people do for some fun at night?"

John knew Juan Carlos was propositioning him then, and he softened.

"Well," he said, "I'm not really in the know."

"Two well-dressed men like you and me can find out," Juan Carlos said. "We've done business together, John. We can do more."

"I hope we can."

Juan Carlos walked around the table so there was nothing between them. Looking into John's face. "We're all lonely," he said.

"Yes, Juan Carlos, we are, but I don't think I have in mind what you have in mind."

"What do I have in mind, John?"

"More than I can provide, my friend."

Juan Carlos waved his hand. "Don't worry about that. Come with me tonight. We'll have a grand time."

"You probably don't need me to say this, Juan Carlos, but I think it's a good idea for both of us to go home."

Juan Carlos shrugged before moving away. Over his shoulder he said, "Thanks, John," and kept on, past the registers, to the front door. In a better mind he might have turned and seen John differently. Instead he zipped up his Gucci jacket, pointed his chest forward, and didn't look back.

As Juan Carlos walked down the stairs into the street John caught a glimpse of his body receding in the darkness lit by streetlamps. John hoped he'd done right by him but felt ashamed thinking he might have wounded him.

Juan Carlos walked south.

Home was in the opposite direction.

MARY IRENE HIGASHI, formerly Mary Irene de la Cruz, knew her former husband Juan Carlos didn't love her anymore.

She didn't love him anymore either.

But she still cried sometimes thinking of what they might have been.

AS JUAN CARLOS WALKED to the waterfront he imagined lights strung like pearls from here to Canada. The buildings went black into the sky, windows glossy or dimly lit. He could be borne by concrete as much as water. A shroud of jagged horse in his mind.

He'd tried enough. He wasn't going to try anymore.

At The Gull he degraded himself until 4 a.m. Afterward, he went to the alley behind the establishment and ended up clutching at the few men there, paying exorbitantly for nothing, a kiss or fondle that went nowhere. He slept against the wall until the rain woke him, a dull light among gray buildings covered by clouds.

He moved under an overhang in the alley a few blocks further north and curled his jacket under his head, a satin bomber embroidered in light blue with sequin detailing and metallic thread, raglan sleeves, zip closure, welt pockets. A coat fully lined in pink silk that cost him eight grand.

He slept into the afternoon.

When he woke he rose and beat his coat into shape. Capturing rain from the corner overhang, he ran his hands through his hair and wiped them on his pants. He brushed his teeth with a finger. There was still a hint of cologne to him. He searched his wallet. He hadn't been rolled, though he kept a thick clip of cash and a motherlode of exclusive cards—the Dubai First Royale, the Eurasian Diamond, the Centurion, the Octave Black. He also carried a single photo of his daughter. Her face framed by black curls, her brown skin, and cupid bow lips. Ana Luz was delicate. He felt she deserved a real father.

In the photo she was in his arms, gazing into his face.

She trusted him.

He took the photo from his wallet and placed it in his shirt pocket.

He ate dinner at El Jardin Verde on the twenty-third floor of the Cosmopolitan.

At his table by the window he set the photo of his daughter on white linen above a gold-leaf charger and Tiffany Bone China, cow bone ash in the ceramic. The food was tasteless. His stomach didn't sit well. His mind felt bruised. He found it challenging to sit at the table and wake up.

Taking a cab to Capitol Hill, he browsed Elliot Bay bookstore one more time, moving with effort among the stacks, hoping to see someone he knew.

He sat in the café for an hour and drank hot tea with sugar. He didn't know why. The last customer to emerge before closing, he didn't look at the books he bought and set them in a neat stack in a doorway a block from the store, leaving them there. He paused beneath a high industrial streetlamp, took two thousand in century notes from his wallet, and placed it in a hidden zip pocket in the hem of his shirt. On coke, whiskey, and not a little acid he stayed awake for six days, napping on occasion. Laughing, crying, a body could survive. He entered the seventh day trembling and looking unrespectable.

He had money, but people questioned him.

"Are you okay?"

"Yes."

"You look strung out."

"No."

"No? You're higher than the stars."

"Thank you," he said. His eyes felt touched to live wire, current pulsing through him with such force he couldn't seem to keep still.

"Yes son, you're strung out," said a stout bartender with a crisp goatee and a soul patch.

Juan Carlos reached for the goatee, saying "I'm not your son," but the man took a step back.

"You will be," he said, "if you puke or flatline in here. Dead or not I'll take you out back and beat you good before I haul you back in and make you clean it up."

"You're such a nice boy," Juan Carlos said.

"Shut your mouth," the tender said, lifting a sawed-off pool cue from below the counter.

"Nice comb," Juan Carlos said, reaching out again, this time for the man's hair.

The tender slapped Juan Carlos's face so hard his neck felt torn.

"Time to go," the tender said as Juan Carlos righted himself.

The final word sounded foreign to Juan Carlos, like snow, or blow, but his legs managed to turn and lift, moving him back to the door and out into the night again. He felt alive now, the connections between here and there expanding and contracting as he entered the street. A man hollered at him and he tumbled forward, regaining his balance twice before reaching the far side where he stood hugging a tar treated telephone pole, his face pressed to wood and paper.

He pricked his cheekbone on a loose staple and envisioned blood bubbling, hives of bees beneath his skin, pods of spiders, maggots stewing flesh. His body seemed jointless and he imagined himself an Olympic sprinter. When someone asked him to get out of the street he pushed off from the pole and tried running up the sidewalk. It's my race, he thought, my race to win, as he fell face first into a parked sedan, denting the hood and knocking himself unconscious. Half on the curb half in the street he looked like a butterfly.

When he regained consciousness he had no conception of time. A great fire burns within me, he thought, staring upward. No one stops to warm themselves at it and passersby see only a wisp of smoke. The streetlamps hummed. His stomach turned inside out and he vomited. His face had blood on it, oozing from a wet gash over the bridge of his nose.

On all fours he paused, and finally stood. The light above was haloed in rain. He checked his belongings. Coat and slacks, shoes, wallet, shirt, everything still there, along with the money hidden in his shirt, and his daughter's likeness in his chest pocket.

I'm fine, he thought, and walked slowly, touching the brick of storefronts up to the corner where he entered another bar, went into the bathroom and cleaned himself up. Being almost decent in the dark he was able in broken Spanish to convince a young Latino boy from Guatemala to offer him a place for the night. The boy was gentle, transporting him to a trailer in southwest Seattle, a place with no electricity. The boy gave him the bed and took the couch, and Juan Carlos slept for two days.

HE WOKE at night not knowing where he was, and entered the streets again for meth, ecstasy, and coke in rotation, popping acid to bridge the downs, staying awake on varied drug cocktails for thirteen straight days with naps when needed. The money he pulled from the ATMs fluttered from his hands like leaves.

He didn't touch the two thousand.

He loved jargon. Meth P, amp, or amphetamine monikered his mouth, and every sweetness had an idiot basket of names: window pane, sugar cubes, and back breaker for acid; Elvis, white lightning, Superman, and ever, always, Lucy in the Sky with Diamonds for his pretty little LSD. When he went candy flipping, blending acid with ecstasy, it was troll or mossback, for acid and coke or heroin together, frisco and speedball, and for acid and crack, two-snort, pull, outer limits, sheet rocking. He hated jargon.

"I'll have acid," he said, or "cocaine please," or just "meth."

Keep it straight.

His brain a roman candle.

He hated crashing and convinced himself not to.

Accept what comes. Take death like a man. Whatever that meant. Stay high until you die. He'd wanted death so many times. All the way back to the years his father owned him.

He spoke directly to his father in his mind's eye. You've succeeded, he thought.

You've killed me.

In his death wish he saw only his own darkened head and body from behind, and this bothered him. Not his face or hands. Not his heart, though he believed firmly he had a sacred heart in his chest. Crowned by thorns. Made of chrome and fired red.

A gift from his grandmother Maria Celeste perhaps.

He saw a woman's wrinkled face, not unkind. It was her face, or Mary Irene's.

And he saw another face of similar eye color, with concern on her lips.

His Ana Luz.

PEOPLE WERE SHOT FORTH like stars, Juan Carlos thought. But when reality came their bones were ground to dust.

STILL HIGH, he slumped against the back wall of a strange bar. He believed good men lived truthfully, if fallen, and what rankled him were the most distressing questions.

If there is a God why do people suffer?

Why do they not only die but die terribly?

Why was I raped?

How come women hate me?

Why do I hate women?

FOURTEEN DAYS into his second up cycle, amped and dreaming of silt in his veins, he woke on his back in an alley. Late morning in a light drizzle, the sun behind clouds over the Olympics, he opened his eyes. At first he thought he was naked, but noted he had pants on. His body stank. He numbly searched the area, finding his shirt but nothing else. No coat, socks, shoes, or wallet. He gripped the shirt, feeling it through, exhaling to find the money safe along the hem. His feet were cold.

He came out on Governor Street, walked a long while and entered an old haunt barefoot, shirt in hand.

"Worse for wear?" the bartender asked, shirtless himself but for a leather vest that revealed a swollen belly ensconced in black hair.

"Yes I am," Juan Carlos mumbled. "Should I go?"

"Stay," the man said. "Your money's good, if you have any."

"I do."

"Happy to take it then," the man said, motioning with his nose. "Back room."

Juan Carlos could almost feel his veins arch wanting heroin.

He walked shoeless through the bar to an open doorway in the back that led to a hallway lit by a single bulb. The light was funky. Someone had painted it black. He thought of Ana Luz, and the photo. He rifled the shirt, clenching the chest pocket before turning everything inside out. The picture was gone. He went to his knees.

His grandmother called her child of God.

God, he asked openly, please help. He used his grandma's religion unabashedly now. He didn't know if he was asking for Ana Luz or himself. He balled the shirt, coiled himself around it on the floor and wrapped his head in his hands. His mind felt blank.

A fist knocked on his spine.

He stiffened, observing the sound, a persistent rapping as if on an oak door. Dull pain increased with each knock.

"Get up," he heard.

He didn't move.

"Get up, fool."

The voice kicked him in the ribs.

"Get up! You're blocking the way."

The voice gripped his hair and lifted him, propping him against the wall.

"Stay the hell up!" the voice said.

Juan Carlos kept his eyes closed, his hands over his face, bracing, but the body moved away. He trudged forward, opening a door at the end of the hall, his grip effortful on the round silver handle.

"Welcome," he heard. "Shut the door."

A gaunt man sat behind a simple metal desk. Juan Carlos thought he should know this man, his thin lips and mouthful of teeth. Gold-plated revolver on the desk near his right hand.

"It's been awhile," the man said. "Good to see you again."

"You see me?" Juan Carlos asked.

"You look blown to the moon and back."

"Blown," Juan Carlos said.

"How long you been up?" the man asked.

"Long," Juan Carlos said.

"You look cold," the man noted, directing him to put his shirt on.

Juan Carlos fumbled with his shirt, the task proving impossible until the man rose and helped him. Juan threaded his arms through the holes. The man buttoned the front for him.

"How much you need?" he asked.

"Two thousand," Juan Carlos said.

"Hand it to me."

"Do you know me?" Juan Carlos questioned.

"I do," the man said.

Juan Carlos pressed both hands at the hem of his shirt until the man lifted the hem, unloosing the inner seal and lifting the bills out, counting them on the way back to his seat.

"Twenty true," the man said, placing the bills in a bag on the floor next to his chair. He opened one of the desk drawers, sliding a tray of needles across the desk, plungers extended and full-juiced, tiny wax caps on the tips, an old length of surgical tubing, a thin plastic grocery bag neatly folded.

"Fresh cooked," the dealer said.

"Is it clean?" Juan Carlos asked.

"Who gives a shit," the man said, "look at the condition you're in."

Juan Carlos stared at the needles. Mexican horse. His own tar and honey dragon.

The man showed his lower teeth. "Nice and clean. No muck in the juice. Skimmed it already. Go ahead," he said. "Do your thing."

Juan Carlos started to roll the sleeve on his left arm.

"Not here," the man said. "Outside." He placed the needles and tubing in the bag, securing it with a double knot. "Don't lose this," he said.

"Penelope, come in here," he called over Juan Carlos's shoulder.

A large White man in a metallic gold tank and white tight pants entered.

"Help him," the dealer said. "He needs you to walk him out. Nothing rough. Just get him out back and let him go."

"Happy to," Penelope said, taking Juan Carlos's hand and the bag from the table, walking him down the hall into the metro beats of the bar. Penelope moved people aside until he and Juan Carlos went out the front door where he directed him around the corner and handed him the heroin, saying, "Take it easy."

"That's my horse." Juan Carlos shouted in the man's face. "My horse!"

"Liquid hell dust," Penelope said.

MOVING THROUGH the alley in search of something she'd lost but couldn't name, Alberta McBane overheard the exchange. Her husband in jail, her daughter was safe, but the opium was gone. She looked yearningly in the direction of the two men who talked of heroin. They didn't return her gaze.

JUAN CARLOS WENT EAST, bag in hand until he slogged uphill and positioned himself behind the Pioneer Club, sitting down in front of a green dumpster. He filled his veins and felt his skin flush. His tongue stuck to the top of his mouth. He pumped in all he could before the swings started him nodding in and out of consciousness. His arms and legs were heavy.

The roof of the world opened. The stars showered him with light.

He didn't feel the thud of his skull on the pavement.

He woke staring sideways at the asphalt, the bag near his left arm, the two needles inside still wax-tipped. A pool of bile reeked near his left ear. He sat up, tied and tapped his arm and sluiced the double flow, a final train that arced from his cerebellum through the occipital lobe to the trough of the corpus collosum where it shot free at the apex of the temporal lobe. This made him stand and he walked, experiencing a moment of frightening clarity as he entered the street experiencing auditory and visual hallucinations that terrified him, followed by his grandmother Maria Celeste who appeared to him as real as rain. She motioned with her hand to a woman beside her, the Queen of Heaven in whose eyes he felt all-encompassing love. He received this love with his whole being. His feet were raw but his heart was open as he noticed the cursive N of Nordstrom's above and to his right. He thought he might enter and buy himself a suit. Instead he projectile vomited, toppled sideways, and knocked his cheekbone on the concrete wall.

He landed in a heap near the front doors.

Five in the morning.

If not for his head bent to the side over his outstretched arm he might have drowned in his own fluids. The body overdosed and it was the continual jerking movement before he went still that caught the eye of a man mopping floors in the department store. Sober twenty years, night shift crew for nineteen, Oliver Chantos called 911, rushed outside and held Juan Carlos in his arms, praying over him until the ambulance arrived. A female paramedic leaped from the vehicle, touched Juan Carlos's neck, opened his closed eyes, and slammed first one naloxone needle and then another into his chest. A bigger, taller, male paramedic stood by. She put her ear to Juan Carlos's mouth. "He's breathing," she said. "Let's go."

The ambulance lit the city with sound.

A FEW MINUTES earlier, striding down Fifth Street on his way to work, John Sender cut across Pine before the light changed. To his right a few car lengths away he saw the back of a man prostrate on the sidewalk. The man was convulsing and for a moment John thought he recognized him but John needed to get to work early.

When someone emerged from Nordstrom's, he moved briskly on.

Walking fast he noticed through the latticework of the city a small hoard of birds pecking the lawn of a bank building two blocks from his and he was transported to the world of his father again, place of witness where blackbirds roosted in snags and thickets or among the vast tree canopies, sheltered by forest, sleeping close to one another near the trunk heat as they tucked their beaks into a wing. Because of his father he had knowledge of the wilderness. The birds placed their nares into the plumage where the air heated their bodies, warming them. Those on the edge of their number stayed awake, watching for predators.

Men and women were seen moving on the landscape too. In America, he thought, those who were so inclined had vision to find each other, and being so inclined, they also had velocity, projection, pretense—they had need. He provided loans for them. The birds, however, were provided for by God, he thought. In their innumerable sorties they ranged near and far because of hunger, or survival, or simply for how flight produced a lightness the body knew well.

FROM THE INITIAL night gone, Paulo searched every bar in the area. Endless calls with no answer. Text silence. His cell phone unlocatable. People said they'd seen Juan Carlos but after the first few days the reports grew thin and Paulo started to think Juan Carlos had finally left him completely, or worse, he feared him dead.

Sleeping during the day, Paulo searched at night, finding nothing. He hated the scene. Drink and drug like a fountain overflowing. So much wantonness. He bit his nails to the quick making them bleed.

After seven days he searched the hospitals, increasing his reach from the downtown corridor, north and south along the coast, and inland further east. He left his name and contacts, insurance information, and a photo of Juan Carlos along with Juan Carlos's birthdate. After two weeks his body began to hive, and imagining he'd lost Juan Carlos entirely he went to the King County morgue. At the front desk he pleaded, shedding more tears than he thought he should.

On day twenty-three, seated on the edge of his own bed, gray light etched on the window, he received a call from Pacific Medical Center on Beacon Hill. He fled the apartment, breakneck through the streets, gaining the hospital doors then directions to the room. The elevator's brushed steel chilled his hands. Emerging, he ran down the hall, cutting the H pattern to reach the south-facing wall and the door where he gathered himself and tousled his hair to be presentable. He took deep breaths and walked through the door to where Juan Carlos was wired in, tubes curving from his face and arms.

Juan Carlos dreamed he walked a broad flood plain among those who walked unseen beside him. People who hoped for healing. People who believed in love.

Blackbirds flew among them.

Paulo knelt at the bedside and held his hand, weeping inconsolably.

A male nurse entered. Large arms, bald head. Latino like Juan.

When Paulo calmed, the nurse questioned, "Is he yours?"

"He is," Paulo said.

"He's lucky," the nurse said, "and very strong. I've seen people die from far less than he put in his system."

"He's here," Paulo said, clutching Juan Carlos's hand in both of his. "I can't believe he's here."

"He's been awake on and off. He'll be glad to see you."

"I hope so," Paulo said.

"Coming back from where he's been he's got a long road ahead."

"You saved him," Paulo said. "You brought him back to me."

"Wasn't me," the nurse shrugged.

WHEN THE NURSE left, Paulo closed the door and crawled into the bed, positioning himself carefully alongside Juan Carlos.

When Juan Carlos woke his body shook and Paulo held him.

Juan Carlos's esophagus and stomach lining were distressed. He'd collapsed some of the vein work transporting his lifeblood. He felt gravely unwell, but his body was calm in Paulo's arms. "So much dark," he whispered.

"Shhh," Paulo said, putting his palm to Juan Carlos's jaw, "don't talk that way."

Juan Carlos had begged God to keep him in the world. He wanted to live. He wanted life. He knew his grandmother Maria Celeste and even Mary the mother of Christ had helped him. From a boy he'd been hated and despised.

He'd only ever wanted love.

With the warmth of Paulo beside him, sleep enveloped him.

WHEN HE WOKE, he tried to set his feet on steady ground.
His shins, during detox, felt tumbled by large rocks.
He vomited near constantly, accompanied by diarrhea.
He thought constantly of death.

PAULO NURSED JUAN CARLOS through detox in the hospital to a treatment facility in Edmonds called New Hope where Juan Carlos remained for ninety days, Paulo visiting on weekends, bringing baked goods. Juan Carlos's counselors recommended a long-term approach in which the bridge from New Hope would be a place in Kentucky called Vitalife.

"Don't use methadone or suboxone to lessen the blow," they said. "If you break free of addiction you do it on your own volition."

"And if I die?" he questioned.

"Then you die," they said. "But you're not going to die."

Juan Carlos wasn't sure. They'd just finished giving him the speech on opium deaths in America. Seventy thousand in one year alone. More than the American death toll in Vietnam.

In Kentucky he underwent a full year of treatment. He did grounds work involving snow removal in winter and mowing grass and tending flowers in summer, along with some minor mechanical work. Paulo called each night from Seattle, telling him he loved him. They talked of the future.

Juan Carlos had many dreams then, most of them featuring his grandmother Maria Celeste. She'd been a professor at Cal Berkeley in the fifties. She'd gone back to Mexico to serve at the Universidad Nacional Autónoma de México though the country's machista smothered women. She wanted to change Mexico. He woke with salt on his lips. She died too young. He was thankful for the time he had with her as a boy. She understood men and violence. Fighting and loving.

"El alma está en los ojos," she told him.

The soul is in the eyes.

He couldn't find his ancient family, but he knew he was from both old Mexico and new America. Maria Celeste had sat him down when he was only fourteen and told him of a boy who stood up to tyranny during the fascist atheist purges in the Cristero War. From 1926 to 1929 violent leaders in Mexico cut the population of Mexican priests from forty-five hundred to less than four hundred, eliminating them through assassination, emigration, and expulsion. In response thirty thousand Cristero fighters gave their lives defending God. "His name was José Luis Sánchez del Río," Juan Carlos's grandmother said. "He was a boy just like you. Only fourteen. Joselito gives you his heart, Juan Carlos."

Feeling both guilty and inspired, Juan Carlos remembered José Luis Sánchez del Río. In 1928 José Luis's death was witnessed by two childhood friends. Government commanders ordered him to renounce his belief. To break him they forced him to watch the hanging of another Cristero. José Luis called out to the man, saying, "We will soon meet again in heaven after death." They threw José in prison, where he proceeded to write heartfelt letters to his mother. On the evening of February 10, 1928, they took him from prison, cut off the soles of his feet, and forced him to walk through the town toward the cemetery. As he walked they cut his body with a machete so that he bled from multiple wounds. He cried out in agony but would not submit.

"If you shout 'Death to Christ the King' we will spare your life," they said.

"¡Viva Cristo Rey!" he shouted.

At the execution site the government soldiers stabbed him over and over with bayonets. He was a boy. He went to his knees and drew a cross in the dirt, putting his face to the dust, kissing it with his lips. The commander, piqued by the resolve of José Luis, drew his pistol and shot him in the head.

Juan Carlos prayed to have the heart of that boy.

"Por favor, Dios misericordioso, dame un poquito del corazón valiente y apasionado de Joselito."

Paulo moved to an apartment near the grounds and kept up the basic details of Juan Carlos's realty business. Despite Juan Carlos's absence, the thirty to forty realtors that made up the core of his Seattle realty empire sold commercial and residential holdings in record numbers. Being that Juan Carlos had turned toward life, and being that the facility was drug, alcohol, sex, and lewd-internet free, he gained his first full year of abstinence from his major vices. Upon his return to Seattle, this paved the way for three additional years of twelve-step sobriety and opened passage into a more humbly realized life with Paulo. His fatherhood to Ana Luz stabilized.

Back in the condominium overlooking waters the color of a mountain jay, they sat in their bedroom in the white leather loveseat watching the sea and sky.

"Thank you," Juan Carlos said, kissing Paulo's head.

Paulo remembered van Gogh . . . art consoles those who are broken by life.

He liked being called Juan Carlos's husband. He didn't like the word "spouse."

Juan Carlos relapsed for two days in year five. And a day in year seven.

After this he did not relapse again.

Book 6

You will feel good inside those voices
with two sentences left,
the first made of my rib,
the second of yours.

—Kateřina Rudčenková

JOHN AND SAMANTHA

BACK BEFORE John's career took flight, before marriage and children, before the climb—the scent of bear musk was in the air and his life depended on a single moment. He thought it a big female, her cubs nearby. She was downwind, he reckoned, and called himself a fool. His face was in the dirt and bleeding. His hip out of kilter. Sow grizzly, he thought, but when he heard the muzzle snorting loudly in the earth beside him, up under his ribs, and when he let the bear turn him over, he knew he was mistaken.

The size astounded him, a massive silvertip boar.

He marveled at how he felt almost calm until the wind shifted. At this, his horse screamed and ran up the mountain. John rolled to the side and the bear raked a set of furrows in his back that made him arch and lose breath and woke him like a babe from the womb. He howled and gathered himself inward, clutching the bear's throat. Teeth ribboned John's skull and opened his face. Blood poured into his eyes and he shut them and fumbled upward, reaching the bear's nose where he dug his nails into the softness of the flesh and ripped downward with great force. The bear flinched and barked, coughing sharply as he leaped from John's body. With awkward vision, John saw the animal, a blur moving over the terrain north where it disappeared into a wrinkle in the land.

I will bleed out right here, he thought.

He wiped his face with his forearm but his sight kept filling with blood.

He sat up and raised his head and used the tail of his shirt to clear his eyes. For a moment he saw the mountain side and a chip of blue sky before he needed to shut them again. His hip was undone, perhaps out of socket, his ribcage harmed. He rose and held his side and the movement made his mind blacken. With his eyes closed he took off his light flannel shirt, peeling it from the wound on his back. He tied it by the sleeves tightly around his head and used a loose end to wipe his face again. He knew he had to calm himself. He didn't have the luxury of time. His heart rate and adrenaline would kill him if he didn't slow down and breathe easy. Forget the blood, he thought, move.

He could see some now and he gimped forward, trying by awkward gesticulation to offset the pain. Pausing twice, he gripped his side and tried to breathe. He whistled once, weakly, and called out to his horse, Charlie. When he reached the tent he saw Charlie's head peering at him from behind a tree.

"Good Charlie," he said, and the horse came on.

He discarded thought of tack or saddle.

He felt lightheaded as he hoisted himself onto Charlie's back, yelping at the torque to his hip. Gripping the mane, he laid himself forward over the shoulders and neck. His lungs felt pinched and he moaned. Charlie grew twitchy from the blood.

"Home," John said, and Charlie turned and walked toward the gap. "Good Charlie."

The go was rough and too slow and John clucked his tongue and gave heel so the horse cantered some in the two hours it took to reach the downslant, causing him great agony. The jostle at pace was intolerable and when his mind closed he bit his tongue to stay conscious. He figured on three or four more hours this way before he'd be in sight of the ranch house. His throat was raw and he kept his eyes shut, needing to clear them each time to see and thinking sight largely unnecessary now anyway.

Going down the mountain he blacked out twice, and when he came to on the plain, his breathing had shallowed. Unbeknownst to him an eagle circled above, peering sidelong at the blood that glistened from his head and face, down the horse's neck in a broad scarlet swath from the shoulders to the chest. The sheen and coppery odor attractive, the quarry too big and alive. The bird swept upward and rode a thermal into the blue until the wings tilted and the eagle banked on a circumference that covered half the sky.

John continued to lose consciousness, but woke again three times, seeming to feel the horse stumble. He saw two red-winged blackbirds lift from a juniper and flit away south. He thought of God and felt he should live if he didn't die soon.

Near dusk his father, Jack, spotted the horse and knowing something was wrong he retrieved the glasses from the kitchen, stood on the porch and lifted them to his face. What he found made him shout: the body of his son slumped on the horse's neck, the horse's front quarters covered in blood.

He ran to his truck and gunned it over the plain to where he halted and removed John and set him into the front seat where he couldn't revive him though he found a pulse. The blood had coagulated on the wrecked face but still ran more freely than Jack wished. Pressing a cloth into the wounds, he fishtailed onto the dirt road, John's mother, Pamela, already in the sedan behind him. They sped to the hospital in Choteau where emergency workers moved the body with such speed behind closed doors, Jack and Pamela stood stunned in the emergency room lobby. A big male nurse appeared from a side hall and ushered them to a couch in a private room where Jack's upper body shook as Pamela placed his head in her lap and stroked his hair saying, "John will be all right." She didn't want it to but her voice waivered. "He's like you, he's strong."

"We'll bring word as soon as we know," the nurse said.

Three hours passed. The doctor entered. The families knew each other, had for decades. Doc Jordan, white-haired, heavy set with a big jaw. "John's alive," he said, "He'll survive just fine." His gloves and apron were bloody. "Wanted to let you know before I clean him up the rest of the way. He lost a lot of blood but he's stable. We've got it flowing back in now. He has a shattered cheekbone. Displaced hip. Five broken ribs and a punctured lung. Ugly back wound where the bear opened him up. I've stoppered that one for now." He paused. "I'll need to restore the cheekbone and reset the hip."

Jack stood and hugged him, clenching, refusing to let go, as if the doctor was John himself. "Thank you, Doc. Mighty good of you. Thank you."

Pamela shook his hand soberly.

"My pleasure," he said. "Tough as hell. His face will be worse for wear. He might have a limp, might not. But he's back in the land of the living."

He clapped his hands once and said, "Back to it," before he pivoted and walked from the room.

TETON HOSPITAL in Choteau, Montana, was a single-story L-shaped building. In the evening they were alone in John's room when his voice came to them hushed, as if he was in awe of them or the world or something beyond perception. He was lying on his side in the hospital bed, his face bandaged but for the eyes and mouth, and swollen.

His mom sat in the chair beside him.

"Samantha will be here tomorrow," she said.

"Thank you," he said.

His father looked at Pamela.

"Are you still afraid?" she asked John.

He thought of his broken face. What would Samantha think of him now?

WHEN SHE ARRIVED in the hospital room the next day near sundown she confirmed his mother's intuition. He'd slept much of the day and was asleep when she entered. Samantha embraced his mother and father together and he woke to see the three of them in a tight circle, their heads touching as she and his mother cried and his father set his cheek on the back of John's mother's head.

When Samantha turned, she ran to him and gently kissed his lips.

"You're awake!" She drew his hand to her face.

He cried and couldn't speak.

"Dead before I met you," he managed. "Alive now."

He grimaced, smiling through his injuries.

They were at the beginning of it all.

HE SLEPT through much of the next three days. Samantha and his mother stood watch.

His father went back to work.

John slept beneath the sound of their voices.

"I'm hoping we can talk about what I told John." Samantha said.

"Please do," Pamela said. "I hope you feel safe enough to talk with me. I also need to tell you about my life." She glanced at John. He was still asleep. "I was also raped," she said. "John doesn't know."

Samantha exhaled. "I'm sorry."

They sat next to each other at the foot of the hospital bed.

"I am too," Pamela said. "For us both. I told Jack I want John to know. I'll tell him when he wakes. You've opened this door for us. Jack and I are grateful."

Samantha loved Pamela. She ran cattle, branded, shot elk and cleaned them. She was not weak in any way. She held fierce tenderness for her and John.

"We love you so much, Samantha. You've brought John such love. I want to know your life and I want you to know mine."

Samantha held Pamela's hands in hers, saying "Te amaré por siempre. I'm so glad I'm here. I love this family. I will love you forever."

Pamela pressed her head to Samantha's.

"Love is all," she said, and began.

"I WAS fifteen when my uncle raped me. He was thirty-two. My mother's brother."

"I was twelve," Samantha said. "My brother was twenty."

The room had a small lamp near the headboard, the windows were coal black.

"He'd been awkward since he was young," Pamela said. "Somewhat violent until he joined the army. The discipline mellowed him and made him more respectful of people. Still the women tended to keep themselves between him and their children. He was a loner. Stayed over the garage at Miller's Gas Station near Four Corners. When he came home from military duty, he kept mostly to himself."

"I was walking to see my mother at the post office on Highway 2. She and her best friend Betty were the postmasters, had been for years. They split time to be with their families and help with the ranch work. Most days after school I helped Mom finish up and close the office. Before I got there he pulled his truck in front of me on the shoulder of the road."

"Did you know it was him?" Samantha asked.

"I did but I was oblivious. I didn't think anything until he got out. His face looked wrong. He grabbed me and put a handkerchief over my mouth. I screamed, but he muffled it. The cloth smelled like gasoline and turpentine. No cars. No people. Just cattle in the fields off the road. The post office only five minutes from me. I bit his hand before I went unconscious."

"He could have killed you."

"I believe that. Something kept me here."

"Yes," Samantha said.

"We're tough," Pamela said. "You and me. Tougher than what bad men do. I woke in the woods a mile above town. One shoe on. The other ten feet away."

"Was he still there?"

"Yes."

"Oh no." Sam's face tightened.

"It's all right," Pamela said. "I've had my share of trouble, but I've been blessed. Very blessed. My husband. My son. You." She gestured to the window. "These mountains. This life."

John slept, breathing heavily.

"Your uncle was still there?"

"He was. I remember my body face down. My eyes blurry. I kept still. I thought he didn't know I was awake. He sat against the base of a tree. He had his head down, his knees in his arms."

"Bastard," said Sam.

"No broken bones but my body hurt everywhere. He looked over. We made eye contact and he rose and knelt next to me. As I see it now his face was forsaken. He was distressed. Evil, yes, and also scared like a cornered animal."

"I felt that way with my brother too," Samantha said.

"They're predators," Pamela went on, "and they're prey. 'I'm sorry,' he said. 'I won't touch you now.' I didn't move. Couldn't run if I wanted to, for fear or shock. 'Don't tell anyone,' he said, crying. 'I don't want to have to kill you.'

"Then he moved away, heading back to his truck. I waited there on the ground before I brushed myself off and put my clothes back in order. I took a route to the edge of town and quickly walked down main street. I didn't want to see anyone, but I wanted people near. I went home immediately, being careful to walk as normally as I could."

"Did your parents find out?"

"Neither of them were home yet. My dad was in the fields, my mom still closing the post office. I ran a bath. Cried. Felt I couldn't tell anyone."

Samantha cried, holding Pamela's hand.

"I sewed my dress before Mom came home. Burned my underpants in the barrel by the barn, threw some wet grass in after to cover it, dampen the smoke. They came home and I ate with them and as usual we didn't talk a lot. Now I'm not sure how, but then it seemed unthinkable to speak of. I went to bed and didn't sleep. Didn't sleep well for years. I never told my parents. I told Jack, but as my parents aged I didn't want to burden them.

"The next week my uncle left town for more military service. Within a year, news came that he died on a mission overseas. We never knew how he died. I didn't attend the funeral. My dad and mom fought over that. She thought I should. Dad gave me the choice. I was glad for it."

They were silent for a moment before they sat back and looked at John.

"He's a good one," Samantha said.

"Like his father," Pamela said.

"You and Jack have made a beautiful family."

"We've had our burdens," Pamela said. "We've got flaws. I hope we bear each other up though. We're here for you, Samantha." Pamela nodded and moved nearer to Samantha.

"Growing up, I believe my mother hated my father," Samantha said. "They hardly touched and only laughed together when they were drunk. She told me he was more unfaithful than faithful. That may be true. They're divorced now. Regardless, she despised him, and often despises him still. I don't remember a time she didn't. Before it was over she had her own affair with his closest friend, Steve. Simple revenge, I think, but I saw her brighten up when she was in it, until she began hating Steve too."

"Likely hated herself," Pamela said. "I've certainly hated myself."

"Yes," Samantha said. "her and me both. We hated ourselves."

"Made me vengeful toward myself and my abuser," Pamela said. "I wanted to die or kill him or both, even after he was long dead. Often I shunned loved ones and friends both."

"Me too," Samantha said. "I only have one brother. His name is London. He started babysitting me when my parents went out. My dad was a happy drunk, so Mom and Dad had some good times despite themselves. They came home loud and slept hard.

"In any case London watched me and at first it was just a game. Like my dad, he could have a fun personality when he wanted to. When I was twelve the game started to feel dirty. Touch this. Show me that. Let me touch this. It's nothing. It's natural. It's just our bodies. He didn't even ask me not to tell Mom and Dad.

"Late fall I remember walking to school the day after he crossed the final line. The leaves had lost color and blown from the trees. Even then I knew he raped me and I wanted to kill myself. Specifically, I wanted to drown. Jump from a bridge. If I'd have understood guns or pills I don't think I'd be here. I handled our kitchen knives, but dying that way seemed too slow, too drawn out."

"Did he keep on?"

"Yes, and the dread too." Samantha looked at Pamela. "I got quieter and quieter. Through their alcohol haze my parents sometimes asked why, but it was easy enough to avoid them. They fought every night, yelled, slapped and pushed each other, bit into each other like dogs."

"How long did it go on?"

"On and off for about two years. He'd failed in community college. Dad wanted to kick him out. London's friends were all drunk or high. The ones who finished college left him behind. When I was fourteen the police physically removed him, taking him into custody."

"Who turned him in?"

"My mom. I finally told her. She didn't believe me, but I'd been cutting pretty much from when it started. I always wore jeans and long-sleeved shirts. I cut on my stomach or upper thigh, or my arms. What he did, he did in the dark. I cut in the light and it kept me sane."

"It's something no one should have to carry," Pamela said.

"Some never get free," Samantha said. "I still feel guilty."

"I felt the same for a long time," Pamela said.

A nurse with her hair in a French twist touched the door frame and peered in. "Everything okay?" she whispered.

"Yes," Pamela said, "thank you."

The nurse's steps receded down the hall.

"My mom believed me when I lifted my shirt and showed her my stomach," Samantha said. "She was horrified. 'No,' she said and just started weeping. I stood there with my cuts, crisscrossed and ugly. 'London,' my mom said, walked to the phone and called the police. My dad was at work. My brother in the basement. The police came and knocked on the door. They talked to me and my mom for about ten minutes on the porch. They looked at the cuts on my stomach and asked my permission and took a picture. They asked where London was and went to the basement. They questioned him directly. He confessed. They cuffed him and hauled him up the stairs. He was crying, even at twenty years old. My mom tried to slap his face but the police held her back. They took him down the front steps and drove away with him, my mom screaming after him from the driveway.

"I sat in the house and cried."

"I'm so sorry," Pamela said.

"It got worse before it got better. When Dad came home my mom and dad almost murdered each other. She jumped on his back and raked his neck with her nails. He threw her to the ground but she clung to his ankle. He cursed her and hit the back of her head until she released him. He was ignorant. She was a cyclone. They split that night and I went with her and they never came back together."

"And your brother?"

"Being twenty he was tried as an adult. My exam was humiliating. Gratefully the doctor was female. The court case hung on too long. My father disappeared. My brother looked lost. No one stood for him. I'd enclosed myself in a different way now. I wanted him to suffer. I didn't want him to be my brother.

"London was to serve five years in prison due to what the judge called his 'perverted and oppositional nature.' Mom wanted us to visit him so we visited him once a year and he just looked sad. 'Please get me out of here,' he said. His eyes were empty. 'I wish we could,' Mom told him, and it was true. By then we saw the abyss in him. We wanted him to get help. He had controlled me totally and now he controlled no one. He seemed unlovable or he was unlovable, but after everything, we still loved him.

"When he was finally released we met him at the gate. My father wasn't there; he'd been nowhere for years. My brother's parole officer helped him get set up in a halfway house the state arranged for him in south Seattle. We bought him a hot plate, a small refrigerator, a few cups and bowls and utensils but in a month he was on the streets. We went to look for him but couldn't find him. The state didn't find him either. The parole officer said in a city of that size men just disappear. It's true. We haven't found him since. And that's it, that's my life."

Pamela gripped Samantha's shoulders and looked into her eyes. "Thank you, Samantha. We've been taught women were meant for abuse, given the message to loathe our own bodies, our histories, ourselves." She spoke directly. "Don't believe it. One of the hardest things to do is to paint the darkness which nonetheless has light in it. We were made for love. We were made for light. We learned to fear, but we've overcome fear. We've chosen well. Under healthy circumstances, we've risked love. Women and men can't live without love."

"Es verdad," Samantha said. "I'm so glad we're with each other."

"Me too," Pamela said.

AS SAMANTHA ROSE and turned down the light, the night outside came close. They made themselves ready and the nurse brought them each a pillow and a throw blanket. Samantha took the reclining hospital chair beside John, Pamela a slender couch near the wall. The room had begun to feel better, smell more like home.

John slept in the dark between them.

THE NEXT DAY with Jack and Samantha present Pamela told her son.

After she spoke, John didn't know who among them held the other more closely.

THE NEXT EVENING, John's father spelled the two women so they could get better rest. Toward nightfall he saw his boy's spirits were good. He had in mind the encounter with the bear.

"What was it like, son?"

Jack sat in the chair beside the bed.

John took his father's hand and held tightly. He spoke as he was not used to speaking but felt driven to now that beyond fate or expectation everything was new.

"Dad, I love you more than I've been able to say."

"I love you too, son," Jack said. "The good Lord saw fit to keep you here. I'm wholehearted grateful, and equally grateful your mom had the chance to tell you about her life."

John was propped up in bed, his cracked ribs aching as if hit with a hammer. He leaned to his side, facing his father. "The bear was heavy, Dad. Like dead weight."

"Was it muscled, or more thick?"

"Both. It smelled like carrion and mud. There was so much movement and it was so quick and strong I just told myself to act. Not wait."

"In that situation most people get killed," Jack said.

"I can't believe I'm still here," John said.

"What were you thinking when the bear was on top of you?"

"All I thought was 'I'll fight until I die.' That's it. 'I'll fight until I die.'"

TIME WENT FORWARD and back, and the days were like one day.

The bear had changed him.

His face marked forever, his back opened and ribs broken. His hip so misaligned Doc Jordan had to reset it. John hated bandages and removed them as soon as he was out of the hospital. The stitching's tracks made Samantha grimace, and in fact the scars shifted his bodily presence. John and Samantha married in a high-windowed contemporary cathedral in Edmonds, Pamela and Jack joining Samantha's mother, Alma Victoria, their families and friends for the wedding.

A few years later, in the spring after John and Samantha's second daughter was born, John's father died of a stroke.

JOHN THOUGHT HE and his family, and all those he'd loaned money to in small or great amounts, these and millions more, borrowed from the past for the present.

He loved his father.

He found himself driving the highway north toward Edmonds, as lonely as he'd ever been. The blackbirds flew in immense clusters, one-hundred to a million-fold, and when they moved this way, fluid, darting, luxurious, twilight was transfigured and he knew them to be emissaries of his father's beckoning. Along the wing line, carpometacarpus and phalanges, flesh and blood bent skyward beneath flight feathers asymmetrically shaped, symmetrically paired. Fused clavicles. Scapula and coracoid. Beak and mandible. The keeled breastbone and sleek neck. Remiges and rectrices, wing and tail feathers propelling thrust and lift.

Thus powering flight, the blackbirds were strong and agile fliers. He followed them with his eyes among the fields that lined the coast. The world below them shifted and moved. They flew high before banking across the sky, descending to the water and up through the land. They went southward, where they dispersed before reaching Seattle to glide through the city, the people merely objects they flew among. People borrowed hope, John thought, and even the design of their own wedding rings. On the day they were married Samantha gifted him a ring made of metal from a thrown shoe, melted down, rounded, polished to a light gray shine.

AURORA GAVE Elias a ring intricately beaded by his grandmother Catherine.

PHIL MCBANE had Alberta's name tattooed on his ring finger as she giggled with delight.

John hadn't seen Phil for a long time, but on a day when Samantha took their second baby for a stroll, her path crossed Phil's like the transit of planets over the disk of a distant star.

The sun a wide flare above the Olympics, Samantha was in downtown Seattle.

She didn't know Phil from anyone.

But she would have lost the baby, and herself, if Phil had not walked behind her.

"TODAY WAS different," Phil said when he got home.

This before Alberta left him, before he'd gone to jail a second time.

"Why?" she asked.

He thought maybe he should keep it to himself.

He told her anyway.

"When I was out panning, a white van ran a red light and a woman with a baby in one arm and her other hand on the empty stroller wasn't paying attention. I pulled them back. The van pounded the stroller and threw it a hundred feet in the air. Driver just kept going."

"You saved that woman and her baby," Alberta said and started crying.

She held him tightly to her chest and kissed his head.

WHEN SAMANTHA called him, John was there in minutes.

He ran for her and she met his open arms. They held the baby between them.

"¡El ángel se ha ido! The angel is gone! ¡El ángel se ha ido!"

"She's right here, alive," he said.

John touched and kissed their daughter Mercedes.

John absorbed his wife's tremors, enclosing Samantha and the baby fully, his body almost entirely concealing them in the haven his chest made.

"The man who saved her is gone," she said.

ANGELICA PRESENTED Gabriel with a ring of black gold.

JUAN CARLOS DE LA CRUZ received a weighted platinum band ordered by Paulo direct from Hatton Garden of London and set with Cartier diamonds in a cobblestone pattern.

AS JOHN AND SAMANTHA'S daughters entered their teenage years, the gulf between Roark and John grew wider. John still brought in big dollars, but also made sure he got home on time.

Roark called, wanting to meet at the strip club again and John said flatly no. Roark relented. "Meet me in my office then," he said. Though he hadn't mentioned it his admiration for John's scars was overt. "I'd like to have those," he said this time. "Make me look even stronger."

The lines patterned the side of John's face from his temple to his jaw. Though people stared he wasn't self-conscious.

Roark lifted his hand to touch the scars.

Giving Roark a vicious look, John moved him back.

Roark showed John a new business card and read it aloud:

R.R. Freeman, Owner, CEO

National American Bank

5,300 Branches Worldwide.

The 'Greatest' Bank, The Greatest CEO

Seattle to New York. London to Hong Kong. All Points Between.

"What'ya think, Montana?" Roark asked. He liked calling John, Montana.

"Seems like you," John said. "What do the Board of Investors think?"

Roark waved John's critique away. "Are they making good money? Yes. Do they want anything else? No. Don't be dense, John. The question isn't who's going to let me do what I do, it's who's going to stop me. Besides, I couldn't care less.

"Do you fear me, John?"

"Never," John said.

"Well show some respect. Where do you think your job comes from?"

UNLIKE THE SPEED of light, the speed of time was immeasurable. As Samantha and and John's daughters grew older, they marveled at the uniqueness of each. Mercedes, curly-headed and compact compared to her taller straight-haired sister Lourdes. John's mother Pamela moved to Seattle to help with the girls. John leased out the land and had the ranch house and outbuildings weatherized, paying a foreman of a nearby operation to look in from time to time. John and Samantha step-laddered into a great house overlooking the Sound. Junior high and high school like a whirlwind. Pamela had ten good years with them before she died of lymphoma.

She died with Samantha, John, and the girls haloed around her.

Samantha's brother surfaced a few times after that, twice with his gait lingering on the front step, a slight knock at the door. On both occasions Samantha and John invited him in for dinner and he accepted. Like a starved dog, John thought. His eyes were red-veined, the slant of his shoulders echoing a void hard to bridge with conversation. But before he left he thanked them. In prison he'd become a loner, he'd been altered by what he'd done, or from being locked up like an animal, treated with scorn by guards and inmates, mistreated, bodily. They didn't see him again until years later when they found him at a homeless shelter in Tacoma. London didn't speak, and rarely lifted his head. Destitute and weepy in the eyes. To John it was apparent the man had nothing to live for and seeing Samantha's sisterly tenderness, John had no hate for him.

Samantha wrapped London's head in her arms and kissed the top of his head.

John cried.

After that they saw him on and off for a few months before he disappeared.

When they finally found him again he'd hung himself from the rafters inside an old mill outside Ellensburg.

"He wasn't meant for this world," Samantha said on the drive to retrieve the body. Samantha was in her forties. John found her as striking as when they first met, her black hair in tendrils at her neck, the wisps of hair along her hairline.

"He was meant for so much more," she said.

A week later, on the ferry from the Port of Seattle to the Strait of Juan de

Fuca, Samantha held her mother as her mother scattered London's ashes in the ocean. John held them both, watching the ash turn to a cloud of smoke under the surface before it faded into the deep.

WITHIN A FEW GENERATIONS everyone is forgotten, John thought.

Samantha's mother had chosen against burial, preferring to keep her son's after-trace in the urn with a few pictures of him in gilded frames on an altar to Our Lady of Guadalupe in the main room of her apartment. When she died unexpectedly in her sleep a few years after London, they released her ashes in the Strait of Juan de Fuca too, just as she requested.

Honoring her mother, Samantha made an altar to Our Lady of Guadalupe and surrounded her mother's urn with beloved photos, setting it next to her brother's urn in an alcove off the kitchen. Her mother's theology, her adoring Mary, was also a reckoning. Love is that you are the cross on which I willingly crucify myself, her mother said. Samantha couldn't fully receive it until her own children had come into the world. Now she took it to heart. As newborns the nurses placed them on her chest. Skin to skin, she'd held them close and watched their color come up.

Now they were young women and she saw her mother in their eyes.

"Que Dios siempre esté con nosotros," she whispered.

God be with us always.

JOHN'S GRANDPA had been a Colonel in the Pacific Theater. He was on the ground in the first wave after atomic warfare.

He carried his body with exactitude until he suicided.

John knew that what we witness, or what our mothers and fathers witness, changes us. What John's grandpa witnessed in war he took with him to the afterlife.

John's cyclical depressions were hard on the family but he got by.

AS ROARK'S EMPIRE continued to ascend, he sat at his desk, took out his moleskin, and outlined his plans for Sky City:

1) Powerful upswing, easy on the back end,
2) financing through my own development arm,
3) loan backed by my personal guarantee
4) and the completion guarantee,
5) Certificate of Occupancy,
6) long-term mortgage,
7) tenants clamoring to be in early,
8) skyrocketing revenues,
9) ungodly return on investment,
10) my name in lights above it all.

HIS URGES overwhelmed him now. Down from the city onto the track for undesirables along Pacific Highway South past 2 a.m. he picked up what looked like a Native girl walking the shoulder. From his window he gave her a twenty-dollar bill and listened to the lilt in her voice as she got into the passenger seat.

He didn't want her.

To his own disgrace he had wanted Aurora.

But Aurora humiliated him, and he hated her with a deadly hatred.

He drove the girl into an alley behind a lightless motel. His sex was haphazard. With his ugly hand he beat her before he placed his good hand over her face and pressed down until her life went out.

WITHOUT A SECOND thought he went home to sleep, got up early in the morning and drove to work. At his desk he removed his book from the drawer, went to the back page and drew a small triangle in the middle between the other two, pressing firmly, following each edge and vertex inward until the shape held no light. He pressed his forefinger over the one for the young prostitute from years back, then over the triangle for the one from last night, and finally over the triangle that stood alone in the top corner under AAH for Aurora American Horse.

THE GIRL WASN'T found until late the next day.

The body went unclaimed.

After sixty days she was declared "Indigent Dead."

The coroner released the body to a funeral home with a government contract where the body was cremated, the ashes scattered at a common site.

The police didn't open a murder case.

WHEN SAMANTHA met John he loved love.

He borrowed the love of dancing his father shared with his mother.

He borrowed his father's steady hand.

John remembered when Jason Shobe called the square dances on Saturday nights at the dance hall in Rock Springs or the school gymnasium in Cohagen. The people locked arms and hooted for joy. There was great delight in the pairings. The seventy-six-year-old Whitney couple with smiling eyes, still light on their feet. Young Joseph Hatton, afraid to dance with Jacine Zook. It took Joseph up until the last song but when he asked and she said yes, Joseph's chest swelled with pride. John remembered the quick step of his father. The elegance of his mother, her face to the light, a sheen of sweat on her neck.

When he took Samantha dancing in the Seattle country dance clubs she moved like something untame. Variations of jitterbug, but a little different. Up and down a slotted line, or in more of a triple step. Be it West Coast or East Coast or the swivel hip movements of salsa, John never tired of moving with her, holding the small of her back, feeling her spirit in his hands, renewing him.

AS ROARK and John grew apart, John and Elias grew closer, meeting not only at the bar for the Seattle Rodeo Club events, but a couple of times a week throughout the city for lunch or happy hour. Though Elias was a good deal younger, the friendship grew more and more powerful. They laughed together, remembering their glory days in Montana. Team roping. Saddle broncs. John with two daughters becoming professionals. Elias on the rise, and childless. John complained about work and sadness, Elias about marriage.

"I can't reach her, John. She's lost to me."

"Stay strong, Elias. Aurora's worth it all, here or in Montana."

"I don't know why I get so down," John said, internal deficit putting him on the rack more than he'd admit to Samantha. "Way too much, I feel like dying."

"My Uncle Clayton says we shouldn't block life, John. We should befriend life."

True advice, they both knew, but hard to realize.

MEN TRIED to be unselfish, Samantha thought.

Every Friday she and John met at five thirty, had dinner somewhere downtown and danced past midnight. He was so conflict averse they almost never fought. His stubbornness, though, infuriated her.

In the early years of marriage she'd found his sexual greed tempered but keen beneath the surface of his angers. In recent days though, his energy waned.

His depression generated disturbances that took a long time leaving.

She loved his face, even kissed his scars openly, or secretly as he slept.

She knew him through and through.

But her own weaknesses, the ones paired perfectly to his, she rarely brought up.

AS FOR JOHN, more and more he ruminated over his grandpa. He hoped others would not have to experience the dejection and hopelessness that blanketed his mind.

Men hold the keys to the abyss, he thought.

Men are the architects.

BUT HE LOVED Samantha beside him, the friendship, the conversations, the union of their bodies and minds. Evenings, her arm against his, he read about World War II. He thanked Mary Irene de la Cruz for that, for how a chance meeting in the library had unearthed new worlds. People should know more of their own history. He wondered what Mary Irene was doing now. He wanted to know Samantha's Puerto Rico, and began to find his own history important too.

The war had ranged throughout Europe, but he paused on the German invasion of Czechoslovakia. As Samantha slept, what he learned broke him open. 1942. Prague. Place of John's people. Place of his origins. Over the wide gray ocean his reading carried him to the River Vltava, to the Mother of Cities, the Golden City, City on the Threshold of Stars: Praha. To Nazi occupation where he discovered more of where he came from.

Jan Kubiš and Jozef Gabčík, soldiers, sons of Czech, born for a day when the body rises and kills and the mouth long silent shouts to the sky. They rose and killed the Blond Beast, Reinhardt Heydrich, Hitler's henchman in control of Moravia and Bohemia. In response Hitler razed a small village called Lidice to the ground, killing the men, concentrating the women, sending eighty-two of the youngest children to Chelmno where they were gassed to death in Magirus vans known in Russian as *dushegubka*: soul killers.

My two daughters were not yet born, he thought. My two daughters were yet to be when these children were lost. Removed from the face of the earth. For them, for every child, Christ a silver aspen whose leaves are placed on their foreheads for the healing of the nations. My grandfather is German. My grandmother is Czech. The cloth they wore was common.

The suits John wore were less and less common.

THE SAME YEAR the Nazis invaded the Czech lands, John's Czech grandmother Katerina married his German grandfather Detlef in New York City where they danced and heard little word of their home countries but let their bodies flare in the dark of the dance hall as they tipped their heads to the light and kissed fiercely.

He reckoned no one knew the fullness of the lives that came before their own.

Fascism cycling again, in space and time.

Bloodline could be as sweet as sugar, he thought, or like a steel bit that rubbed the mouth raw.

A RHYME his grandma taught him as a boy stayed with him, the tune in Czech, melodic from her mouth: Beruško, kam poletíš, do peklíčka nebo do nebíčka. In English the words were grim: Ladybird, ladybird, fly away home / Your house is on fire / Your children shall burn! In the old days the rhyme was sung by farmers when burning their fields after harvest, urging the ladybird, or ladybug, to fly home, where only one of her children remained, hidden, unburned, under a stone. The ladybird, a sacred symbol of safety from pestilence, beckoned a blessing, so your family and children would be protected. His grandmother had often soothed him with song, and the truth that the world is not safe.

"Miláčku," she called him, the Czech word for "darling."

He called each daughter Miláčku too.

Past 2 a.m., the reading light on, John paused, staring at Samantha sleeping in shadow beside him. Her face and curved jawline. I am German, he thought, I am Czech, and I am also Cheyenne, and she carries her own countries.

Our children carry all of us.

Our daughters are Puerto Rican, he told himself, our daughters are German and our daughters are Czech and Cheyenne. Lourdes. Mercedes. Stunning Puerto Rican names given in honor of Samantha, and Samantha's mother.

He treasured the shape of his wife, the calm he heard in her breathing.

BUT BACK IN HIS OFFICE where he tallied ledgers many floors above the city, John couldn't stop his depressed thoughts. His window faced west and had for some time now, not east toward the brick and concrete high-rises, but west toward the water where offices were reserved for the higher-ups. John knew something about financial history, and always, it was tied to deficit followed by war. Being a loan officer and a leader of loan officers, he reckoned the debt.

America has never not been at war, he thought.

Each war laced with massacres, the rise of the war machine, the concomitant fall.

Other major sources of American "public" debt?

Recession. Despair.

Not surprising, John thought, regardless of presidencies and party affiliations, from 1950 on, American public debt rose into the trillions of dollars, generally staying below two trillion until the 1980s when precipitous climbs made public debt surpass the ten trillion mark after the 2008 recession.

The ongoing gross federal debt would apex forty trillion in due time.

$40,000,000,000,000.00.

An unfathomable number.

John knew about collapse.

The country couldn't pay its debts.

The country would never again be able to pay its debts.

We're culpable, he thought, all of us.

Like him, America borrowed against life, and borrowed against oblivion.

John remembered days with his father, pinching ticks from the skin of the blue heelers if the ticks weren't too fat. When they were, they looked like garlic cloves and his dad had to burn the bulbous sacs until the ticks backed out of the skin. He threw them in a bucket of gasoline because ticks were hard to kill. Unpleasant work, but just seeing the joy in the dogs' faces, John never minded the removal because it made them healthier and it was always better than just waiting for the ticks to drop off, engorged with the dogs' blood.

What did money mean?

He wished he could alleviate suffering.

Often, he increased it.

Despite all, he hoped for his daughters, and everyone he'd been given to serve.

Always, he imagined blackbirds in flight among them.

MARY IRENE moved on and didn't look back.

Emerging with Paulo, Juan Carlos found himself anew.

ANGELICA WITNESSED the stars with great affection.
The diaphany of the Divine at the heart of a universe on fire.
His song as smooth as satin, utter loneliness inhabited Gabriel's eyes.

ALBERTA QUESTIONED her life and wanted more.

Phillip didn't know where he was going and often forgot why.

BEFORE AURORA left Seattle, she helped the most compromised babies in the world.

Elias rode the dawn to Mankato.

JOHN'S FAMILY forewent their Northern Cheyenne bloodline three generations back. The story passed to him through his matrilineal line, a single name and date in the front pages of an old Bible. We displaced or misremembered, he thought, distanced, cut off, and ultimately erased our great-great-grandmother, Winona Killsnight.

Birds flew from east to west and disappeared at the edge of existence.

ACROSS SEATTLE, in the luxury apartment Juan Carlos de la Cruz shared with Paulo, Juan Carlos remembered he'd nearly begged John Sender for sexual attention during what Juan Carlos referred to as his own descent into hell.

John had rebuffed him in a direct but polite manner.

Juan Carlos told Paulo if he'd have listened to Sender, it would have saved a lot of heartache. "A year or two at least. And when I was all the way down, I kept hearing what he said to me . . . that I was lonely, that I just needed to go home. I kept imagining one day I'd be home, like I am now, and everything would be okay. Even though we barely know each other, I love that man.

"After this place, never did another loan with him. I can't say why."

"Why don't you do something nice for him now?" Paulo suggested.

"Like what?"

"Like give him money out of the blue without his knowing the source."

A WEEK LATER, when John Sender returned to the office after lunch, he found an envelope addressed to him set squarely in the middle of his desk. When he opened the envelope, he found a check in the amount of one million dollars.

He questioned the bank's lead accountant, a woman named Diane Inbody, a friend of Samantha's, and she told him yes, it was true, the check was his.

He thought it a cruel joke from Roark to further enslave him.

When he asked who it came from, Diane informed him she was not at liberty to say but verified the money was real.

ON A BRIGHT sky day a few months later, John found a handwritten note in the pocket of his suit jacket. It read, "Urgent: Ask R.R. about your stock options." The note was signed D.I. Diane again, who worked in Roark's central office on the floor just below the top floor. John asked Roark, and he appeared to be found out, but immediately switched his face from guilt to stone and informed John the five hundred thousand in stock options he'd promised hadn't been processed correctly and so could not come into effect for at least ten more years if at all. A ploy, John knew, to bleed him dry.

He considered litigation.

Raork can't understand love, John thought, because he has no organ for understanding. The next day, he told Roark goodbye, foregoing the stock options.

Roark had been a long thorn. John was glad to be rid of him and tried not to focus on the despondency that lurked behind betrayal.

With the million from the unknown giver he made his move.

He and Samantha would retire early and go back to the ranch in Montana.

ROARK WAS NOT pleased. Roark's worth was unassailable but he'd imagined John a bone from which he could perpetually suck marrow.

He was wrong. When John left it goaded him.

Roark took solace in deception.

In the years of presidential debt-gathering by blue and red presidents Aurora had been here in Seattle and he'd shadowed her without her knowledge. Maddening how he couldn't find her now. But he'd find her. He knew where her husband lived, the third loan John closed for American Horse was half of an entire floor in The Towers near Capitol Hill. Seattle like a forest, beetle-dead, he thought, ready to burn, the streets encamped now for too long with homeless pillagers handfed by the city.

Black Lives Matter. Antifa.

The turbulence made Roark stronger: Cities engorged with blue-red hate and Roark ready to buy large plots and service more loans in the fattening. Government and business acolytes of the rationalist persuasion all the way to the heights of Wall Street and the bedroom of the White House. But the banks own the world, he thought. With near fifty-five hundred branches he was ready now. In his mind's eye he saw himself not as a son of God but a son of industry, a son of sky. A son. "Our son," his father and mother had said. Arson. They'd been a house on fire in the night. In the morning she was gone. His off-hand ached. He didn't care about that anymore. Specifically, if he could engulf the cities in flame, high-rises and other large private holdings along with government operations, police stations, federal buildings, he'd buy those who would need to sell, secure the new build on properties that burned, and lock in gargantuan loans with government debt written in on the tide of paranoia.

He'd launch his mile-high Sky City, the 528-story single-tower megalithic skyscraper envisioned by Frank Lloyd Wright in 1956 but bettered by Roark in the present day. Thermonuclear powered. Balanced by Tuned Mass Dampers for amplitude reduction of mechanical vibrations. Housing a hundred thousand workers, climbers, achievers. A fifteen thousand electric-car parking structure embedded inside. Sky City would dwarf the Space Needle, being nine times its height, twice the height of Burj Khalifa in Dubai, the tallest building in the world, and taller still than the forthcoming Jeddah Tower in Saudi Arabia.

He'd beat the Japanese to it too, with their futuristic ocean mega-city designs, the Arab world with their glimmering masterpieces—a mile-high race he knew they all visualized but wouldn't have the guts to accomplish before him. The physicists had taken care of the colossal wind loads, the earthquake stress, the typhoons. Atomically fixed sustainable zero net power draw came of wind, sunlight, and geothermal mass. The shadow his Sky City cast would be substantial. He didn't care about the critics. With enough money he'd follow Wright's vision to the end.

Tenuity. Continuity. Balance. Elastic stability. Enlightenment.

People loved heroism. They worshipped heroic achievement.

His off-hand grew cold. He rubbed it with his good hand and perused the architectural drawings for Sky City: five-story base structure and transition of a central reinforced concrete core into a taproot foundation set deep into the earth; cantilevered floors and a tensioned tripod made of steel rising skyward; very small in the background, Lloyd Wright's scale silhouettes of the Washington Monument, the Great Pyramid, the Eiffel Tower, the Empire State Building.

Roark's vision was a great vision.

He'd be informed by Japan, the United Arab Emirates, and the Saudis but would transcend all with multiuse sky decks, three-level high-speed elevators, the highest sky terraces in the world, water treatment through gravity acceleration, an articulated face for cloud harvesting, Tokyo's vertical openings base to apex combined with the Saudis' smooth sloped facade for wind vortex shedding, incremental steps and tapers for more breakup of wind vortices, allowing wind both to be disbursed and to pass through, all in a design like a spear hurled from deep space.

2040. He would beat Tokyo by five years.

He pictured himself again standing on the threshold at the highest point of the building. Wind in his hair. The world below.

From there he'd look into the stars.

See the darkness within the light.

Roark had made a few calls that day.

The dream was incremental. More land, more development, more billions. The team would be in position when the time was right. They'd set some fires. His kingdom would increase. At the same time, he'd rid himself of what ailed him. Push Elias too far. Then take Aurora.

JOHN MET ELIAS at Picket's before the move. They took a table in the back away from the screens. Wood chairs, wood paneled walls. They were by themselves.

"I'll miss the time together, John, I'm not lying."

"Me too, Elias. Please, let's stay in touch."

Elias had been down for some time with Aurora gone, his own will caught in an eddy he couldn't seem to navigate. Tears welled in John's eyes. Elias couldn't believe John was leaving.

"I don't know that there's many true friends left," Elias said.

John looked at his face, acknowledging him. Certain decisions carry infinite weight, he thought. Unavoidable, and terrible. He loved Elias. Closer than a brother. And Elias loved him. But John was steeled to what lay ahead.

He also warned Elias. "My boss, Roark Freeman, he'll try to come after you for more money, loans, investments. He's scum. Find another bank. Someone you can trust." John pictured the strip club again, Roark's disregard and drunken questioning after Elias's wife, Aurora, even Samantha.

"I remember him," Elias said.

"He's got a thing for your wife," John said.

"Well she's gone, John. It doesn't matter."

"All right, but there's ill will in him, about you and Aurora. Watch out."

"I'm not worried," Elias said. "But will you consider staying?"

"I can't," John answered.

They spoke of the years. They blessed each other with their words.

As the night closed they walked to the parking lot and before parting they threw themselves on one another's necks and wept together.

John promised to be in touch.

Elias went back in the bar and didn't leave for a long time.

AFTER THE MOVE to Montana, John didn't stay in touch at all.

Even from the first months of retirement he was not well.

The removal of work was like the removal of worth. The fact that his money had come to him solely on the backs of others burdened him, and distinctly, how he'd cheated life by feeding Roark's ambition and staying silent about it until too late.

Just after his birthday, he lost three million in a steep market drop. Like a fool he got out. The government changed or stayed the same. All the grimness he held at bay rushed in. He didn't call Elias. Before retirement, when his stocks were strong, he'd been better, telling himself he'd be giving that money to his children. He'd still be giving them a lot of money but three million couldn't be replaced. The one million from the secret giver plagued him as well, all of it lost too. He cursed himself. The back of his hands were roped with thick veins. His ruminations closed in and though Samantha didn't want him to he kept falling into himself.

Yes he'd suffered low-grade to significant depression much of his life. This, however, was a different, more invasive species. He didn't get out of bed some mornings. He gained weight. Even his bones felt heavy.

Like an old enemy his childhood predilection for wanting to die returned.

He was afraid of becoming his grandfather. A self-loathing recluse. The brown recluse, he thought, only he was White, or gray. Poisonous. Short for this world. He was beginning to think too much. His life insurance would restore some of the money he'd misplaced. All she needed to do was present his death certificate at the claim office.

He couldn't say why money meant so much to him.

He found his own self-pity disgusting.

IN LATE AUGUST of his sixtieth year, Samantha decided to say what she needed to say. The whole family was home: the oldest daughter, Lourdes, from State Department work in Beirut; the youngest, Mercedes, from her visual art studio in Las Cruces, New Mexico—Mercedes painted faces mainly, and some figures, the bodies misaligned in a way that made viewers feel at odds with themselves and yet also buoyed. Her work had gained some small critical acclaim, while Lourdes had steadily advanced toward diplomat status in the Foreign Service.

The children brought their whole families, their spouses, the young grandchildren. Everyone thriving but him. Samantha couldn't believe how far a man could turn in so little time. They had all they needed, be it love or money. He'd lost three million, yes. All in a stupid stock decision during the downturn. But it was their three million. In fact, she'd made more than him, and her stocks had started to recover some. She thought he'd weather it. They still had meaningful funds they'd be giving to the children, whether the children needed it or not. Maybe he'd lived too much for her and for them. And his misguided effort was strangling him now. Maybe they should have given all their money away. He didn't know his real value, she thought.

"How will you survive when I die?" he asked. "I have nothing for the kids."

"I'll survive just fine," she teased, but it made him grimace.

"What are you saying," she continued, "you have your whole life ahead of you." If she'd have been ready for this, she thought maybe she could have saved him a little anguish. But his mind kept burying him. Last year, he'd elected for surgery to remove prostate cancer but lost his sexual functioning. Wanting to wake himself up, he told her he'd tried to think of her naked during the day. He even admitted he'd thought of other women but felt too guilty and stopped doing that. Finally, his body didn't respond, and she could see he only felt alone. He'd gained girth through his chest and around his waist. He slept more, or panicky, didn't sleep. She believed this should be the prime of his life, having given all for her and their daughters, and he should know they loved him, powerfully, each in their own way. He should stop wallowing, she thought.

But he didn't. Or wouldn't. Perhaps couldn't.

FEELING NUMB JOHN further berated himself.

"He's so self-enclosed," he overheard Samantha tell their oldest. "He doesn't hear me."

The children knew and didn't know. They moved in his presence like worlds in orbit to the sun of Samantha while he felt left to the outer dark.

"I love you," she'd said continually. "I don't want you to think this way."

But no one could stop him. The thoughts were stubborn. Hopelessly he wished he could go back and retrieve the money and make himself good again.

Just before the kids came home she'd taken a harder line, "You need to change if we're to be together. You're still young. Stop acting like you're dead."

She was no-nonsense. Loyal to a fault for three decades now, but she had to be tempted just the same, he thought, he'd left the barn doors wide through winter. No hay or even the fragrant hint of hay. Good way to kill your horses.

Now she brought him to the bedroom alone, with all of them moving in the space beyond the bedroom door, talking and playing games, preparing and making meals, entering and returning, on horseback or by truck, from the wilderness. She sat with him on the edge of the bed. He'd gotten that far, and would gather himself for dinner. He tried to keep up appearances when the girls were present.

"Your shoes," she said.

He left them unlaced.

"I don't love you anymore," she said.

She hoped it might break him loose.

A tear rolled from her left eye and she wiped it away and pinched her eyes shut before opening them and staring into his face.

He felt blank. The Montana weather had aged him, but not ungracefully even if hardened by his depression and the marks that scored his face.

"I know," he said. "I've made myself unlovable."

"No you have not, dammit," she said.

"Is it someone else?" he said.

She shook her head no, but she knew where he went now despite both of them wishing he hadn't. He'd hoped, against his own logic, she'd keep him close, even in his despair. But he felt convinced her body had displaced him.

He'd been telling himself they'd continue to perform their tacit separation in this bed, before these windows and this wilderness.

"It's Hank Thompson," he said.

She was angry now, and cried more, though she tried to stop. He was so obtuse. She didn't reach for his hand and he was grateful she didn't. He wasn't prepared. He felt the slow build of hate in his frame and kept his face unmoved. She wiped her tears with her sleeve. John touched his thumb to his earlobe.

"No," she said. "There's nothing there."

Hank Thompson, he thought, former National Park forest ranger. Ten-year widower. Five, maybe six years older than John. They'd had him over numerous times for dinner. Hair cut tight to his head like a badger, but one that smiled too much. John hadn't killed Samantha's brother. He thought he should kill Hank. His chest felt a jolt. His face revealed nothing.

"Say something," she said.

He lifted his eyes and looked at her.

She slapped him. Too gently, he thought.

Her hand like the beat of a drum seeking to rouse him.

She watched his eyes after and he held her gaze. He was granite.

His scars, she noticed, grew enflamed from how she hit him.

She rose and left the room.

He watched her go before he rose and pulled his father's .357 Smith & Wesson revolver from his upper closet where no child could reach. He lifted his flannel shirt and placed the stock in his armpit so the barrel lined his upper ribs. He clutched the firearm to his side this way, concealing it as he walked through the living room, smiling at his wife at the kitchen table with their two daughters.

When he walked out the front door, the men on the porch nodded and lifted their beers to him. A steady gait took him to the barn half a football field south and through the barn doors, past the stalls where the horses sensed him and twitched and the big roan glanced at him white-eyed with her ears back.

You know, he thought, don't you.

The animal kicked a back leg once against the stall, the sound like thunder. He went out the far doors, turned the corner and sat down with his back to the west-facing wall. Green barn, white trim. She'd wanted it that way to catch the color of the fields in spring, and he'd painted it happily and she'd helped him. His halcyon days when they first moved. Short-lived now.

He set his legs straight and leaned his head against the wood. He drew the weapon from under his shirt and didn't look at it. He pressed the barrel to his face just under the cheekbone. He moved it, placing it under his jawbone, then up under the orbital bone. He touched the metal to his temple. The bridge of his nose. The steel was heavy and cold.

He lowered the gun, resting it on his thigh.

He'd won her, he thought. He'd healed her of rape. Or she'd healed herself. Or God had healed them both. But she wanted to give herself to another, he thought. Maybe he was wrong. He didn't think so. Samantha was made of many great women, but she was singular. Resplendent of mind and uncommonly attractive even after all these years.

Their children he never failed to find lovely. He'd defended them against racism like the bear that nearly mauled the life from him. But he couldn't protect them entirely, he'd learned that soon enough and so had they. They needed to face the furnace of America, she'd told him. And they had, with great dignity. They'd tried in their own small ways to tear that oven down and replace it with a sanctuary of their own design. He thought of Samantha, her Puerto Rican blood. He thought of their lives in the first years, skin to skin. Of how she'd tried hard, recently, to move him. He thought of her being false, disloyal now after everything. He couldn't bring himself to hate her. He saw how with an infected selfishness he'd spurned her. He hadn't acknowledged it enough and now that he did, the laceration was ineradicable.

Far below, where the road bordered the great field and met the river he saw a long black line of movement. A flock of yellow-headed blackbirds and starlings at play between the land and sky, he reckoned, a few redwings mixed in. Up close the cacophony would be deafening but from this distance the flow was simply a gesture that called to him as if flight were his home and earth only a memory.

He pressed the gun barrel to his eye again, chalking up against himself his hands disjointed from rodeo and ranch work, the tuft of hair on his head, the lank bangs long for cutting, the stink of his armpits, his disheveled appearance and hooded eyes.

With the malady in his mind, his parents would be disappointed, but they were long passed now. He blamed and didn't blame God. Samantha had hung in there all she could. Increasingly she'd said he needed to change. But he didn't listen. Admittedly, he'd coveted this moment for so long and now that it was here he was at peace. He could finally allow his anger, at himself and the world, and how below it was the overwhelming desire to be free of pain.

He wouldn't be his grandfather.

He'd be himself, in the same place behind the barn but not with a rifle.

The handle of the revolver felt light in his hand compared to the density of his bones. His age and bearing and lethargy. She'd mentioned it of the nation and of him, but it was concrete now. Yes, he thought, I'm angry. The clear-headedness surprised him. So angry with himself and God, and Samantha. It was a victory to say so. He touched the metal to his lips once before he placed the barrel in his mouth, closed his lips over the curvature, and closed his eyes.

He had to breathe heavily through the discomfort. He cocked the hammer, his hands more steady than he imagined. A voice kept saying *kill yourself. Do it now.* He inverted his hand, placing his thumb on the trigger, breathing out and in one more time through his nose. When he pressed his thumb slightly into the metal he heard grass rustle from around the corner, and a child's voice singing.

Gabriella, the light-haired one. He opened his eyes, uncocked the hammer and set the gun behind him just as she rounded the corner and came bounding toward him. Young and not afraid. Singing a made-up tune about the clouds she leaped into his arms. He held her as if holding his own life, carefully, closely, and with all the tenderness he could bear.

"I'm singing at the clouds!" she said. "Do you love my song?"

"I do," he said. "Very much."

"Is that why you're crying?" she asked him.

"Yes, Gabriella," he said.

Her name made him shudder.

"Good tears," she said, "happy tears."

She wiped his cheeks with her hands and kissed his head.

"Happy tears," he echoed and held her close, her frame so light in his arms.

A cousin shouted her name and she laughed and ran away.

Her name was Gabriella Blue. She wanted everyone to call her Gabriella. "Not Gabby. And not Blue." She smiled as she corrected people. His oldest daughter's child.

She ran like a young deer into the lower field.

When she disappeared over a grassy lip he shook his head, wiped his eyes and stood. He lifted the revolver from the grass and placed it under his belt above the right front pocket of his jeans. His shirt covered it. He saddled the roan he called Bluebell for how the horse's sheen came full in certain light, and rode the ten minutes down to the river. The water was smooth and deep even in late summer. Clarity in it like glass. He stood next to his horse and threw the revolver far into the river, the effort making his shoulder socket ring with pain. He rode back to the barn, unsaddled Bluebell, and patting her down spoke kindly to her. He put his face to the animal's forehead. Pressing his cheek to Bluebell's cheek he smelled the rich scent of wheat and horsehair. The horse breathed calmly and looked on John with a pleasant eye.

Returning to the house John's chest felt lighter. He drew a glass of water from the kitchen faucet and one for Samantha and sat next to her as she sat with Mercedes and Lourdes. He placed his hand on hers and she moved her fingers into his, the curve of their hands something he recognized.

He didn't know if they could regain each other.

Book 7

La muerte y yo dormimos juntamente . . .
Cantarte a ti, tan sólo, me despierta.
Death and I sleep together . . .
When I sing to you, only then, I awake.

—Julia de Burgos

JOHN KNEW AS men aged they lived like blown fuses. Society didn't help, its speed and disregard contributing to a man's perceived uselessness.

And below it all was moral vacuity, disquieting, absolute.

In the coming months he tried to win her back.

But each time he broached the topic she refused to listen.

Through effort extended over time he flushed the depression from his system, getting up early to work the fields, handling the horses, keeping his appointments with the doc in town and taking his meds, seeing an old friend who was a former psychologist twice a month in Great Falls.

He stopped wanting to kill himself.

He released her, but she didn't leave.

After everything, he thought her more loyal than him though he'd never wanted other women and didn't know what may have passed between her and another. Whenever he wanted to dwell on his failures he told himself to love and serve someone else: Samantha, the horses, a note of encouragement mailed to a daughter or son-in-law or grandchild, a helping hand to a neighbor. He fought less. Asked forgiveness more. He talked more, and slept less.

He listened to those around him.

THEY CONTINUED IN the same house.

She didn't seem too attached to Hank after all, and after a year or so she turned more readily in John's direction. He loved her, and their children and grandchildren. Smiling, she said he was succeeding in winning her over.

He held a special place in his heart for Gabriella.

IN WOLF POINT, Aurora American Horse felt an acute sensation in the evening as she watched a peck of tiny birds, each smaller than her hand, walk vertical and sideways, upside down and right side up among the limbs of the pine tree outside her window. A feeling in the body along her jawline, not at the skin level only, but in the blood and down through the chest and below, to the stomach, where the fire resides. Her intuition told her she should return to the city and check on Elias.

Her child had grown strong.

She could leave her with her father and feel good now.

She borrowed his 1967 black satin Cadillac Eldorado, the one with the restored floorboards and the beautiful body. The engine was remade. New steel coil shocks. She cut south to I-90 and rode the interstate through Montana to Idaho and into Washington, the car on an oceanic glide west.

IN SEATTLE ELIAS hadn't moved for far too long.

He didn't sing anymore. He needed to get closer to Clayton again. In the corner of the closet he found an empty jewel case of his Seattle drum group. He needed to get on his feet. If not at work he was mostly in bed since Aurora left him. He stood and walked to the window where rain and dark skies made him want to call his mother. He felt too mortified to call. He saw his reflection, called himself a pig. He'd done it to himself. Left both him and Aurora empty. He was faithful now. Likely she wasn't. He didn't care. Or he cared too much. His mind was filled with a fearful gravity.

Millions of birds are born every day, he thought, but few of us see the miracle.

Who of us by worrying can add a single hour to our lives? They were her grandmother's words, or Aurora's. Who knows why birds rise one moment and descend the next—why they swirl in patterns, who leads and who follows, and how they know to do so? He watched the rain. How long was she gone now? He held the turtle shell in his hand and pressed the leather pouch to his cheek. The old woman at Mankato smiled, laughed at him. Blessed him. He needed to go back to the rez. But the job kept binding him, and Aurora's leaving had taken his will. He was afraid she didn't want him anymore. But in his dreams she gazed on him with kindness, walking with him on the high plains north of Wolf Point toward the edge of the world across pale fields dimly illumined, into a wind that carried flocks of birds high overhead.

He decided to quit his job and go back to Montana whether she wanted him to or not. He'd give notice by week's end.

He called his mother. She prayed over him.

He slept better, woke at dawn and started running again.

He went to work, but came home early to set a plan for just how to see Aurora. He went out again to get dinner and when he entered the hall that led to the elevator she was there walking toward him. She approached directly, held his hands, and said, "Te hu wan ci yun ke sni. I didn't see you for a long time!"

"Tan yan yahee ya yea," he said.

"I need to get right," he said. "I'm all wrong."

She touched his chest and then hers. "You're here. You're here now."

Happiness filled him and when she brought him close, he sobbed.

WITHIN THE HOUR, Roark's hired surveillance of Elias informed him of Aurora. Roark proceeded immediately to meet with two men who led neo-Nazi cells rooted in the south and east precincts of the Seattle Police.

They were off duty, clean cut, both in their forties, and White as the Klan.

THAT EVENING AURORA and Elias drew close, holding each other as lovers do.

On this, a night gravid with unknowns, their bodies met in a mosaic of hope and renewal. The composition of their hands and faces in the half-light gave an incandescence to the evening and Aurora remembered why she loved him.

"I love you," she said, and he wept again.

"I receive you with gratitude," he said.

They slept then as if cocooned from the world.

In the deep dark they woke and she told him of their daughter. The past was the past. They looked into each other's eyes, their hearts full of joy. Aurora laughed about the child, so alive, and Elias couldn't stop smiling now that he knew he had a daughter and she'd been named after his grandmother Catherine. The one they called The Great One. They spoke of home, of making a life together and serving the tribe. As they held each other Elias mentioned John's warning about Roark Freeman.

Aurora listened intently.

"He's been driving by the front entrance on and off since you left," Elias said. "Drives an Aston Martin, silver and white."

"Dirty White boy," she said.

She didn't go back to sleep. She held Elias close.

At sunrise he cooked her breakfast. She told him she'd be back soon. His eyes questioned her. She wore jeans and a Valentino jeweled-lace blouse. Black alligator leather pumps. Black patent leather mid-length coat, belted at the waist.

He'd need to trust her, she thought, kissing him on the cheek.

"I am with you always," she said.

"As I am with you," he said.

She took her handbag, went to the car, and drove to the bank building.

TOGETHER SAMANTHA and John had built a life together, and raised two daughters.

In recent months she often asked him to lay down with his back on the floor. "In the form of a compass rose." He never refused. His arms wide and legs straight, she'd lay over him cruciform, pressing her cheek to his cheek. People wanted to own land, she thought, and land was everywhere but could not be owned by anyone. People also tried to own the souls of others, but the soul was indomitable and it too would not be owned.

"Listen," she whispered, and grew silent, breathing.

He was silent too.

"What do you hear?" she asked.

She'd been a lifelong insomniac until they met, after which she slept as the dayblind stars sleep, brightened of another world. They'd failed together and flourished together: their bodies like dust, like song, like prayer.

We are the wayward daughter, she thought, the wayward son.

We are the beloved one.

JOHN HAD WITNESSED innumerable birds covering the lower field. Between him and his father the heart was sometimes obscured, but his father taught him to read wilderness. In the uplands the blackbirds lived in goldenrod or blackberry bushes, in willows and alder trees, the wing formula describing the distal end of the wing, a mathematical method of distinguishing the difference between species of similar plumage. Over the flatlands and through the concavities and inclines of ranch country, washboard backroads were lined with fences. The fences consisted of old gnarled fenceposts, the forsaken limbs of trees, nailed tight with lines of barbed wire. There the red-winged blackbirds tilted, and when they flew, the wind directed their movement. John saw them on the fence line along the dirt road to the ranch, lifting skyward, their minuscule hearts and wingbeats surmounting gravity. The knowledge came to him again. Sevenfold. Fly, blackbird, fly. Seventy times seven. Even with their mutual faults, his father had been to John a safe haven, his mother a place of well-being. The birds lived free, without violation or punishment. In striking red, yellow and black plumage, glossier in spring, less so in winter. Passerine and carinate, steady and skyborne. Often they escaped predation, but predators moved on the ground and from the sky. Snakes, mink, and wildcats, foxes, eagles, hawks. The blackbirds were flushed from earth to air. They dove and swooped to prevent their children from being consumed. They fled to keep from being torn asunder.

What made such dynamism attainable? Who reached from heaven to earth?

He thought of Gabriella again.

Women and men walked hand in hand or alone. They died separately or together.

The red-winged blackbirds flew among them, the people generally unknowing.

Driven by instinct or hunger, the birds' lifespan was meager.

But their flying gladdened the sky.

PHILLIP MCBANE SERVED his debt to society and when he emerged from the metal doors of King County Jail in the middle of Seattle his wife, Alberta, got out of her car and greeted him sheepishly and took him into her arms saying, "My baby, Baby, good baby. It's okay now, Baby. Good baby boy. I'm here now."

"I didn't think you'd be here," he said. He had the same twenty dollars in his pocket.

"I'm here," she said.

Her eyes smiled on him and he held her face in his hands and kissed her long and hard and with his tongue.

GABRIEL KENNEDY REED locked himself in his bathroom for three days after he'd had sex twice in one night with two different prostitutes. Old bodies. Tired faces. His wife, Angelica, sat outside the bathroom door, trying to draw him out. She didn't tell the Crusade director or the director's wife. She didn't tell anyone. Her intuition piqued, she'd paid the exorbitant costs for her two oldest to fly to Alabama and stay with her mom for the week. She had Tamar with her. Gabriel lay on the bathroom floor on his side of the door in old sweats, cheekbone to cold tile, wishing he could become like marble, inert and unknowable, unable to hurt or do hurt, unable to harm.

Opening the door and stepping over her, he left the bathroom for one hour, put on his old wrinkled Covid mask and bought a twenty-foot coil of rope from True Value Hardware in the U District. As he reentered the house he hid the purchase under his sweat top and returned to the bathroom where he closed and locked the door again. He felt capable of nothing. The rope was half-inch nylon boating rope, a smooth triple-braid with high tensile strength. He didn't acknowledge Angelica anymore, or her pleas. At night she made a bed for herself and Tamar and he heard them breathing. They didn't need him. They needed each other. He remembered looking into Angelica's eyes back when the piercing he underwent by receiving her was almost bearable. The color a dark richness outlined in the kind of black that humbled him. He'd been held to this world by what he knew was a real woman. Now he was nowhere.

WHAT WAS THE feminine soul of God, she thought, but a wombing the universe conducted in which light ingested and obliterated darkness. Angelica got up and lifted Gabriel's clothes from the informal closet he tended to make of the folding chair beside the bed, navy-blue tailored suitcoat, slacks, and cinnamon oxford shirt bought on sale. Striped Carolina and navy-blue socks. Cognac wingtips. He was a fine dresser. She loved his outline in tailored clothes. Shaping the creases with her hands, she hung the clothes in the closet and returned to hold Tamar on the floor outside the bathroom. She wasn't worried anymore. The evening had gone still. They had no money. Who cares, she thought. Who can purchase the stars or the beauty of the beloved's gaze?

Past midnight she gave a loud knock on the door.

"Please," she said, "talk to Daryon."

Daryon Vigil was a youth pastor in Dallas, Texas. Gabriel and Daryon completed the first two summers of Crusade training together. When Gabriel cracked the door he didn't look at Angelica. She placed her phone on the bathroom floor. He pushed the door shut. On the other side she sat cross-legged, listening. The child slept in her lap.

Angelica prayed.

"Are you having sex with prostitutes again?" Daryon asked.

"Yes," Gabriel said, and his chin quivered.

He opened the door and sat down next to Angelica and the child. His tongue felt thick. He handed her the phone. "Gabriel has something to tell you," Daryon said. She put the phone face up on the carpet between them. Crying, he told her everything.

MEN ARE CHURCHGOERS, she told herself, criminals, judases. Little Christs. *And nations shall come to your light*, she thought—whether of herself or him or God, she wasn't sure. She wasn't hurt anymore. She was hurt more than ever. Men are flesh and dust. Here, then gone. God is for them. God is against them. They deny, forfeit, feign, beguile, betray. They're loud and physical. Quiet. Undone. She thought of Alabama and of her family and friends and their sons. Men use shotguns. Point blank. They blow holes in one another's chests, and nothing is stronger than love.

Men badly need women, she reasoned.

They put guns to their heads and annihilate themselves.

She looked beyond Gabriel's shoulder to the rope on the bathroom floor.

Or they hang themselves.

When they murder they murder life, and love is eternal.

The aspect may change but the essence remains the same.

A man and a woman are one, she thought.

A man and a woman and a blackbird are one.

ANGELICA KENNEDY REED pursued a PhD in astrophysics, her specialty the infinite blackness of colliding dark matter billions of light years away. She started working for one of NASA's remote space labs, telling Gabriel of a sky dotted with the dense remnants of collapsed stars. Merging supernovas. Black hole stellar violence generating unforeseen gravity. Time was undetectable.

Gabriel lost his ministry appointment with Crusade. She and he went farther now, taking some years to gain a more resolute existence. Him working odd jobs, carpentry, road work, sand and gravel. Mentoring, sponsors, recovery, vulnerability, responsibility; seeking to be true, hoping to be.

They knew themselves better. Their sex with each other was generous. Passing annual polygraph tests without defensiveness, he remained loyal to her. They weren't anti-love anymore, she thought. She saw her head, her hair, her wigs, all her body for what it was—splendor and power.

The same year she finished the PhD, there was a public laying on of hands with his reinstatement as worship leader at the University of Washington. Same Crusade director, new flights of students, Gabriel kept praying for courage. At night in his study working out the chord progression to a gospel song called "I Look to You," he paused. He rarely spoke of heaven, and this was good. Healthy. Picturing himself going to his wife, he was afraid. He'd go anyway, later tonight he told himself. He'd speak directly into her eyes, saying "I have a strong will to love you for eternity."

Now he whispered as he prayed, "Have mercy."

From the kitchen he overheard Angelica on the phone talking to a friend.

A man wrestled the divine antagonist for a blessing, she thought, and though his hip was displaced the blessing came. God dwells in thick darkness. God is also called The Awful One, she noted. The wrestling occurred in the night. The man didn't let go and the blessing arrived with the dawn.

When Gabriel heard his wife speaking from the next room, dread filled him.

"He's beautiful," she said. "He's beautiful now."

And Gabriel felt beautiful, and believed he might be beautiful forever.

THEY LIVED SOBERLY into the future.

Their daughters moved like black swans through the city's dark waters, but before they finished high school Gabriel was driving home late night through ice and fog when he crossed the median, hitting an eighteen-wheeler head-on, breaking his neck. He felt a trace of pain like an arc of light before the wick of his life went out.

WHEN ANGELICA called, John didn't know what to say.

She'd told the bank she needed to reach him. John's voice caught, listening. Gabriel had no life insurance, but John couldn't help. Consuelo Ibarra, a contact he'd kept who was VP of Loans for Bank of America now, could. With three eager bidders, the house, on the east edge of gentrification, sold for three times the original price. Angelica purchased a smaller flat and put the difference into college accounts for Ruth, Hagar, and Tamar.

YEARS FROM HIS overdose, Juan Carlos de la Cruz felt better than ever. Long divorced from Mary Irene, years married to Paulo, he sat with Mary Irene at a table in a hall lit by chandeliers. On the dance floor, their daughter Ana Luz danced in slow solitude with her partner Lee Anne, an army pilot who flew Black Hawks. The wedding was sublime.

Mary Irene held Juan Carlos's hand. "I was too hard on you," she said.

He looked at her. "And I you."

"You're happy with Paulo. I can see that."

"Thank you."

"Our daughter," she said, looking out.

"Yes," he said, "our daughter."

She nodded. "I'm convinced the best way to know God is to love many things."

"What an exquisite sentiment," he said.

She studied his eyes.

He leaned in and kissed her cheek gently and with the love we all knew when we started, alone and alive in this world.

AMERICAN RATIONALIST CONVERGENCE, like many White nationalist groups, prided itself on largely leaderless resistance due to FBI and police scrutiny, but remained from its inception, unequivocally purposeful and virulent. After the Capitol insurrection and the new regime, law enforcement ramped up security but the nation itself bespoke the subtle if not fully conscious White supremacy extant not only in government but also in the police throughout America. In fact, ties between ARC and law enforcement had grown. Roark pictured the former president. The man's bloated face, bagged eyes, and vulgar wing of hair. The diminishment of law enforcement intelligence, of people and funding dedicated to uncovering groups like ARC had resulted in a rash of neo-Nazi activity within the force, individual and large-scale, aimed at violation of the weak by the strong. The neo-Nazi groups ARC funded in the Seattle Police, fully operative, remained undiscovered by the higher-ups even when overtly meeting at local bars or in a dark lounge on Aurora Avenue North as they did today with Roark. ARC had its own government double-men who worked for the FBI but whose allegiance was also theirs. It wasn't hard to get away with what he wanted. Under the former president's apparent elimination of police intelligence, policing the police had nearly gone away.

He bought the men 7 Crown American blended whiskey.

To Roark his long funding of ARC affirmed his rational self-value and girded his ability to make further gains. He wouldn't call himself racist. He'd call himself one who wasn't afraid to get dirty to keep the leeches from leeching. His associates in American Rationalist Convergence understood as well as anyone: Leeches are segmented, parasitic, predatory; soft and unmuscular; weak-willed; they lengthen and contract in order to push into the skin and feed on the host.

They do not remove themselves. They must be removed.

"All right, men, let's get started."

"Yes sir," the men said.

"Tomorrow night," Roark said. The streets were agitated again over the death of a Black boy in Mississippi. Weaponless. Gunned down in his front yard by undercover policemen and recorded by phone by a grandmother in her living room across the street. The feed went viral worldwide. Seattle too was incensed.

"A concerted, five-prong effort," Roark said. "Three buildings aflame. Two people targeted. Permission to target more." He'd waited so long. Inconceivably, Aurora had shown her face. He wouldn't lose her this time. "Coinciding riots incited in the streets near Capitol Hill. Chaos, with abundant opportunity to do harm."

"What people?"

"An Indian from Montana and his wife. Take him. Leave her to me."

Roark proceeded with the plan, informing the men what buildings were to be set fire just south of Capitol Hill after the riots were in full swing on the Hill toward midnight: two large federal holdings and the high-rise called The Towers that housed Elias and Aurora. He counted on the alarms leaving ample time for most but the elderly to get out before the buildings were consumed. He was getting old himself, but he hated old people. Hangers on, sucking on Social Security. "In the blocks north, have your men lob Molotovs toward the White crowd. Make it appear to be Antifa. Don't get bogged down by the National Guard. There will be troops. Avoid them. When the fighting starts, come to The Towers. Seek out the one I show you. I'll provide the room number. Do what you want with him but separate him from his wife. I'll take care of her from there."

He'd eyed The Towers since it was built by a rival not ten years back. The building received critical acclaim not only in Seattle but San Francisco and New York. Seventy-seven floors. Two pillars of glass with a glass connecting bridge at the top. To Roark, destroying The Towers would be an orgiastic endeavor. He'd rebuild in their place, on a much larger footprint his cantilevered mile-high Sky City, perhaps man's greatest achievement. From above and below they'd set the North Tower aflame first as he and these two watched from the South Tower. As it started to take hold they'd simply descend to Elias's floor, kill him, and take his wife. The police cells would do damage in the streets five blocks on toward Capitol Hill and he'd drive her to Pacific Highway North and treat her like the last one. She'd pay more dearly though. We the killers, he thought, exalted for our beautiful souls, whose dawning and setting arrives without a trace of social instinct or herd feeling, deserve what we deserve. A strong man eventually tramples society underfoot. He was strong enough.

He'd use a suitcase for her body. A vat of acid in the woods.

IN THE BANK building Aurora arrived at the executive suite on the top floor and was greeted by Roark's secretary, an old flinty White woman with high platinum hair who eyed her with contempt.

"No, you may not see Mr. Freeman."

Back in the ground floor lobby, Aurora sat in a chrome chair and located his city mansion through a simple search, drove the coast and found an impregnable fortress north of downtown that looked silent but for security detail. No longer so affected by the pandemic, traffic was gridlocked again; the drive two hours instead of one. She inquired at a fifteen-foot metal gate where a low-gloss screen revealed an old White man no less contemptuous.

"No, you may not see Mr. Freeman. Leave now or you will be summarily dismissed from the premises."

She returned to the bank building, but with traffic more entangled it took three hours. Her mind grew tight. Far off she watched the Olympics go dark. When she arrived it was late, a smoke-blue tone on the glass of the facade. This time she stopped one floor below the executive suite. The area was outfitted in steel and partitioned by glass, the people still at work, hours after closing, some with masks, some without, their heads down but for a woman in a black satin dress-suit who noticed her, rose from her chair, and walked toward Aurora.

"Hello, I'm Diane. Diane Inbody. Can I help you?"

Kindness passed between them. Aurora decided to be direct.

"Aurora American Horse. I knew John Sender. I'm trying to reach Mr. Freeman."

"Is there trouble?" Diane asked.

"Yes. Do you know where he might be?"

"Give me a moment," Diane said, and walked back to her desk.

She returned and handed Aurora a small piece of paper. A few words in fine cursive: *The Towers, South Tower, rooftop terrace, near the glass bridge.*

"Dispose of it, please," Diane said.

"I will. Thank you."

As Aurora drove she hated that he'd been in their building all along.

A sky under cloud cover, the night had come, the city lights framing roads and buildings in dim obsolescence. From above, Elias saw her car, black and angular, so fine-looking in the streetlight below. He was encouraged by her return. He waited the requisite time then entered the hall. The elevator numbers ascended, then passed his floor and went to the final floor, the seventy-seventh. He pondered this, and finally he pressed the button thinking it was her in the elevator, perhaps wanting to see the view, and he'd meet her at the top.

He was unaware she had disembarked earlier at the sixty-seventh floor, one below his. She didn't know he'd seen her car. She'd reach the top through the emergency stairwell. The elevator he watched did not house her but others who'd come to meet Roark.

Elias waited until the elevator sounded, entered, and rode to the seventy-seventh floor.

At the top of the stairs Aurora cracked the door. The rooftop was open to the sky, a place where people gathered for corporate events, family parties, or merely to watch the sun die. There was no one here but three men in the distance facing away from her in electric light: Roark and two with him, their mouths wide in what could only be shouting or laughter. Roark in suit and tie, the other two in S.W.A.T. uniforms, submachine guns hung crosswise at their chests. Something wrong with the air, she thought. She saw a brightness emerge from below the men, heard the low roar of fire consuming oxygen, the whip of wind and shattered glass. The darkness was lit by slender overhead lights and the illumination of the bridge between the towers. She quietly closed the door, opened her handbag and removed the .38 Special her father had given her. She took off her coat and heels, set the coat, shoes, and her handbag against the wall, and placed the weapon in the small of her back, wedging it under the beltline. When she cracked the door again Elias emerged from the elevator.

A mistake she thought. He had no weapon.

He ignored all and she could see he would confront Roark but what happened took her aback. Roark motioned with his hand. One of the men raised his weapon by the barrel and set the stock into Elias's temple with such force Elias tilted and fell face to the ground and didn't move. Her mind went numb. She witnessed them lift his body, hoist it, and throw it over the edge. She gasped.

Tears traced her face. She covered her mouth in her hand.

Roark directed the men to the elevator and the two walked to where the doors opened and closed, enveloping them.

He turned and looked over the lip.

Aurora moved quickly.

When he turned back, she stood in front of him not ten paces away.

Seeing her now, he smiled.

She removed the .38 from the small of her back and as she lifted the revolver, she watched his mouth form the word "I . . ." The entry wound would be small. The exit wound ugly. She held the weapon steady, fired, and placed the bullet cleanly on the left side of his forehead. His head swung violently back. His hair went sideways. He fell to his knees as the torso turned and the curve of the skull met the roof's surface. The face stared upward at an oblique angle. Drawing near, she put the second round in his mouth and heard it ring off the steel below.

She positioned the barrel left chest. The third round entered his heart.

Walking briskly to the door, she took her coat, shoes, and handbag and descended the stairs. She entered a flow of screaming people on the lower floors. She pressed herself to the wall of the stairwell and worked slowly lower until the mob emerged into the dark and ran from the building. She went to the car and maneuvered north. At a distance from the structure she passed through crowds of gawking people and lit emergency vehicles. She paused when the path was clear.

Stirring a wonder against the night The Towers erupted in smoke and flame. The base of them became completely engulfed as firefighters on ladders shot water in great parabolas calming nothing. She thought of Elias. I gather your spirit. We go now. Her body shook. Be still, she told herself. She followed side streets and ascended onto the interstate, entering the stacked speed of the cars. As the road crossed the water and rose upward helicopters emerged from the south. She looked in the rearview mirror at a sky of smoke under a ceiling of cloud, the atmosphere blurred to gray and black.

A red gash marked the core where the city burned.

AURORA POINTED THE car to Wolf Point.

She put her hand on her neck. Her body shuddered.

Elias had been thrown into the fire. His life emptied.

Her cheekbones felt cold.

She called forth. "Elias! Elias American Horse! Tecihila! Cantecikiya!"

She drove through the night into day without stopping. She'd killed the man who wanted her and Elias dead. Her thoughts grew condensed, flattening vision, the mess of them seeming to coagulate at the base of her brain. The night gathered and fled, the day came and flew away. A vacancy entered her, followed by great sorrow. The wicked man's death was needful. Her thoughts unified as she pictured Elias, the answers to her search found, finally, in a rightness between them, a oneness she had not foreseen. Arise, shine, she told him. She felt mortal sickness. The spirit world spoke. He was lost to her until she could walk hand in hand with him again, moving beside him with many blackbirds entangled like stars in her body. Through the back window, dusk blackened the skyline. The road blurred. There was peril in what she'd done, she thought, peril for her and her child, an illness lower and less defined, that nauseated her: She knew murder severs the soul. She put her hand on her neck again. She couldn't tell anyone. From the centerline bright dashes sped toward her. She could only tell the Great Spirit.

Who would bear with her the horror?

She could only tell God.

Where her neck met the jawline her heartbeat raced. When a husband dies who is one with you, does your own spirit die of grief? And what of life and breath? No one sees from where we arrive, she thought, or to where we return.

The land ahead lay broken by coulees.

When night fell again she entered the dirt lane of her father's house. Turning off the car lights, she rolled her window down. The sky was open to the north, a long translucence vivid in the firmament. Around a bend she saw the house in its low arrangement below a hill. The kitchen light. The blue glow of the television.

When she emerged from the car her father came out onto the porch with her daughter asleep in his arms. Stone-faced, Aurora met him there and they embraced.

"Elias is dead," she whispered.

Her father looked up, his eyes welling. "He walks now with all our relations."

She loved her father's kindness.

"I killed the one who killed Elias."

Solemnly, her father held her.

The child woke and leaned into Aurora.

Aurora gripped her father's shoulder and wept into his chest as he cupped the back of her head. She turned and kissed her daughter's forehead. "You are the daughter of Elias and Aurora American Horse," she said. She pressed her cheek to her daughter's cheek and kissed the soft skin at her temple.

"I am," her daughter said.

Crickets sounded from the tall grass near the house.

In a gentle voice her father spoke, saying, "Catherine American Horse."

They walked into the house together and sleep came late, the child nestled into Aurora's body, Aurora's hands at rest on her daughter's arms.

The night sky through the window appeared close and full of light.

The child was the child of Aurora and Elias, and the child was the nation.

IN THOSE DAYS there were only two races of people, John thought, those who believed in love and those who denied love. Tired, electrified, poor and rich, infected, robust, unwell. They were everything and nothing. Men borrowed not only money but also the skills of other men. They borrowed, or bought as they were able, talent at carpentry and handiwork, a neighbor's hammer, his band-saw, his understanding of power panels and pilot lights, his wrench, his tool belt, his box of screws, nuts, nails.

Men borrowed ideas, attitudes, actions.

Always, they took more than they knew.

Yet he believed the American family, embodied in multiple and unexpected forms, was one.

He'd held the barrel of a .357 in his mouth.

His wife had saved him.

She called him back, he thought, when Gabriella touched his face.

Afterward he might have been fine if he stayed in the mountains, but he and Samantha needed to go to Seattle to meet Lourdes who was stateside for furlough before flying to Lebanon again. With State Department clearance she was granted time with family during what the U.S. government called "threshold uncertainty" due to Lebanon's potential failed state status. He dreaded the city, but when he and Samantha followed the water on the light rail from Sea-Tac, he remembered how much he loved people, especially the people of Seattle. He'd been a part of their humanity, helping them finance a home. He loved their tenacity.

Who knew the souls of others?

No one but God, he imagined.

After a late dinner at Las Duedas with Lourdes, they walked her to her hotel, one of the finer boutique hotels near Pioneer Square. The scent of the sea in the air, he kissed her forehead. Holding her shoulders, he asked her as he had before: "Do you feel deeply loved?" A ritual of assurance since she was a girl.

"Yes," she said, smiling. She hugged him and turned to hug her mother.

"I'm glad," Samantha said.

A few minutes past ten Lourdes hugged them again and said goodbye, blowing them a kiss. With news warnings of the events near Capitol Hill they knew to stay away. Walking with Samantha to their own hotel, John thought he might call Elias in the morning. Thinking this way John's step was more sure.

As he and Samantha continued down Dogwood Street they were tired and quiet. Not five minutes on, they passed an alley and heard a ruckus against the near wall. Peering into the dark they saw two men in a struggle, a larger man in a leather coat wrestling another, holding his victim by the neck as he brandished a knife.

"Stop!" John shouted.

The victim's face was obscured.

John thought he recognized him.

"Wait," Samantha said, but John leaped forward, pummeling his body into the two men. The movement unhinged them, and John lost balance. He fell to one knee as the smaller man scrambled free. Without hesitation the taller one turned, stabbing John once in the throat, twice through the ribs. The assailant looked up, his head creased by shadow, then took a step backward and ran down the alley. John leaned toward the noise, a clacking sound, arrhythmic as it receded. He placed one hand on his midsection, the other on his neck, went to both knees and folded inward. Samantha shouted as he slumped forward and lay on his side. John felt asphalt against his cheekbone. His windpipe was compromised making his breath rattle. She cried out again, a harsher, sharper cry. Blood seeped between his fingers. The largest amount came from his neck. Samantha rushed forward, trying to speak. Trembling, she placed her body over him and touched his lips.

Before she could say his name the light left his eyes and he was gone.

PHILLIP MCBANE, HAVING eluded death, fled south.

He had no recognition of who saved him. He scrambled through side streets, working his way to the water. Murmuring of luck, he told himself he needed to live better. But in the ensuing years he moved as he always had between homeless and near homeless, drug hungry and drug addled.

He lost Alberta and found her again three times, pursuing her for the happiness she gave him. As a New Year's resolution, she stopped drugging and left him again. He followed her anyway, even as his own burn for opiates ascended. With his hunger edging between dim-eyed and comatose, she saw him only here and there, but when she did she ran to him, sweeping him up, kissing him.

She needed to leave him for good, and she did.

She worked as a hairdresser, went back to the community college, graduated with a C average. She worked as a caregiver in an elderly home. Her sons moved to Seattle and came around more. Her daughter didn't hate her. She thought they might turn out all right.

But the memory of Phil haunted her, and she kept searching.

She never found him again.

An unremarkable span of years after John Sender saved his life, Phil lay in a drug hovel off First Avenue. He looked like an old man. There was nothing left of him. In the haze of an overdose he thought he saw Alberta enter in the dark and sit on the floor next to him, stroking his hair as his eyes rolled back in his head.

She held him to her chest.

He dreamed she called out for help, but no one came.

He felt her lips on his.

How openly his upper body took the shape of her arms before he died.

EARLY EVENING the week before John died, he'd called to Samantha and she came to him and lay herself down over him in their bed.

This time it was him asking her, "What do you hear?"

"The wind outside our window," she said, "and my heart saying I love you."

In the years of his agony he had hurt her, being so absent. She had hurt him too. But everything was behind them, she thought, drawing herself into his arms.

"Don't be afraid," he said, waiting for her.

"There are these feelings I have," she said, "and I wonder if you have them too."

"I do," he said.

"Maybe we can have them together."

"Yes," he said.

She touched his hand. "I'm afraid, and also happy."

"Me too," he whispered.

She'd ridden her horse that morning and returned with fresh wildflowers for the vase at the window: paintbrush and dust flower, lupine, lily, wild rose. "I rode Water, our Appaloosa. Glassed the fields and saw a meadowlark and four magpies, two fat hawks on fence posts not a hundred yards apart, and a redwing among the cattails. I chewed timothy stems. Admired the sky. Whistled, and thought of you. Clucked my tongue and returned home."

John listened. Her voice soothed him.

The day ended like this, with them holding each other in bed next to the long window, looking out on fields and mountains. The comfort he felt from her brought him joy, waking as he did in the night with her asleep, her hipbone in his hand, her body so familiar and good to him as he watched the constellations stride forth—the Bowman Sagittarius, Aries the Ram, Cygnus the Swan, the Northern Cross, Taurus the Bear.

Ursus arctos horribilis, he thought, the silvertip, the bear made of night. For those who borrowed, who could never pay back what they'd taken but who wanted to make it right, life led toward greater life. Here, between her and me, here where we are loved, there is peace. She moved closer, entwining her body with his. Thinking her asleep he said, "Remember we are dust."

She was listening. "And to dust we shall return."

He didn't know why they were speaking of death.
"Que Dios te acompañe," he said.
"And you," she said.
He beheld her face. The line of the eyebrow. The arc of the mountain swift.
He fell asleep to the sound of her breathing.

AT THE HEAD of an alley in south Seattle as John passed from his body, the body went still, a vessel inert and without knowledge. There, in her anguish, Samantha had felt the soul immutable, uncontainable. She was convinced then intimacy from one to another was also presence and memory and future, myriad unfoldings from their youthful beginnings to now. Physical. Tasteful. A breath, a glance, the way they looked at each other, how they'd held each other. As they aged their skin aged with them, brown, white, moist, dry, marked, stippled, wrinkled, and they'd loved each other's skin, kissing on the day he died, and painfully for a moment after.

In the dark of the alley she'd cupped his jaw in her hand. She'd felt the soul release. Pressing her face to his, she heard the sirens, and when the paramedics came she'd held fast. With her eyes closed she saw the light of water between the buildings on the descent to the bay. The light was their light, she thought, the same light of the great rocks that lifted from the plains of Montana through stands of aspen, white pine, and juniper, a thousand feet beyond the tree line. The light of the house, their voices when they were young or old, the way they spoke or grew silent, how they touched or grew still.

In another part of the city, riots had erupted.

On a Sunday dubbed Seattle's "Night of Fire" three major structures burst into flame and the carnage left forty-three dead, ninety-seven wounded: the *Seattle Times* reported twenty-two elderly and two other men unable to escape the fires at The Towers; the rest killed in the streets near Capitol Hill by vigilantes.

Back home, the funeral was quiet and simple. The body burned, the ashes sprinkled over the ridge below the summit of Wolf Mountain. The day beautified by his daughters, their husbands, his grandchildren's faces lit by twilight.

In the dressing room at the church before the wedding, she'd heard him come in. She cracked the dressing room door. He hadn't seen her. She held close what her tía Sofía said over the phone when she'd called the previous day, housebound in Puerto Rico. She was in her bungalow overlooking the strand of La Playa de Los Tiburones. "Here's to your life, my love! Speak to your husband as Julia de Burgos speaks! 'Dime, en tormentas, que me amas.' And don't be afraid to shout! 'Yo soy vida, fuerza, mujer!'"

"Dime, Tía," she'd said.

"El amor lo es todo," her tía said. "Everything. As we advance in life, love becomes more difficult, but in knowing the difficulties the inmost strength of the heart comes forth. Be vulnerable, my child. Let your soul be laid bare. Be well. Take his soul unto yours!"

John's eyes had been to her like the lakes of these mountains, dark blue and all-encompassing. She believed he walked now in the next world. Her chest felt hollow.

She thought of their first days. His face full of wonder.

Alive, desiring to marry her, he was his own and anything but his own.

On their honeymoon in their bed she'd spoken to him.

"Te canta mi alma de amor por tí."

My soul sings of love for you.

JOHN'S SPIRIT was free, and from his vantage he watched those he'd seen—those he'd loved, and those he'd known. They were all sisters and brothers, and in their hands they held the reconciliation of people and nations.

Lifted one by one into a vast murmuration over the fens in northwest Montana and in the Cascades above Seattle, blackbirds rose from river drainages, from the habitat of mountain lion, grizzly, spider, and wolverine, from the forests below the great rocks. As if beckoned they flew upward toward the light and their number grew until they swept the horizon at dusk, blotting out the sun. They rose with abandon above the plateaus, voluminous in their undulations to the heights of the mountains. They flew until the wind lifted them farther, sending them north and west where they dispersed as they met the vanishing point and the cloud of their presence was seen no more.

FROM THE PLACE where he stretched out his hand to Samantha, time being of no consequence, he remembered their wedding day.

At four in the afternoon under a blue sky, a Saturday, John drove his truck to the modern cathedral in Edmonds. He sang a rousing tune his grandmother taught him as a boy. He glanced in the rearview mirror at his dad in the olive-green Chevy sedan, his mom next to his dad on the bench seat, his dad's arm around his mother's shoulders.

What we borrow who can repay? he thought.

He entered the heavy wood doors of the church on the corner of Olympic and Maple. He wore his grandfather's wingtips polished bright black. Next to his heart in the silk-lined pocket of the tuxedo, he kept the ring in its velvet box. He'd be giving it to the ringbearer, receiving it back in front of over a hundred witnesses and placing it on Samantha's finger. When it came to borrowing, beyond the appeal of money was a reality harboring deeper secrets and even deeper deficits.

The birds have ceased their songs, he thought, all save the blackbird.

We are emptied of all. Given all in return.

In stirrings of desire or great dreams, in the mundane and the fateful, they loved each other. In the wake of history, gruesomely, grotesquely, his people and hers had been harmed. Pierced and hung. Desecrated. Mutilated. Raped. Silenced. Left on the threshing floor. Burned alive or buried in mass graves. His people and hers had been executed. Her people and his had put them to death; the paradoxes and divinations were never ending.

Have mercy on our souls, he thought.

He and she were at the beginning, Samantha still new to him, as he was to her. But what life they knew was enough. Her mother loved him. His mother loved her. This too was enough. He felt great joy. In front of the dais he turned to face the people. He still hadn't seen her. He carried a limp. Scar lines angry on the right side of his face. The color of love was silver, he thought, the exact hue of atmospheric clarity comprising all the colors of the spectrum—absorbing color and reflecting color, where all that becomes visible is light. In the new morning silver light ascended, and in the evening the same light descended. At midday the blackbirds along the Rocky Mountain Front were red-winged or yellow-tailed, dun or gray or forest black awash in the same silver light. They were solitary, a whisper from heaven, or communal like star fields awheel through space and time. They were vocal or silent, immanent, wildly given, lovely to the eye and born of shadow, a darkness treasured of God. From thickets and willows, from grasses, meadow, tree, and thorn, and uniformly from the cattails among the marshes they rose and filled the sky. When she emerged at the head of the aisle he exhaled and felt for a moment lost to all but the dark, afraid and unknowing. She'd walk the aisle arm in arm with her mother to be given away. Before the altar he'd promise to honor, cherish, and obey her until death. With all his faith he'd say it out loud in front of everyone.

Say it with all his heart, all his love.

I do, I will.

Acknowledgments

Gratitude to Mel and Shelby Four Bear and their family for their love, and to M. L. Smoker, Andrew Krivak, Karissa Naslund, Dre Castillo, Jessica Maucioni, Travis Helms, Charles Finn, Chris Dombrowski, Stefani Ferris, Alyson Hagy, Maria Esther Zamora, Bruce Holbert, John Whalen, Jonathan Johnson, and CooXooEii Black for kindness, friendship, and discerning reads of this novel in draft form. To Layli Long Soldier, bell hooks, Delores Huerta, Cesar Chavez, Nazim Hikmet, Coretta Scott King and Martin Luther King Jr., Lin-Manuel Miranda, Helena Maria Viramontes, Ross Gay, Angela Davis, W.E.B. Du Bois, Vaclav Havel, James McBride, E. M. Forster, Héctor Abad, and Paula Gunn Allen for more truth. To Milan Kundera for the words "I have a strong will to love you for eternity" from *Immortality*; to Sherman Alexie for thoughts on hippies, and for the words "these White men forgot to love their own mothers"; to Tulele Faletolu and Taya Smith for understanding we are "shadows and portraits, empires of light and clay"; to J. K. Rowling for thoughts on the lunatic fringes of one's religion; John Steinbeck for "monsters born in the world to human parents"; and James Baldwin for "writing the common history . . . ours." To Pierre Teilhard de Chardin, for the words, "The diaphany of the Divine at the heart of the universe on fire" from *The Divine Milieu*. To my agent and good sister in art, Kathy Helmers, for the peace you've given me. To Mako Fujimura, for brotherhood and the refractive soul of your paintings. To my editor Clark Whitehorn, for blackbirds, Montana, y por el sí sagrado.

Por la Reina del Cielo, siempre.

To Charles Johnson for dark gravity, for *Middle Passage*, and for the light.

I want to credit artists and thought leaders across multiple disciplines who have informed this work. Thank you, Natalie Diaz, for the wisdom you spoke into my life of the non-White indigenous body forced to be a pleasure bordering on violence, harmed, traumatized, erased, and your poetry of yearning to "disappear, not into violence but into love, into church and darkness." To Cinnamon Kills First, for friendship, and for leading the nations into justice and truth. To Debra Magpie Earling, for generosity, kindness, and love. In creating characters who are descendants of real Cheyenne and Lakota people, I want to acknowledge with humility and respect the crucial impact leaders such as American Horse, Killsnight, Black Kettle, and others have had on the human family. I also want to acknowledge the grace of Lakota spiritual leader Jim Miller, for his dream of the Dakota 38 + 2, and for healing the heart of the world with forgiveness.

Audre Lorde's warrior-poet conception of darkness shaped this novel's movement toward centering the dark, decentering the White: "the woman's place of power within each of us is neither white nor surface; it is dark, it is ancient, and it is deep." Robin Coste Lewis's discoveries on "the Holy Black virgin mother of God, the mother of the world," influenced my view of women and men, children, and God. My gratitude to Tony Doerr for friendship, the poetry of being and the golden boat, Viktor Frankl for the nature of the eye, Michael Cunningham for the elegant structure of *The Hours*, Jim Harrison for meditations on the death of birds, Elizabeth Barret Browning for her poem "A Man's Requirements," and T. S. Eliot for the shirt of flame.

To Maya Angelou for her dialogues on human evil, for the words "the power of hate is almost as strong as the power of love," and for the words surrounding the words. To Claudia Rankine for *Citizen*, and her vision of forgiveness as "a bottomless vacancy held by the living, beyond all that is hatred or love" from *Don't Let Me Be Lonely*; Dorothy E. Roberts on Black women's bodies, justice, and reproductive freedom; Alison Scott-Baumann on Ricoeur and orientalism in reverse; Michelle Chaplin on Derrida and feminism; Julia Siccardi on intimate relationship as shelter and home in Zadie Smith's women of the diaspora; Judith Jarvis Thompson for her thoughts on the unconscious famous-violinist, people seeds, and the ever-expanding child; Leslie J. Reagan's study of ambiguous and interactive private and public spheres; Hilary Plum on choice; and Albert Camus on choice and the invincible summer; Susan Brownmiller, Lisa Duggan, Ann Heller, and Masha Gessen for their insights on Ayn Rand; as well as Sujatha Jesudason and Anat Shenker-Osorio's research in *The Atlantic* on son preference in sex selection in America. Ta-Nehisi Coates's work indicting America, and his warning to be "wary of every dream and nation" were influential, as was James Cone's, Cornel West's, and John Coltrane's discernment that power is everywhere but love is supreme through Christ's crucifixion and sacrifice on behalf of humanity.

Research on banking, debt, rodeo, objectivism (including direct quotes from Ayn Rand and Friedrich Nietzche), Frank Lloyd Wright's mile-high Sky City, opium addiction, neonatal nursing, atomic theory, space, and astrophysics all informed the novel, as well as specific historical accounts of genocide.

Mary Szybist's view of angels in the poem "Invitation" from *Incarnadine* introduced me to the angel of abortion and helped shape my views of mercy. To E. E. Cummings for praising love. To Toni Morrison, for vision, for *The Bluest Eye* and *Home*, and for *Playing in the Dark: Whiteness and the Literary Imagination*. To Elizabeth Alexander for kindness and *The Light of the World*, Ishmael Reed for The Before Columbus Foundation, Mary Oliver for "The Uses of Sorrow" and "On Thy Wondrous Works I Will Meditate" from *Thirst*, Ursula K. Le Guin for ideas on authorial voice, The Notorious RBG for devotion to gender well-being and freedom of choice, Rudolf Otto and F. W. Robertson for the mysterium tremendum et fascinans, Joy Harjo for the poem "She Had Some Horses," and Julia de Burgos for the infinity in your words "I am life, I am strength, I am woman" and for fathoming love's fortitude in storms. The novel contains lines from Wallace Stevens's poetry on blackbirds, and more on blackbirds from Debra Magpie Earling, dg nanouk okpik and Heather Cahoon's honoring her, Jean Toomer, David Macbeth Moir, W. E. Henley, C. Bernard Jackson, James Hatch, Ray Henderson, Mort Dixon, Alfred Tennyson, John Lennon, Paul McCartney, and Leila Chatti. Each main character herein speaks or thinks at least one line from Vincent van Gogh on love or color.

I wish to thank the following publications where excerpts of this novel previously appeared, and their respective editors, Allen Jones, Tom Jenks, and Brianna Van Dyke, for their support of my work:

Big Sky Journal, Winter 2017

Narrative Magazine, Spring 2022

Ruminations, Summer 2015

www.ingramcontent.com/pod-product-compliance
Lightning Source LLC
Chambersburg PA
CBHW031303060825
30672CB00002B/2

* 9 7 8 1 4 9 6 2 4 3 5 7 7 *